the light

[A NOVEL]

#1 *NEW YORK TIMES* BESTSELLER

MIKE EVANS

TimeWorthy
BOOKS

P.O. Box 30000, Phoenix, AZ 85046

Published by TimeWorthy Books
P. O. Box 30000
Phoenix, AZ 85046

The Light
Copyright 2011 by TimeWorthy Books
P. O. Box 30000
Phoenix, AZ 85046

Design: Lookout Design, Inc.

USA:	978-0-935199-43-7
Canada:	**978-0-935199-44-4**
Hardcover:	**978-0-935199-45-1**

dedication:

To you, a follower of The Light,
I acknowledge The Light in you.

* * *

Sadness flies on the wings of the morning
and out of the heart of darkness comes the light.

~Jean Giraudoux

the light

Scientists in a laboratory attempted an experiment to measure the power of attitude in rats. They wanted to see how attitude affected the will to live.

One rat was placed in a large tub of water with sides so high it could not get out. The tub was placed in a dark room. They timed how long the rat would keep swimming before it gave up. The rat struggled to survive for a little over three minutes, then it gave up.

The researchers then placed another rat in the same tub. This time, however, a bright ray of light was allowed to shine into the room. The second rat swam more than thirty-six hours, seven hundred times longer than the rat with no light.

Why was that? The rat with no light had no hope. He saw only darkness. There was no reason to keep swimming.

It is my prayer that as you read *The Light*, new hope will flood your heart and life.

chapter 1

Darkness cloaked the cellar, broken only by the amber glow of the streetlight filtering through the narrow windows high up on the wall. David, eleven years old, lay helpless on the damp, earthen floor. Wally, his father, glared at him through blue blood-shot eyes that smoldered in the pale light. "Think you can look at me like that?" Wally's breath was heavy with the sick-sweet smell of liquor. "Think I'll let you get away with that? In front'a my friends?" He lifted a coil of electrical extension cord from a hook on the wall. Gripping the plug in one hand he spread his arms wide apart and stretched the length of cord between them. He moved in measured, deliberate motions and transferred the plug to his opposite hand, doubling the cord and letting it dangle menacingly at his side.

"Dad, please," David pleaded. "I didn't look at you. I didn't do anything."

Whap! The biting sting of the extension cord landed across David's back. "Don't talk back to me, boy!"

Whap! The cord struck him again. "Ya' stupid lyin' moron," Wally growled. "Ya' think I'm blind?"

"No," David begged. "Please!"

Whap! The cord ripped into David's flesh again and again. The young boy's body jumped and twitched with every strike. Wally glowered over him. "Ya' think I'm that stupid? God hates liars—and I do too! Ya' stupid Jew bastard."

Whap! "I'll teach ya' some respect." Wally drew back the cord and brought it down against David's back once more. And then something inside him snapped. Again and again he drew back the cord and whipped it across the boy's legs and back, his arms and shoulders. On and on he went, sweat dripping from his forehead, his arms swinging in maniacal rhythm, the cord ripping through David's shirt, tearing it to shreds as each stripe took Wally deeper and deeper into the grasp of anger, hatred, and lust.

"Stop!" David screamed. "Stop! Please!"

Trapped now in the pleasure of his drunken frenzy, Wally ignored the young boy's cries and plunged further and further into the agony of his victim. Driving with all his might to release the tension that welled in his body, he worked the cord from side to side, whistling it through the air and then jerking it back at just the right moment to make it pop against the boy's flesh. With each lash against David's now bared back, bright red blood splattered against Wally's hands and face, setting his body aflame with the intensity of an animal on the attack, conquering, and spending itself in the pleasure of inflicting pain.

Finally, winded and spent, his arm aching with fatigue, Wally let the cord slip from his fingers. He bent over and propped his hands against his knees, gasping for breath.

David, still clinging to life, listened to Wally panting in the dark. A heavy, musky smell filled the room. Not quite urine, not quite sweat, it had the scent of something uncontrollable and raw. David knew what was coming next. He'd been through this before. Always it was the same. His father drank himself into a stupor then turned on his oldest son. Sometimes on the kitchen floor, sometimes in the cellar, but always with the extension cord, or his belt, or his fist. And when he had exhausted the muscles in his arms, he turned to the ones in his legs. A whimper slipped from David's throat. And then it began.

"Humph!" he gasped as the toe of his father's boot crashed against his side. Searing pain shot through David's limp body. A warm trickle of blood oozed from between his ribs. David squirmed to the right, brought his knees up close against his stomach, and curled his body in a fetal position.

"Humph." His father's boot struck again. David's heart pounded as he gasped for breath, but no breath would come. Panic seized him as he struggled to fill his lungs with air in quick, short gasps.

Then his father's hands locked around his neck. David was plucked from the floor and lifted into the air, higher and higher. So high he was certain he would bang his head on the kitchen floor above. Instinctively, David clutched at the hands that held him, trying to relieve the pain that shot through his side, desperate to pry loose the fingers that quenched the flow of air to his lungs.

Wally's laugh shook the timbers above. "What do you think now, you moron? I'll kill ya! Yer nothin' but a piece a garbage." David twisted from side to side and kicked his legs furiously. With his last breath he cried out in a raspy voice, "Let me go...I don't want to die!"

✱   ✱   ✱

Suddenly, a hand nudged his shoulder, jiggling him from side to side. "David, David," a voice repeated softly. "Wake up. Wake up."

David's eyes popped open. He stared up at the ceiling and blinked, trying to remember where he was. He turned his head and looked blankly at the woman lying beside him in bed. She smiled at him. "It's me. Sue."

David rubbed his eyes. "What time is it?"

"Three in the morning."

"I can't stand this," David sighed. He took a deep breath and tried to relax. "Night after night. It just won't go away."

"What was it this time?"

"The cellar." He rested his head against Sue's arm. "He was beating me with that extension cord." David shuddered. "It was that awful dream...but one I've actually lived." He ran his hands over his face and pushed his dark hair back from his forehead. "Why would a father do that to his son?"

"Wally Ellis is a sick man."

"And why won't these dreams go away?"

"Because deep inside you there's an eleven-year-old boy, and he's feeling a lot of pain. You've buried him deep inside your mind, but he's still alive. You need to learn to love him, David."

"You are the second person who ever believed in me. I love you, Sue."

"I love you too." She wrapped both arms around him and pulled him deeper beneath the covers.

chapter 2

Hours later David felt the bed shake. His eyes opened to find the room filled with brilliant morning sunlight streaming through the windows. He squinted against the glare and glanced around, trying to remember what day it was and why he was still in bed. Slowly, his eyes focused on a form lying a few feet away. His twelve-year-old son, Joel, was grinning back at him. "Mama said it was time for you to get up."

"She did?"

"Uh huh."

David rolled on his side and wrapped his arm around Joel. "Why do I have to get up?"

"Vacation."

"Vacation?" David dug the tips of his fingers into Joel's back to tickle him. Joel laughed and squirmed. "Where are we going on vacation?"

"We're going to the beach," Joel shouted. "Stop tickling me." His eyes sparkled.

David ran his hand over his son's back and gave him a hug. "You think we could fish from the surf?"

"We tried that last year, Dad. It didn't work too well."

"Yeah," David grinned. "But there's a pier down the road. We could try that." Behind them, Sue entered the room. David rolled over and glanced at her. "We were going to leave by eight. What time is it?"

"Almost ten."

David threw back the covers and raised himself to a sitting position on the edge of the bed. "You let me sleep."

"You needed it." Sue draped her arms across his shoulders and hugged him. "The car is packed. The kids are ready. If you get in the shower now we can be gone before lunch."

David stood and rubbed his eyes, then stretched his arms wide apart. "We could stop at that café in Laurinburg."

She swatted him. "Only if you get moving."

David started toward the bathroom. "Vacation!" He reached for the door, and then glanced back at Joel. "Two weeks at Carolina Beach."

For ten years he had served as pastor of Belmont Baptist Church, a congregation on the western edge of Charlotte, North Carolina. He loved the ministry, but each year, as winter turned to spring and the afternoons grew longer and warmer, he counted the days until he and Sue could pack the car, load up their two children, and head off to the coast. Now that time had come again. Steve Smith, his associate, would handle the services and run the office. Life Group leaders would take care of any other details that arose, leaving David and his family two weeks of nothing but glorious sunshine and plenty of time to lie aimlessly on the sand, eat fresh seafood, and enjoy the roar of the waves as they crashed ashore.

By ten-thirty David was out of the shower and ready to go. As he came down the hall he saw Sue in the kitchen making one last check of the refrigerator. "I think that's everything out of here that would spoil."

Megan, their sixteen-year-old daughter, leaned against the doorway. "Come on, Mom. Let's go. It'll be midnight before we get there."

David stood behind her and squeezed her shoulders. "Relax, sweetie. We have two weeks to enjoy the waves and the sun. And who knows? You might even see a boy or two."

"Oh, Dad," she groaned.

A moment later the back door burst open and Joel shouted, "C'mon! We gotta go! At this rate I won't get the raft out today."

"Raft?" Megan shook her head. "That old thing's probably long gone by now."

Joel's eyes darted to David. "You think it's still there?"

"I don't know," David shrugged. "Other people use that house, you know. We're just renters."

"But it's our house."

David crossed the room and grabbed his son in a playful headlock. "That's right, buddy. It's our beach house. Same house every year for as long as you can remember." He pulled Joel toward the door. "Come on, Sue," he called over his shoulder. "Let's go." Megan followed her father and brother outside. The door banged closed behind them.

Their home had no garage, and the driveway came around the side of the house to the back, ending at the patio. The three walked around the corner of the house where the 1978, dark blue Chevrolet Caprice was parked in front. David had bought it new the previous fall from a dealer in midtown. Billy Jones, one of the church's Life Group leaders, knew the sales manager. David had never owned a new car before, and at first he did his best to limit its use in an effort to make it last, but the car was fun to drive, and soon he decided he should exercise some of the faith he encouraged others to show. Over the ensuing twelve months the mileage began to mount as he visited members and traveled to meetings. Sue used it to attend classes at Queens College, to carry their children to school, and to attend a growing list of activities. The Caprice had become like another room in the house. This summer morning it was loaded with swimsuits, towels, inflatable rafts, and everything they needed for a trip to the beach.

As they neared the car, Joel broke free of David's grasp and scampered around to the passenger side. He flung open the rear door and jumped in the back seat. Megan got in beside him from the driver's side. David dug in his pocket for the keys and then slid in behind the steering wheel. As he reached out to pull the door closed he saw Sue coming around the corner of the house. The look on her face told him something was wrong. A couple of sighs came from the back seat.

"She's got 'the look,'" Joel grumbled.

"This always happens," Megan complained.

Sue came around the open car door and leaned close to David. He looked up at her. "Whatever it is, they can call Steve. Or Alan Scruggs. He's chairman of the board. He politicked for the job and now he's got it. Let him deal with it. I'm going on vacation."

"Virgil Ellis is on the phone."

David felt his heart sink. Virgil lived in Massachusetts, just across the state line from Connecticut. Although he was David's cousin, they hadn't seen each other in twenty years. Still, they talked occasionally on the phone. Long after David's parents divorced, his mother moved back to Indian Orchard, where they had lived when he was a child. As a result, Virgil had become the sole point of contact between David and his mother. If he was calling, David was certain it wasn't good news. "What does Virgil want?"

Sue's face softened. "He said he had something important to tell you about your mother."

David's shoulders slumped. "What's wrong? Is she sick?"

"I don't know." Sue laid her hand on his shoulder. "You'd best not keep him waiting."

David turned, walked quickly into the kitchen, and picked up the phone lying on the counter.

"Hey, Virgil. How are you? What's going on with Mom?"

Virgil cleared his throat; his voice caught when he finally spoke: "David, your mom collapsed at home. They took her to the hospital in an ambulance. She...um...was pronounced dead in the emergency room. I'm so sorry to have to tell you that."

David's heart sank. As a pastor, part of him wanted to move ahead with automatic responses to the death of a loved one. But this was different. This was his mother. Finally he said, "Thanks, Virgil. Have any arrangements been made?"

"Yes, she made all the arrangements herself several months ago. She gave me a copy of her wishes. Her funeral will be day after tomorrow."

"I'll fly up there as soon as I take care of some things here at home. I really appreciate your calling me, Virgil. Will I see you at the funeral?"

"I'm not able to drive right now, David. I fell and broke my leg about three weeks ago. I'm in a full cast from my thigh to below my knee."

"I'm sorry to hear that. But, hey, thanks for taking care of the funeral details. I really appreciate it."

The two men said their goodbyes, and David replaced the receiver in its cradle. He hung his head in sorrow, turned, and walked down the hall in a daze. Alone in the bedroom, he picked up his Bible and dropped to his knees beside the bed. He laid his open Bible on the bedspread and dropped his head into his hands. "Oh God, please give me a word of comfort. My mom's life was so sad and painful…she suffered so much…how could her life end this way?"

He raised his head and looked in his Bible. The words of Proverbs 3 fairly leapt off the page, "Trust in the Lord with all your heart; and lean not unto your own understanding." As the scripture sank deeply into David's spirit, he flipped the pages of his Bible to the New Testament. Again, God's Word in II Timothy, chapter 1, seemed to have been chosen especially for him at this moment, "For God has not given us a spirit of fear, but of power and of love and of a sound mind."

David rose from beside the bed, grabbed a couple of tissues from the box on his bedside table, and mopped the tears from his face. He slipped his wallet from his hip pocket. Tucked in the corner was a dog-eared, black-and-white photograph—a picture of his mother and her sister, Eliana. He took it out and held it in his hand. The picture had been taken when they were girls. Both of them wore dark coats and had scarves tied around their heads. They stood stiff and unsmiling in front of a large bush.

He had been curious about the picture, but every time he had asked, his mother seemed to drift off to another world or quickly change the subject. He stared at the picture a moment, wishing now that he had asked more questions. He returned it to the corner of his wallet and slid it back into his hip pocket. "I need to get moving," he said to himself. *Joel wants to get to the beach before sunset, and I need to get to the airport.*

He slowly walked back down the hall and out to the car. With one look Sue knew.

He reached for her. "My mom died early this morning."

She slipped her arm around his neck. "I'm so sorry, honey. What happened?"

David gave her a tight-lipped smile and told her about his conversation with Virgil.

With tears in her eyes Sue whispered, "When's the funeral?"

"Day after tomorrow."

"Wednesday?"

"Yes. In Massachusetts."

Sue looked past him toward the back seat. "Joel, Megan, y'all need to get your stuff and take it back in the house. We need to let your father …"

"No." David held up his hand, interrupting her. "I don't think we should do that. There's no need for them to go." He bounced the keys against the palm of his hand. "You take them to the beach. I'll go up to Massachusetts for the funeral, and then come to the beach in a few days. I'll get Billy to take me to the airport as soon as I can get a flight. Since he retired, he's volunteered at the church nearly every day. He's always ready and willing to help out."

Sue propped her hand against the doorframe. "Don't call Billy. We can drop you at the airport on our way out of town. You think it's wise to make this trip by yourself?"

"I won't be alone, honey. God has given me two promises to comfort and strengthen me."

"What if your father's there?"

"All the better reason for me to go alone."

"Are you sure?"

"Yep." He leaned toward the back seat. "You wait in the car. I'm going to see what kind of flight I can get. Shouldn't be long."

"Okay Dad," frowned Joel.

Megan shrugged her shoulders, leaned back to rest her head against the seat, and closed her eyes.

David glanced at his watch and started back to the house.

chapter 3

David and Sue walked past the corner of the house and up the back steps. As they entered the kitchen, she turned to him. "Look, I know you want the kids and me to go on to the beach, but this could be a really difficult trip for you. I'm still not sure you should go up there alone."

"You're right." He leaned over and kissed her forehead. "It could be a tough trip. But this would just be too hard on the kids. Besides, they're all set for the beach." He turned away and started toward the hall. "Call the airlines for me?"

David made his way back to the bedroom. He crossed the room, took a suitcase from the closet, and set a pair of black, wing-tipped shoes in the bottom. He took out a golf shirt and laid it on top of the shoes. Then he added a gray suit, two white dress shirts, a couple of ties, and another golf shirt. He would travel in the jeans and shirt he was wearing. Across the room, he opened his dresser drawer and took out socks and underwear. With everything in place, he patted the front pockets of his jeans and did a quick check. "Keys and money." He touched his hip pocket. "And my billfold. Shoes, socks, underwear, shirts, suits. That should be everything."

Suitcase in hand, David turned toward the door and then remembered his Bible. He had packed his study Bible in the suitcase for the beach. He turned back to the night table, picked up two slips of paper, jotted down the scriptures God had just given him, and shoved them into his reading Bible. He opened the suitcase, tucked the book beneath his suit, and snapped the case shut.

When he returned to the kitchen, Sue was taking one last look in the refrigerator and freezer. She looked at him askance. "You're going dressed like that?"

David nodded. "I want to be comfortable during the flight. What they see is what they get today." He put his suitcase down. "Did you get a flight?"

"Delta. Two o'clock."

"What time does it get into Hartford?"

Sue leaned back against the counter. "Six. You have to change planes in New York."

David glanced at the clock on the stove. "We better get moving."

"Plenty of time."

"Not if you're going to have lunch at that café in Laurinburg."

"You have other things to worry about besides where we eat lunch."

David put his hands on her arms and pulled her to him. "Listen to me," he said softly. "My father made many, many mistakes with his children. I'm not repeating them with ours."

Sue laid her head on his shoulder. "David, you are a wonderful father. But there's more going on inside you than most people could handle." She kissed him. "And I'm not letting it get the best of you."

David grinned. "I sure hope not." He took her hand and stood. "Come on. Our children are waiting."

David held the back door as she stepped outside, followed her out, and then pulled it shut behind them. "When is my return flight?"

"I left it open."

"Why?"

Sue reached the bottom step and glanced up at him. "You don't know what will happen once you get there."

"Yes, I do." David took a key from his pocket and locked the door. "We'll have the funeral, and then I'll get on a plane and come home."

"David." Sue's voice took a serious tone. "I know you want to get down to the beach to me and the children, but take your time in Massachusetts." David jiggled the doorknob to make certain it was locked. "There's a lot from your past that's been pushed aside. By you. By your sister and brothers. The whole family. This might be a time when some of it gets pulled to the front." David moved from the steps. She hooked her arm in his. "I want you to make certain you let God do whatever it is He wants to do with you."

David squeezed her arm against his side. "Okay," he sighed. "But I'm not hanging around up there any longer than necessary."

*　　*　　*

An hour later David stood outside the entrance to Charlotte Douglas Airport and watched as the Caprice drove away. Through the back window he saw his son seated on the passenger side. Megan rode up front with Sue. A feeling of sadness swept over him at the thought of not being with them when they arrived at the beach house. He stood there watching until the car disappeared in traffic. When it was out of sight, he leaned over and gripped the handle of his suitcase. *On to Indian Orchard, my old home town.* He sighed. *I've dreaded this day for a long time.*

Half an hour later he moved through check-in and started the long trek down the corridor toward the gate for his flight. As he walked along, his mind wandered to Sue, the children, the beach house, the sound of the surf at sunset …

The brush of something against his leg interrupted David's thoughts. He glanced down to see a young boy walking next to him carrying an ice cream cone. A white streak on David's jeans told him what had happened. Farther ahead of them, a woman stood in the center of the corridor waving and gesturing in the little boy's direction. "Come on, Scott," she urged. "We have to hurry." She glanced up at David. "Sorry about that. Our plane's about to leave." Then her eyes caught the ice cream on his trouser leg. "Oh," she stopped. "Your pants."

David smiled and nodded. "No problem."

"You're sure?"

"It'll be fine." David reached down and brushed the ice cream off. The lady took the little boy's hand and turned away. David watched as the child hurried to keep up with her. As he stared after them, he thought about his mother. Through all of his childhood she never once laughed with him, held his hand, or bought him an ice cream cone.

A few minutes later David arrived at the gate. The plane didn't board for an hour. Rows of empty seats lined the waiting area. He chose one near the window and sat down. Outside on the tarmac planes moved back and forth. Some rolled toward the runway for takeoff, while others taxied into place at the gates. Baggage carts loaded with suitcases and boxes of every kind zipped past. David watched for a moment, trying to imagine where the owners of the luggage might be going.

The little boy with the ice cream had reminded David of Joel at that age, and he thought about what Sue had said that morning: "You're a wonderful father." In his mind's eye he could see five-year-old Joel standing in a small rowboat. It had been Father's Day, and he and Joel were camping together for the very first time. David woke Joel early. After they dressed warmly, David drove down the trail to the little excuse for a store near the turn-off to the campground. David had forgotten to bring milk for their morning cereal. Creeping to a halt in front of the gas station, store, and bait shop, David spied a pay phone outside the front door. On the spur of the moment, he decided to call his father to wish him a happy Father's Day. Wally cursed and yelled, "Moron, why'd ya wake me up so early? Don't even come to my funeral. I don't want no Jew bastards there!"

David had been devastated. He woke Joel and tried to hide his hurt and disappointment. He helped Joel into the boat, put a lifejacket on him, pushed away from the shore, and puttered out into the middle of the lake. He baited his best fishing rod and handed it to Joel. When he tried to cast, the backlash caused the line to become hopelessly snarled.

Joel tried bravely to cast three different times with three different rods. Each time he would ask, "Daddy, are you mad at me?"

David would reply, "No, son. I'm not mad at you."

When Joel began to complain about being hungry, David pulled up anchor and the two rowed back to shore. His son went into the tent to change out of his wet shirt while David cooked a breakfast of bacon, eggs, and roasted bread—thick slices of toast cooked on a fork over the fire.

"Dad?" David turned to see Joel standing behind him with a piece of yellow paper clutched in his little hand. He took the paper from his son, opened it, and inside found a drawing of two stick-figure fishermen—one big and one small. Each had a fishing rod in one hand, and the two were holding hands. On the page in wavy childish lines, Joel had painstakingly written, "I love you."

The wadded piece of paper held $5.28—all the money Joel had. Tears sprang to David's eyes as he knelt and pulled the little boy to his chest. "Thank you, Joel," he whispered. "But isn't this your birthday money?"

"Yeah Dad, but I love you more than all the money in the world." Tears began to etch themselves in rivulets down his little dusty face.

"Joel, you're only five, and you may not understand now, but God has used you to heal my broken heart today. Jesus is big in you, Son."

"Thanks, Dad. It's cold out here. Why did we camp out in the cold?"

"Well, I promised you I would, and I didn't want to break my promise."

"Dad, next time break your promise."

David chuckled at the memory. He reluctantly returned to the moment at hand and remembered the mother he had tried hard to understand but knew so little about. From the few stories he had heard, he knew she had been born Leah Levintov, sometime around 1920—she would never say for certain. She was born to a Jewish family in a tiny village near Kishinev, an area of Moldova that was part of the Russian Empire.

In 1917 Orthodox Christians descended upon the Jews of Kishinev, unleashing a bloody persecution. Soon after that Leah's father, a tailor, brought his family to America. She was Jewish, though David had never known her to attend services at the synagogue, and she did not like Christians. He could hear her voice scolding him, "Christians kill Jews. Christians hate Jews. Jesus died, David, Don't dig him up."

While still in college David had reconciled his mind to living with that irreconcilable tension: a fundamentalist Christian father who hated Jews and a Jewish mother who hated Christians. Nevertheless, he still bore in his heart the emotional scars of their violent and abusive relationship. Even now, bits and pieces of memories tried to push their way into his conscious thought. The whistle of an extension cord. The biting sting on flesh. He winced at the sudden onslaught of these thoughts.

Though David's father had professed to be a Christian, Wally drank himself into a demonic rage every Friday night at the Twilight Café. On Saturdays he continued to slake his thirst for alcohol with Jack Daniels while gambling with his buddies. He usually paused only to beat his wife and children. After a day of drinking he would shout, "Line up!" They all knew a beating was in the offing. Wally would grab an extension cord and scream, "No use tellin' me you ain't done nuthin'. Jest line up and git it over with. The Good Book says, 'Spare the rod and spoil the child.' I ain't gonna have no spoilt young'uns sittin' on my pew when we git to church tomorrow!"

Sunday mornings, Wally awoke to a throbbing hangover, guzzled three cups of coffee to dull the ache, and sucked on a lemon to hide the lingering odor of whiskey. Then, with his hair slicked in place and his shirt buttoned all the way to the top, singing "Ghost Riders in the Sky," he dutifully marched his children from their home at 77 Pasco Road to a church four blocks away.

As awful as his childhood had been, David grinned at the memory of those Sunday mornings. They all followed the same pattern: Shake hands with the saints and take a seat on the third pew from the front, everyone sitting quiet and still. Midway through the service, the children were excused from the sanctuary and sent to Sunday school. In spite of all that might have happened the day before, Wally smiled at each of his children and doled out coins for them to place in the Sunday school offering plate. Women in the congregation nodded approvingly at the way he doted on his children. Coins in hand, they filed out in a line. Henry and Peter, David's younger brothers, were in front, followed by his sister Anna. As the oldest, David brought up the rear.

One Sunday morning David took the lead. Instead of going down the hallway toward the classroom, he led them outside. Anna looked frightened. "What are you doing? We shouldn't be out here. Someone will see us and tell Dad."

"Hush," David snapped. "We aren't going to Sunday school today."

"Where are we going?"

David pointed over his shoulder. "There," he said, gesturing toward the Dunkin' Donuts store down the block.

Anna was eager, but nervous. "You think he'll find out?"

Henry, the youngest, spoke up. "He'll beat us if he does."

"Well," David suggested, "I'm not telling. Are you?"

"No." Anna shook her head.

Henry looked like he was going to cry. David put his arm around his brother's shoulders. "Don't worry about Dad. Aren't you hungry?"

"Yes," Henry sniffed in response.

"Me too," David nodded soberly.

Anna squinted as she looked longingly down the block. "Do we have enough money?"

David held out his hand. "Give me your change." Each of them dropped their offering coins into his palm. David counted it up. "We have a dollar and thirty-five cents. That ought to be enough for one doughnut apiece."

Anna took him by the elbow. "Let's go, before someone sees us out here." Then, as they started down the street, she recited in a sing-song voice, "Don't take me home to 77 Pasco, until I've had my dough-no's, from Dunkin' D's church."

"That doesn't rhyme," Henry groused.

"Close enough," Anna replied.

"Leave her alone," Peter retorted, and punched Henry on the shoulder.

Tears filled David's eyes as the images rolled through his mind. He could see Henry, Peter, and Anna standing with him. The detail of each face was sharp and clear. The moment was as vivid as if it had happened that very day, and the risk seemed so real. *Wally would have beaten us senseless if he had found out.* And then he wondered why that never had happened. Surely a teacher noticed they were in the service and never made it to class. *Maybe they knew. Maybe they knew more than I thought they knew.*

A gate agent's voice blared over the loudspeaker, announcing the flight to New York. David brushed the tears from his eyes and stood to find the waiting area filled with passengers. A line had formed near the door to the jet-way, and they shuffled past the gate desk. David moved around the rows of chairs and joined the others.

chapter 4

When the plane landed at Hartford, David retrieved his suitcase from the baggage claim area and walked across the lobby to the Hertz counter. Twenty minutes later he steered a rental car away from the terminal and drove north toward Springfield and Indian Orchard.

The countryside looked lush and inviting. It had been years since he had returned to the area, and seeing it again brought back memories of warm summer days at the municipal pool, baseball games in the park, and long walks in the afternoon—anything to avoid the terror that awaited him at home. But the farther he drove the darker his mood became. Half an hour from the airport, he felt a gloomy cloud of depression settle over him. Tension worked its way up the back of his neck. Before long he had a throbbing headache and felt on the verge of tears. Going home, it turned out, wasn't so easy after all.

David's mind turned to the two scriptures he had marked in his Bible that morning, and he began to quote them under his breath. As he did, he felt a deep peace settle over him.

Just north of Enfield, he passed a sign for Agawam. Seeing the sign reminded him of the summer he and his friend, Johnny Bowles, joined the army on the buddy system. They hitchhiked up to Springfield from Indian Orchard so no one would know what they were doing, only to find out they were too young and needed their parents' permission.

David's father was all too happy to sign his. He snarled, "Glad to be rid a ya."

Johnny's dad took them back to Springfield the following week with the signed forms. Then they discovered they both were too skinny. "Gain some weight," the sergeant barked at David, and then he explained. "Ya need to weigh at least 132 pounds—the scale shows 111 now. Try eating bananas. They'll put some weight on you. Come back in about a month, and we'll weigh you again."

David shrugged into his clothes and headed for the door. Outside in the bright sunlight, Johnny was waiting for him beside his father's car. The two boys climbed into the back seat for the return trip to Indian Orchard.

"Hey Ellis, I can't come home with you. I told my mom I'd mow the lawn this evening."

David nodded. "Mr. Bowles, would you drop me off at the corner? I need to stop by the store." The car rolled to a stop and David climbed out. "See you later, Johnny."

David walked to the A&P, where he filled a shopping cart with dozens of green bananas and started eating them. He would make the trip to the market several times before going back for his next weigh-in. At home, he eased open the front door, sneaked the bananas up to his room, and stashed them at the back of the closet. He knew they wouldn't last if his two brothers found them.

All that month he ate every banana he could get his hands on—he thought he must have purchased more than one hundred pounds of them. He prowled the back doors of the local grocery stores and fruit markets looking for ripe bananas too old to sell. He sighed every time he peeled yet another one. Finally, at the end of the month he stepped on the scales. To his horror, he had not gained a single ounce.

At Ryan's Sporting Goods store a few blocks from the house he bought four five-pound weights encased in rubber and three stretch belts. He took them up to his room and worked all afternoon to fashion a harness for the weights that would fit around his waist, hold the weights in place between his legs, and allow him to walk. Finally, after several attempts, he succeeded. The weights were in place and he could walk, sort of.

David sat back on the bed. Then he remembered that they made him strip down to his underwear at the examination. His heart sank. *It's a good thing I wear boxer shorts, but the only ones I have are white. The weights are gray. Guess I could paint them, but they could still be seen.* Desperation took over. *I gotta try something. I can't stay here anymore. And besides, I already told Dad about joining, and he signed the papers. If I don't make it, he'll just laugh and get drunk and....*

Then David had what he thought was a brilliant but embarrassing idea. He had seen some boxers at Ryan's with huge flowers on them. He could buy a pair and wear them over the weights. The guys would tease him, but it would be worth it. At least it would get him away from 77 Pasco Road.

Unable to think of anything better, David decided to go ahead with the plan. On a Friday morning two months later, with the weights strapped between his legs, he rode with Johnny and his father to the recruiting office in Springfield. He followed Johnny from the car into the recruitment office. He did his best to steel himself against the news he was about to receive, but inside he wanted to run and hide. The sergeant recognized the two as they came in the office and guided them to the back.

"Kick off those shoes and step up on the scales."

Johnny took a seat and reached down to untie his sneakers. "Don't we need to undress?"

"Nah." The sergeant shook his head. "I weighed you two last time. I can tell if you gained weight or just filled your pockets with lead."

Johnny set his sneakers beside the chair and stepped up to the scales. The sergeant checked the number for the weight, but David was certain the effort was futile. Johnny hadn't gained more than two or three pounds. "Hey," the sergeant smiled. "Look at that." He pointed to the number on the scales. "Just right."

David was astounded. Johnny had been eating and eating, but he still wore the same clothes as before, and they still looked a size too large. Then David noticed the sergeant had the toe of his boot against the platform of the scales.

Johnny stepped from the scales with a triumphant grin. "Your turn, David."

"Ellis," the sergeant growled. "Step up here. Make it snappy. I got a hundred other things to do today."

David inched his way toward the scales. To keep the weights from clanging together, he took short, slow steps, like some of the little Chinese ladies he saw on the streets.

The sergeant shouted, "Hurry, Ellis. We don't have all day!"

As he stood up to step on the scale, disaster struck. Two of the weights bumped together. David fell to his knees and hung his head in pain and embarrassment. He slowly arose from the floor, mumbled, "I'll be right back," and inched his way toward the bathroom. He unbelted the weights and dropped them into the trash can.

Then, red-faced, he made his way back to where the sergeant was waiting and slowly stepped on the scales. The sergeant smiled as he checked the numbers and slapped David on the back. "Two pounds extra," he chortled. "I guess you ate all those bananas I suggested?" The sergeant turned away and started toward the front of the office. "Get your shoes on and come out here. We got some more papers for you to sign."

When David sat down at the desk the sergeant leaned toward him and smiled conspiratorially, "Next time, son, wear a cup. It could save the family jewels."

David blushed, ducked his head, and mumbled, "Thanks. There won't be a next time."

"Son, where would you like to go? Europe? Hawaii?"

"No, I want to go as far away from 77 Pasco Road as I possibly can."

"Well, how about Japan...or South Korea?"

"South Korea; that's where I want to go." And just like that, they were in the army.

Remembering that day made David chuckle to himself, but just as quickly he remembered the day he actually left home for basic training. He said goodbye to Henry and Peter in the bedroom. Anna met him in the hallway and kissed him on the cheek. Then he went downstairs to the kitchen for one last moment with his mother. She sat at the table with her back to the room, just like she did when Wally was on a drunken rampage. "I'm leaving now," he said.

"They should have sent a car for you."

"They gave me bus fare. All I have to do is walk to the station."

"With your suitcase?"

"Yes." He gave her a hug. "I love you, Mom."

"Me too, but you better go. You'll miss the bus."

Wally was waiting on the front stoop. David held out his hand, but his father knocked it aside and laughed. "You'll never make it in the army. You screw up everything ya' touch, moron!" David lowered his head in shame and started down the steps. Wally continued, his voice loud and belligerent, "In six months you'll be in the stockade. Six months! When they see you the way I see you, they'll kick your no-good butt out! You're nothing but a failure. You hear me? Nothing but a miserable, low-down, good-for-nothin' failure! And don't come crawling back here. Don't think I'll take ya' back. No sir. You're on your own now, boy! And good riddance, ya' piece'a Jew crap. You'll fit in real good with all them black recruits. They're running the country and the Jews 'er payin' for it."

David hadn't looked up to see, but he knew the neighbors sitting outside in the warm July sun were watching. With tears in his eyes and clutching his suitcase, he had turned his back on his childhood home and had trudged off to the bus station.

Now, years later, the memory of that day brought tears to David's eyes once again. He wiped his cheeks with the back of his hand. "At least I got away," he sighed, "which is more than I can say for some."

* * *

Thirty minutes later David reached the outskirts of Indian Orchard. He followed the highway to the east side of town and located a Holiday Inn not far from the neighborhood where he had grown up. He parked the car near the lobby entrance and went inside. The clerk put him in a room overlooking the swimming pool.

It was already seven o'clock. He bought a newspaper from the dispenser near the front desk and took it with him to the motel restaurant. While he ate dinner, he read Leah's obituary. Funeral arrangements were being handled by Kline Brothers Funeral Home with help from the Temple Emanuel Chevra Kaddisha. The wake was scheduled for Tuesday evening. The funeral service would be held on Wednesday morning. "Good," he said to himself. "If the service doesn't last too long, maybe I can get an afternoon flight back to Charlotte."

After dinner David went to his room and flopped down on the bed. Back in North Carolina, with Sue and the children by his side, news of his mother's death hadn't seemed that important. The notion of traveling alone to her funeral seemed like the right thing to do. Now that he was here, the whole thing seemed much too real. He felt as if his childhood were still alive and reaching for him with long, spiny fingers, trying to pull him back to the horror that had threatened to end his life almost before it had begun. David rolled on his back and stared up at the ceiling. He had the sudden urge to talk to Sue. He flipped on the light and reached for his wallet. A scrap of paper inside had the phone number for the beach house. He had scribbled it down the year before. Sue answered on the second ring. "Sue," he whispered, "I know you're praying for me. Please don't stop."

Sue gripped the phone tightly. "David? Are you okay? I can barely hear you."

"I'm as okay as I can be, honey. I just needed to know that you were praying for me. This is harder than I imagined it might be."

"Oh David! Of course I'm praying for you! I haven't stopped since you got the call this morning. Let's say Psalm 23 together. Let the word of the Lord speak peace to your spirit."

After they recited the Psalm, Sue whispered, "I love you. Now get some rest."

Her words seemed prophetic. David had a restful night's sleep and awoke feeling refreshed. He spent the morning lounging in his room, reading and watching television. Shortly before noon he slipped on a pair of jeans and a golf shirt, then drove up the street in search of a place for lunch. He came to the Indian Orchard Diner and slowed the car, craning his neck to see through the front windows. "Seats are full," he mumbled. He glanced toward the far end of the building and surveyed the parking lot. "Lot is almost full." He turned the car from the street. "This must be the place to eat." He squeezed the car into an empty space and went inside.

Opposite the front door a counter ran to the left and right. Behind it, a cook dressed in a white t-shirt and white pants worked the grill. The smell of onions and hot grease filled the air. Waitresses moved back and forth through the room, bringing dishes to waiting customers and shouting orders as they walked. David stood there a moment, feeling out of place amidst the crowd. A waitress brushed past him. "Sit anywhere you can find a seat, honey." David spotted an open stool at the counter and slid onto it.

A few moments later the cook turned to him. "What'll ya' have, pal?"

"What's good?"

"Everything."

"Hamburger and fries."

The cook grinned, "My specialty."

A waitress appeared behind the counter in front of David, scribbled something on a notepad, and then glanced down at him. "Whatcha drinkin'?"

"Coke."

"One Coca-Cola." She scribbled on the notepad again then

disappeared. A moment later she returned with a glass of Coke and set it on the counter. Five minutes later she came back with a plate holding a hamburger and fries.

As David ate, he thought about the wake for Leah later that evening and wondered if he would know anyone there, or if anyone would attend. He wasn't certain his brothers, Peter and Henry, would be there. Anna maybe, but not his brothers. To his knowledge, they hadn't seen their mother since they had each left home. He wiped mustard from the corner of his mouth and glanced at the waitress. She turned in his direction. "You need something, honey?"

David nodded. "Can you tell me how to find Kline Brothers Funeral home?"

The waitress looked puzzled. "Kline Brothers. I don't know. I'm not from around here."

A man seated next to David nodded. "I know where it is." He swallowed. "Go down here to the traffic light." He pointed with his thumb. "Turn right, and it's a couple of blocks on the left. You'll see it."

"Oh. Not far."

"Nah. You're almost there." The man wiped his mouth with a napkin. "Got a funeral today?"

"A Wake. This evening."

"Sorry. Relative of yours?"

"My mother."

"Oh, man. That's tough, losing your mother."

"Yeah, it is."

"She lived here? What was her name?"

"Leah Ellis. I think she still used that name. She and my father were divorced."

"What was her maiden name?"

"Levine."

The man smiled and nodded. "Kline Brothers does a lot of Jewish funerals. I thought they might be having one today."

"What made you think that?"

"I go by there every day on my route." He pointed to the logo on his shirt. "They had some extra cars in the parking lot this morning."

"Extra cars?"

"Yeah. You know, people staying with the body."

"I don't follow you."

"Aren't you Jewish?"

"Half. My father wasn't Jewish. We grew up going to a Pentecostal church."

"Jews won't leave a dead body unattended like that. Somebody stays with it until they put it in the ground. You didn't know that?"

"No." David shook his head. "My father wouldn't let our mother tell us anything about what Jews believed. He hated Jews."

The man frowned. "But he married your mother."

"Yeah," David said thoughtfully. "Now you see why I live in North Carolina."

A man seated to David's left spoke up. "That's the trouble with relatives. You can't move far enough away to get rid of them."

Everyone chuckled, but the words touched a spot deep in David's soul.

chapter 5

When he finished lunch, David left the diner and drove up the street. He was curious to see what the funeral home was like and what final arrangements for Leah's service Virgil had made. At the traffic light he turned right. Three blocks later he came to the funeral home. Four cars were parked near the front entrance. David parked in a space beside them and stepped out. As he reached to close the car door, he glanced down at his pants. Suddenly, he was self-conscious about the way he looked. Blue jeans, a golf shirt with a few wrinkles, and topsiders with no socks. "Not exactly what you should wear to a funeral home," he mumbled. "Oh, well. Plenty of time to change before tonight." He pushed the door closed and started toward the building.

As he came through the entrance, a man dressed in a black suit met him. "May I help you?"

"Is anyone from the Ellis family here?"

"Ellis?"

"Leah Ellis. Maybe, Leah Levine?"

"Oh." The man's face brightened. "Yes. They're back here." He gestured toward the hallway. "I'll show you. Are you with the family?"

"I'm her son."

"I'm Harvey Kline." They shook hands. "I'm sorry for your loss."

"Thanks."

David followed him down the hall. A little way past the first parlor, he heard voices. As they continued on, the voices grew more distinct. A moment later Harvey came to a stop and gestured toward an open door. "They're in here." David acknowledged him with a nod and stepped inside the room.

A plain, wooden casket sat on a bier along the far wall. David noted that it was closed. Chairs lined the walls to the left and right. Three men occupied the chairs to the right, all of them dressed in black suits with white shirts. Each wore a yarmulke.

Across the room to the left, an older woman was seated in a chair near the casket. Her face was creased with wrinkles and her white hair was disheveled. Standing before her was a tall, broad-shouldered man. Like the others seated across the room, he wore a black suit with a white shirt and black tie. And, like them, he wore a yarmulke on his head, though it had slid to one side. He reached up with his hand to push it back in place. "Look, you shouldn't be here," he insisted. "This is the job of the Chevra Kaddisha."

"I'm her family." As the woman spoke, her eyes met David's. Her face lit up. "Here is her son." She gestured to him with a wave of her hand while she continued to talk. "Let him decide." She gestured once more and patted the seat beside her. "Come here, David."

David had no idea who she was, but he immediately felt comfortable with her and crossed the room to join her. She stood and slipped her arm around his waist. "It's good to see you, David." Instinctively, David looked down at her and rested his hand on her shoulder. She nodded toward the man with whom she had been talking. "This is Lee Zeidman. He's from the Chevra Kaddisha. He's trying to tell me I can't sit *Shemira* for my own family." The old woman dismissed Zeidman with a wave of the hand. "We can't talk now. I must talk to Leah's son now." She looked up at David again, and they sat down together.

Reluctantly, Zeidman turned away and took a seat with the men on the opposite side of the room. When he was gone, she rested her hand on David's leg. "I knew you would come." She gave him a kind smile.

"Of all the children, I knew you would be here. Will your brothers and sister be able to come? I know how much they loved your mother."

"I haven't had a chance to talk with them yet, but I hope they'll be here soon." He looked away awkwardly.

She leaned back, her eyebrows arched. "You don't remember me?"

"I'm sorry," David said, sheepishly. "I don't."

"I am Yona." She gave him a knowing look. David shrugged in response. "Yona," she repeated. "Yona Kanievsky."

"I'm sorry." David shook his head. "I just don't remember."

"Well." She leaned closer. "It's okay. I remember you. I was there when all the events of your life occurred—some great, some not so great. I remember them all."

As she spoke David heard a low, mumbling sound from across the room. He glanced in that direction and saw Zeidman and the others sitting with their heads bowed. David nodded in their direction. "What are they doing?"

"The Psalms," Yona replied. "They are reciting the Psalms."

"Who are they?"

"They are men from the Chevra Kaddisha."

"What is that?"

"The burial society. From the Temple. They look after the dead until they are buried."

"I thought the funeral home did that."

"Not for us. The Chevra Kaddisha wash the body, anoint it, and dress it for burial. Then they sit with it until the funeral. I was with Leah when she died. Now they try to send me home."

"I don't know much about those traditions."

"That was because of Wally, your father."

"You knew him?"

"I knew them all. Your sister and brothers. Your mother. Her sister Eliana. But your father, Wally ..." She shook her head. "He was real trouble."

"Wally was a lot things," David sighed.

"Your father would not let Leah teach you the Jewish ways. He forbade it. She had no energy to train you after he started beating her. She did her best just to stay alive." Her voice trailed away, as if the words had brought to mind a memory she would have rather avoided.

"Our house was a very dark place."

"But your aunt and uncle, Eliana and Jacob, were a light." Yona patted him on the leg. "They tried to teach you some of the things. As best they could."

"I remember they took Anna and Peter and me on a trip." David smiled at the thought of it. "We went to New York, I think."

"Yes." Yona's face came alive. "We drove to Brooklyn to Barry Friedman's bar mitzvah. Anna and Peter were with us."

David frowned at her. "You were there?"

"Yes, I was there." She gave him an incredulous look. "I was the one who grabbed you when the door came open. You do not remember?"

An image flashed through David's mind. They stopped for a break on the way to New York. When they got back in the car, he was seated on the passenger side, by the rear door. Uncle Jacob made a sharp turn with the car, and David's shoulder banged against the door. It flew open, and he tumbled out toward the pavement. He was certain he would die, when a hand caught hold of his shirt collar and jerked him back inside.

David looked at Yona. "I thought that was Anna who grabbed me."

"No," Yona said, shaking her head. "Anna was a little girl. She was not strong enough to do that. Besides, she and Eliana were up front with Jacob. I was in back. Sitting between you and Peter." She gestured proudly with her thumb upward. "It was I who pulled you back inside the car."

"Hmm." David glanced away, his mind racing to make sense of what she said. "I don't remember that." He looked back at her. "But I remember we got some new clothes."

"Ahh. The rags they dressed you in." She touched her hands to her cheeks. "Leah would never have done such a thing, but Wally wouldn't give her money to buy clothes for you."

"I remember the food too, at the bar mitzvah. They had a lot of food."

"Oh, my. You kids ate like you hadn't had anything for days."

"We probably hadn't," David said resolutely. "We didn't have much."

"Your father spent it all on beer and gambling."

"Where did we eat that day?"

"The Friedman's. We went to their house in Bensonhurst."

"They had so much food."

"But do you remember what happened when we took you home?"

"No." David shook his head. "What happened?"

"Oh. It's a good thing you don't remember."

"Something happened?"

"It was late, and we were all laughing at some joke your Uncle Jacob had told us. He was like that. Always with a joke. Leah went up the steps of your house, opened the front door, and motioned for us to be quiet; but it was too late." She shook her head. "Wally was standing at the top of the stairs, shouting, 'Shut up! Shut up you stupid, loud-mouthed Jews!' He was the one who looked stupid. Had on nothing but his underwear. But he was shouting at us, 'I'm tryin' to sleep up here.' Ahh." She had a pained look on her face. "It was awful."

As she spoke, David saw the angry, drunken look on his father's face, the extension cord in one hand, a bottle of beer in the other. The memory sent a shudder through his shoulders.

Yona squeezed his leg. "Poor Jacob. 'We didn't mean to disturb your sleep,' he said. 'We'll bring the kids' things in and then be on our way.' But it wasn't good enough for your father." Yona shook her head. "Once the rage got hold of him, nothing would do but to let it out all the way. He came down the stairs, grabbed Jacob by the collar and hit him."

"Hit him?"

"Yes. Hit him so hard, he flew into the screened door, sent that door flying, and both landed in the front yard."

Now David could see Jacob lying on his back, motionless, with Aunt Eliana screaming at Wally and clawing at his back. Wally brushed her aside and stomped into the yard. Uncle Jacob was a small man. Wally picked him up and slammed him into the wooden fence that separated the yard from the sidewalk.

"I remember that now," David said softly. "I was terrified."

"Fortunately for Jacob, a neighbor called the police. Wally could have killed him."

"I don't remember Dad getting arrested."

"He didn't get arrested," Yona said, wagging her finger again. "The policeman who came to the house was one of his drinking buddies." She threw her hands in the air. "After all of that, Jacob almost dead, and they still didn't do a thing to Wally."

"Was Uncle Jacob all right?"

"Bruised and stunned. His nose was broken, and two teeth were knocked out." She leaned closer to David. "But after that, he and Eliana never came back to your house." Tears filled her eyes. "I knew it was bad for you." She patted David's leg again. "I knew it was bad. But they would not come."

Yona dabbed her eyes with a handkerchief. David slipped his arm across her shoulder. "It's okay." He rubbed her shoulder lightly. "We all made it out alive."

"Only by God's blessing."

"You are right about that."

They spent the afternoon alternately talking to each other and listening to Zeidman and the men as they recited the Psalms. Finally, a little before five, David said to Yona, "I have to go back to the motel to change clothes."

Yona nodded. "I will stay here until the others arrive. Then I will go home. But I will see you tomorrow."

"You won't be here tonight?"

"I don't think so," she said, shaking her head. "I have seen most of Leah's friends already, and I am tired. I will see you tomorrow. Keep meditating on those two scriptures."

David was puzzled. *How could she know about that?*

chapter 6

David drove back to the motel. He took a shower and dressed in a gray suit with a white shirt and red tie. By six o'clock he was ready to return for his mother's wake. That left him enough time to eat dinner and get to the funeral home before seven.

He was glad for the extra time and used it to walk down to the motel restaurant, where he ordered a salad. As he ate, he thought about his conversation with Yona. He had enjoyed meeting her and was happy for the memories, though painful, that she had brought to mind. The sound of her voice, her hand patting his leg to emphasize a point, and even the sweet aroma of her perfume reminded him of special occasions and trips in the car to New York. Most of all, he was excited to finally talk about the Jewish side of his family. Throughout his childhood he had been forbidden to discuss the matter. Finding it now was like throwing open a window on a bright spring morning. Fresh air blew through his soul and left him eager to learn more of what it meant to be the son of a Jewish mother.

True to her word earlier that day, Yona did not attend the wake. David spent the evening introducing himself to people he had never met before. Most of them were members of Temple Emanuel where, he learned, Leah had been quite involved. According to Rabbi Kunstadt, who presided at the synagogue, she was active in a Sisterhood group and in one of the Chavurot groups that met for dinner and study. Though

David didn't know much about Jewish synagogue practice, he knew enough about congregational life to know that his mother was much different than she'd been when he was a child.

Back then, she would hide in the kitchen when his Dad began to drink, and then hurry to the bedroom if he brought out the extension cord or the wide leather belt. She seemed not to notice the bloody beatings he gave to David, Peter, and Henry. And when Wally turned his wrath on her, she never defended herself. David couldn't remember her having friends. Obviously, she had changed, becoming a woman who spent a good deal of time caring for others. Still, it struck him as sad. All those wasted years, when she could have been alive and involved, when they all could have benefited from it. He wondered how his life would have turned out if she had asserted herself more.

From seven to eight that evening, the parlor that held Leah's casket had a steady stream of visitors, but by eight fifteen only Rabbi Kunstadt and David remained. The empty, silent parlor left David feeling empty too, and sad. Leah had five children and a husband. As far as David knew, all of them were still alive. Yet on this final night, he alone was with her; he alone had returned to say goodbye. He was sure his siblings weren't aware of the Jewish custom. The thought that her life would end this way left him feeling lonely and abandoned.

David stood there for a moment and tried to remember something besides the image of her at the kitchen table with her back turned toward him. All he could grasp were small snippets from here and there...pushing her grocery cart on Friday nights, glad to be out of the house for a light, carefree moment, and reminding him not to mention the trip to his father...playing in the backyard on those rare occasions when his father worked late, interrupted by her warning not to get his pants dirty. "You know what your father will do." David shook his head, as if by jostling his brain he might bring to mind a more peaceful memory; but none came. Finally, he turned to Rabbi Kunstadt. "I think I'll—"

David's voice caught when he saw Anna in the parlor doorway. She was only a little over five feet tall and looked amazingly like Leah. He started toward her at once. Tears filled his eyes as he wrapped his arms around her. "I wasn't sure you could come."

"I wanted to make certain Dad wasn't here," Anna replied.

"I don't think he's coming."

"Does he even know?"

"I don't know," David shrugged. "I didn't tell him."

Anna leaned away. "I can't stand the thought of seeing him."

"Well," David smiled. "He isn't here tonight. Come on," He hooked an arm in hers. "Let's sit over here by the wall." He escorted her across the room to a chair near the casket.

As she took a seat, Anna lowered her voice. "Is there a reason why the casket is closed? Was something wrong with her?"

"I think it's one of the traditions," David replied.

"Traditions?"

"Not to have the casket open. I think I overheard someone say that earlier."

"It's all the same to me," Anna said, her voice as emotionless as her face. "I haven't seen her in so many years. One more night won't matter. But still, she was our mother …" Anna sniffed.

David nodded. "It was tough—"

"No," Anna retorted. "You don't know the half of it."

A frown wrinkled David's forehead. "What does that mean?"

"It means you got out. You joined the army. Went to school. Had a career."

"And you didn't?"

"I—"Anna suddenly stopped. She took a deep breath. Her face softened. "I'm sorry." Her shoulders relaxed. "It wasn't your fault. You did what you could." She squeezed his arm. "None of it matters now anyway."

Men from the Chevra Kaddisha again took their places in the chairs along the opposite wall. Anna nodded in their direction. "Who are they?"

"Official mourners. Every synagogue has a burial society," he explained. "They make sure the body is prepared according to Jewish custom. They provide someone to sit with Mom until she's buried."

Anna looked at him. "You learned about this as a preacher?"

"No," David replied. "Yona told me."

"Who is she?"

"Someone who says she knows us."

"I've never heard of her."

"I hadn't either, until today. But she knew me, and she insists she was there for all the important events in our lives."

Now Anna's face was wrinkled in a frown. "And you believed her?"

"She'll be here tomorrow for the funeral. You can ask her about it yourself. Are you staying?"

"As long as Dad's not here. If he comes, I'm going back to Chicago. But I don't remember a Yona."

"I talked to her all afternoon, and I still don't remember her. I think I've buried a lot of those memories."

Anna nodded. "I know the feeling. And the strange thing is, I don't even remember consciously doing it."

Anna stared blankly across the room. "One of my therapists said it's the way the mind survives. Like we know it was awful, but admitting how awful it was is worse than the things we suffered in the first place."

"You're seeing a therapist?"

"Not now. I did for awhile."

"Did it help?"

"Tom, the guy I'm seeing, thinks it did."

Anna slipped her arm through David's. "Have you been by the house?"

"No." David shook his head. "But it isn't far from here."

"I never want to go back there again," Anna offered. "I wouldn't mind seeing the neighborhood, but I wouldn't want to go inside the house."

"I wonder if the house is still there."

They talked a few minutes longer. Anna described her life in

Chicago, then Rabbi Kunstadt appeared. "The funeral home is closing now. And I need to get on home."

David sat up straight. "What time is it?"

"Ten."

David checked his watch. "Wow. I didn't know it was that late."

"You can stay as long as you like. There's an exit door available to family at the rear of the building" Kunstadt nodded over his shoulder toward the men across the room. "They'll be here until the funeral tomorrow."

Anna stood. "I think I should leave."

David pulled himself up from the chair and held out his hand for Anna. "Where are you staying?"

"At the Holiday Inn. It's not far from here."

"Good," David smiled. "I'm staying there too." He turned to Kunstadt. "We'll see you tomorrow."

"Very good," Kunstadt nodded. "I'll be gone in a few minutes myself."

David led the way toward the door. As they reached the hallway, he glanced back to see Kunstadt standing with the men near the casket. He could not deny a new, insatiable curiosity about what it meant to be Jewish.

chapter 7

The following morning David rose early. He dressed, packed his suitcase, checked out of the motel, and then met Anna for breakfast in the restaurant. They talked quietly about what to expect at the funeral, but the conversation was not as engaging as the night before. When they finished eating, they walked together to the parking lot. David put his suitcase in the trunk of the car and turned to Anna, "You know how to get back to the funeral home?"

"Yes. I'll be fine. I have a map in my car."

"Okay. I'll meet you there."

As David drove to the funeral home he thought about what they had endured as children and the effects it had on them. Anna seemed much more calm, and he wondered how he appeared to her. *What does it matter how I appear? Why do I care what others think of me? It only matters what God thinks of me.*

Gradually, his thoughts gave way to a prayer, which he prayed aloud as he turned the corner beyond the diner. "Lord, you have taken me so far from where I began, and yet it seems like I have only begun. Help me to avoid the traps of the past—the ones I know about and the ones I don't—and let me never subject my family to the kinds of things I endured as a child." He repeated the two scriptures God had given him the morning before then continued, "Help Anna to find peace, and help her to love You with all her heart. Amen." He parked near the front entrance of Kline Brothers, switched off the engine, and got out. Anna parked next to him.

"Not many cars," Anna said, glancing around the lot.

"Probably won't be many people here," David replied. "I thought maybe some of the Ellises would come. Virgil was the one who told me she died."

"They won't come," Anna said, shaking her head. "Virgil always acts like he cares, but he's just waiting for something bad to happen."

David gave her a skeptical look. "That's a little jaded, isn't it?"

"Think about it." Anna came around the rear of the car. "When did he call you?"

"Well, the other day when Mom died."

"And before that?"

"When Henry's son was arrested."

Anna cocked her head. "And before that?"

"When Peter had a wreck."

"That's what I'm talking about." Anna jabbed his chest with her finger for emphasis. "He's not concerned about us or Mom or anything. That's just his way of saying, "Oops, they messed up again.""

"Maybe so," David shrugged. "You might be right."

"You know I am."

Just then, a black Mercedes turned into the parking lot and came to a stop a few spaces away. The driver's door opened and a woman stepped out. Anna mumbled under her breath, "Who is that?"

"Yona," David replied. "That's Yona Kanievsky. Says she was there when we were children."

"She looks familiar," Anna whispered. "I think." She craned her neck to see. "I can't really tell."

David leaned his head in Anna's direction. "Why would we forget her?" He watched as Yona looked in their direction.

"I knew you kids would be here. Something told me this morning you would be here."

"Yes," Anna said in a pleasant voice. "We were just talking about you. How are you?"

"Fine." Yona stopped and surveyed the sky. "Such a beautiful morning." She started forward again, and when she reached them she slipped her arm around Anna's waist. "So good to see you again."

"Yes," Anna replied courteously. "It's good to see you."

Yona gave them each a kiss on the cheek. They continued to chat as they made their way into the funeral home. Rabbi Kunstadt met them in the lobby and escorted them to the chapel. They took a seat on the front row and sat quietly while waiting for the service to begin. A few minutes later, a couple arrived and took a seat on a pew across the aisle. Moments later, several more entered. David heard the rustling as others came down the aisle and entered the pew just behind them. He turned and looked up to see the solemn faces of Henry and Peter.

David jumped up and gripped Henry's shoulder. "I wasn't sure you would be able to make it."

Henry wrapped David in a bear hug and replied, "It was touch and go. I wasn't sure the boss was going to let us off, but in the end he did. We work for the same guy, so Peter was in the same boat."

Peter reached out to David and grasped his forearms in work-hardened hands. "The boss wasn't real happy about giving us the morning off. I told him, 'Look man, it's our mother!' He just shook his head and waved us out of the room. He's a little short on compassion."

"Come and sit with us here in front," David beckoned, and they stepped into the center aisle and came around to join him and Anna and Yona. Yona scooted away and David followed her lead so the brothers could sit between David and Anna. It was good to see them, and he knew they would probably have little time together. Anna gave each of her brothers a quick hug as she moved down the row to make room for them.

Promptly at ten o'clock attendants wheeled the casket into the chapel. Rabbi Kunstadt followed. When it was in place, the attendants stepped away and Kunstadt turned to face the pews. In his hand he held a length of black ribbon to symbolize the loss of a loved one. "We have gathered here today to pay tribute to the life of Leah Levine Ellis and to mourn her death." He paused to tear the ribbon into four pieces. Holding them between his fingers, he stepped forward and handed one piece each to Anna, Henry, Peter, and finally David. With each piece, he said in Hebrew, *"Baruch atah Hashem Elokeinu melech haolam, dayan ha'emet."* Then in English, "Blessed are you, Lord our God, Ruler of the universe, the true Judge." When he finished, he turned back to the congregation. "Join me in reading Psalm 14." He held up a folded page. "The words are on the service bulletin you received as you came in."

David felt Anna nudge his side. He glanced in her direction and saw a bulletin in her hand. "I got one for you," she whispered, handing him the paper.

"Thanks," David whispered. He took it and opened to the inside page.

Kunstadt paused a moment then began. "The fool says in his heart, 'There is no God.'" As the familiar words slipped from David's lips, he noticed the sound of the congregation was louder than he had expected.

After the psalm, an elderly woman made her way up the aisle and stood near the casket. Kunstadt stepped aside. The woman cleared her throat and began. "Leah Levine was my best friend. I met her several years ago when she returned here to live." She nodded toward David and the others. "I am sure many of you shared her bitterness and sorrow over the earlier years of her life." The woman paused a moment, and in that break David realized his mother had talked about her past, and she had done so with regret. A lump rose in his throat. The woman continued. "But she did not wallow in it. Instead, she used her energy to help others. The first time I met her was when I was sick. Some of you remember I was confined to bed for three weeks." She placed her hand to her brow and shook her head. "It was awful. But," her face brightened, "there was Leah, with a pot of soup and a smile. She didn't talk too much, which I was glad." Laughter twittered across the room.

"Yes," she said, acknowledging the response. "She wasn't much for talking. She was more for doing.

"After I got better, she continued to visit me, and then we worked together in the Sisterhood. She told me I needed to get involved. I did my best to convince her that I wasn't able, but she told me I couldn't spend the rest of my life lying in bed. So," she shrugged, "what could I do? She wasn't going to leave me alone if I didn't." While the audience responded with more laughter, she took a step back and turned to face the casket. "Leah, I thank you for being my friend." The room was quiet. "I will miss you," she said softly." Then she turned away and started back down the aisle, tears rolling down her cheeks.

Rabbi Kunstadt moved back to his place in front of the casket and folded his hands near his waist. "Let us pray," he said, then closed his eyes and bowed his head. The room became still. Moments passed and no one said a word. David opened his eyes and took a peek to his left. Anna, Henry, and Peter sat with their eyes closed.

After what seemed a long time, Kunstadt lifted his head. "O God, full of compassion, who dwells on high, grant true rest upon the wings of the Shechinah to the soul of Leah, who has gone to her eternal world. May her place of rest be in Eden, and may the All-Merciful One shelter her with the cover of His wings forever and bind her soul in the bond of life. The Lord is her heritage; may she rest in peace. Amen."

The congregation responded with another amen. Then Kunstadt gestured with the service bulletin in his hand. "Join me now in reading the Twenty-third Psalm."

There was a rustling sound as the congregation stood. Yona stood and nodded toward David to do the same. He and his siblings rose from the pew and opened the bulletin as Kunstadt began to read. "The Lord is my shepherd, I shall not want. He causes me to lie down in green pastures." While the congregation continued to read, attendants from the funeral home appeared on either side of the casket. Carefully, they scooted it out from its resting place and turned it toward the aisle. With the words of the psalm filling the room, they wheeled it down the aisle and out of sight.

The psalm finished, Yona glanced down the pew once again in David's direction. "We may go now," she said, gesturing with a wave of her hand.

David and his brothers and sister stood and turned to follow the casket down the aisle. They looked in amazement as they surveyed the room. Almost fifty people had gathered for the service. "I didn't expect this many," David whispered to Anna, who was right in front of him.

"I know." She glanced around. "There are quite a few." Peter and Henry looked dazed and nodded in agreement.

Yona leaned close to David, her arm through his. "The woman who spoke was Abigail Meyer. The words she said were true." As they entered the hallway she said, "Walk me out."

*   *   *

From the funeral home they drove across town to the cemetery. None of the crowd followed. Only Yona, David, Anna, Henry, and Peter attended. Rabbi Kunstadt led them in a psalm and offered a prayer of thanksgiving to God. When he was finished, workmen from the cemetery lowered the casket into the grave. Once it was in place, they stepped aside and waited.

Yona tottered over to a pile of dirt at one side of the grave. She picked up a few clumps and tossed them into the hole. They landed with a plop atop the wooden casket. She turned to David. "You and your siblings should do the same." David, Anna, Henry, and Peter dutifully complied, each one tossing a clump of dirt atop their mother's casket.

Anna hugged Yona and then reached up to slip her arm around David's neck. "I miss you," she whispered as she kissed his cheek. Then she turned to Yona. "I need to go. My plane leaves at one. It's almost eleven. But it was wonderful to see you again."

"You too, dear," answered Yona with a hug.

Anna turned back to David. "There is still a lot of pain."

"I know," he sighed. "I thought I had dealt with it myself. Now I'm not so sure."

"Call me!" Anna turned to Henry and Peter as she made her way to her car. "It's so good to see you. We don't stay in touch like we should. Can I take you somewhere on my way to the airport?"

"Thanks, Anna," said Peter. "If you could drop us back at the funeral home, we'll be on our way back to work. We left Henry's car there. We'll both have to work overtime to make up for the lost time today. That's the kind of guy our boss is." Then they shook hands with David and gave him the kind of hugs guys share.

As they drove away, Yona turned to David. "I have something to show you. Follow me to my house."

David glanced at his watch. If he left for the airport now, he was certain he could get a flight back to Charlotte that afternoon. If he went with Yona, he might have to wait until tomorrow. He saw images of his children on the beach, playing and laughing in the waves and running across the sand. His heart longed to be with them.

Yona interrupted his thoughts. "You have something else to do?"

"No," David said, shaking his head.

"Good. You can follow me." She turned away and started toward the car. "The house is on Davis Street. I will drive slowly. You can keep up."

chapter 8

David followed Yona across town to a white frame house, which stood on a quiet street in a nice neighborhood. She parked the Mercedes in the driveway, and he parked at the curb out front. He crossed the lawn and followed her up the steps to the front porch. Yona took him by the hand and looked up into his eyes. "You need something to eat."

"I'm all right," David replied. He was hungry, but if they had lunch he would never make it to the airport in time.

Yona turned and unlocked the front door. "I think we should eat." She pushed open the door and pointed to the left, toward a hall. "The bathroom is down there. Use the towel on the counter by the sink. I put it out for you this morning before I left." She moved through the living room, calling, "Come to the kitchen when you are done!"

This woman seems to know what I need before I do, mused David as he walked briskly to the bathroom. Five minutes later he stood in her hallway looking at the photographs on the wall. Most were of people he had never seen before, but two were of him and Peter and one was of Henry and Anna. At first blush they looked so young and innocent, but as he looked into their eyes, he saw traces of the pain they all tried so hard to hide—yet desperately wanted someone to see.

Yona called from the kitchen, "Everything okay?"

"Yes," David replied. He walked through the warmly furnished living room and leaned against the doorway to the kitchen, watching her as she prepared lunch. A sink and counter ran along the wall opposite the door. Natural light filtered through a window above the sink. The stove and refrigerator stood to the right. To the left, a table sat in the corner. Two plates were arranged with napkins and silverware on either side. Yona worked at the counter. "Have a seat. This will be ready soon."

David walked over, pulled a chair from the table, and sat down. She set a glass of iced tea at his place. "Drink," she said. "I know you must be thirsty." David took a sip from the glass and was surprised to find it sweet. Over her shoulder she said, "Yes, it's sweet. Your friends in the South got that part right. They missed many things, but they got the tea correct." A moment later she placed a bowl of chicken salad on the table. "Anyone who takes good, lovely water and makes it bitter with tea has an obligation to make it sweet with sugar." She seemed to glide across the room, and then returned with a bowl of sliced fruit. "There," she said, setting the bowl on the table. "I think we are ready." She moved to the opposite side of the table and took a seat.

Yona reached across the table and laid her hand on David's. "I have something to tell you…a message from Leah."

"A message from my mother? How? When? What did she say?"

"I was with her in the ambulance on the way to the hospital. I held her hand and sang the Twenty-third Psalm to her. She said, 'Tell Davy I saw Him, and I talked to Him…to the Messiah. It's okay now. I'm not afraid.' Do you know what she meant by that?"

David gasped. He slumped back in his chair, and tears were soon dripping from his chin. Yona got up, set a box of tissues next to him, and sat down again. He appreciated her silence. When he regained his composure, he sat forward and leaned his elbows on the table. "Every time we talked I asked if I could pray with her. Sometimes it seemed as if it were a game between us. I'd ask; she'd refuse. But the last time we talked, it was different. She said, 'Sure Davy; it couldn't do any harm.'

I was almost speechless. It was the opportunity I had prayed for year after year, and I was determined not to mess it up. So, I prayed:

"'Jesus…Savior…Messiah…Redeemer, thank You for Your love for us. The prophet Isaiah wrote, "The people who walk in darkness have seen a great light." Thank You for giving us the Light. Thank you for giving Your life on the Cross for me…and for my mom. I know You love her as much as I do, and You want only what is best for her. Please show her Your love. Open her understanding so that she may know You in all of Your light and truth. Come to her as You did to me, and show her the reality of Your sacrifice and salvation. I ask this in Jesus' name, Amen.'

"Mom whispered, 'Thank you, Davy. I'll talk to you next week.' But there was no next week." David jumped up from his chair and began to pace the floor. "Yona, do you know what this means? It means I'll see her again! She has been redeemed!" He pulled Yona up from her chair and wrapped his arms around her. "Thank you! Thank you for delivering my mom's message to me. Praise God! Praise God!"

After they had rejoiced and wiped their tears, both sat back down at the table. Yona lifted the bowl of chicken salad from the table and handed it to David. "Now, here. I know you're hungry. I knew that when you came from the car," she continued. "You were just saying no because you thought you could leave early." She tilted her head. "I have something to show you that is more important." Again he was amused at how accurately she understood his thoughts. He took the bowl from her and scooped chicken salad onto his plate.

"How was it you knew my mother?"

"I knew her from Russia. I have always been with her."

Yona reached behind her to a shelf and took down a box. It was the size of a cigar box, made of tin and painted with a pastoral scene. A man and woman were seated on a blanket, having a picnic in a green meadow.

David shook his head. "Yona, I have tried and tried, but I can't remember knowing you."

She lifted the lid and reached inside the box, then handed him a photograph. "You have seen this?"

"Yes." David nodded, taking the photograph from her. "I have one just like it in my wallet."

"Good. Your mother gave it to you. I am glad you kept it all these years." Yona closed the lid and set the box aside. "But she did not tell you anything about it."

"No. She wouldn't tell me much about her life. All I know is that she was born in Russia, her parents were Jews, and she hated Christians." He laid the photograph on the table.

"So, you do not know about the bush?"

"The bush?"

Yona tapped the background of the photograph with her finger. "That bush."

"No." He looked more closely at the photograph. "I never thought about the bush. Only thing I noticed were the coats. It must have been cold that day."

"Ahh," Yona grinned, wagging her finger. "It was not cold. Look at the bush." David looked again. Yona tapped it with her finger. "See those white dots on the leaves?"

"Yes, what are they? I never noticed them before."

"Flowers," she said, letting the word slide slowly from her mouth. "They are flowers. It was springtime."

"So, why the coats?"

"For that, I must tell you something else." She took a sip of tea. "In Kishinev where they lived, your mother's grandfather—your great-grandfather—was a rabbi in the synagogue. So, they were there on the Sabbath. The whole family. They were all there. Then Leah said to their mother, 'Ima, I have to go to the outhouse, please.'"

"The outhouse?"

"The synagogue had an outhouse out back, made of wood, with a hole in the ground. So her mother said, 'Leah, you are too small to go alone. Eliana will have to go with you.' Eliana didn't want to go. She wanted to sit there with everyone else and hear her grandfather read from Torah. But Leah was very uncomfortable, and Eliana could see she was going to…you know…have an accident. So, she went outside with her."

Yona took another sip of tea. David swallowed a bite of chicken salad. "What does this have to do with the bush?"

"I'll get to that. The outhouse was in a grove of trees behind the building. It was cold. Dead of winter. Snow everywhere. But she had to go, so out they ran. Leah opened the door and went inside. Eliana waited a few feet away." Yona pointed to David's plate. "Are you eating? I've only seen you take one bite." David took another bite of chicken salad, and she continued.

"While they were at the outhouse, an angry crowd formed in front of the synagogue. They were shouting, 'Christ killers! Filthy Jews! You drink the blood of babies!'" Yona clasped her hands together and her shoulders shook. "It was a terrible time. Leah was inside the outhouse, and the mob couldn't see Eliana, but she could see them." Yona leaned back from the table. "When Leah came out, they huddled by the trees and watched as the mob hammered the windows closed so they could not be opened and nailed boards over the doors so no one could get out." She paused a moment to collect her thoughts. "Then some of them came with torches and set the building ablaze."

David's mouth flew open. "They burned it?"

"Yes."

"With everyone inside?"

Yona nodded. "Your grandmother, your great-grandfather. Their brothers and all their cousins and friends." Tears streamed down Yona's cheeks. David reached across the table and took her hand. "It was terrible," she sobbed. She let go of David's hand and dabbed her eyes with her napkin. "And that is why Leah felt the way she did about Christians. The people in the mob were all Christians, from the Orthodox church down the street." She wiped her nose and took a deep breath.

"Where was her father?"

Yona's countenance changed. "He was not there that day."

"Why not?"

"He did not think it was necessary to keep the Sabbath. He was a tailor. He spent his days making a living."

"How did you know this?"

She looked David in the eye. "I was there. I saw it. As I told you before, I was with them in Russia."

"How do—"

She cut him off. "The girls ran home and told their father, but there was little he could do."

"Was anyone saved from the building?"

"No," Yona shook her head. "By the time their father and the others got to the synagogue, all that was left was a smoking pile of rubble." She held the napkin to her mouth. "The next year, he brought the girls to America."

David glanced at the black-and-white photograph. "And the bush?"

"What?" Yona suddenly looked very old.

"The bush," David repeated, tapping the photo with his finger. "What about the bush and the coats and spring?"

"Oh, yes. The bush." She took another deep breath to calm herself. "There was a bush near the synagogue. They called it an olive but... it was for decoration. Not an olive tree. People in the village called it a Russian olive. It got burned in the fire, but the next year it came back, healthy and green. Everyone said it was a sign. An olive tree, growing from the ashes. When they left to come to America, their father stopped and took a little piece of it. Wrapped it in tissue." She made the motion with her fingers on the napkin. "When they got to America, he rooted it in a pot. And when they moved to a house in Springfield, he planted it in the yard."

"So, why the coats?"

"Leah's father did the best he could. He got a job in a factory. Changed their name to Levine. Tried to fit in." She glanced inside the box. "He thought if their name was different, maybe people wouldn't hate them the way the Christians had in Russia. It helped, I suppose. No one burned the house or the synagogue, but children still made fun of the way your mother talked."

"But life was better."

"Yes. It was better, for a time. Her father remarried, but his second wife died in childbirth. Then he started drinking and...then he became abusive." She looked at David, her eyes dark and heavy. "In every way possible."

"My mother was abused by her father?"

Yona nodded her head slowly. "It was bad for her. One day at gym class, a friend noticed Leah's bruises and the welts on her back. She persuaded Leah to tell the school nurse. The investigation that followed uncovered that she had been sexually abused since the age of thirteen. Not long after that, Child Welfare took the girls away from their father."

"And the bush?"

"They came back for a visit one day to see their father. By then the bush was big. He wanted to take their picture in front of it, but he made them put on their coats and hats. He said it would remind them of the day the synagogue burned." Yona rolled her eyes. "As if they would ever forget."

"He sounds like a strange man."

"He *was* strange. Very strange." She nodded her head slowly. "And tormented." She paused a moment and looked at the photograph. "But he was not always so strange. Before the fire, he was very different. I remember him laughing and dancing with their mother—your grandmother. But after the fire he was never that way again. After the fire he became as cold and gray as that winter afternoon when the mob burned the synagogue." Yona leaned across the table and looked David in the eye. "He refused to deal with the past in terms of the present, but he could not go back and change the things that had happened to him, and so he was trapped. The past haunted him all his life. And in the end it destroyed him too, just as what happened that day destroyed those who were trapped in the synagogue." She took David's hand. "You have a past that haunts you, David. And you must address the past as it is today. You cannot change it; and if you try, you will only end up reliving it. Do you understand me?"

"I think so."

"The Light shined on you when you were eleven; you saw His eyes and heard His words. That Light has made all the difference in your life. The Enemy is doing all he can to extinguish it. Follow the Light, David, and you will be blessed." There was a sound from the front of the house. Yona's eyes darted in that direction then back to David. "Come." She stood. "We have said enough." She folded her napkin and laid it beside the plate. "Come."

David pushed his chair back from the table and followed her into the living room. Near the front door, she abruptly turned to face him. She wrapped one arm around him, and with the other pulled him down to kiss his cheek. "You must go now. I think if you hurry, you can make it to the airport in time to leave and rejoin your family. I know they have been on your mind, and you miss them." She squeezed him tight. "Remember what I said. You must deal with the past as it is today. You cannot go back and change it."

"I will try," David replied. "But I'm not sure what that means."

"It takes time to understand these things, but you will learn. God has heard your prayer. He is at work in your life. You need not do everything at once. Just follow the Light. You have only to do the next thing."

David was curious. "But what is that? What do I do next?"

"Your past is tied to your father. You must go to see your father. Trust in the Lord. You know that He has not given you the spirit of fear. Follow the Light, David…just follow the Light. When you see your father, you will know what to do."

"My father?"

"Yes, your father. When you see your father, then you will know." She opened the door and held it as David stepped past. "Wally does not have all the answers, but when you see him, you will know what to do. Now hurry. You don't want to miss that airplane."

chapter 9

David left Yona's house feeling puzzled and confused. As he crossed the lawn toward the car, Yona's words echoed in his mind, "When you see your father, you will know what to do." The more he thought about it, the more astounding those words seemed. How could Wally Ellis help him find anything? Wally knew nothing about God, except for the smattering of words and phrases he had picked up in church. The god he really worshipped lived in a bottle, and the only thing he ever gave any of his children was beatings and verbal abuse. David muttered to himself as he opened the car door. "This makes no sense to me at all."

And then there was Yona's comment about the Light. "The Light shined upon you." She had said it as if she was talking about a specific event that they both understood. He knew what she was referring to, but there was no way *she* could have known about it. David closed the car door and glanced out the windshield as he put the key in the ignition. "No one knows what happened that night. I never told a soul, not even Peter or Henry, and they were asleep in the room when it happened."

David drove to the airport in Hartford, returned the rental car, and rode on a shuttle bus to the terminal. Much to his surprise, he learned that Yona was correct. A flight left for New York in less than an hour. He would arrive with time to spare for a connecting flight that would get him to Charlotte by nine that night. David hurried down the concourse and through security. The plane was already boarding when he reached the gate. He handed the agent his ticket and walked onto the jet-way. When he reached the aircraft, he found the flight wasn't crowded. He had a row of seats all to himself. He reclined the seat and rested his hands in his lap. With his eyes closed he returned again to what Yona had said about the light, which triggered a memory.

He had come home late one evening after playing up the street and found his father seated in the chair between the fireplace and the stairs. An empty beer bottle sat on the floor, about an arm's length from the chair. Wally gripped the neck of a full one and tipped it up to his mouth. In a hurry to get past him, David struck the empty bottle with his foot. It spun across the floor and crashed into the table by the sofa. Wally barked at him. "Ya' stupid moron!"

David stooped to pick up the bottle, but when he raised his head he struck the shade of a lamp that sat on the table. The force of the blow knocked the lamp onto the sofa. He caught it before it rolled onto the floor, but by then Wally was out of his chair. "Ya' clumsy idiot. You're gonna wreck the whole place!"

"I d-d-d-didn't me-me-mean to," David stammered. He stuttered all the time, but it was always worse when Wally glared at him.

Before David could move, the back of Wally's hand struck his cheek. Wally drained the bottle of beer he was holding and shoved the empty bottle toward David. "Get me another one." When David reached for the bottle, the lamp rolled from the sofa and hit the floor, chipping one corner of the base. In the rush to retrieve it from the floor, drops of beer dribbled from the bottle onto the shade. "Now look at that!" Wally roared.

"Bu-bu-but it wasn't my fault," David protested. "I di-di-didn't do nothing."

"I've told ya before, boy. God hates liars and I do too!" Wally slapped him twice, then continued hitting him again and again.

David raised his hands to protect his face and retreated toward the staircase. Then he heard the sound of the belt as Wally pulled it free of the loops on the waist of his pants. The beating that followed left David's young body bruised and bloody. When it was over, he crawled up the stairs to his room and lay on his bed quietly, so as not to wake Peter and Henry. As he listened to their deep, regular breathing, he wondered why he had ever been born. Searching for answers, he looked through his window and saw the stars. He quietly prayed aloud, "God, if you're really there, show me why I was born."

The room suddenly filled with a radiant light so brilliant David covered his eyes with his hands. Not hearing a sound, he peeked through his fingers. He could see the form of a man standing in the midst of the light. Suddenly two hands reached out to him. The palm of each hand bore an ugly scar. David was both frightened and mesmerized by the sight before him.

It can't be Him, David thought. *My mother said He was dead.*

As David lowered his hands and looked into the face of the One in the light, like iron to a magnet he was drawn to His eyes. Every color in the rainbow sparkled back at him. *Why, His eyes are smiling. I didn't know eyes could smile. I've never seen a man with such kind eyes.* David felt as if he were being drawn into the very depths of those shining eyes. Waves of unspeakable joy washed over him as he realized he was in the presence of Jesus.

David whispered, "Jesus!"

Then Jesus spoke words David had never heard before—words that would change his life forever. "Son...I love you...and I have a great plan for your life."

As suddenly as they appeared, Jesus and the light were gone. Once again the room was dark and filled with silence, broken only by the gentle snores of Peter and Henry as they slept in their beds a few feet away. David wondered how they could have slept so soundly through the whole incident.

"He loves me...He loves me!" David cried softly with joyful abandon. "I am His son, and He has a great plan for my life."

The following morning David awoke with no pain from the beating he had received the night before. When he spoke at breakfast, he no longer stuttered. His brothers were amazed, but Wally never said a word.

David knew that hopelessness had disappeared from his heart, but that wasn't all. His speech impediment, his fear of death, darkness, heights, and people—all were gone. His terrible self-image was replaced with a sense of divine destiny and value, and in the days following, the ulcer no longer plagued him.

It was that night in the Light that David Ellis experienced joy unspeakable and was filled with glory for the first time in his life. However, although he had changed on the inside, his father still beat him. His frightened mother still ignored the terror that ruled their house. His outside circumstances remained unchanged, but David had found the purpose and meaning he needed to survive.

David still struggled to earn his father's approval, still wrestled for an understanding of why he was born into such a life, but on his darkest days he remembered the night when the Light shined through his bedroom window and Jesus appeared to him. As he grew up, David kept that moment to himself. He was certain no one would believe him; and if Wally found out he would beat him for lying. But it wasn't a lie. It was the most truthful moment he had ever experienced.

There was no way Yona could have known about it.

Somewhere in that childhood memory, David dozed off. The next thing he knew, a hand touched his left arm. His eyes popped open to see a flight attendant smiling at him. "You need to bring your seat upright. We're preparing to land in New York."

Inside the terminal he located the gate for his next flight and found a telephone booth. He placed a call to the beach cottage. Moments later he heard the phone ringing. Then Sue's voice came on the line.

"Hey, where are you?"

At the sound of her voice, a flood of emotion swept over David. "I'm in New York," he managed.

"Are you all right? You sound like something's wrong."

"I'm okay. Just glad to hear your voice."

"How did it go?"

"Better than I expected. I'll tell you about it when I get in."

"What time do you arrive?"

"Nine. In Charlotte."

"Okay. We'll be waiting in the terminal."

"No. Don't do that. I'll get my bag and meet you on the curb. Just be there around ten."

"Ten? I thought you said nine."

"I don't want you to wait for me. I'll wait for you."

"No," she insisted. "We'll be there when you get there. Just get your luggage and come out to the curb. You let us worry about the timing."

"Okay."

"I'm glad you're on your way. It's been lonely here without you."

"It's been lonely without you too."

David hung up the phone and walked back to the gate. He took a seat near the windows and stared into the night. Airplanes of every shape and size moved back and forth across the tarmac. Catering trucks and other equipment zipped in and out between them. He watched them a moment, then let his mind drift back to the events of the past three days.

David felt Anna didn't seem to be entirely at peace with herself or with her past. Yona was right, he thought. Anna appeared to address the past in terms of the present, rather than trying to change it; but Anna also was carrying more hurt and anger than she was willing to talk about. That left him wondering how much unresolved conflict he held inside. Was he really as serene as he tried to show, or were the recurring nightmares a sign that something else was going on inside?

Perhaps Sue was right. Maybe there really was more happening in him than he could admit—or see. He had gone to Indian Orchard out of a sense of obligation and responsibility. Leah was his mother. He hadn't seen her in several years, although he had talked with her regularly on the phone. Once he was at her funeral, he had seen how important her

Jewish heritage had been to her. She had returned to it and had been changed by it. She wasn't perfect, but thank God, in the end she had found a saving relationship with her Messiah. Furthermore, he had seen the Jewish side of her life and family, and he had found it intriguing.

He wondered about Yona. As hard as he tried, he could not remember her, yet she seemed to know the most intimate details of his life, things he had forgotten and things he had never remembered knowing. Talking to her had ignited a new curiosity in him. He was more interested than ever in the role his Jewish ancestry played in shaping the events of his life. And, for the first time in his adult life, he was determined to resolve the tension he had felt about why he was born and why his father hated him. But who was Yona?

*   *   *

By the time the plane landed in Charlotte, David had moved on to thoughts of the beach and the remaining ten days of vacation with his family. When the plane came to a stop at the gate, he was all too eager to get moving. He bounded up the jet-way to the corridor and walked quickly to the baggage claim. Twenty minutes later, he was standing outside at the curb as the Caprice came into view.

When the car came to a stop, David walked around to the back. He took his keys from his pocket, unlocked the trunk, and placed his suitcase inside. With the lid closed, he hurried around to the passenger side and jerked open the front door. In one quick motion, he leaned across the front seat and kissed Sue. The kids giggled from the back seat. David pulled away and turned toward them. "I missed you guys," he grinned.

"We missed you, Dad," they replied.

"Better buckle up," Sue cautioned. "We need to get moving. Traffic is backing up behind us."

David tousled Joel's hair, reached over and squeezed Megan's hand, then he faced forward in the seat and snapped his seatbelt into place. Sue glanced in the rearview mirror, then steered the car from the curb. "Did you have a good flight?"

"Yes," David nodded. "As much as I remember."

"You slept?"

"From Indian Orchard to New York."

"That's a good sign." Sue glanced over at him. "You usually can't sleep on the plane."

"I know."

"Were any of the family at the funeral?"

"Anna, Henry, and Peter were there."

"Good. How were they?"

"About like they've always been. Anna seems okay, but I didn't get to spend a lot of time with my brothers. Both had to get back to work right after the funeral."

Megan called from the back seat. "Do we know them?"

"Not well." David answered. "You've only met them once, and you were both pretty small."

"That's all right," Joel piped up. "We have the best part of Dad's family with us every day."

"Ahh," Sue smiled. "That's sweet."

"Thanks, son." David felt a lump in his throat. "I want to be."

"You're the best, Dad."

As they rode out of the airport to the highway, Sue glanced over at David. "I think we ought to spend tonight at home. Go back to the beach in the morning."

A chorus of boos went up from the back seat. David shook his head. "No way."

"It's late."

David glanced at his watch. "It's not ten yet."

"It'll be one by the time we get there."

"Later than that."

"Later?" Sue frowned. "It doesn't take that long."

A grin broke across David's face. "It does if we stop at Tony's Ice Cream."

"Yeah," Joel shouted. "Chocolate milkshake."

David looked pleadingly at Sue. "I'll buy you a strawberry shake."

"Okay," she smiled. "If you all insist."

David reached over, captured Sue's hand, and said loudly enough for all to hear, "I have some wonderful news to share about my mother. You know we've all been praying for her to come to know Jesus. Well, guess what?"

chapter 10

It was well after one in the morning when David, Sue, and the children arrived at the beach house. Everyone trudged off to bed and went quickly to sleep. The next morning David awoke early. The house was quiet. He lay there a moment, watching Sue sleeping next to him and listening to the sound of the waves breaking on the beach. After a few minutes he gently rolled back the covers and eased out of bed.

In the kitchen, he loaded the coffeemaker and turned on the switch. He found a pair of his sandals that Sue had placed near the door and slipped into them, then stepped outside to the deck that ran along the back of the house. He leaned against the rail and stared into the gray light of dawn. *This is the best time of day.* As he watched the sun peek through the clouds, the words of Solomon burst from David's mouth, "Trust in the Lord with all your heart, and lean not unto your own understanding. In all your ways acknowledge Him." David whispered, "I acknowledge You, Lord. I acknowledge Your leadership in my life."

Behind him the door slid open. He glanced over his shoulder to see Sue coming from the house. She pulled her robe tight and slipped her arms around his waist. "Talking to yourself again?"

"I always talk to myself," David chuckled. "Some of my best conversations." He turned toward her and gave her a kiss. Sue shoved her hands in the pockets of the robe and rested her head against his chest. David held her in his arms and leaned back against the railing.

Sue sighed contentedly. "That was great news about your mom, honey. What a happy reunion you'll have one day, and it is a great lesson for the kids to see God answer what seemed like an impossible prayer. Your persistence paid off in a huge way."

"Sue, I know who the real prayer warrior is in this house. You prayed as intensely as I did for my mom. Did anything exciting happen here while I was gone?"

"No, not a thing. We walked on the beach and ate seafood and played in the waves."

"Sounds like fun."

"Alan Scruggs called to say he was sorry your mother died. How did he have this number?"

"I gave it to Steve. I'm sure Steve gave it to him."

"They're spending a lot of time together. They have lunch together every Monday."

"Good. Steve needs to get more involved with the board."

They were silent a moment, then Sue asked, "So, tell me about the trip. Get a chance to talk to Anna?"

"A little. Anna's seeing a guy named Tom."

"Is that working out?"

"I don't know. She didn't say much about him."

"Think she's going to church?"

"I don't really know."

"Did they ask you to participate in the funeral service?"

"No. I didn't really want to. At the grave, they have this tradition where they put the casket in the ground, then everyone comes by, scoops up a handful of dirt, and tosses it in."

"I've seen that before."

"You've been to a Jewish funeral?"

"No. They did that at my grandmother's funeral, down in Georgia."

Sue took her hands from the pockets of her robe and wrapped her arms around David's waist.

"Yona went first, then Anna, the boys, and I tossed in a handful."

Sue's head popped up. "Wait, who is Yona? Is she a relative?"

"Oh. I forgot to mention her. I'm not really sure who she is. She was at the funeral home. She said she was Mom's friend. Knew her from Russia. But she also knew me and acted like I was supposed to know her."

"But you didn't?"

"Not a clue." David shook his head. "I've thought and thought, and I can't remember ever seeing her."

"What kinds of things did you talk about?"

"At the funeral home we talked about Jewish traditions and that sort of thing. But at her house we talked about things that happened to Mom and Aunt Eliana when they were kids."

"You went to her house?"

"Yeah. She had a house there in Indian Orchard. I wanted to get on to the airport, but I didn't want to be rude. And I had this sense in my spirit that I was supposed to go with her. So I went." He looked down at Sue. "You want some coffee?"

"Yes, but first tell me more about this woman. What was her name again?"

"Yona."

Sue's eyes narrowed, "And how old was she?"

David laughed. "*Very, very old.*"

"Okay, okay. What kinds of things did she know about?"

"She knew about a time when my mom and her family were in Russia and a mob surrounded the synagogue. They burned the building to the ground with everyone in it. Eliana and Mom had gone to the outhouse just before it happened. They saw the whole thing."

"Did you know that before?"

"No."

"What else did she have to say?"

"She talked about a time when Aunt Eliana and Uncle Jacob took me and Anna and Peter to a bar mitzvah in Brooklyn."

"You remembered it?"

"A little. But she reminded me of more details."

"Like?"

"On the way down we stopped to take a break. When we got back in the car, I was sitting by the door in back. Uncle Jacob had to swerve the car, and I banged into the door. It flew open, I started to fall out, and just before I reached the point of no return, somebody caught hold of me and pulled me back in. I always assumed it was Anna, but she was in the front seat."

"And Yona says she was there."

"Yes. Sitting between Peter and me, but I just don't remember her." David leaned forward and rested his cheek against the top of Sue's head. "Have you ever seen an angel?"

"Not the kind with wings."

"Me either."

"There was that time when I was stopped on the road with the kids and the car wouldn't start. This guy in a pickup truck stopped and jump-started the car."

"I remember you telling me. The car started, and you turned to see about Joel. When you looked back the guy was gone."

"Yeah. It was strange but it seemed perfectly normal."

"That's the way I felt about being with Yona, and she said something else that surprised me." Then David told Sue about his prayer before she had taken him to the airport and about the two scriptures. "Yona knew about the scriptures. How could she know that?"

"You think this Yona person is an angel?"

"Well, I didn't see any wings, but it was as if she were an angel. It was strange, seeing her and talking to her and going to her house. But it was peaceful too, like I was doing exactly what the Holy Spirit wanted me to do."

"How did it end with her?"

"She told me that a great light had shined on me from a time when I was a child."

Sue looked up. "How did she know about that?"

"I don't know. You're the first person I ever told about it. I hadn't mentioned it from the pulpit until we came here to Belmont."

"Did she say anything else?"

"She said the past haunts me, that trying to change the past is a trap, and that I should deal with the past in terms of the present."

"That sounds good. What does it mean?"

"I think she meant I shouldn't try to go back and make the past different, but I should accept it for what it was and deal with it in terms of now."

"Any suggestions about how you should do that?"

"She says I need to talk to my father."

"She said that?"

"Actually, she said, 'When you see your father, you'll know what to do next.'"

"How do you feel about that?"

"I don't know what good it will do. It'll just be another one of his screaming tirades."

"Did she think you could actually talk to him?"

"She said he wouldn't have all the answers for me, but when I talked to him I would know the next step."

"The next step."

David sighed. "Yeah, but the next step toward what?"

"Toward an answer to whatever's behind those nightmares."

"You think all this is related?"

"Have you had any nightmares since you went up to the funeral?"

"No."

"Four days of sound sleep. I think the Holy Spirit is working in your life. You should yield to whatever He's doing. It seems like He's using those two scriptures to bring peace to you."

"I don't want to see my dad."

"I know."

"The way I learned how to be a father and husband was by doing the opposite of what he did."

"You can see him without becoming like him."

"Sometimes I'm not so sure."

Sue pressed her head against his shoulder. They stood there side-by-side, arms around each other, with nothing but the roar of the waves to break the silence. "David, can I ask you something?"

"Anything."

"Is Wally Ellis really your father?"

"Why do you ask?"

"I don't know." She looked up at him. "But I've wondered about it for a long time. You keep saying he beat your mother on Friday nights and kept calling her a Jew-whore and you a bastard. And he never called your brothers or sister a bastard. Maybe—"

The door slid open and Megan appeared. She squinted against the glare of the rising sun. "Wow." She stared past them into the distance. "I love the sunrises here."

Sue let go of David's waist and pushed back her hair. She and David turned to see the sun, orange and round like a giant ball, rising above the horizon. They stood there a moment, enjoying the view. Then, as the sun made its slow climb into the sky, David turned away and started across the deck. "Anyone hungry?" He slipped his arm across Megan's shoulder. "Come on." He smiled at her. "You can help me."

* * *

A few nights later David went for a walk on the beach alone. Overhead, the sky was ablaze with stars. Off to the left waves crashed onto the sandbar. Foam from the surf swirled around his ankles. In the solitude of that moment, he prayed about what he had encountered in Indian Orchard and the past that seemed to grip him so tightly.

"Lord, I don't want to be like Wally, but I have no idea how to break free from it." He smiled. "And I don't know who Yona is."

Memories of the time at his mother's funeral played in his mind: Yona in the funeral home with the casket, Rabbi Kunstadt and the men who accompanied the body, seeing his sister and brothers, and then having lunch in Yona's home. "I just don't remember her. What does it mean?"

In that instant, words from the prophet Isaiah, chapter 43, came to mind: "See, I am doing a new thing! Now it springs up; do you not perceive it? I am making a way in the desert and streams in the wasteland." As he remembered that scripture, David felt a refreshing presence in his spirit.

He felt something touch his hand and jumped. Sue was standing beside him. "Scare you?"

"Yes," he laughed. "You did."

She looked up at the sky. "It's nice out here."

"I know."

"Too bad we can't just live down here all the time."

"I agree totally. Where are the kids?"

"Joel's in the shower. Megan is reading a book." She looked up at him. "You okay?"

"Just praying."

"What did you hear when you were praying?"

"I heard a verse. 'See, I am doing a new thing in you. Do you not see it?'"

"Isaiah. What do you think it means for you?"

"I'm not sure. But I think that trip to Indian Orchard was about more than just burying my mother."

"I had a sense something was happening."

"I mean, look at the way it happened. I didn't go there looking for reconciliation with my father or with my past. I didn't go there on a quest to understand my Jewish heritage. And I didn't go there hoping to see my sister or brothers. I only went there because I am Leah Levine Ellis' son, and that's what sons do."

"Honor."

"Yes. I was honoring her as my mother. But in doing that I think I encountered something from the Holy Spirit that is turning my life, our lives, in a new direction."

"Any idea what that direction might be?"

"No," he said, with a hint of laughter. "But I think things are changing."

"Well," she put an arm around his waist. "The ten years at Belmont have been good," she sighed. "But I trust you to hear God's voice."

"Do I detect a note of reluctance?"

"Not reluctance. I just know that change will probably alter everything. And that means moving. And I don't like packing all those boxes."

David pulled her close. "We'll see about all of that. Let's just concentrate on hearing His voice."

∗   ∗   ∗

For the rest of that week and all the next, David and Sue enjoyed the beach with Megan and Joel. They dove in the surf, played on the sand, and took long walks in the evening. Then, all too quickly, it was time to leave. As they packed the last of the suitcases in the trunk of the Caprice, Sue took David's hand. "You want to drive out to your dad's house on the way home?"

"No," David said, shaking his head. "It's too far out of the way." He shot a glance toward Megan and Joel, standing on the sand twenty yards away. "And I'm not taking them anywhere near him."

"Well, I think you should consider a time when you can see him."

"I'll think about it."

Sue, still holding his hand, turned away. "Come on," she said. "Let's go have one last look at the beach."

chapter 11

Back in Charlotte David spent the following week catching up on all that had happened while he was away. Although he had only been gone two weeks, it seemed like he was returning to someone else's life.

As he prepared his sermon for the following Sunday, he found himself drawn in two directions—one toward his rediscovered Jewish past and the other toward reconciliation with his father. Learning about the Jewish traditions he had missed as a child sent him to the bookstore and the public library. There, he found a number of books on Jewish history, the resettlement of modern Israel, and a thousand variations on the historic themes of Judaism.

The thought of going to see his father, on the other hand, was far from inspiring. For one thing, seeing Wally brought up more painful emotions besides those he already had. There was his mother, who sat by quietly while his father beat and berated David and his brothers and sister, the neighbors who surely must have heard what was happening and yet did nothing, and even Aunt Eliana and Uncle Jacob, who were well aware of their circumstances. Eliana was the one person who could have stepped up in dramatic fashion and changed things, but she didn't.

As the week unfolded, David was led deeper into the notion of reconciliation with the past. He kept returning to a passage in John, where Jesus said, "You will know the truth, and the truth will set you free." That seemed to be the point of what Yona had tried to say, and what the Holy Spirit was saying to him. The past wasn't something to fear; it was something to confront and to define in terms of the present. It was what it was, and there was nothing he could do to change it. All he could do was address it as it affected him now.

Sunday dawned bright and sunny. David left the house early and arrived at the church before anyone else. Located on a beautiful campus on the west side of Charlotte, the buildings included a large sanctuary, a separate education building, and a gymnasium. The congregation was composed of mostly upper-middle-class professionals who lived in nearby communities and subdivisions. For many of them, the church was only a place to go on Sunday; but David had developed a strong corps of dedicated believers, who were committed to discipleship. He met with them throughout the week in a rolling schedule of small group gatherings. Then, every Sunday morning, regardless of what had happened the week before, anyone from any of the groups was free to join him to pray. They met in a room off the basketball court in the gymnasium.

David parked the car near the gym and unlocked the back door of the building. Inside he switched on the light and made his way down the hall to a meeting room on the right. He turned on the lights, arranged chairs in a circle, and then walked out to the snack bar. There, he filled the coffeemaker with water, put coffee in the drip basket, and flipped a switch to turn it on. As the coffeemaker heated up, he heard the back door open. Moments later Billy Jones appeared in the doorway.

"Welcome back!" he called, as he came into the room. "Have a good vacation?"

"Yes. It was nice."

"I was sorry to hear about your mother. Where did she live? I don't remember seeing her here."

"Massachusetts. She lived in Indian Orchard, Massachusetts."

"All your family go up for the funeral?"

"No. Just me." David checked the coffeemaker. "You want a cup?"

"Yeah, sure."

David took a cup from the counter, filled it with coffee, and handed it to Billy. "I'll let you fix it."

"I like mine just like it is." Billy took a sip. "I've been thinking about you all week."

"Oh? What about?"

"I keep remembering this scripture from John. "You shall know the truth, and the truth shall set you free."

"John, chapter eight. I'm preaching about it this morning."

"Hmm," Billy said, thoughtfully. "Interesting."

"Yes," David chuckled. "That's a word I've been using a lot lately."

Billy set the cup aside and leaned back against the edge of the counter. "I think it's more than that." He folded his arms across his chest and stared ahead with a pensive look. "I think it's personal."

"What do you mean?"

"I think it's a personal word for you." Billy unfolded his arms and picked up the coffee cup. "I don't know how it applies." He took a sip of coffee. "But I think it has something to do with you."

"Yes," David replied, his mind suddenly filled with memories of the last two weeks. "Maybe so."

Billy set the coffee cup aside. "This is important." He crossed to David. "Let's pray about this before anybody else gets here." Before he could react, Billy had him by the shoulder with one hand and rested the other hand atop David's head. "Lord, we keep hearing this scripture, 'You shall know the truth and the truth shall make you free.' I declare that word over David this morning, and I ask You to show him what it means. Show him how to apply it to his own life. Let the truth—whatever truth You have for him—truth about Scripture, about You, about himself, about the circumstances he faces—whatever truth he needs, let him see it, embrace it, and allow it to have its full effect in his life. Amen."

"Thanks."

Billy gave David a pat on the shoulder. "I believe something will happen." He turned back to the counter and picked up the coffee cup. "Y'all went down to Carolina Beach?"

"Yes." David was glad for the change of subject. He took a cup from the counter and filled it with coffee for himself. "We've been renting the same beach house down there for the past ten years."

"That's a good place. I used to go down there when I was a kid. A little quieter than Myrtle Beach."

David chuckled. "Not quite as many tourists. Although I guess, in our case, we are the tourists."

"Yeah," Billy nodded. "I guess so."

In a few minutes others from the discipleship groups arrived. As the crowd grew, David guided them down the hall to the prayer room. Soon they were each sharing what they had heard God say during the week, then they moved seamlessly into worship and prayer. David heard the words they were saying, but his mind kept replaying the words Billy had prayed over him, "Let the truth have its full effect in his life."

David wanted that. He wanted God to work in whatever way necessary to make him whole and fully alive. Nevertheless, as he thought about those words, a sense of dread swept over him as well. Talking about confronting the past was one thing; doing it was quite another. Dark secrets lurked in the shadows of his past. What would happen when he confronted them?

chapter 12

On Monday morning David awakened feeling rested and refreshed. He rolled on his side and lay there staring at Sue, thinking about how blessed he was to be married to her. His mind wandered back to the first time he had seen her. Even now, he could see her walking across campus, her silky blonde hair blowing in the breeze. When he moved past her that day on the sidewalk, she smiled at him. He looked into her big, blue eyes, and that was it. He was hooked. It took him three weeks to get up the courage to ask her out, but when he did he knew he had found the love of his life.

Suddenly Sue's eyes popped open. She looked at him, startled to find him staring at her. "What are you doing?"

"Looking at you."

"And what do you see?"

"I see a beautiful girl coming across the quadrangle."

"Hah," she chuckled, patting her stomach. "That girl doesn't live here any more."

"That girl," David leaned close, "is more beautiful now than she was back then."

"You have been in a really good mood since you got back from Massachusetts."

"I have?"

"Yes. And you've slept well too."

"Yes, I have." David rolled away and stood. "That is why I'm going out to see Wally."

"Today?"

"Yes. Yona said the next thing I should do is see my father, and so that's what I'm going to do. It's Monday. My day off. I can be out there in an hour."

David turned away and started toward the bathroom. Sue called after him. "Want me to go with you?"

"No, thanks." he called in return. "I need to go by myself."

✳   ✳   ✳

Two hours later David turned the Caprice from the Charlotte Highway and drove through Mooresville, a mill town north of Charlotte. On the east side of town, he turned left onto Wiggins Road and wound through the countryside. A few miles later, he came to a dirt road that led off to the right. He turned onto it and let the car roll slowly down to the third driveway on the left. A mailbox hung precariously from a rotten post. David turned onto the two-rut drive beside it.

At the end of the drive, a mobile home sat beneath a large oak tree. Limbs from the tree sprawled across the top, covering it with shade from one end to the other. The ground around it was littered with dried and decaying leaves. Weeds grew in the spots where sunlight filtered through. Tiny oak sprouts grew in the shade.

David brought the car to a stop near the front steps and got out. As he closed the car door, he heard the sound of the television from inside the trailer. *Probably stayed on all night*, he thought. He rapped on the door with his knuckles, then backed away and waited.

To the right of the trailer were rows and rows of Bantam roosters, each one chained to a stake in front of a small shelter just large enough for a single chicken. As much as Wally enjoyed cockfighting, he loved trading and selling roosters even more. The sound of their clucking and crowing filled the air with a constant chorus.

An overgrown fencerow separated Wally's yard from the house

next door to the left. Through a gap in the bushes David could see it was a frame structure with lapped siding that had once been painted white. The little paint that remained was peeling from it in long streaks that dangled in the air like confetti. Beneath it, the exposed wooden siding was weathered to a dull gray. Kudzu vines laced their way up a downspout, and windows on the end were broken. Shingles on the roof curled up along the edges. Out front, a pickup truck sat on concrete blocks. Pine saplings grew up through rusted holes in the rear bed.

After a minute or two David banged again on the door with his fist, this time hitting it harder than before. When Wally still didn't answer, he gave the doorknob a jiggle, and the door swung open. Startled at first, he leaned forward and carefully stuck his head inside for a look around.

Across from the door, Wally was sound asleep in a recliner. The armrests were torn and tattered, and the footrest was held up by a stack of magazines. David stared at his father, thinking about why he had come out here and what he planned to say. The old man was eighty-eight now. His head leaned to one side, drool coming from the corner of his mouth, and a shotgun lay across his lap. He didn't look much like the man who had beaten David and his brothers to a bloody pulp. Still, David could not quell the fear that rose inside him. As he stood there gripping the doorknob, he felt his chest grow tight. His heart raced faster and faster. His throat was dry, and he found it all but impossible to breathe.

Suddenly Wally pitched forward in the recliner and pulled his shotgun to his shoulder. "What's that?" He rose from the chair and started toward the door, mumbling as he went, "Better not be that sorry coyote stealin' my prize roosters. I'll make mincemeat outta ya!"

Just then he saw David standing on the porch. "Whacha doin' sneakin' up on me like that, ya sorry piece a road kill? Ya ain't nothin' but a phony preacher takin' people's money. Git yer sorry rear off'n my property before I shoot it off!" Wally raised his shotgun and aimed it at David.

David turned and walked quickly down the steps. He staggered to the car and leaned against the front fender, gasping for air. After a moment, he made his way to the car door and jerked it open. He dropped onto the seat behind the steering wheel. With his heart pounding against his chest, he started the engine, backed the car away from the trailer, and steered it toward the dirt road.

"I can't do it," he whispered to himself between gasps. "I just can't do it."

At the mailbox he turned right toward Wiggins Road. As he turned onto the pavement, he stuck his head out the window and let the air blow over his face. Down the road a little way, his heart rate slowed. Breathing came easier. "I don't want to do it," he said, at last able to fill his lungs with ease. "And I won't." He shook his head. "I won't do it."

Mooresville went by in a blur before he came to the highway and turned south toward Charlotte. By then, his heart rate was normal and he was breathing as usual. In his mind, he was more resolute than ever. Whatever the next step might be, he would have to find it without the help of his father. He had no intention of ever going back to that trailer.

*　*　*

When David returned home that afternoon, he found Sue waiting for him at the kitchen table. "How was Wally?"

"Asleep."

"What did he say when you woke him up?"

David told Sue about Wally aiming the shotgun at him and ordering him off the property. "I didn't talk to him. I just stood there and let him intimidate me again. I really thought he was going to kill me this time. Look, Sue. Yona said I should see him. I saw him. She didn't say I had to risk life and limb to talk to him. I just got out of there."

"Well," Sue said quietly, "at least you went. That's something. And, we'll just have to pray harder that things will go better next time."

"I'm not going back."

"Okay."

"You should have seen him, lying there in his La-Z-Boy, sound asleep, as if everything was right in the world."

"I'm sure he carries his own baggage."

"Yeah, as well as a shotgun! But I'll just have to work this out another way." He sat down at the table and rested his head on his arms. "I'll just have to figure it out another way."

chapter 13

That night David and Sue went to bed as usual. Sue lay with the light on to read. David turned his back to her and closed his eyes. As he tried to sleep, he felt her arm slide over his side. She nuzzled close to his ear. "I am with you, no matter what," she whispered.

David turned to look at her. "I was so scared."

"I know."

"I'm an adult. Why was I so frightened of an old man?"

"The wounds he gave you run deep. And they go to places a parent is supposed to protect. Your identity as a boy and a man. Your physical life. He did his best to destroy them, and you know how close he came to doing it."

"But I'm as big as he is now."

"Yes, you are physically, but you didn't have a shotgun in your hands. I think when you see him, you see yourself as that vulnerable little boy. And that's what Yona was trying to tell you. You can't go back and fight that fight as a little boy. The past is gone. What you have are memories. You have to address this in the present as it affects the man you are now."

"I just want to be free."

"I know. And God is taking you there. God is taking you there," she whispered. David turned away again and closed his eyes as she began to stroke his back.

*　*　*

Suddenly he was twelve years old, standing in the kitchen at the house at 77 Pasco Road. Images in shades of black and white appeared around him. Light streamed through the window near the sink. Without warning his father shouted from the living room, "Get in here! All of you!" Fear shot through David. His heart dropped to his stomach. From the corner of his eye he saw his mother turn away. She moved past his line of vision, but he could sense her behind him and knew she had taken her familiar seat at the table with her back turned to the door.

An instant later David was on the living room floor in front of his father's chair. Anna sat to his left. Behind him were Peter and Henry. Their father flopped into his chair. An extension cord dangled ominously from one hand. In the other he held a plug of chewing tobacco. He shoved the plug into his mouth, clamped it with his teeth, and ripped off a hunk. He worked it with one side of his jaw then switched it to the other. He nudged a coffee can out from the wall with his foot, then leaned down and picked it up. He set it in his lap and wrapped a hand around it to hold it in place.

"We're gonna have devotions." From his slurred speech, David knew he had been drinking.

Little Anna asked, "What's that?"

"It's readin' the Bible and prayin'," Wally snorted. "Devotions. Don't y'all know nuthin'?" He leaned forward and spit a stream of thick, brown tobacco juice into the coffee can. "I gotta explain everything?" David felt his legs tingle as tension rose in his body.

Wally reached over to the table beside the chair and grabbed a Bible from it. He thrust it at David and barked, "Read." David took it from him and let it fall open in his lap.

"Read John 3:16," Wally grumbled. David flipped through the pages quickly as he searched for the right place. Nervous and scared, he struggled to find it. After what seemed like forever, he heard the chair creak and then, "Whap!" the extension cord struck his wrist with a biting sting. "In John, ya' moron. In the New Testament." Wally leaned closer. "You're way over in Joshua. Idiot."

The image vanished from David's mind as quickly as it had come, and in its place he was standing on the porch the day he left for the army. He held out his hand to his father, only to have it knocked away with a laugh. "You'll never make it in the army. You screw up everything ya' touch. You're nothin' but a moron."

From out of nowhere the extension cord appeared in Wally's right hand. David couldn't see it, but he sensed its presence. Then he felt it strike his back. "Worthless! Ya' hear me?" David jumped from the porch and started across the yard. The cord struck him again on the left shoulder. "Worthless. Look at me!" Again and again the cord struck his back, alternating between his left and right shoulder. All the while his father continued to scream at him. "You won't find it! You won't find it! I have it in my pocket, and I ain't givin' it to no stupid Jew bastard like you!" David continued across the yard toward the street, rolling his shoulders to the left and right with each lash of the cord.

✳   ✳   ✳

"David, wake up." Sue's hand touched his shoulder. "Come on, David. Wake up."

David's eyes popped open to see the clock on the nightstand. His heart raced wildly as he rolled onto his back and gasped for breath.

"It's okay. It was only a dream."

"A dream." David rubbed his eyes.

"It's okay."

"I never should have gone out to that trailer." A chill ran over David's body. He patted his chest to find his clothes were soaked with sweat. "I should have stayed right here at the house."

"You did what you thought was right."

David threw back the covers and rolled to a sitting position on the side of the bed. "But the dreams have returned." He stripped off his shirt and walked across the room to the dresser.

"What was it this time?"

"More of the same." He took a fresh shirt from the dresser drawer then reached for his Bible on the nightstand. "I'm gonna read a while."

"You ought to come back to bed."

"I can't sleep now," he sighed. "I'm wide awake." He tucked the book under his arm and padded from the room.

chapter 14

Later that morning David arrived at the church. He parked in the lot near the sanctuary and went inside to the office suite. The receptionist greeted him as he entered. "Good morning, Pastor Ellis."

"I've told you before," David smiled at her. "Call me David."

"Yes sir."

As David moved past the desk he saw a brochure lying in the mail basket. On the cover above the address box was a picture of a domed temple, gleaming in brilliant sunshine. He paused and picked it up. "What's this?"

"That came to us by mistake."

David let his eyes scan the front and found it was an announcement about a trip to Israel. He flipped it over to see the back. "Why do you think it came by mistake?"

"Look at the address."

David flipped it back to the front again. The flyer had been addressed to Temple Beth El. A frown wrinkled his forehead. "They missed it big, didn't they? Beth El's on the other side of town."

"It was stuck inside another piece of mail."

David tossed the flyer into the mail basket and started down the hall. As he walked toward the office he thought again about his Jewish roots and his desire to learn more about what that meant. At his office door he turned around and retraced his steps to the receptionist's desk. He reached in the mail basket and scooped up the flyer. "I'll take care of this."

"Okay," the receptionist chuckled.

Back in his office David dropped into the chair behind his desk and studied the flyer. The brochure advertised a trip that was sponsored by Israeli Jewish Tours. Most of the copy had been printed in advance, but a block on the back had been printed specifically for Beth El. David felt his heart skip a beat as he read about a Jewish tour of Israel, "designed to put Jews in touch with their historic past." Temple Beth El was organizing a two-week tour for the fall. They would leave September 14th.

The brochure had been folded multiple times and sealed on one side with tape. David clipped the tape with his thumbnail, unfolded the flyer, and laid it across his desktop. Squares on the page highlighted each day—arrival in Tel Aviv, travel to Rosh Hanikra, Mount Gilboa, the Western Wall, water tunnels beneath Jerusalem. David was enthralled. Much of what the brochure touted as important meant nothing to him—towns and sites that dealt with the resettlement of modern Israel—but he was certain it would have great meaning if he took the trip and learned about the country from a Jewish perspective.

"This would be perfect," he said to himself. He opened the desk drawer and took out his calendar. With a flip of his finger, he turned to September and checked the dates. "Great," he grinned. "Steve is already set to preach one of those Sundays. I'll get him to take the other one too."

David laid the calendar on the desk and spun the chair around to face the credenza. He took a phone book from the shelf and opened it to the Yellow Pages. After a quick search he found an entry for Temple Beth El. Mark Cronfeld was the rabbi. He reached for the phone to dial the number then thought better of it. Instead of calling, he could drive over and see Cronfeld in person. He glanced at his watch. It was a little after nine. "Almost two hours before staff meeting," he mused. "I could go now and get back in time." He folded the flyer, stuck it in his pocket, and started toward the door.

As he stepped into the hall, Alan Scruggs appeared. "Hey, David. Glad to have you back. I was just on my way down to see Steve. Think you could join us?"

"I'd love to, Alan, but I'm on my way out."

Alan arched an eyebrow. "Okay, David. Maybe we could talk later."

"Yeah, sure." David moved past him. "Give me a call. We'll get together." He stepped quickly down the hall. "I need to run."

David drove across town to Temple Beth El on the east side of Charlotte. The drive took less than fifteen minutes. As he turned into the parking lot he noticed only one car. "I should have called first," he said to himself. "I really don't have time to run around the city looking for a rabbi." He parked in a space reserved for visitors and went inside.

As David entered the building he saw a short, slender man with balding head and dark, intelligent eyes standing partway down the hall. He looked up as David entered. "May I help you?"

"I was looking for Mark Cronfeld."

"That's me. How may I help you?"

David thrust his hand forward. "I'm David Ellis, pastor over at Belmont Baptist Church."

Cronfeld's face brightened. "Yes," he said, shaking David's hand. "I recognize you now. I see your picture every weekend in your advertisement. In the Saturday paper."

"Yes," David smiled. "We get an unusual number of responses to that ad."

"What brings you to Temple Beth El?"

"This." David pulled the flyer from his pocket and handed it to Cronfeld. "It came to us by mistake."

Cronfeld took it and glanced at David. "You came all the way over here to bring me this piece of mail?"

"No. I was wondering if I could go on the tour."

"I suppose," Cronfeld shrugged. "But why do you want to go?"

"My mother was Jewish, and she recently died," David began to explain. "I went back for her funeral and became interested in my Jewish roots." He pointed to the brochure. "I thought that tour would be a good way to find out more."

"Hmm." Cronfeld gestured with the flyer in his hand. "You realize this is a Jewish tour."

"Yes."

"I mean, we won't visit any of the Christian sites."

"Right."

"Won't go to Golgotha or the Garden of Gethsemane."

"I understand."

"But you may have free time to visit them on your own."

"I know, and that's okay with me."

"We'll probably spend most of our time in Jerusalem and Haifa, and a few sites around Tel Aviv that were important to the development of modern Israel, not ancient Israel or Israel in Roman times."

"I understand," David nodded. "I know a good bit about ancient Israel, but not much about modern Israel."

"And you'll be traveling with a group of Jews."

"Great!" David exclaimed. "I want to see Israel as a Jew. I want to find out what it means from a Jewish perspective. I know what it means for me as a Christian. I don't know what it means to be a Jew."

"Okay." Cronfeld handed the brochure back to David. "Send your reservation to the tour company. They'll notify us for approval."

The answer caught David off guard. "I have to be approved?"

"Yes," Cronfeld smiled. "But don't worry. I'm the one who issues the approval."

"Great," David beamed. He grasped Cronfeld's hand. "This will be great."

As he turned to leave David caught sight of a poster tacked on a bulletin board. In large, block letters it announced formation of a Torah Study group. David paused and pointed to it. "Torah Study?"

"Yes," Cronfeld replied. "We meet each Thursday morning at eleven."

"And you study the Torah?"

"Yes. The weekly portion. From the reading in Shabbat worship."

"Can anyone attend?"

"You would like to attend our Shabbat worship service?"

"No. Torah Study."

"I suppose."

David gave him a quizzical look. "You are hesitant."

"I understand your interest in learning what it means to be Jewish, and I am not unsympathetic to that; but Torah Study is not a place for an argument over Christian theology."

"I wouldn't argue Christian theology. I wouldn't argue at all. I just want to learn what the Torah means from a Jewish perspective."

"You may attend if you like. But let me inform the class first. Perhaps if you go on the tour you could come to one of our sessions afterward."

David nodded. "That's a good idea. I'll do the tour, and then I'll come to Torah Study. We can see how it goes from there."

"Very good."

David turned away then stopped a few steps down the hall. "And you'll tell me if I'm disrupting class and causing a problem."

"Yes, I will." Cronfeld chuckled.

"Great." David continued down the hall toward the door. "Looking forward to it."

* * *

That afternoon David drove home to tell Sue of his plans. He found her in the backyard, sitting in a lounge chair beneath the shade of a pecan tree.

A glass of iced tea sat beside her on the ground. "You look like you're in better humor."

"I am," he grinned.

"I suppose you better tell me what happened."

"I went to see Mark Cronfeld." David pulled a lawn chair next to hers and sat down.

"I don't know him."

"He's the rabbi over at Temple Beth El."

"You're becoming Jewish now?" she quipped.

"I've always been Jewish," he countered. "Half of me, anyway," David chuckled. "When your mother is Jewish, you're Jewish. Otherwise Jesus would not have been Jewish."

"What did Mark Cronfeld have to say?"

"They're organizing a tour of Israel for the fall."

She glanced over at him. "And you want to go?"

"Yes," he nodded. "I do."

"Why?"

"I think it's a way to find resolution to whatever's going on inside me."

"A trip to Israel will resolve your conflict with your father?"

"I know it sounds crazy, but I think it might."

"I think you should make another trip to Mooresville."

The comment aggravated David. "I thought you wanted to help me find another way."

"I was talking about inviting him to dinner, or meeting him at a restaurant, or going to his house again. I wasn't thinking about a tour of Israel. How'd you find out they were going?"

"That's the neat thing about it." David's countenance softened. "I didn't find it. It found me."

"Okay." She gave him a skeptical look. "How did it find you?"

"When I went to the office this morning a brochure about the trip was lying on the desk out front. The mailman had delivered it to the wrong address."

"And you took it over there to the rabbi?"

"After I read it."

"They don't mind having a preacher on their tour?"

"I don't know about the members of the synagogue, but the rabbi doesn't mind." David leaned closer to Sue. "I need you with me on this."

"We both can't go, David. Someone has to stay here to get the kids off to school. And we can't afford to spend the money for both of us to go."

"Well." He settled back in his chair. "Maybe not. I just think this is part of what Yona was talking about. She said I would know what to do when I saw my father."

"And you think this is what she meant?"

"Sue," David snapped. "I think I have to do this."

"Okay. Go on." She looked him in the eye. "But sooner or later, you're going to have to face the fear that grips your soul."

David sighed and leaned his head back against the chair. For an instant, he knew she was right. Then just as quickly, he pushed the thought aside.

chapter 15

That evening after dinner David retreated to the den and
buried himself in *Exodus*, the book by Leon Uris. A few hours later,
Sue came in and turned on the television. Laying his book aside, David
glanced over at her. "This book is making me think about things I hadn't
considered in awhile. For instance, did you know that the ancient histo-
rian Josephus and Theodor Herzl were both influenced by anti-Semitism
to become advocates for Israel?"

"No," she grinned. "I didn't know that."

"Josephus saw the destruction of Jerusalem, and Herzl encountered an anti-Semitic mob in Paris when he was a journalist."

"Fascinating," she smiled.

David's shoulders sagged. "You're being sarcastic."

"Yes," she chuckled. "I am. Who is Theodor Herzl?"

"A famous music composer. Just kidding! He's the founder of modern Israel."

"He must be pretty important if he started a country."

"Okay. Make fun."

Sue slapped his leg. "I'm just being silly. I know it's important to
you."

"But not to you."

"I'm not that interested in the history of Israel." She leaned toward
him. "But I am interested in you. So tell me about him."

"Theodor Herzl developed a plan for the Jews to return to Palestine. He said it would happen within fifty years, and it did. The Jewish people had been dispersed following the destruction of Jerusalem. Some went west into Spain and Portugal. Others went north into what later became Germany. The Diaspora took them to other countries in Europe and Asia and around the world. In the 1800s Herzl thought they should return as a way of escaping anti-Jewish mobs in Europe." David glanced around. "Where are our children?"

"They're in bed."

"In bed? What time is it?"

"Eleven."

David checked his watch. "Wow. I didn't realize it was this late. Joel and I were supposed to watch a show on television."

"He watched it upstairs."

David set the book aside. "I better go up and see him. He'll think I forgot."

"You did forget."

"No. I just got busy." He stood. "There's a difference."

Sue grabbed the leg of his trousers. "It's okay. He's asleep. You can apologize to him in the morning. He wasn't upset. He saw how interested you were in that book and didn't want to bother you. I checked on him. He's fine." David's countenance fell. Sue shook his pants leg again. "It's okay. Really." She pointed to the chair. "Sit down and tell me more about Theodor Herzl and that other guy."

David dropped onto the chair. "I feel like a moron."

"You're not a moron. You're an inspiration. It's all right. Now, tell me more about Theodor and the other guy."

"I know what you're doing."

"What am I doing?"

"You think I should go back out there and see my father, but you know I don't want to go and would rather resolve this thing inside me a different way. You disagree, but rather than fight me on it, you're taking the opposite approach and just diving in headfirst." He gave her a knowing look. "I'm onto you."

"Would you rather have a fight?"

"No."

"Then tell me more about Theodor Herzl and that Josephus fellow."

✹ ✹ ✹

Sleep did not come easily for David that night. He tossed and turned, and when he finally got to sleep he was transported back to the kitchen inside the house at 77 Pasco Road. Color was gone from the room, leaving only shades of black and white. His mother sat at the kitchen table, her back to him. David stood near the sink, his body frozen in place, held fast by the grip of cold, hard fear.

Just inches away Wally glared from behind a twisted, sneering scowl. His eyes were focused and sharp, and while they bore into David's soul, his long, powerful fingers slowly closed around his throat, squeezing tighter and tighter. He felt Wally's fingers press into his flesh, felt his fingernails sink deep into his skin. "Breathe now, ya' moron," Wally seethed through clinched teeth. David gasped for breath. "That's right," Wally nodded. "It ain't so easy is it, big boy?" David flailed his arms and shook his head from side to side as he tried to wiggle free, but that only served to amuse Wally all the more. His sneer became a grin. "Breathe, Jew-baby! Breathe if'n ya' can."

Suddenly David was off the floor, lifted by the hand around his throat, his head rising higher and higher until it almost touched the ceiling. He dangled there, kicking his feet and thrashing about with his hands, his head twisting from side to side in a desperate struggle to break free.

At the last possible moment, as he was slipping into the darkness that closed around him, stomach acid rushed into David's throat, burning like molten fire and taking his breath away. His eyes popped opened. He lay on his back, staring up at the bedroom ceiling and gasping for air.

Dazed and disoriented, his eyes darted around the room. Numbers on the clock on the nightstand glowed in black and white. He heard them flip over and saw it was four in the morning. His chest was tight and heavy, as if a great weight was pressing down on him. His t-shirt was soaked with sweat. His body was cold and shivering. Waves of nausea washed over him.

David had been plagued for years with acid reflux, and he had to sleep with his head elevated, but this felt different from a usual bout of reflux. He rolled on his side and swung his feet to the floor, only to find the room spinning round and round. He collapsed backwards on the bed, gasping again as his heart raced out of control. "A heart attack," he whispered. "I'm…I'm having a heart attack." He groped with his left hand and called out in a raspy voice. "Sue." His hand struck the mattress near her side. "Sue…help me."

"David. What in the world?" She jerked upright in bed and snapped on her bedside lamp. "Stay right there and don't move." She grabbed the phone from the nightstand and jabbed the keypad with her finger. "Don't move," she repeated. "Just lie still. I'm calling 9-1-1." Despite her valiant attempt to remain calm, David could hear the tremor in her voice.

The next few minutes went by in a blur. Megan came to the door. Sue guided her into the hall and sent her downstairs to let the EMTs inside. Red and blue lights flickered across the ceiling. Two men dressed in dark blue uniforms raced up the stairs. One leaned over the bed. "Mr. Ellis, can you hear me?"

"Yes," David replied.

"We're EMTs. We came with the ambulance. We're going to place you on a stretcher."

"I can walk."

The EMT took him by the hand. "See if you can sit up."

David grabbed hold of the man's arm with both hands and raised himself to a sitting position. The EMT shook his head. "Mr. Ellis, I don't think you can walk." David groped with his left hand for the man's shoulder, then forced himself to stand. "Are you sure about this, Mr. Ellis?" David took a step from the bed and caught sight of the stretcher on the floor a few feet away. A second EMT came to his side. David took another step, and then lowered himself to the stretcher. As his head reached the pad, the room went dark.

chapter 16

A voice called through the darkness. "Mr. Ellis, can you hear me? Can you open your eyes?"

David forced his eyes to open and squinted at the glare of a bright light hanging from the ceiling of a stark, white room. He struggled to move his lips. "Where am I?"

A nurse leaned over him. "You're at Carolinas Medical Center. In the Emergency Room." She smiled. "I'm going to take some blood from your arm. I need you to hold still. Okay?"

"I'll try."

David felt something cool against the bend of his elbow. A hand touched his forearm. "Okay," the nurse continued. "I'm going to stick the needle in now. It might sting a little. Hold still."

David closed his eyes and thought of the last day at the beach. Megan and Joel were standing at the water's edge watching waves crash against the sand. He came up behind them and slipped his arms around their shoulders. They leaned against him. Now he wondered if he would ever see a day like that again.

"Okay," the nurse said. "That's it. You can rest now."

David took a deep breath and tried to relax. A hand touched his right arm. He opened his eyes to see Sue standing beside him. "It's okay," she said softly.

"Why did they take the blood?"

"To run tests. They'll know more in a few minutes."

David shook his head. "I can't believe this is happening."

"Were you dreaming again?"

"Yes," David nodded. "I was—"

The beeping from a machine on the table to the left interrupted him. A nurse appeared at the doorway. She had a concerned look on her face as she stepped into the room and pressed a button on the machine. The beeping stopped. She waited a moment, studying a graph on the machine's tiny screen, and then glanced over at David. "You need to lie quietly, Mr. Ellis. That machine monitors your heart rate. Just lie quietly and it will slow down."

David turned his head to look at the machine and saw an IV bag hanging from a pole beside his bed. A thin plastic tube snaked from the bag to a needle in the back of his left hand. "What's in the bag?"

"Just an IV solution," the nurse replied. "We gave you something to calm you down. Just lie there and let it work." She shot a look at Sue and then stepped out.

Thirty minutes later, a man wearing a white lab coat entered the room. Tall with short, thinning hair and broad shoulders, he stood near the foot of the bed. "Mr. Ellis, I'm Dr. Mark Perry, the resident on call tonight. How are you feeling?"

"Better."

"Good. We ran some tests. Looks like you didn't have a heart attack after all. That's good news."

"What was it?"

"Probably a panic attack."

"What can you do about that?"

"We'd like to run some tests. Make certain we're right before we put you on any treatment."

"How long will I be here?"

"Two days. Maybe three. We'll just have to see how it goes." The doctor backed away from the bed. "Someone will be here in a few minutes to move you to a room."

"Can't I walk?"

"No. You just lie right there and relax. They'll wheel you upstairs in a few minutes." Dr. Perry stepped through the doorway and disappeared down the hall.

When he was gone, David looked at Sue. "I guess you better call Steve."

"I already did."

"What did he say?"

"They'll take care of everything."

David gripped Sue's hand. "Whatever happens, don't cancel my trip to Israel."

Sue's voice took a matter-of-fact tone. "We'll talk about that after we find out what's wrong."

An hour later David was in a room across from the nurses' station on the hospital's sixth floor. Nurses moved in and out, positioning the heart monitor, checking the electrodes on his chest and arms, and changing the IV bag. When they were finished, David looked at Sue. "What time is it?"

"Six o'clock."

"Don't you need to get the kids to school?"

"It's summer, David. They don't have school."

"Oh, yeah. I forgot."

There was a knock at the door. Alan Scruggs entered the room. "Glad to see you're still with us."

Sue's face lost all expression. David looked at Alan. "Glad I'm here too."

"Quite a scare."

"Yeah."

"Are you feeling better?"

"Yes."

"Good. Steve said it wasn't a heart attack."

"Yeah," David replied, with a wry twist. "It was just a panic attack."

"Stress is a subtle thing. Creeps up on you before you know it. Have they said anything about an exercise program?"

Sue stood. "We aren't that far in the diagnostic process yet."

"I just know it helps me to work things off at the end of the day. Gets rid of all that extra energy so I don't take it home."

"I'm sure we'll get to the bottom of it." David shifted positions in the bed. "I'll be back at the church in a day or two."

"Yeah," Alan nodded. "Listen, I know this is a bad time to discuss business and all, but I've been talking to Steve about expanding his role at the church. With you out for a while now, I think this is a good time to do that."

"Expanding his role?"

"Bringing him into the day-to-day decision process."

"I won't be out that long."

"Still, I think it would be a good idea. Take some of the pressure off you."

"We should talk to the board about this."

"I've already done that, informally. They agree that it's a good idea. Can't hurt to have everyone participating in the way things operate."

"I don't know," David sighed. "I really can't talk about that right now, Alan."

"That's okay. We'll have plenty of time later." Alan backed toward the door. "I hope you get to feeling better."

When he was gone, David frowned at Sue. "What was that all about?"

"I don't like this. Why did he come in here now to talk about that?"

"I don't know."

"How did he get to be chairman of the board?"

"I'm not sure. He's good friends with Steve and some of the others."

Sue shook her head. "I don't trust him."

David cut his eyes at her. "Tell me, Sue." He smiled. "How do you really feel about Alan Scruggs?"

"He wears nice suits," she grinned.

"He's a little tough to handle."

"No kidding."

David shifted his legs to a more comfortable position. "I'm more tired now than I was when we went to bed."

"You should get some sleep."

"I don't want to sleep."

"You look tired."

"Terrible things happen when I sleep."

"You go to sleep," Sue insisted. "I'll sit here with you and make sure nothing happens."

David's eyes filled with tears. "I've got to get past this. I've got to!"

"Shhh. We'll talk about it later." She reached over and patted his hand. "Get to sleep now. God's got everything under control."

chapter 17

Later that morning a stress test confirmed what Dr. Perry and others suspected—David was suffering from tachycardia triggered by panic attacks. An echocardiograph that afternoon showed his heart was in good condition. David returned to his room and lay on the bed, thinking about all that had transpired. He remembered the conversations he had had with Yona and found himself longing to talk to her again. "I should have asked for her phone number."

Billy Jones appeared in the doorway. "Heck of a way to get a few extra days off," he quipped.

"Believe me," David said, "I would work double duty if I could avoid this."

Billy came into the room. "I heard the tests came out okay."

"Yeah. Everything looks good."

"What happened?"

Of all the people in the church, Billy was the one person with whom David felt comfortable talking. David was certain he could tell Billy anything, and it wouldn't change Billy's opinion of him. But if he told Billy everything, it would change David's opinion of himself. Admitting to someone else how awful his past had been, how it reached out through the years to plague him almost every night, would be admitting to himself that the past was something he couldn't handle.

"They don't know for sure," David replied.

Billy pushed the door closed, then moved up beside the bed. "But you do."

David frowned. "What do you mean?"

"I'm no doctor, and I'm not a trained counselor, but I know this: Things this traumatic don't simply happen. Something was going on that threw you into a panic so severe you thought you were having a heart attack. Your body was geared up for a fight. It dumped adrenaline and a bunch of other chemicals into your system to get ready for that fight, only the fight never occurred." He paused a moment. "So, I think you need to tell somebody what that something was."

David looked away. "I'd rather not talk about it."

"I'm sure you wouldn't, but that's the kind of thing you have to talk about." Billy stepped back to the foot of the bed and propped his hand on the frame. "You remember the other Sunday I told you I had a word for you?"

"Yes."

"You remember what it was?"

"You shall know the truth and the truth shall set you free."

"That's right. I was thinking about that on the way over here, and I think the Holy Spirit gave me a little more for you."

"What is it?"

"God already knows the truth about your situation, and He loves you in spite of whatever that truth is. He knows what you're worried about, or what you're afraid of, and His love for you surpasses all of that. Whatever it is, He knows about it already and He loves you. He is with you, no matter what." Billy stood up straight. "And I'm going to tell you something else."

"What?"

"I am too." Billy ran his hand over his chin. "Whatever it is that's bothering you, whatever you're carrying around—a past you can't handle, financial problems, or wife problems." Billy glanced away, and then looked back at David. "Whatever you've got going on inside, I'll help. And if you aren't comfortable talking to me about it because I'm a church member, I'll quit and go to church somewhere else, and you can just talk to me as a friend and not a parishioner. Or I'll drive you to wherever it is you need to go to get the help you need."

Tears ran down David's cheeks. "I appreciate that, Billy."

"I mean it." Billy pulled a chair up beside the bed. "So tell me, what's going on that threw you into a panic?"

They sat in silence for a long time, Billy looking at David, David staring into space. Finally, David looked at him. "Billy, my father treated us worse than awful. Beat us regularly. And almost every night, when I go to sleep, I have the worst nightmares you can imagine."

"Your dad comes back in your dreams, doing all those things to you all over again?"

"Yes."

"The past is a terrible thing. It's always there in your mind, but there's no way to go back and make it right. You don't get a do-over." Billy's words sounded familiar. "You remember a few months ago you preached about how the future is forbidden to us? We're not supposed to go to fortune tellers and all that to figure out the future, you remember that?"

"Yes."

"And you said Satan tries to get us to fight battles in the future, and that leads to worry."

"Negative faith."

"That's right. Negative faith. Well, the past is just the same. Satan tries to get us to fight battles in the past too." Billy leaned forward. "I'm sure you'd like to go back to the past as that little boy and just knock the …" Billy cleared his throat. "Pop your dad right between his eyes. But you can't. You gotta deal with the past as it comes to you in the present."

David's eyes opened wide. Those were the same words Yona used. "Say that again. The last part."

"You have to deal with the past as it comes to you in the present."

"Where did you hear that?"

"I don't know. Why?"

"Someone else told me the same thing."

Billy stood. "That's a smart person! I hear you're going to Israel."

"Yes I am, if the doctor'll let me after all this."

"Didn't you tell me your mama was Jewish?"

"She was."

"That makes you Jewish too…as Jewish as Jesus."

"It does. And that's part of the reason I want to go over there. To find out what it means to be a Jew."

Billy nodded. "Let me pray for you, and then I'll go." He stepped closer and laid his hand on David's shoulder. "Lord, bring peace to David right now, in the present. Let him find You wherever he goes, and let him not be able to avoid Your truth and the freedom You bring. Amen."

David reached out to shake his hand and smiled at Billy. "Thanks for coming."

"Glad to see you, though I'd rather visit at the house and have a drink of tea." Billy squeezed his hand and winked. He started toward the door and then turned back. "I believe God has another word for you. It's in II Timothy 1. You know it, but I think He wants me to remind you. "For God has not given us a spirit of fear, but of power and of love and of a sound mind.' Now, slide down under the covers and get to sleep. I don't think you'll have any trouble tonight."

David lay awake long after Billy was gone, thinking about what he had said. From deep in his spirit he sensed God speaking to him and repeating to his spirit what Billy had said. "I am with you, no matter what." Billy had come in person to deliver that message, not just through words but also through himself, through his own expression of personal commitment. "If you can't talk to me because I'm a member of the church, I'll quit and go to church somewhere else and then we can talk." As David rolled those words around in his mind, a sense of peace swept over him. Maybe Sue was right. Maybe what he really needed to do was to try to see his father again. Still, even if he was wrong in not going, God was with him, and He would make things work out right.

chapter 18

David arrived home from the hospital with a prescription for *Tenormin*, a beta-blocker to interrupt the panic attack signals. He also had a medication to help him sleep. He set the bottles on a shelf in the medicine cabinet and reached up to close the door. As he did, the red and white labels caught his eye. "I've never been sick more than a day in my life," he sighed, "and now I have a shelf full of medicine because I'm scared of my father."

Suddenly, an image of Wally sitting in the recliner flashed through David's mind. In an instant, he was not an adult but a little boy again, staring through the open door of the trailer, looking over at his dad. David felt his heart rate quicken. Veins in his neck pulsed. His palms were damp. The skin on his forearms was clammy. "This isn't right," he whispered. "I have to get beyond this." He pushed the door of the medicine cabinet closed and stared at his reflection in the mirror. What he saw there was equally upsetting.

Deep lines creased David's forehead. Tiny crow's feet spread out from the corners of his eyes. Dark circles ringed his red, puffy eyes and hung like bags beneath them. David ran his hand over his face. "I look old," he muttered.

"You look tired."

David turned to see Sue standing at the doorway. "I am tired," he replied.

"Take a nap," she suggested.

"It's the middle of the afternoon."

"You've had a rough two days. Take a nap. I'll call you in an hour."

David moved from the bathroom to the bed and flopped down on his back. "I'll just close my eyes," he sighed.

After what seemed only a minute, he felt a hand gently shaking him. He opened his eyes to see Sue standing over him. "Time to get up."

David blinked his eyes. "I've been asleep?"

"Two hours."

"I thought you said one."

"Think of it as a gift." She sat down on the bed beside him. "Rabbi Cronfeld called. They received your deposit for the trip. He's sending the information you need to get a visa."

"Good. I don't even have a passport."

"They're sending something about that too." Sue ran her hand over his arm. "Do you really think this is a good idea?"

"What?"

"Going off to Israel."

"I want to find out what it means to be Jewish."

"Don't you need to know what it means that one of your parents was Jewish and the other Christian?"

"I know what it means to be Christian."

"Your father's version of Christianity and what you believe are two separate things."

"What are you saying?"

"That's a really big conflict. I mean, having one parent who's Christian and the other who is Jewish would be a big deal, even if they loved each other and got along great. But your parents hated each other. Not just Wally hating Leah, but Wally hating Jews and Leah hating Christians." She arched an eyebrow. "That's a lot for a child to carry into adulthood."

"And I've been carrying it?"

"What do you think?"

David laced his fingers together behind his head and looked toward the windows. "There certainly was a lot of conflict."

"And that's where the nightmares come from. Your mind just can't hold all that tension without finding a way to release it." She laid her hand over his heart. "All that conflict inside is taking a toll on your body. So, don't you think going to Israel is just running from what's really bothering you?"

"I'm not running." Tears formed in his eyes. He looked over at her. "I'm not running."

Sue scooted up on the bed and lay down next to him. With one arm draped across his chest, she rested her head on his shoulder. "Okay," she whispered in his ear. "Go to Israel. See what it's like." She nestled her head to a comfortable position. "I trust you and I trust God. Only promise me one thing?"

"What?"

"You won't bring back a bunch of slides and make us watch a slide-show about it."

David laughed and pulled her closer.

chapter 19

The next two months were a whirlwind of activity as David obtained a passport, visa, and up-to-date inoculations. He bought new luggage, a few clothes, and then made sure a thousand details at the church were covered. Finally, August gave way to September and the day arrived. It was time to leave. He made one last survey of his open suitcase, closed it, and lifted it from the bed.

Sue, Megan, and Joel were waiting for him at the car. Joel grabbed the suitcase. "I'll take that for you, Dad." David let go of the handle and watched as Joel lugged the suitcase to the rear of the car. While he hoisted it into the trunk, David looked over at Sue. "He wants to grow up."

"He is growing up. And Megan will be finished with high school before you know it."

"I don't want to think—"

Sue cut him off with a touch of her finger to his lips. "Don't get maudlin on me."

David grinned. "I'm going to miss you."

"I'm going to miss you too. But we're not going to mope about it. This is a big step in your life, and you're going to find whatever there is to find in it. You hear me?"

"Okay."

"Besides, you'll be back in two weeks." She leaned forward and kissed him. "It's not that long."

* * *

The flight to Israel proved long and arduous. David did his best not to sleep for fear he would have another "Wally-post-traumatic-stress" nightmare. If Sue was right and it was the way his mind found relief, the stress of leaving home and traveling to the Middle East would be more than enough to touch off an awful dream. Somewhere over the Atlantic, however, David's effort to stay awake fell short. With the airplane's engines rumbling in the background, he drifted off to sleep. Hours later, he was awakened by the nudge of a flight attendant.

"We will be landing in Tel Aviv shortly. Please bring your seatback upright."

David raised his seat and glanced out the window. Below, the blue water of the Mediterranean Sea shimmered in the sun. He thought about his mother and Aunt Eliana, huddled by the outhouse in Russia, their mother and grandfather—his grandmother and great-grandfather—burned alive in the synagogue by people who claimed to love Jesus more than life itself. And then he thought of Wally, a man who claimed to be a Christian yet hated Jews and blamed them for all the bad things that happened to him. David shook his head and muttered, "I am one messed-up individual."

The man seated beside him leaned over. "Did you say something?"

"No." David shook his head. "Just talking to myself."

"I do that all the time. Your first trip to Israel?"

"Yes."

The man held out his hand. "Then, welcome." They shook hands. "I hope you and your companions have a lovely time."

David nodded. "I'm sure it will be enlightening."

Getting off the plane and through customs took several hours. David was one of the last in the tour group to make it through. He collected his suitcase and joined the others near the front of the airport terminal. Rabbi Cronfeld stood at David's side. "You ready for this?"

"I hope so."

"I have been to Tel Aviv many times. It is never the same twice. But one thing is almost always certain."

"What's that?"

"Septembers are always hotter than the tour books suggest." Cronfeld nodded toward the doors. "Let's go find out."

David followed Cronfeld through the doorway. As they left the building, heat and humidity enveloped him like a hot, wet blanket. Almost immediately, sweat trickled down his back. He glanced over at Cronfeld. "I see what you mean."

"Yes," Cronfeld nodded. "And this is a cool day."

The group took a bus to the Yamit Plaza Hotel, a modern structure on the beach overlooking the Mediterranean. The hotel staff was ready and waiting when they arrived. David was in his room in less than thirty minutes. When the bellman was gone, he pushed back the curtain and looked out. Beneath his window, the blue Mediterranean stretched out to the horizon. A wide sandy beach lined the winding coast. Waves lapped ashore, the surf shimmering in the sunlight. Palm trees along the roadway provided a tropical backdrop. "Wow," he whispered. "This view was worth the trip."

For the next seven days, David followed the tour as they criss-crossed the country. From Tel Aviv, they worked their way up the coast to Caesarea, then over to the Golan Heights. They traveled to the Syrian border, then down to Safed and into western Galilee. Along the way David learned about Jewish mysticism, the struggle against the Romans, and the return of Zionists in the 1800s. He toured the places where battles were fought in the 1947 War for Independence against Israel's Arab neighbors and looked across the border into Lebanon, with whom Israel continued to struggle to maintain that freedom. As he viewed the sites and heard the guide's lectures, he became aware of how Jewish life had been defined by struggle, for each individual and for the nation.

He was struck by how much his own life had mirrored that same conflict—a conflict against racism and hatred.

Midmorning of the eighth day the tour reached Jerusalem. They would spend the last week of the trip visiting the Temple ruins, crawling through tunnels beneath the city that dated from the time of David, and then out to Masada and the caves of the Dead Sea. As they entered the hotel lobby, Rabbi Cronfeld called them together.

"We've arrived a little earlier than expected. The hotel is not quite ready for us to check-in. So we're going to leave our luggage here in the lobby and have lunch in the dining room. We'll be joined there by a group of people from Jerusalem. I know we've seen some interesting people along the way, but this will give you an opportunity to meet some of the locals who live and work in Jerusalem every day, those you might not otherwise get a chance to meet on such a short trip."

David added his suitcase to the growing stack in the lobby and followed Cronfeld to the dining hall. The room was abuzz with voices, punctuated by the tinkling of glasses and clanging of silverware. David scanned the room and located a table near the center of the room. He crossed the room to the table and pulled out the chair. A man seated to the left rose and scooted his chair over to make more room. Pointing at David's name badge, the man said, "You are Mr. David Ellis."

"Yes," David grinned. His eyes searched for a badge that would reveal the man's name.

"Hello! I am Avi."

They shook hands and took their seats. "This is quite a treat." David glanced around the room. "Do you participate in these events often?"

"Whenever I can," Avi answered. "One of my relatives owns your tour company. He often makes certain I am here to greet you Americans." He took a sip of water from the glass at his place. "Tell me, have you enjoyed your stay in Israel so far?"

"Yes, I have. We've seen some interesting sites and met some interesting people."

"What about them struck you as interesting?"

"Their struggle for survival."

"Oh," Avi nodded. "You have been looking with the eyes of your heart."

"Yes." The comment struck David as odd, but he didn't want to be impolite. "Everywhere we've been we've seen conflict, struggle, against the Romans, your Arab neighbors."

"You did not realize we live in the midst of conflict?"

"I've read about it, but reading and experiencing are two different things."

"Rather like one's own life."

"Exactly."

"And the accommodations? They have suited you?"

"Great."

"How did you sleep last night?"

"I've slept well each night so far. No complaints."

"I am glad to hear that," Avi smiled. "Rest is important, is it not?"

"It certainly makes the day much better." David scooted his chair closer to the table and changed the subject. "So, Avi, tell me, what do you do?"

"Actually, I make inferior interiors superior."

"Ah, then you are an upholsterer?"

"Actually, I am a counselor, but I do a little bit of everything. Whatever the need is, I try to fill it."

"That's a lot for one person to cover. Most counselors I know try to stay in a particular area. Marriage and family, substance abuse, that sort of thing."

"I find they are all related. The complexity of the human soul never ceases to amaze me."

"I'm sure you have enough to keep you busy."

"Here in Jerusalem we get several each week claiming to be prophets." Avi had a twinkle in his eye. "A few days ago we had two who claimed to be Jesus. They showed up at the same time at the Western

Wall, each of them rebuking the other 'in the name of Jesus.' They spent twenty-four hours rebuking each other and claiming, 'I am the real Jesus; Satan, I command you to go.' And the other one saying, 'No, I am Jesus. I bind you in my name.' Finally they sat down, completely exhausted. One looked at the other and said, 'I'm George from Detroit.' The other responded, 'I'm Bobby from Australia. Let's get some sleep.'"

David laughed. "You're making that up."

"No," Avi shook his head. "True story. But most of the people I see are not quite so entertaining. They are simply suffering souls in need of light."

"I'm sure your patients—"

"Not patients," Avi interrupted. "I prefer to call them my *chaverim*—my friends."

"I'm sure your friends sense the way you care for them."

Avi gave a little shrug. "I do not know, David. With people you can't always tell. I do not base my efforts on their appreciation. I want them all to receive what they need. And speaking of needs, here are our salads." Avi smiled as the waiter placed a salad before him. "*Eizeh yofi! Toda raba, adoni.* How lovely. Thank you, sir."

The waiter bowed and turned away. David took a napkin from the table and placed it in his lap. Avi slid a dish toward him. "Try this hummus on the pita bread. It is wonderful."

As they continued to talk, David grew more at ease with his new acquaintance. Avi seemed to notice everything—the expression on the face of a woman seated two tables over, the color of the tomatoes in the salad, the sound of a passing waiter's voice. David began to notice them too. He looked at the faces of the people as Avi pointed them out, trying to imagine what their lives were like. David enjoyed himself in a way he couldn't remember.

All too soon Rabbi Cronfeld passed between the tables. "The hotel is now ready to check us in. So, as you finish eating you can make your way to the lobby, and they will get you to your room. We'll have some free time this afternoon, then meet back here for dinner to get things organized for tomorrow."

"I guess that means me," David said, gesturing in Cronfeld's direction. "Avi, I have enjoyed talking to you." He took a business card from his pocket and handed it across the table. "If you're ever in the United States, give me a call. I'd love to see you. You can stay at our house."

Avi took a card from his pocket. "Here is one of mine."

The card was made of plain white stock with the words, "Counseling Services" in block letters and a Jerusalem phone number below it. Across the bottom of the card, in much smaller type, was a Scripture reference to Isaiah 61:3. David pointed to it. "This quote... isn't it the one about beauty for ashes?"

"Yes," Avi beamed. "You say it that way in your King Jimmy's Bible. A very lyrical translation, by the way."

"My first Bible was a *King James Version*. We don't call it King Jimmy's Bible."

Avi's eyes lit up. "Smile, David. He's Jimmy to me. Do you still have it?"

"Yes. I think so. Put away somewhere." David glanced around. Most of the others from the tour group had already left. He took one last sip of water from his glass. "Well, I suppose I should get going."

"Do you have something scheduled for this afternoon?"

"No." David shook his head. "I don't think so."

"Good," Avi nodded. "I am going to a lecture at Hebrew University. Would you like to join me?"

"Sure. What's it about?"

"I like that," Avi grinned. "You said yes before you knew what it was about."

"Gets me in trouble sometimes."

"Opens you up for unexpected opportunities too."

David pointed over his shoulder with his thumb. "I guess I should check in first with the front desk. What time is the lecture?"

Avi glanced at his watch. "We should go now. The main campus of the University is just down the street from here, but where we are going is to the Mt. Scopus campus, all the way across town. Traffic is sometimes a problem. We do not want to be late." He wiped his mouth with the napkin. "Come. We will ask the bellman to hold your luggage. You can check in when you return."

chapter 20

Back in North Carolina the sun was just breaking over the horizon, but Sue was hard at work. With David gone she found it difficult to sleep. Many nights it would be two or three in the morning before she nodded off. She filled the extra hours doing laundry and straightening the downstairs, reading her Bible, and paying bills. Working kept her hands busy, which left her mind and spirit free to pray.

As the new day dawned outside, she opened the dryer and took out a load of freshly laundered clothes. She placed them in a clothes-basket, lifted it with both hands, and started toward the bedroom. She dumped the clothes on the bed and began sorting through them, mindlessly dividing hers from David's and placing them in piles on either side of the bed. With David gone, her pile was noticeably larger. Once she had the clothes sorted, she sat on the edge of the bed, folded them flat, and stacked them neatly at her side.

While she folded clothes, she thought of David and what he might be doing. She glanced at the clock and calculated the hours in her mind. Jerusalem was seven hours ahead of Charlotte, which meant it was past noon there. David wouldn't let noon go by without eating lunch. If he had a choice in the matter, he was sitting at a table somewhere enjoying a meal.

The image in her mind brought a smile to her face. David was tall, lean, and ruggedly handsome. She could see him now, seated at the table, enjoying the conversation with his tablemates as much as he enjoyed the food. She always said she first noticed him when they were at Southeastern Baptist Seminary in Wake Forest and she passed him on the sidewalk. She next noticed him in the cafeteria, sitting with a group of guys, all of them laughing and joking as David entertained them with a story. Even then he had a deep reservoir of intriguing experiences and an engaging way of recounting them.

With the clothes folded and stacked, Sue moved to the dresser. In her left hand she held David's socks. With her right, she opened the top drawer and put them away. When she was finished she noticed a trace of dust around a jewelry box that sat near the mirror on her side of the dresser. She ran her fingers over it and left an outline on the top. "I just dusted this a few days ago," she frowned. She walked to the kitchen for a dust cloth then returned to the bedroom.

Working methodically she removed items from the dresser and set them on the bed. As she moved across the top she came to David's side. An old *King James* Bible lay at the far side. On top of it were a comb and a pair of cuff links. She scooped up the items from the top, then picked up the Bible and set them on the bed with the box. After a few swipes of the cloth, the top was clean and shiny. "There," she smiled. "That looks better."

In quick order she moved the jewelry box to her side of the dresser top. With it in place, she gripped the spine of the Bible in the palm of one hand and grabbed the cuff links and comb with the other. As she turned toward the dresser, the Bible flopped to one side, revealing the first page. Handwriting on the page caught her eye.

Sue slumped back on the edge of the bed and rested the Bible in her lap. Its faux leather cover was worn along the spine and crumpled at the corners. Crudely carved into the imitation leather was "Words of God." Carefully she peeled back the front to see the title page. David's name was scrawled in a child's handwriting near the top right corner. As she looked at it, an image flashed through her mind of David as a young boy, seated on the edge of the bed with the Bible on his lap. The room was dark, but he had a flashlight in his hand. Head bent over the book, he held the light with one hand and a pen with the other as he wrote his name on that page. The image brought tears to Sue's eyes. "So much pain," she whispered. "And that little eleven-year-old boy is still hurting." She wiped her nose. "Lord Jesus, please hold onto him and help him hold onto You."

For the next half hour Sue slowly leafed through the pages of the Bible, reading notes that had been scribbled in the margins. Along the way she found scraps of paper, church bulletins, and an assortment of candy wrappers that had been tucked inside the book. Like a trail of crumbs, they marked a path across David's childhood as he wrestled with the notion of God as Father, what it meant to love, and the hope love could instill.

Then, wedged against the spine of the book, she found a small leather strap. Using a fingernail, she pried it loose from the spine and held it in her hand. As she studied it, she saw there were two small metal loops on one end. "This looks like a cat collar," she mumbled. "But I don't remember anything about a cat." She turned it over. "Why did he keep this?" As she continued to study it, she noticed one edge of the collar was darker than the other, and there was a stain near the clasp. She flicked the edge with her finger. A fleck from the collar lodged beneath her fingernail. "There's something on this collar." Her face wrinkled in a frown as she thought of the possibilities. Then her eyes noticed the page marked by the collar.

"Isaiah," she whispered. She saw a circle drawn in a child's hand around the verse. *Behold, I will do a new thing; now it shall spring forth; shall ye not know it? I will even make a way in the wilderness; and rivers in the desert.* Her hands traced lightly across the page and she read again the melodic words of the *King James Version. He marked this a long time ago, when he was just a boy of eleven. He even printed the date next to it.*

Suddenly she had the overwhelming sense that she needed to pray. She laid the Bible aside and slid to the floor on her knees. "O Lord, wherever David is today, continue Your work in his life. I have no idea what this new thing might be, but You do. Bring it to pass, and make us ready for all You bring our way. Give David wisdom, insight, and courage. Strengthen him as he allows You to lead him. And keep him safe. Amen."

chapter 21

Avi and David took a taxi from the hotel and rode across Jerusalem. Thirty minutes later they arrived at Hebrew University's Mount Scopus campus. As the car pulled to a stop at the curb, Avi glanced at his watch. "The ride was much quicker than usual. We are early." David opened the door and stepped out onto the sidewalk. Avi paid the driver and glanced around, as if checking. "Let us walk down the street a little ways. There is a café on the corner where we can talk."

David walked alongside Avi as they made their way down the sidewalk. "Is it safe to be out like this?"

"Yes," Avi chuckled. "It is safe. As safe as Jerusalem can be. We have more bombings than Americans see on the news, but we do not let it stop us. Personal safety is simply a way of life here. Personal safety is a personal responsibility." By then they had reached the corner. Avi laid his hand on the small of David's back, steering him to the right. "We can sit in here."

David glanced up to see they were in front of a small café. Tables lined the sidewalk out front, but Avi opened the door and gestured for David to go inside. "It will be a little cooler inside."

They found a table in the corner near the door and took a seat. A waiter appeared and took their order. In spite of the warm weather, David asked for hot tea. Avi ordered coffee. When the waiter was gone, Avi asked. "So tell me, what was it like growing up in America?"

"Well," David sighed, "if you're looking for a typical American experience, you'll have to ask someone else."

"Yours was not typical?"

"No."

"How so?"

"To begin with, my father is from the South. Grew up in rural North Carolina. He hates blacks and Jews and thinks of women as an object to service his sexual desires."

"Oh." Avi looked puzzled. "He is not a Christian?"

"He claims to be."

"You are a minister, are you not?"

"Yes."

"But you are unsure if your father is a Christian?"

"All my life he has claimed to be a Christian—Bible-believing, Spirit-filled—but the things that come out of his mouth are...quite a contradiction."

"And your mother?"

"My mother was Jewish."

"This *is* quite a contradiction. A father who hates Jews, married to a Jew."

"Yes," David nodded. "A Jew who hated Christians. It made for an awful childhood."

"He was abusive?"

"That would be an understatement." The waiter returned with their drinks. They waited while he set the cups on the table, then David continued. "It wasn't so bad through the week, most of the time. But on Friday nights he started drinking, and when he drank he got really mean. Beat us with a coat hanger, extension cord, his fist, whatever he could find."

"He hit all of you?"

"All of us boys. I never actually saw him beat my sister."

"And your mother?"

"He beat her too. It was horrible."

"Have you ever thought about why it was always worse on the Sabbath?"

"No, not really."

"Did he ever talk about dreams? Perhaps that would be a clue."

"No, he wasn't much of a talker. He just yelled a lot. Some nights, though, I could hear him screaming like a crazy man. And one time I heard him tell his brother that he kept having this really strange dream. He said it was about black rocks. His great grandfather would hand some black rocks to Wally's father, and his father would hand them to Wally. He didn't have a clue what that meant, and neither do I."

"Maybe someday that answer will come to you, David. But how did you escape Wally's abuse?"

"I joined the army."

"Yes, but you escaped more than that. You've escaped to a life of love. I can see it in your eyes. The Light has shined upon you." The words struck David like thunder. They were exactly the words Yona had said to him that day at lunch. Before he could say anything, Avi continued. "You have a family?"

"Yes."

"I am so sorry for all you had to endure. A father is supposed to protect his children."

"Well, he was just the opposite. And our mother…she was never really there. I think she gave up very early in our lives."

"Fear can live a long time, David. Fortunately, love stays alive much longer."

David was unprepared for the tide of emotion that washed over him. He thought of Sue and knew that love could endure, but just as quickly he remembered the day he went out to the trailer to confront Wally, only to slink away like a scared little boy. He stared down at the table through a veil of tears and carefully lifted the cup of tea to his lips. He took a sip. "When I was in the sixth grade, the teacher asked us what we wanted to be when we grew up." He paused to wipe his eyes. "All the other kids said they wanted to be doctors, firefighters, police officers, nurses, things like that."

"And what did you say?"

"Twenty. I said I wanted to be twenty." David took another sip from the cup, trying to get control of his emotions. "I couldn't imagine growing up, having a family, a career. I couldn't imagine anything. The only thing I could think of, the only thing I dared to hope for, was just to live long enough to get to my twentieth birthday. I was certain my father would kill me before I got there." He set the cup on the table. "That's how bad it was at my house."

Avi put a hand on David's arm. "I am sorry."

"It seems strange telling you all this." David glanced at his watch. "I only met you two hours ago, and here I am pouring out my life story to you."

"You needed to tell someone. We are far from your home, and no one will ever know we talked. There is peace for you in that anonymity."

"I suppose."

"Your father sounds like a terrifying man."

"I was terrified of him," David nodded. "We all were. Always afraid of what he might do the next time he had too much to drink—which was every time he drank. And my mom…when I told her I was going to school to become a minister, she said I'd be better off if I were a drug dealer or a homosexual."

Passion filled Avi's eyes and a lone tear slipped down his cheek.

"Do you have a picture of them?"

"I have one of my mother when she was a little girl." David reached for his wallet and took out the faded, wrinkled photograph. He handed it across the table to Avi. "That's her on the left. Leah. The girl on the right is her sister, Eliana."

"Eliana is still alive?"

"No," David shook his head. "She died several years ago. But I recently saw some of her friends and relatives when I attended my mother's funeral."

"Funerals are like that. We see people we have never seen before."

"Yes, that's true. I met someone like that. Said she had known my mother and Eliana when they lived in Russia. Said she knew me when I was young, but I have no recollection of her."

"What was her name?"

"Yona. Yona Kanievsky."

"Yona," Avi smiled. "That is a lovely name." He gazed at the picture a moment longer. "You did not tell me your mother was dead."

"She died a few months ago."

Avi pointed to the picture. "She was from where?"

"They were born in Russia. Came to America when they were young girls." Avi handed the photograph across the table. David tucked it carefully into his wallet then took another sip of tea. Suddenly, he felt awkward revealing so much of himself. He had told Avi, a stranger, more than he had told anyone. Only Sue knew more about his childhood. But then, she had not met Wally until a year after she and David were married. He didn't attend the wedding. Later she told David, "I'm so glad I didn't meet him before we married. If I had, I probably would never have married you. I would have been too afraid that you would be like him. My family are wonderful Christians, and I have never met anyone like Wally." David didn't tell her about his childhood until he was thirty-three, eleven years after they were married.

He took another sip of tea and changed the subject. "So, what is this lecture about?"

"Lecture?"

"Didn't we come over here for a lecture?"

Avi glanced at his watch. "Oh my. Time is getting away from us." He took a hurried sip of coffee. "I want to keep talking, but we should get going if we are to make the lecture."

"But what's the lecture about?"

"Simeon Katz is giving a lecture on ancient Babylonian art." Avi stood. "He is an expert in several fields of study, but the development of life along the Euphrates is one he really loves." Avi tossed some money on the table and ushered David toward the door. "You will find him most interesting."

chapter 22

David followed Avi from the café to the opposite side of the street and up a sidewalk through the campus to Atzmaut Hall. The lecture was held in a classroom on the ground floor. When Avi and David arrived, the room was half full. They took a seat near the back. Avi glanced around. "It is a good thing we arrived early."

"Early? I thought we were late."

"No," Avi smiled, shaking his head. "We were late to be early. I wanted to get here before now. But this is good."

Twenty minutes later the room was filled to capacity. The door opened, and a slender man with graying hair and dark, intense eyes entered. He was over six feet tall and, although he appeared to be in good shape, David was sure he was at least seventy-five. Avi leaned close and whispered. "This is Simeon Katz. I will introduce you to him later."

Katz crossed the room to the podium, where his eyes quickly scanned the crowd. He began, "Babylonian art was first and foremost a means of political and religious expression. Art is much the same today, but it was even more so six thousand years ago. In order to discuss Babylonian art, we must first take a moment to discuss the Babylonians, and for that we must begin with the Sumerians and set the context."

For the next hour David listened as Katz told of the rise of civilization at Sumer, the spread of civilization up the Tigris and Euphrates valleys, the capitulation of Sumer's neighbors to the rise of the Babylonians, and Sumer's subsequent fall—a story he traced through examples of art from the period. David had expected a tedious, boring lecture. What he found was so intriguing, the time flew past.

As Katz ended the lecture, many in the audience moved from their seats to the front of the room. They formed a semicircle in front of him and peppered him with questions. David stood and started toward the aisle. Avi laid his hand on David's arm to stop him. "Wait here. We will speak to Simeon after they have left." David settled back into his chair and watched as Katz patiently listened to each question then carefully explained in greater detail many of the points he had only mentioned generally in the lecture. Forty-five minutes later, the last student walked from the classroom.

Katz glanced up at Avi. "I see you have brought a friend."

Avi tapped David on the leg and motioned for him to move. "Yes," Avi replied, as he and David made their way to the front and up the steps to the podium. "I found him in a tourist group at the Park Hotel. Thought you might find him interesting. Simeon Katz, this is David Ellis."

"I am pleased to meet you," Katz stared intently at David as they shook hands.

"Fascinating lecture," David offered. "I didn't realize Babylonian art was so intriguing."

"Not many do."

"While you were talking, I couldn't help but think of the current political situation in the Middle East. It's not much different from that of the Sumerians."

"Yes. It has been much the same here throughout all of history."

"I was thinking about how Sumer's fate rested on the willingness of its friends to defend it."

"We do not have many friends in the region."

"Israel may not have many friends in the region, but it does have a friend in America."

"So far."

"And that got me to wondering: If Israel is weakened, will the terrorists you have over here be free to launch an unrestrained attack against America? Which raises the question, isn't the defense of Israel a key to America's survival?"

Katz glanced at Avi. "You are right. This is an interesting man."

"I'm not trying to sound smart," David continued. "I'm just learning. I had this idea while I was listening to you and thought I would ask."

"Well, to answer your question, what happens here with the security of Israel is far more important to America than most Americans realize. Many in America see the spiritual connection between Judaism and Christianity, but they fail to see the strategic nature of that connection. Israel is the buffer between Islamic terrorists and the West. If America abandons us to our enemies, Islamic radicals will see it as a sign of weakness. They will see the West as vulnerable, and they will be empowered to act on their radical beliefs. America and its allies will be the next target."

"That makes sense."

"We are the only democratic nation in the Middle East that is armed and ready to defend itself against the onslaught of hatred and bigotry that I feel is about to be unleashed."

"Most people in America aren't really paying attention. I mean, we know the Russians invaded Afghanistan in December of '79 and we boycotted the summer Olympics in Moscow the next summer, but we don't see the connection between that and Israel."

"Many in the West do not see it, but trouble will come." Katz's eyes narrowed. "And make no mistake about it, radical Islam does not bring a message of peace. They want you to think they come in peace and only want the freedom to reach their own destiny. They call it self-determination, but they come for only one purpose: to destroy all the West holds dear." His face softened. "We desire to live at peace with our neighbors in the region, but we are prepared to do whatever is necessary to defend our people."

The two men talked at length about Israel's relationship with other countries of the region and with the United States. Finally, Avi interrupted them. "You two could talk for hours about this topic, but David needs to get back to the hotel to check in and meet with his tour group."

"And I need to get moving myself." Katz glanced at his watch. "I did not realize we had talked so long." He paused, thinking, then glanced over at Avi. "I am attending a reception for Menachem Begin this evening. Would the two of you like to join me?"

"Sure," Avi replied. "We would be delighted." He looked at David. "Right?"

David tried not to look completely blown away. "Certainly. It would be an honor."

Katz took a business card from his pocket. "Give me your name and address, David. I will have to phone the prime minister's office and let them know you will be joining us."

Thank you, Joseph...uh...Simeon," David shook his head, terribly flustered. "I'm sorry, Simeon. My mind wandered for a moment."

"Wait! Why did you call me Joseph?" Simeon demanded.

David was even more startled by his reaction. "I don't know. It was a mistake...jetlag, I guess."

Simeon said quietly, "No, I think it was not a mistake. When my father, a shipbuilder in Geneva, Switzerland, was dying, I held his hand, and he whispered his last words to me: 'Joseph, Joseph, the nation of Israel will be born, and you will feed it bread.' The year was 1943; the date March 11. I sold his shipbuilding business and built granaries with the proceeds. Joseph fed Israel bread. Now I feed Israel bread." He stared intensely at David. "I have told no one this story!"

David could barely get his business card out of his pocket and hand it to Katz, and then he marveled at what came out of his mouth in response to Katz's admission. "You know, I've heard you meet some people for a season, others for a reason, but very few for life. I have a feeling that our meeting is for life."

Without another word David rose and silently made his way out of the office and down the steps.

chapter 23

David and Avi took a taxi from Mount Scopus back to the hotel. Avi sat in the lobby while David checked in at the counter and put his luggage in the room. He was seated on a bench near the elevator when David arrived downstairs. "All done," David announced. "Ready to go? What time is the reception?"

"We have plenty of time," Avi replied calmly. "Do you need to see Rabbi Cronfeld?"

"Oh, yeah. The meeting. That shouldn't take long." David turned away and started across the lobby. "I'll be right back!" he called.

The tour group was gathered in the dining hall reviewing the next day's schedule. Rabbi Cronfeld handed David a copy. "Glad you made it. I was about to send out a search party for you."

"Sorry," David shrugged sheepishly. "The guy I sat with at lunch invited me to a lecture. It was all the way across town."

"Good," Cronfeld smiled. "But alert me next time, so we'll know where you are."

"Okay." David glanced over his shoulder nervously.

Cronfeld looked in the same direction. "You have somewhere else to go?"

"Actually yes, I do. The lecture was given by a guy named Simeon Katz. He invited us to a reception this evening."

Wide-eyed, Cronfeld pulled David aside. "You met Simeon Katz?"

"Yes. Why?"

"David, he is one of the most respected men in all of Israel. He is an expert on ancient history, and he was instrumental in founding this country. I heard him speak once in New York, but I've never met him. How did you meet him?"

"The guy at my table at lunch knows him. He introduced me, and we started talking. Katz invited us to a reception."

"What time?"

"We're leaving as soon as you say it's okay."

"So go!" Cronfeld exclaimed. "And enjoy! This is why you came here. Just be in the lobby in the morning at eight."

"Great." David gave Cronfeld a friendly slap on the shoulder. "I'll see you then."

"Knock on my door when you get back, so I'll know you're here."

"Okay."

*　　*　　*

The reception for Begin was held at the King David Citadel Hotel, an elegant new establishment overlooking the oldest portion of Jerusalem. The taxi dropped Avi and David at the front entrance. Katz was waiting for them in the lobby. *"Shalom, na'im meod."*

"And peace to you as well," Avi replied. David was unsure what to say, so he just smiled.

Katz led them down a hallway to the right. "This reception is in honor of Prime Minister Begin's work in reaching the Camp David Accords. They were signed in September 1978. Each year since then, those of us who were present that day have gathered to remember the achievement and to encourage ourselves to continue working toward regional peace and security."

A little way down the hall they came to an open doorway on the left. Two soldiers stood on either side. Additional security officers dressed in business suits lingered nearby. Inside, near the center of the room, Menachem Begin was surrounded by a group of men, all of them laughing and talking. Katz leaned close to David. "Do not be intimidated. Just follow my lead."

Katz started across the room. Avi followed with David close behind. When they reached the center of the room, the prime minister acknowledged Katz with a tip of his head. Katz stepped forward. "Mr. Prime Minister, may I present Avi Davidson." He waited while Begin shook hands with Avi, then he turned to David. "And our friend from the United States, Pastor David Ellis."

Begin smiled broadly as he shook David's hand. "An American preacher on his first trip to Israel. Welcome to our country. Be sure to call God while you're in Jerusalem. It is a local call. People worry about being killed when they are here. Do not worry; Jerusalem has the highest rate of resurrections. And you get to go up with some of the nicest people." Begin laughed at his own jokes.

"Thank you," David laughed. "I am honored to be here." He wondered how Begin knew it was his first trip.

For the next ten minutes David listened as Begin talked about his health—he had suffered a heart attack—and about his grandchild. David was grateful for the monologue and used it as an opportunity to think of something to say. Finally, Begin looked kindly at him. "I have done all the talking, Mr. Ellis. Now it's your turn. What brings you to Jerusalem?"

"Well, Mr. Prime Minister, my mother was Jewish. I came hoping to find out more about my roots and what it means to be Jewish."

Begin laughed. "I can tell you what it means. If you have two rabbis you will have three synagogues. Everyone in Israel thinks they are the chief rabbi or the prime minister. If your mother was Jewish, you are Jewish." He moved closer to David. "Leah Ellis. She died a few months ago, did she not? I am sorry for your loss."

David was taken aback. "How did you know about her?"

"My security detail lets no one near me who has not been fully vetted. We know about you—that your mother was Jewish and Wally Ellis was not."

"Remember," Katz said. "I asked for your name and address."

"Yes, but I didn't realize they would be that thorough."

Katz and Begin laughed. "So," Begin continued, "you came to find your Jewish roots."

"Yes," David replied. "But beyond that, I feel deeply that God sent me. I don't know why."

"What? God sent you and didn't tell you why?" David was surprised when Mr. Begin threw back his head and laughed. He called to his assistant, "Kadishai, shake hands with an honest man. He flies nearly eight thousand miles to come to Jerusalem and doesn't know why; only that God sent him." He turned back to David. "When God tells you, come back and let me know. *Ani ish sakran meod.* I am a very curious man."

"I will be sure to do that, Sir," David grinned.

"And Mr. Ellis, have you discovered those roots?"

"I'm not sure."

Begin laughed heartily. "I really like you, David Ellis! This is the country where Judaism began, and you do not know if you have discovered your Jewish roots? That is too funny. If you want to find your Jewish roots, just look down. You have the feet of a big man. Do you know why you are so tall, Mr. Ellis? The righteous shall grow like the cedar in Lebanon."

David felt his cheeks blush with embarrassment. "Well, I have discovered many things about Israel, but I have not yet figured out what my Jewish heritage means to me, personally. Or what it means that I am Jewish."

"You mean half Jewish."

"Yes. Half Jewish."

With a twinkle in his eye, Begin laughed uproariously. "Which half? The front half, or the back half?"

David liked Begin's humor. "I think you could find some who would agree with either."

"I suppose that is true for us all. Even those of us who are completely Jewish."

Begin extended his hand. "I am very glad to meet you Mr. Ellis. I hope you have a wonderful time during your stay here, and I hope you find the answers you seek." He pointed to Katz but his eyes remained fixed on David. "Simeon knows a lot about our country. He can answer many of your questions and point you in the right direction." He patted David on the shoulder and turned away.

The conversation moved on to other topics as Begin drifted around the room. David listened a little longer then slowly retreated. He found Avi standing near a table where a bartender served drinks. "I have never felt so awkward," David grumbled.

"Relax," Avi replied. "You said what was in your heart."

"It sounded naive."

"It sounded genuine."

"I should have been better prepared."

"Questions like the one about your roots sometimes reach deeper into our soul than we expect."

"What do you mean?"

"It is a reception. You were meeting a head of state, perhaps the first head of state you have ever met. He asks an innocuous question, the kind one might ask of a person one does not know as a way of engaging them in conversation. He does not know the things with which you struggle. In your mind you are farther from that struggle than you have ever been. It is nowhere near your conscious thoughts. And, although you are nervous for the occasion, the defenses you've spent a lifetime developing and maintaining are at their lowest point. Then, at a moment when you least expect it, a simple question, one you could easily deflect at any other time, flies unmolested past all those brilliant psychological defenses and strikes you at the core."

David gave Avi a quizzical look. "Do you talk like that all the time?"

"Only when surrounded by such a magnificent setting." Avi took David by the elbow. "Come. I know a place where we can have dinner."

David hesitated. "Avi, I suddenly know why I came to Israel—or at least one of the reasons—and I need to tell Prime Minister Begin."

Avi nodded thoughtfully, touched David's elbow, and began to lead him back to the prime minister. As they approached David caught Begin's eye and heard him say, "Excuse me one moment, while I say goodbye to my new American friend."

"Mr. Prime Minister, I know why I'm here, and I believe I'm supposed to tell you."

Begin smiled, but his eyes were serious. "Please. Tell me."

"I'm supposed to be a bridge builder."

Begin chuckled. "A bridge builder, huh? A bridge like the Brooklyn Bridge?"

David was suddenly resolute. "No, Mr. Prime Minister, a bridge of love between Christians and Jews, and between America and Israel. That's why God sent me to you."

Begin stretched out his hand and David clasped it eagerly. "I will help you build that bridge, Mr. Ellis."

David was just saying, "Thank you, Mr. Prime Minister!" when several gentlemen came up to direct the prime minister's attention elsewhere. David turned to Avi, who had a smile of extreme pleasure on his face, and asked, "Should we say goodbye to our host?"

"Yes," Avi nodded. "You are quite right. We shall bid farewell to Simeon Katz, and then we shall be off." He steered David across the room toward Katz, who was standing near the door.

Katz turned to face them. "Gentlemen, I am glad you were able to join us this evening."

"Thank you for inviting us," Avi replied.

"Yes," David added. "Thank you."

"David ..." Katz laced his fingers together and held his hands near his chest. He seemed suddenly nervous and uncomfortable. "David, it has been a pleasure making your acquaintance. I hope to see you again one day."

"That would be good," David replied.

"We should get back to our earlier conversation." He cleared his throat. "I am sure we would find that and many other things to talk about." His eyes darted in Avi's direction, then back to David. "I hope you enjoy the remainder of the tour." He shook David's hand and stepped away.

When he was gone David looked over at Avi. "That seemed a little awkward. Did I do something to offend him?"

"I am certain it was an indication of the pleasure he found in meeting you and the discussion you began this afternoon."

"I hope you're right."

"Trust me," Avi urged. "I am right. I know Simeon and I know you. It had nothing to do with anything you said or did." He gestured toward the door. "Come. Let's have dinner."

chapter 24

Avi hailed a taxi in front of the hotel and held the door open while David slid inside. As the driver steered the car away from the curb, he glanced over at David. "You are going to a restaurant that has the best fish in the city." David gave him a skeptical look. Avi grinned. "Believe me. You will love it."

Fifteen minutes later they arrived in front of Beni's, a restaurant on the edge of old Jerusalem. As David stepped from the car he smelled the aroma of grilled trout mingled with a hint of spices. He took a long sniff. "Smells good."

"Tastes even better." Avi opened the restaurant door. "Let us go inside and you will see."

They took a seat at a table in the corner. A waiter brought them a basket of bread and took their order for drinks. Avi took a slice from the basket and looked across the table at David. "That was an interesting question the prime minister asked you."

"Don't remind me."

"I was wondering that myself. Why did you come to Israel?"

"Like I said, when my mother died I wanted to know more about what that it meant to be Jewish."

"That was difficult for you? Being Jewish in America?"

"I never thought of myself as being Jewish. I didn't know what it meant to be a Jew. My father took us to church on Sunday. Christianity was all I knew. He wouldn't allow our mother to tell us anything about her religion."

"Your father seems much more a part of your life than your mother."

"I suppose," David shrugged. "In a negative way. She was very withdrawn. He gave us attention, in the form of beatings, but it was attention."

"So why do you want to find out about being a Jew?"

"Just trying to understand myself. Who I am. What it all means. Like why did my father hate Jews, that sort of thing."

"Do you mean, why did your father hate you?" He pointed at David to emphasize his words. "And have you found those answers here, on this trip?"

"Not really."

"Why not?"

"I don't know." David shrugged. "I guess I just haven't been shown."

"Are you sure?"

The waiter returned with their drinks. Avi ordered salmon. David asked for trout. When the waiter was gone, Avi continued. "Are you sure you have not found the answers?"

"What do you mean?"

"Sometimes people do not hear because it's too painful to listen. And sometimes they do not see because they are afraid of what they will find."

"What would I be afraid of?"

"The world is a scary place for a child. Memories of a troubled childhood become associated with the pain and fear experienced during that time of life. The emotion we experienced then is attached to the memory we have now. When we lock away painful memories from our past, they become a source of great power for the Enemy. As adults, we know there are no monsters lurking in our closet or under the bed, but in our memories, we are still that young child, only now the monsters are not in our closet but in our minds, in the memories we have pushed down deep into our subconscious." Avi took a sip of water from the glass. "You understand what I mean? About the memories?"

"I'm sure I've forgotten many things that happened. What I remember is bad enough."

"But those are not memories of your mother. They are memories of your father." Avi took another sip of water. "I think you came to Israel in search of your Jewish past because it is your mother's past. For you, she was far less intimidating than your father. Because she was not emotionally engaged, the memories you have of her are not as scary as the ones associated with your father. Exploring memories of your father is terrifying. Memories of your mother are not. And so, you think that by delving into what it means to be a Jew you can find a less intimidating path to the resolution you seek."

Avi's words pierced deep into David's soul. For an instant, he realized Avi was correct and had clearly described what he had done. Then, just as quickly, he squelched the thought. He took a sip of water and let it slide slowly down his throat.

"You have mentioned what your father did to you," Avi continued. "How do you feel toward him?"

"My sister and brothers hate him."

"But how do you feel?"

"I hated what he did to us."

"But do you hate him?"

"I hate what he did to me."

"But do you hate him?"

"Okay, I will admit it...I hate him! What are you trying to do, break me down?" Sarcasm crept into David's voice. "Look! Why are you so interested in this?"

"It is who I am," Avi replied. "I am not a counselor because it is a profession I chose. I chose the profession because it is who I am." He wiped his mouth with the napkin. "Hatred is a wild and powerful thing, David. I do not say it is bad—not always. But it requires a great deal of discernment and wisdom, a tremendous amount of strength and will, to keep it properly focused. When it is directed at people, it is almost always harmful. Do you understand what I am saying?"

"I'm not sure," David shrugged. "Sounds like you might be suggesting I let my father off the hook for what he did."

"Not at all." Avi shook his head. "The acts your father committed against you—both the ones you remember and the ones that have not yet resurfaced—were terribly wrong. He is responsible for what he did. I am not talking about absolving him of responsibility. I am talking about you."

"Me?" David frowned. "What about me?"

"Hating your father for doing those things does not rectify those wrongs. The two are not counterweights of each other."

"You mean I should hate the sin but love the sinner?"

"You say that as if you find it objectionable."

"I know that's the proper response. I know it's God's response." David looked across the table at Avi. "But I'm not God."

"I think it is time for you to deal with this."

"What do you mean?"

"I mean, Israel is a great place to visit. Coming here can be a wonderful learning experience, but it is not a good place to hide."

"And you think I'm hiding."

"I think it is time for you to take the next step on your journey."

"Forgiving my father?

Avi leaned forward and lowered his voice. "You must ask your father to forgive *you*."

David was caught flatfooted. "Excuse me?" He shook his head and held up a hand in a defensive gesture. "I have a right to hate him," David snapped.

"An excuse," Avi countered. "You have an excuse for the way you feel toward him. You do not have a right to it."

"He deserves to be hated," David sulked. "And who are you to tell me what to do?"

"Listen to me, David. I know this is difficult, but you must listen. The questions you face, the issues before you, are not just about your father and mother. They are also about you."

"Me?"

"Hatred binds you to him and blinds you to many things. Until you can ask your father to forgive you for the hatred in your heart—even though it arises from his own actions—until you do that, you will remain in the dark. Worse, because of your judgment of him, you stand the chance of eventually becoming just like him."

Avi's statement sounded a lot like Jesus' words concerning judging others. "Are you a Christian, then? Are you a believer?"

"No, I am not a Christian, David; I am a believer. But that is an issue for a different day. You need to focus on the question we are discussing. It is time to ask your father to forgive you for the hatred you hold towards him."

"You have it backwards, Avi. He's the one who did wrong. He's the one who beat me. I did nothing to him. I'm justified."

"That issue may come. But first we must deal with you."

"With me? Look, I barely know you. How is it that you have any right to tell me what to do?"

Avi laid his hand over his heart. "Just listen to what your heart tells you. Judge what I say by your spirit. My words are true. They are acknowledged by your spirit. Your spirit bears witness with my spirit that they are true. Do not be deceived by the pain you carry inside." Avi paused a moment before continuing. "Do you not feel a certain amount of self-loathing because you harbor ill feelings toward your father?"

"It is very hard to admit that I had the kind of childhood I experienced."

"But when you do admit it, at least to yourself, you are angry at him for what happened, and then you are angry at yourself because of the way you feel toward him. You feel justified in hating him, and yet you condemn yourself for those very same feelings. This internal conflict is a major roadblock to experiencing the freedom you desire. It is a dark area of your heart that you keep locked away. You must bring that area into the light."

"You're saying that he did the most awful things to my brothers and me, and that my hatred of him is fully justified, but that justified hatred inhibits my freedom."

"Yes," Avi nodded. "Because of that hatred, you are carrying the weight of your father's abuse on your own back. You carry his guilt and yours. You need to cut the cords that bind you to him and lay that burden on the altar of forgiveness." Avi looked David in the eye. "Beware of the Enemy's schemes. The voice you hear inside, telling you to hold onto the hatred, is a lying voice. You cannot control how your father thinks or acts or the decisions he makes. You cannot force him by your hatred to undo what he has already done. You can only control your own thoughts, feelings, emotions, and decisions. God does not deal with you for your father's sins. He deals with you for your own. Repentance is the first step toward wholeness for you. You must not allow revenge and bitterness to rule you."

David tossed his napkin on the table. "You act like I'm wallowing in self-pity." He stood quickly. "I don't have to sit here and listen to this. My father's heart is so dark I doubt the light could ever penetrate it." He dug in his pocket for some money, tossed it on the table, and then turned toward the door.

Outside the café David flagged down a passing taxi. He crawled in the back seat and barked at the driver. "Park Plaza Hotel." He stared out the window as the driver steered the car through traffic. *I am such an idiot. Meet a stranger at lunch, spend all day revealing my innermost thoughts to him, and then he tells me to ask my father to forgive me—for things he did to me.* He gave a heavy sigh. *I promised myself a long time ago that I would never share these things with anyone. I should have stuck to it.*

Suddenly Avi's voice spoke to David. "That is not what I said." The sound of it was so clear and audible David jerked around expecting to see Avi in the car beside him. "I never suggested you should ask your father to forgive you for the things *he* did to you. I said you should ask him to forgive you for your hatred of *him*. Your hatred of him is as wrong as his actions toward you."

Tears filled David's eyes. He knew what he had heard was true, but the thought of letting go of the hatred seemed more than he could bear and left him feeling sad and lonely, as if he were saying goodbye to a lifelong friend. What would fill the place where the hatred had been? What would define his relationship with his father? What would define him—David—as a man?

And then he heard Avi's voice once more, this time soft and gentle. "Love will fill those places. And love will define you. Abba is closer than you think; more committed than you think. He knows your name and your need, and He is not angry with you. The picture you have of Him was put there by your earthly father. Admit it...and let it go."

chapter 25

Sue parked the Caprice outside the Piggly Wiggly and went inside. She took a cart from the rack by the door and started toward the produce section. Near a table piled high with potatoes she met Steve Smith's wife, Linda. Tall and slender, she had the look of a model and a way about her that gave the impression that being the associate pastor's wife was beneath her station in life. She acknowledged Sue. "How's David enjoying his trip?"

"I'm sure he's doing fine."

Linda cocked her head at an imperious angle. "You haven't heard from him?"

"No."

"I thought he would have called by now to check on how things are going." Linda tipped her head forward in a condescending pose. "He still has responsibilities here, you know. Belmont Baptist isn't a small-town congregation anymore."

"I'm sure everything is fine." The tone of Linda's voice and the look on her face grated on Sue's nerves. She did her best not to let it show. "We knew it might be difficult to call. If anything happens, people at the synagogue and the tour company know how to reach us."

"Well, I guess it's good that Steve is accessible."

Sue ignored the implication. "How is Steve? I didn't get a chance to talk to him last Sunday."

"He's busy keeping things in order."

"He did a good job with the Sunday service."

"Didn't he?" Linda's voice had a snide tone. "Someone asked me afterward why they hadn't heard more of him from the pulpit."

Sue found the remark offensive. David had gone out of his way to make certain they shared time in the pulpit. Still, she refused to give an angry response. "Really? I think we've seen about as much of one as we have of David."

"Hardly," Linda grunted. "But I guess that's how it is when you're the number two person."

"What do you mean?"

"You know, having to take whatever crumbs they give you."

Sue could stand it no more. "Linda, what's wrong? What are you talking about?"

"Nothing." She gave Sue a tight smile and a toss of her head. "It doesn't matter. Steve and Alan are working things out now."

"Working things out? What things?"

"I don't know," Linda shrugged. "They don't tell me anything. I guess we'll find out soon enough." She picked up a potato and checked it. "These things are so dirty." She set it back on the table and dusted off her hands. "Are you going to Minnie Turner's tomorrow?"

"Minnie Turner's?" Sue was puzzled. "For what?"

"Lunch. Didn't she invite you?"

"I have no idea what you're talking about. What's happening at Minnie's?"

"She's having a luncheon for the wives of the Life Group leaders. She invited me to join them. I just assumed she invited you."

"This is the first I've heard of it."

"Sorry. I really didn't know." Linda turned away. "I need to check the meat counter."

"Enjoy your luncheon." Sue pushed her cart toward the canned goods aisle. As she studied the labels on the cans, she thought about what Linda had said. *Something is going on,* she thought to herself. *I don't know what it is, but something is up.* Fear rose inside as she thought of what that might mean. Irritation followed close behind. *I don't trust that Alan Scruggs at all. He will manipulate Steve into doing whatever he wants.* She fought to push the thoughts aside, but as she moved down the aisle she could not escape the notion that things were about to change.

chapter 26

The last five days of David's trip easily allowed him to forget his conversation with Avi. In his free time he managed to walk the path Jesus took to the Cross and sit at the tomb where it is believed Jesus was buried and resurrected. He was filled with an awe and wonder he had never experienced before. As tears coursed down his cheeks, he knew that change was coming, that the new life Jesus had died to give him was going to manifest in brand-new ways.

He had mixed emotions as the tour group boarded the plane at Ben Gurion Airport in Tel Aviv and settled into their seats. David closed his eyes and spent the duration of the flight alternately sleeping and watching the in-flight movie. Whenever his mind drifted back to his conversation with Avi, he reined it in and forced himself to think of something else. What Avi told him in the café might be exactly what he needed to hear, but it would have to wait until later. Right then, he was in no mood to deal with it.

After a long flight across the Atlantic and a layover in New York, he arrived back in Charlotte. Sue, Megan, and Joel were waiting for him in front of the airport. He wrapped them in his arms and held them tight. Sue leaned in for a long kiss. "I missed you," she whispered.

"I missed you," he replied.

"Did you find what you were looking for?"

"Yes," he smiled. "It was right here all along."

Joel carried David's suitcase to the trunk, then they all climbed in the car. David leaned his head back against the seat and closed his eyes. Sue looked over at him. "Long flight?"

"Yes." David's voice had a playful lilt. "But not too long to keep us from one more stop."

"What's that?"

"Anyone up for some ice cream?"

"I am," Joel replied from the back seat.

"Sounds good," Megan added.

David looked over at Sue. "You want some ice cream, dear?"

She took his hand. "I have what I want right here."

"Oh, brother," Megan rolled her eyes and groaned. "Would you two stop it?"

David laughed. It was wonderful to be home.

*   *   *

That evening, after everyone had eaten their fill of ice cream, David lay in bed beside Sue. She rolled on her side to face him. "So, did you find what you were looking for in Israel?"

"I don't know. I met some interesting people. For instance, I met this guy named Avi."

"Avi?"

"It's the nickname for Abraham. Avraham in Hebrew," David explained. "Avi for short. His last name is Davidson. That's a spooky name when you think about it. It's kind of like Abraham Ben David, son of David. When we got to Jerusalem, the tour company had arranged a luncheon for us with people from the area, to give us a chance to meet local folks. He was at my table."

"What was he like?"

"He was a nice guy." David rolled on his side to face her. "He's a counselor and, actually, we hit it off pretty well. He has a wild sense of humor and made me laugh. Most of the time."

"Most of the time?"

"He invited me to a lecture about Middle Eastern art."

Sue raised an eyebrow. "You two must have really hit it off. I've never been able to interest you in art."

"How could I turn him down? I mean, the whole point of the luncheon was to meet people from Jerusalem, and he was there and invited me, so I said yes."

"Was it interesting?"

"It was all right. I mean, it was as interesting as a lecture on that subject could be. I didn't fall asleep."

"Good." There was a twinkle in her eye. "I would hate for them to have heard you snoring."

"After the lecture was over, Avi introduced me to him."

"To who?"

"Simeon Katz. The guy who gave the lecture."

"Oh. What was he like?"

"Katz was an interesting guy. Turns out he's been living and working in Israel since the beginning."

Sue frowned skeptically. "The beginning?"

"Not that beginning," David smirked. "He didn't come in with Moses. He's been there since Israel was reborn. I think he moved there after World War II. He was there when the UN recognized Israel as a nation. We talked to him a while, things were going pretty well, and he suggested we come with him to a reception that evening."

"What kind of reception?"

"Turns out, it was a reception for Menachem Begin, marking the anniversary of the Camp David Accords."

"And you went?"

"Yes. Simeon Katz introduced us to him."

"So, someone you met at a luncheon took you to a lecture and introduced you to a guy who invited you to a reception where you met the prime minister of Israel?"

"Yeah," David grinned. "That's exactly what happened."

"Amazing. What did he say?"

"Who?"

"Menachem Begin! What did he say?"

"He opened up to me during our visit. We talked about a lot of things including his two heart attacks and his grandchild's attempted suicide. Then he asked me why I had come to Jerusalem."

"And what did you say to that?"

"I told him about coming to find my roots."

"And what did he say?"

"Uhhh, he laughed."

Sue frowned. "He laughed at you?"

"Not actually laughed at me. Well, sort of. I said I'd come there to find out what it meant to be Jewish. And he asked if I had found it. I said, 'I don't know,' and he laughed and said, 'You are in the country where Judaism began and you don't know if you've found your Jewish heritage? That is funny.'"

"And you were embarrassed."

David looked away. "Not by him so much as by my own response. I sounded kinda...inept."

"What did your friend say?"

"Avi? He said it was fine. That I was meeting a head of state, probably the first I'd ever met, and that it was right for me to be nervous and to not worry about it."

David laid on his back and Sue snuggled close to him. "Avi was right. I think I like him."

"He's a nice guy."

"A counselor?" They lay in silence a moment, Sue staring at David and David staring at the ceiling.

After a moment he asked, "Do you think I should apologize to my father?"

Sue raised her head and looked him in the eyes. "For what?"

"For hating him."

"I don't know. Do you hate him?"

"I sure don't like him." David sighed. "What do you think of him?"

"I don't really think of him one way or the other."

David looked at Sue. "What did you think of him when you met him?"

"He was scary."

"I can't imagine you being scared of anyone. And now?"

She laid her head on David's shoulder. "He doesn't bother me so much now. I mean, I haven't seen him in years. Why do you think you should apologize to him?"

"Avi said I should."

"Why did he think you should do that?"

"He said hating Dad bound me to him, and that if I remained tied to him, I would begin to be like him."

"Hmm. I never thought about that."

"Me either."

"You were able to open up to Avi?"

"Yes," David nodded. "It felt a little strange—but comfortable at the same time. A little weird."

"Good. You needed someone to talk to besides me. I don't think it was a coincidence you met him."

"I suppose." He held her tighter and brought her chin up to face him. "Did you miss me?"

"Yes."

Her eyes were questioning. David pressed her. "What? What is it you want to say?"

Sue pulled away and lay on her back. "I want to ask you about something."

"Okay. What is it?"

She rolled back the covers and moved from the bed to the dresser. She picked up his Bible from its place on the corner near the mirror and brought it back to the bed.

David sat up. "What are you doing with that?"

David took the Bible from Sue's hand and clasped it to his chest. As he sank back against the headboard, he recalled the day he was given the first Bible he had ever owned. On his way home from school one day he had gone inside Saint Patrick's, a Catholic church located a few blocks from his house. It was a large, imposing building with Gothic arches and heavy oak doors. Once or twice, as he passed by on his way home, he had caught a glimpse inside. It seemed dark and mysterious, and on hot days when the door was open, he had felt a rush of cool air. He wasn't supposed to stop there. His father had warned him about the "Catholics and their Pope-worship." Still, he could not escape the mystery of the building. That day, as he came by the church, he had decided to go inside.

Beyond the oak doors he found the ceiling soared high above an enormous sanctuary that spread out around him on either side—far different from the small, undecorated Pentecostal church where his dad and others raised their hands and shouted on Sundays. David stared wide-eyed at the gilded statues of saints and angels rising behind the altar. He slid onto the end of the very last pew and tried to pray. After a few minutes he realized someone was standing beside him. Slowly, he raised his eyes to meet those of a man dressed in a black suit with a white collar. He had short gray hair, a gentle smile, and kind eyes—not at all like his dad had portrayed.

"Hello, son," he said. "I haven't seen you around here before, have I?"

"N-no, sir. I j-just w-w-wanted to p-p-pray."

"Well, you came to the right place. I'm Father McNally, the priest here. We're glad to have you. Stay here and pray as long as you like." He moved down the aisle and disappeared through a door to the right. A few minutes later he returned, carrying something in his hand. "Son, what's your name?"

"D-D-David."

"David, that's a very good name. You're named after a very important man in the Bible. Do you have a Bible at home, son?"

"N-n-not one of m-m-my own. W-w-we all use m-m-my f-f-father's."

"Well David, somebody left this here last week." He held it out to him. "I believe it must be yours." The priest smiled and handed David the book.

"H-h-how m-m-much is it? I d-d-don't h-h-have any m-m-money."

"There's no charge. This is your Bible now. Just promise me you'll read it."

"Yes, s-s-sir. I w-w-will."

When David had reached home that afternoon he took his jack-knife and carved "Words of God" into the imitation leather cover. He had kept the promise to read it every day. He had many different versions now, but none as special as this one. It had been a lifeline for him, and through it God had spoken many times.

✳   ✳   ✳

"David, where are you?" Sue asked as she gently pried the Bible from his hand and rested it on her lap.

"Sorry," David mumbled. "I was in another time and place."

She flipped the edge of the pages with her thumb. The Bible fell open to Isaiah. She pointed to the page with her finger. "You marked this a long time ago."

David leaned over her shoulder and looked down at the circle around the verse. He remembered finding it a few nights after The Light had appeared in his bedroom. He had been turning the pages and reading verses at random. But when he had seen that verse, he had felt something in his spirit come to life. He had known in his heart God was speaking to him through that scripture.

"This is the verse you told me about that night on the beach. And you've marked many more that you've talked about over and over."

"Yeah," he sighed. As his eyes scanned the verse once more, Sue lifted the collar from the spine.

"Do you remember this?"

"Uh, I'm not really sure," he replied in an evasive tone. He reached over her and took the collar with one hand and lifted the Bible from her lap with the other.

She pressed the issue. "Tell me about it."

"Not now." He sighed and stood.

"Do you remember why it's in there?"

"I don't know." He tucked the book beneath his arm and started toward the door. "I really don't want to talk about this now. I'm gonna go downstairs and read a while."

chapter 27

With the Bible tucked under his arm, David jogged down the stairs, through the kitchen, and out the back door into the night. He plopped down in the patio swing and laid his Bible in his lap. His fingers ran over and over the words carved into the cover…Words of God. The night air was cool and dry against his skin. Overhead, stars lit the sky. A big, silvery moon rose from behind the trees, and in the glow of the moonlight he opened the Bible and stared down at the leather collar. As if by magic, David was transported in time.

It was Christmas day. He was ten years old, standing in the backyard with his BB gun. Overhead, a squirrel darted from limb to limb through an oak tree. David tracked its every move, across one limb, down another, around the trunk. And then it stopped. He raised the gun to his shoulder and squeezed off a shot. The squirrel tumbled to the ground and lay motionless among the autumn leaves.

Excited at the thought of making his first kill, David hurried forward and bent over to pick it up. Suddenly, the squirrel was alive and latched onto his thumb with its teeth. David ran screaming into the house with the rodent dangling from his throbbing hand.

His dog Freckles bounded up the back steps and followed David through the kitchen and into the dining room. Freckles was right behind barking and jumping in a desperate attempt to reach the squirrel. David screamed, "Mom, help!" He turned to avoid the dog, and the squirrel lost its hold on David's thumb. David crashed into the dining table, knocking over the gravy bowl his mom had just set there. The collision sent a river of brown gravy across the tablecloth. Freckles lost interest in the squirrel and turned his attention to the gravy dripping on the floor. He lapped it up, then he caught hold of the tablecloth and backed away, pulling it toward him, along with everything sitting on top. Christmas dinner slid onto the floor.

Wally, who had been drinking all morning, leaped from the chair where he had been dozing. "Moron!" he shouted. He grabbed Freckles by the collar and lifted him off the floor. "Why'd you bring this stupid Jew dog in my house? You ruined dinner; you ruined everything. I'm gonna tend to you, boy." His eyes were like hot coals. "But first I'm gonna tend to this dog."

Freckles shook his head and twisted his body in a frantic effort to escape. As he squirmed, the collar slipped over his head. He dropped to the floor and darted toward the kitchen. Before Wally could react, the dog was outside and gone. Wally threw the collar on the floor and shouted, "Ain't ya' learned no better'n that?"

After Wally finished beating him with a coat hanger, David picked up the collar and dragged himself to his room. Later that night, he tucked it inside his Bible and stared at it as tears ran down his cheeks.

He was pulled back to the present when he felt Sue's hand stroke his hair. "You okay?"

"I'm sorry."

Sue sat next to him on the porch swing, put her arm through his, and rested her head on his shoulder. "It's okay."

"No, it's not." He looked at her. "Why am I so afraid?"

"Those wounds have been there a long time."

"I don't want to see him."

"I know."

"But you think I should."

"I think you'll have to, sooner or later."

"It'll have to be later." David pulled away. "I just can't do it now." He started toward the house. "Come on, we should get to sleep."

chapter 28

Rather than face the issues that confronted him, David threw himself into his work. He thought surely workaholism was better than alcoholism. He spent days at his office researching and preparing for a sermon series he intended to deliver in the weeks before Thanksgiving. He pored over the church's long-range plan and spent hours and hours analyzing attendance trends. The nightmare continued to plague him, and he often awoke in the morning with a throbbing headache, but he refused to make a second trip to see his father and did his best to avoid thinking about his past.

David also was true to his word and began attending the Torah Study on Thursday mornings. Some of the members had been on the trip to Israel with him, and they made him feel welcome. He marveled at the new depth of revelation he was getting from the Old Testament. Although he didn't feel comfortable sharing thoughts with this group, he saw Jesus, the Jewish Messiah, again and again in the Word.

One of the most exciting things about attending the study was what happened afterwards. He would have lunch with a couple of people each week, and the discussion invariably turned to Israel and world events—past, present, and sometimes future. He was drinking in every bit of knowledge and understanding he could get from his new friends. Some had lived in Israel for a time, and most had visited there extensively. But all were passionate about the Holy Land, and he found himself gripped by that same passion.

Three weeks after returning from Israel, David attended a meeting of the worship committee. At Alan Scruggs' insistence, Steve had been named chairman of the committee. From that position he controlled most of what happened in the worship services. David didn't like the encroachment on his role in the life of the church, but he didn't want to embroil the board in a fight about it either. That day, the committee was discussing the upcoming Christmas season. David interrupted the discussion to make a point.

"I don't think we can schedule a Christmas Eve service at seven and then one at midnight. I mean it—" Without warning, David's head jerked to the right. He groaned in pain.

Steve looked at him. "Are you okay?"

"I don't know." David rubbed his neck and rolled his head slowly from side to side. "Must have been a spasm or something. I guess I caught a muscle the wrong way." Just then, his head jerked to the left. "Ouch," he groaned. "That hurt."

"You need to see somebody."

"Yeah," someone else spoke up. "That looks serious."

Steve stood. "You want some help getting to the car?"

"I'm all right." David dismissed him with a wave of his hand. "Let's finish our meeting. We need to get this schedule nailed down."

"No," Steve shook his head. "We can finish this tomorrow. Or next week. We can wrap it up without you. We don't need you here to discuss this." He came from his chair and gestured for David to stand. "Come on. I'll drive you home."

David stood. "I can drive."

"I don't think so. You can't even turn your head."

David's head jerked again, this time forward, tipping his chin down against his chest. For an instant, he was frozen in place, unable to move. "Man, that hurts."

Steve took him gently by the elbow. "Come on. I'll help you."

"Yeah," David rose and shuffled toward the door. "Maybe some heat will help it."

"A doctor, David," Steve urged. "You need to see a doctor."

David spent the remainder of the day at home trying to get comfortable. At first he lay on the bed, but the pillow only made the pain worse. He sat in a chair by the dresser, but holding his head up made the spasms more frequent. Finally, he moved to the recliner in the den. When he was settled in place, Sue handed him three Advil and a cup of hot tea. "Take these."

"Isn't that too many?"

"Not today."

He swallowed them with some hot tea and closed his eyes. An hour later he awoke feeling a little better, but when he tried to stand, his head jerked to the side. He leaned back in the chair.

From down deep in his soul a desperate feeling of helplessness took control. Would he ever get past this? Was this the end of his career? The end of his life? What awful disease had him in its clutches? How could he possibly escape when he didn't even know where it had come from or what it was? As he sank into the depths of despair, Sue came into the room. "I called Dr. Roca. He'll see you at eight in the morning."

"How did you manage that?" Roca was one of the state's best orthopedic surgeons and a member of a large practice.

Sue smiled slyly. "I know his wife."

*   *   *

That night David slept in the recliner. When he awoke the next morning, Sue was dressed and ready. "Better get moving," she said, as she sipped a cup of coffee. "We don't want to be late." David leaned to one side to move the recliner to an upright position. Pain shot through his neck and shoulder. His head jerked to the left.

Sue set her coffee cup on the table by the television and stepped to his side. "You need some help? Can you move?"

"Yeah," David moaned, "but I don't know if I can get to the shower."

"Don't worry about a shower. Just get dressed."

An early-morning doctor's appointment turned into a day of tests, x-rays, and an MRI. That afternoon Dr. Roca met them in an examination room. "Well, it's not a muscle problem."

David asked, "What does that mean?"

"What you are experiencing is not caused by a strain or a problem with damage to the muscle tissue."

"What is it?"

"I don't know exactly," Roca replied. "It seems to be a neurological issue."

"So, what do we do?"

"I'm going to send you to see Craig Peterson, a neurologist. He's in the next building. We're calling now to see if he can see you this afternoon."

"Is it that urgent?"

"You need to get a diagnosis. Besides being painful and disruptive, spasms like yours can damage your spinal column. This sudden, violent twisting is not good."

With Roca's help Dr. Peterson agreed to meet with David that afternoon. He reviewed the test results from earlier in the day and performed a couple more. Late that afternoon he sat with David and Sue in his office.

"You have a condition known as spasmodic torticollis dystonia. We don't see that many cases of it, but of those we do see, yours is the most common form."

"Sounds terrible. How did I get it?"

"There's a genetic disposition for it among some Jews of early European descent. As they moved northward into Russia, they carried the genetic problem with them." Peterson flipped a page in the chart. "I'm right in remembering you are Jewish—your mother is Jewish—correct?"

"Yes. Ashkenazi."

"Duke Medical School has a dystonia research program. I'm sure they'd be interested in taking a look at you. Maybe include you in their study. You seem like an excellent candidate."

"I can control it by holding my chin." David rested his head in his hand to show Peterson.

"Yeah," Peterson nodded. "That's a way of distracting your nervous system. It's not unusual, and it actually confirms the diagnosis." He shrugged and waited for David to respond.

"So I'm a candidate for a study? What about treatment? Is there a cure? I'm a preacher. This really hampers my ability to do much from the pulpit."

"The disease is worsened by stress. Managing stress will help. I can give you something to help with that."

"Drugs," David muttered.

"Yes. And there's surgery. Dystonia patients have had good success with selective denervation."

"Denervation?" Sue repeated. "What is that?"

"A nerve release," Peterson explained. "We would go into the neck and shoulder and cut the nerves. We can identify the muscles that are causing the spasms. Severing the nerves to those muscles will inhibit the spasms. It's not a widely used technique, but it's certainly not experimental. Neurologists began using it in the early 70s."

"Will I still be able to use the muscles?"

"Yes," Peterson nodded. "You could lose some range of motion, but you should also lose the spasms and the pain."

"Should."

"It's not one-hundred percent successful."

"When do I have to decide?"

"Take a few days and think about it." Peterson rose from his chair and escorted them toward the door. "Just give us a call and let us know what you decide."

"Do I have to participate in the Duke study, or can I just have the surgery?"

"You can choose. You don't have to do the study. They would cover the treatment costs, but it would take several months to complete their work before they would actually begin to treat the condition. We can treat you here without the wait."

"Hmm," David sighed. "I'll have to think about it."

That evening David walked gingerly to the den and settled into the recliner. Later, Sue set up dinner trays and the family joined him for supper. Having them in the room left David feeling unsettled. One moment he was encouraged by their presence. The next moment he was anxious and worried they would see how helpless he was when a spasm contorted his neck and shoulders.

When they finished eating, Sue took away the dishes. Megan folded the dinner trays and put them away. Joel came and sat on the floor near his feet. "I'm sorry you aren't feeling good, Dad."

"Thanks, son."

"You think they can figure out what's wrong?"

"I think they know. It's just a question of how to treat it."

Joel looked up at him. "You scared?"

"Nah," David said, bravely. "You?"

"A little."

"It's okay, son. Stuff happens. We endure." He moved his right foot over and rubbed his calf against Joel's shoulder. "I'd hug you, but I can't bend over that far tonight." Joel leaned his shoulder against David's leg and rested his head against his knee.

Sometime after the nine o'clock, Joel went off to bed. When he was gone, David switched off the television. Sue came in and kissed him on the forehead. "Are you all right?"

"As right as I can be."

"What do you think you should do?"

"I don't see how I can do that study. I've missed too much time at the church already."

"You're okay with the surgery?"

"Do we have a choice? I can't keep going like this."

"I know," she sighed. "It just seems like all this has happened so suddenly."

"I think it's been building."

"You felt it coming on?"

"I felt something."

"I wish you'd told me."

"I would have if I'd thought it was important." He pushed against the footrest to shift positions. "Besides, you would have just worried."

"Maybe so," she smiled. "I'm always concerned when something affects you. Call me if you need me." She turned away and started toward the door.

"Sue," he said, sharply.

She turned toward him, her eyes alert. "What is it?"

"You said call for you if I need you." He gave her a mischievous look. "I always need you."

Sometime later that night David fell asleep, and old familiar faces returned in his dreams.

It was night. The moon overhead shone brightly, casting deep shadows all around him. David stood in a clearing with Joel next to him. From the left came the sound of someone thrashing their way through the bushes. Joel inched closer to David's side. "What is it?"

"It's okay," David replied.

"I'm scared, Dad."

"I know. Don't worry."

A moment later the bushes parted and Wally appeared. He was cursing as he came into view, but when he saw David and Joel he stopped. "Ahh," he said, looking over at David. "I see ya' made it." He gestured toward Joel. "And ya' brought your own little Jew boy with ya'." He tipped his head back in a confident pose. "I got my little Jew boy, and you got yours."

"I was right here all the time, Dad. You didn't have to yell and cuss."

"Don't get smart with me." Wally's face turned sullen and mean. "I can still whip you any time I take a notion." He looked over at Joel. "And when I'm finished with him, I'll tend to you. I know how to treat little boys." David did not reply. Wally stepped close and looked up at him. "I brought ya' somethin'."

"What?"

"Hold out your hand."

"Show it to me first," David insisted.

"Why?" Wally stepped closer. His eyes were wide and expressive, his foul breath heavy with the smell of alcohol. "You scared, little Jew boy?"

"I'm not a boy," David replied.

"You'll always be a boy. 'Cause you ain't man enough to be anything else." Wally looked down at Joel. "Your old man ain't no man. He's a little boy, just like you." His eyes focused on David again, his face cold and imposing. "Hold out your hand."

"Show me what's in yours first."

Wally grinned and opened his palm to reveal two black rocks. "Open your hand," Wally repeated. "I got one for you, and one for the kid."

David was unmoved. "We already have ours."

Wally looked puzzled. "What do ya' mean?"

David opened his hand to reveal a single white stone. Wally's eyes grew even bigger than before. A look of terror came over him. "Close it!" he shouted. "Close your hand!"

"Why?"

"I don't wanna see it!" Wally backed away. "I don't wanna see it!"

David slid his left hand into his pocket. "I have one for you, Dad."

"I don't want it!" Wally screamed.

David's eyes popped open. Soft predawn light filtered through the window, casting a dusty glow across the room. "I know what it means," he whispered. "I know what it means." He pushed his heels against the footrest of the recliner and brought the chair to an upright position. "He's not getting my son!" With both hands on the armrests, he pushed himself up and stood.

Sue appeared at the doorway, a worried look on her face. "I heard noises. What's the matter? Are you okay? "

"I know what it means."

"David, are you awake? What are you talking about?"

"Yes. I'm awake," he smiled. "I'm awake, and I know what to do."

"You decided about the surgery?"

"Forget the surgery," he said with a wave of his hand. "I'm going to see my father."

"David," she blurted, "you're in no condition to drive. Let me go with you."

He rested his hand on her shoulder. "I have to do this myself, Sue. By myself. I don't want you there." He moved toward the hallway. "Come on. Help me get ready."

"This is crazy." She trailed after him toward the bedroom. "You can't do this. It's dangerous."

David turned his torso at the waist, bringing his head and neck around in a stiff motion to face her. "Yes, it is dangerous. But it's right."

chapter 29

An hour later Sue was accompanying David to the car. He opened the door to the Caprice and slid in behind the steering wheel. She kept the car door open and pressed, "I wish you'd let me drive you."

"No." David shook his head. "Can't do it. But you can pray."

"I'm doing that already."

"Good." She kissed him and closed the car door. He winked and called out, "See you later." He started the car and reached up to adjust the mirror, then gave her one last smile.

Using the mirror David backed the car down the driveway to the street and drove away. At the corner he stopped and checked for traffic. When he moved his head to see to the right, a spasm jerked his chin to the left. David waited for the pain to subside then lowered the window. He propped his elbow on the window ledge and placed his chin against his palm, then he turned the car to the left and drove toward the highway.

With each passing mile the voice inside his head grew stronger and stronger. *You don't have to see your father. Just forgive him right now, without going all that way to the trailer. And why do you have to ask for forgiveness? Wally was the one who did wrong.* Each time he heard that accusing voice, Avi's voice cut through the confusion. "Your hatred is as wrong as what he did to you. It binds you to him."

Images of the dream flashed in his mind. He saw Joel standing beside him and heard the quiver in his voice. Wally was coming for David, and he wanted Joel too. "Not happening," he mumbled to himself. "I don't care how scared I am. He can't have Joel."

When David reached Wally's trailer, the driveway was empty. He banged on the door and waited then twisted the knob. As before, the door was unlocked. He pushed it open and looked around inside. "Dad," he called. "You in here?" There was no sound but the tick of a clock on the wall.

He closed the trailer door and walked back to the Caprice. A voice called from beyond the overgrown fencerow at the house next door. "You looking for Wally?"

The sound of the voice startled David. He spun in that direction but saw only the bushes. "Yes," he replied. "I am."

"You the law?"

The voice was clearer now, and David realized there was someone standing near the porch. He could just make out the blue of a work shirt through the vines and bushes that separated them. "No," David answered. "I'm his son."

"Oh." The voice brightened. "Are you the preacher?"

"Yes."

"He talks about you all the time."

David could only imagine what Wally might have said. "Any idea where I can find him?"

"He usually hangs out up at Tiny's. It's a bar up the road."

"Which way?"

"Go back up to Wiggins Road and turn right. You'll see it on the left. A couple miles."

David glanced at his watch. "Rather early in the day. You think they're open?"

"Tiny's don't never close."

*   *   *

Tiny's Bar and Grill was located in what had been a service station.

The Gulf Oil sign still hung on a pole at the corner of the parking lot. The pumps were still on their concrete pads, but the building had been painted turquoise, and most of the windows were covered with aluminum foil. Wally's pickup was parked in front.

Seeing the truck made David's heart rate quicken. He pushed aside the fear that threatened him and turned into the parking lot. The car rolled to a stop on the far side of the building. He climbed out and made his way to the front door. A sad string of Christmas lights dangled haphazardly around the doorway. David paused beneath them and took a deep breath, then pulled open the door and stepped inside.

Across from the door a bar ran along the back wall. Between the door and the bar, tables were scattered in a random fashion. David scanned the room and found Wally seated at the far end of the bar, leering at a woman young enough to be his granddaughter. David threaded his way between the tables and moved in that direction. As he came near, the woman looked up and nodded. "Somebody's here to see you." Walking closer to her, David realized she wasn't as young as he had thought.

Wally turned on the barstool. "Well, looky here." His voice was loud and lively. "If'n it ain't my big-shot preacher son. What brings ya' to this neck of the woods, boy? Lookin' for a few more sinners? Don't let 'em know you're a Jew. They don't like Jews out here. Ain't got no use for Jews or blacks."

The sound of his voice grated on David, but he did his best to ignore the irritation. "Hello, Dad. Any chance we could go somewhere and talk for a few minutes?"

"Talk? What do we need to talk about, boy? Whatever ya' got to say to me you can say right here." He glanced at the woman. "Ain't that right, Nancy? Davy boy, why don't ya' preach us a good hell-fire 'n damnation, rafter-shaking sermon?" He winked at the woman. She rolled her eyes and looked away.

"Dad, please." As he spoke David realized he wasn't scared anymore. He had something he wanted to accomplish this morning, and he meant to get it done. "It's really important. Can we go someplace and talk?"

Nancy jabbed Wally's chest with her finger. "Wally, you oughta be ashamed of yourself. At least your kid took the trouble to come find you. Mine don't never come 'round 'less he needs money." She glanced at David. "And from the looks of it, this boy ain't here to ask you for money. So get your sorry hide off that stool and go talk to him like he asked you to."

Wally glared at her. "All right. Fine." He slid off the stool. "A man can't even have a drink without ever'body mindin' his business." He stalked past David and shoved open the front door.

David looked at Nancy. "Thank you."

"Whatever," she shrugged. "I was gettin' tired of listening to his bull, anyway." She gave David a smile. "Now go on. I know he's not long on patience."

By the time David caught up with him, Wally was almost to his battered pickup. "Dad! Wait up a second." David trotted toward his father and laid a hand on his shoulder.

Wally jerked around to face him. "Get your hand off'n me before I break it off."

David stepped back. "Why don't we take my car? It's right over there." He pointed over his shoulder.

"Ya' gonna start chauffeuring me around now?"

"I was just trying to be nice. Are you good to drive?"

"I spent a lifetime learnin' to hold my liquor." He turned toward the truck. "If ya wanna talk, come to the trailer." Wally climbed in the pickup and started the engine, then leaned out the window. "Get movin'. I ain't got all day."

Gravel flew from beneath the rear wheels as he backed away from the building. David's hands jerked up to ward off the flying rocks as he turned toward the Caprice. He heard the truck's engine whining as it headed down the road.

Minutes later David was back at the trailer. He saw Wally slam the truck door closed and walk across the yard to the back door. David parked the Caprice on the grass in front, got out, and climbed the steps. He met Wally in the kitchen.

The place smelled of mildew, stale beer, and scorched food. The countertop was a sea of half-filled prescription bottles. Wally's clothes were filthy, and his hair was dirty and oily. David was certain he hadn't bathed in days. Wally pushed his way past David and sank into the threadbare recliner. He grabbed the television remote, punched the "on" button, and turned up the sound. He sat staring at the television, as if no one else was in the room. "Well," he growled, "ya' come all the way out here to talk, didn't ya'? Get on with it."

Without warning a muscle spasm jerked David's head to the right. He felt his cheeks blush with embarrassment. Wally frowned. "What's wrong with your neck? Sleep crooked? Got a crick in it? Or do you have that stupid neck problem like yer mother had. I heard only mental cases get that."

"Just a little problem, but I didn't come to talk about that." David moved beside his father's chair and knelt on the carpet. For an instant he was back in the house at 77 Pasco Road, groveling beside the chair in the living room, begging his father not to hit him any more. Then just as quickly, he pushed the image from his mind. He reached up with both hands, laid them gently on Wally's forearm, and looked into the old man's bloodshot eyes. "Dad, I want to ask you to forgive me." At the sound of those words David felt something leap inside. From down deep he felt a fresh, light breeze blowing through his soul.

Wally's mouth dropped open. "Huh?" His eyebrows wrinkled in a frown. "Forgive you for what?" He punched a button on the remote and turned off the television.

"For hating you." David took a deep breath and let his body relax. "The Bible says we're supposed to honor our parents, but I never honored or respected you. It was wrong for me to carry that inside all this time. Will you forgive me?"

They sat there, staring at each other for what seemed like an eternity. Then Wally's face crumpled and tears flowed down his cheeks. "I committed the unpardonable sin for what I done to you," he blabbered. "I can't never be saved. I'm damned to hell, Davy."

Shock and awe filled David's heart and mind, but the perfect words flowed freely. "No, Dad. God loves you, and so do I. And this time, I really mean it."

"How can ya' say that after everything I done?"

"God is merciful to all of us."

"Back when I used to talk to God, I asked Him to forgive me a thousand times. I never thought He would, and I never thought none of y'all would ever have nothin' to do with me."

A glimpse from the dream the night before passed through David's mind, of Joel standing beside him and Wally offering them the black stones. He took another breath and pressed the point with Wally, determined to put the matter to rest. "Will you forgive me, Dad? Will you forgive me for hating you?"

Wally stared straight ahead. "That's okay, son. I should be the one askin' you to forgive me."

"I forgive you, Dad. But will you forgive me?"

"Yes," Wally turned to look at him. "I forgive ya." He reached out with his right hand and ran his fingers lightly over David's head. "I forgive ya, son."

"Would you pray for me? Would you ask God to forgive me?"

"Ah, Davy...I don't even know if I can still pray. Lightnin' might strike this old place if'n I was to even try." Wally struggled to get a deep breath of air.

"Dad, are you okay?"

"Oh, I think so." Wally nodded his head. "But, Davy, you don't know all what went on. If you did, you'd be walkin' right out that door."

"What are you talking about?"

Wally's lips trembled and he dropped his head. "Oh, I don't know. I shouldn't a hurt y'all the way I done."

"Dad, all that is forgiven. The beatings, the hitting, the names—"

"There's more, Davy. And it's worse'n name-callin' and beatin's."

"What are you talking about, Dad?"

Wally was breathing heavily. His chest heaved up and down, and his eyes darted around the room. "Sit over there on the couch, would ya?" He pointed with a trembling finger.

"Sure." David moved from beside the recliner and took a seat on the edge of the couch, his gaze fixed on Wally. "What is it?"

"I done some awful things. Worse'n whippin' you with the belt, worse'n hittin' or cussin' or callin' ya'll names."

"What are you talking about?"

"Anna." Wally swallowed hard. He glanced at David then quickly looked away. "There's a reason she don't want nothin' to do with me."

David's stomach roiled as a sudden image flashed through his mind. He had awakened in the night to a sound coming from down the hall. He crept to the door and peered around the doorframe. He heard the rhythmic sound of squeaking bedsprings coming from Anna's room and the muffled sound of someone groaning and crying. Moments later, the bedroom door opened and Wally appeared. David shrank back and watched from the shadows of his room as Wally moved past, buttoning his pants as he went.

Remembering it sent a wave of nausea rumbling through David's stomach. Rage boiled inside. How could he do that? A father, to his own daughter. What sick, twisted person would do something like...David took a deep breath and forced himself to think. *God's grace*, he told himself, *reaches to the depths of sin. Even sin committed by a man against his own children. Even rape.*

"And," Wally continued, "your mother." He looked away, shaking his head. Tears flowed once more. "There's no way a sane woman could'a put up with what I done to her. It was only a matter of time a'fore she'd find somebody who'd treat her right."

"Dad," David choked, "why are you telling me this?"

"I got to tell somebody." Wally implored. "You a preacher, ain't ya? Who else can I tell?"

"Okay," David managed to continue speaking, trying to look at Wally as if he was a stranger in his office. "You've told me. Now you need to tell God."

"I don't think He wants to hear from the likes'a me."

"I think He's been waiting a long time to hear from you."

David slipped to his knees beside Wally's chair again and gently placed his father's hands on his head. Wally glanced down at him, looking self-conscious and unsure. David nodded. Wally began to pray.

"Lord...I guess you're pretty surprised hearin' from me, after all this time. And I guess I'm pretty surprised myself. But this boy here, he...he's a good boy. I ask ya' to forgive him. It seems to me like he oughta be the one prayin' for me, but I'm gonna do what he said, and I'm gonna ask you to forgive him for...for the ..." His voice wavered and broke.

David opened his eyes as Wally reached toward him and collapsed across his shoulders. He cried aloud, "God, forgive me too, if'n you can. If any grace is left for me, please forgive me for all the bad stuff I done. Help me be a better man with what little time I got left. Help me, Lord, please." Wally's body shook as he sobbed. David held him close as he wept.

After a moment Wally let go of David and settled back in his recliner. He grabbed the tail of his shirt and used it to wipe his eyes and nose. "Sorry about that. Got a little carried away."

"Dad, God doesn't run out of grace. And if you got carried away, I'd say it was by the Holy Spirit. That's not a bad thing."

"Last time I cried was when I buried my mother." He took a deep breath and let it slowly escape. "I wish I could see the others and talk to them like this."

"You've done all you can do for now. Leave it in God's hands."

"Better His'n mine."

They talked a while longer, then David stood. "Dad, I need to get back to Charlotte."

"Okay." Wally looked up at him. "You have no idea what this

means to me. You comin' out here like this." He stood and patted David on the back as they walked toward the front door. Wally paused there and glanced up at David. "I guess I shoulda told ya' a long time ago but...Ahh." He hesitated, then shook his head. "It don't matter now."

"What?" David stopped at the door "What were you going to say?"

"It ain't nothin'."

David stepped outside and turned back to face his father. "You sure?"

"Yeah," Wally smiled. "It was good to see ya."

For the first time in his life, David said to his father, "Good to see you too." Then he walked toward the car.

Wally called after him. "Will ya' come back to see me again?"

"Yeah, Dad. I'll come back."

chapter 30

As David drove back toward Mooresville, he lowered the window and let the cool wind blow against his face. He thought about what Wally had said, how he had expressed words of forgiveness and seemed genuinely contrite, and how he prayed. The tears on his face had been like a soothing balm to them both, and as he thought of it again a wonderful sense of lightness enveloped him.

Then he remembered the rest of the conversation—of Anna and the things Wally did to her. It was the most vile and hideous abuse a father could visit upon his daughter. Waves of nausea swept over him, just as they had earlier at the trailer. Each time he thought of it, the familiar weight of hatred stood ready to return; and each time he whispered to himself and to God, "I forgive him. I forgive him for what he did to me, and I forgive him for the anguish he caused me through the things he did to my sister." Each time he said those words, the hatred and anger continued to melt away.

By the time he reached the Charlotte Highway, David realized his neck no longer hurt. "I haven't had a muscle spasm since I was standing by the chair in the trailer." He slapped his hand against the steering wheel. "Jesus is Lord!" he shouted. "This was all from my stubbornness. And all from Your grace."

Sue was standing at the stove cooking dinner when David brought the car to a stop at the end of the driveway behind the house. He could see her through the window above the sink. Her hair was frazzled, and her eyes were red and puffy, but in the fading sunlight she appeared as beautiful as ever. He called to her as he came through the back door. "What's for dinner?"

"Roast beef, mashed potatoes, and green beans."

"Gravy?"

"Yes," she grinned. "Gravy."

"Great. My favorite meal."

Sue tilted her head and looked at him. "Every meal is your favorite. How was your visit?"

"It was good." His voice dropped. "And it was not so good."

Sue's shoulders slumped. "I don't know which to ask for first."

David came up behind her and slipped his arms around her waist, then buried his face in the nape of her neck. "Well," he whispered, "the good part is, I asked him to forgive me for hating him, and he said, 'You should be forgiving me.'"

"And did you leave it at that?"

"No. I pressed him for an answer, and he said 'I forgive you.' Then we cried and prayed."

Sue turned to face him. "You prayed?"

"No." David shook his head. "He prayed."

Sue's eyes sparkled. "He prayed?"

"Yes."

"So things are better?"

"Things are better between me and him." He pulled her close and spun her around, as if dancing. "Things are great for me."

"What do you mean? Stop now! Your neck. You'll hurt yourself."

"I mean," he said playfully, "I drove all the way home without a single muscle spasm."

"Nothing? And no pain?"

"No pain."

Sue threw her arms around him. "David! Honey, that's amazing—miraculous!"

"Yes, it is."

Sue turned back to stir the contents of the pots on the stove. "But what about the bad part?"

He patted her on the hip. "We'll talk about that later."

Megan came into the room, and David gave her a big hug. "How was school?"

"Great." She looked worried and confused at the same time. "How's your neck? We've been praying for you."

"Just fine! In fact, I believe I'm totally healed!"

Megan squealed, threw her arms around David, and hugged him again. "Fantastic, Dad!" She grinned and eyed her father coyly. "Hey, since you're feeling better, can I go to the ball game this weekend?"

David grew serious and held her at arm's length. "And you would be going with…?"

"Gil Watts."

"His daddy's the lawyer?"

"Yes."

"I don't know." He leaned over and kissed her on the forehead. "We'll talk about it after dinner. Isn't it your turn to set the table?"

"You're in a good mood."

"Yes, I am." David glanced around. "Where's Joel?"

"Upstairs."

David walked to the staircase and leaned over the banister. "Hey, son."

"Yeah, Dad."

"Get your football. Let's throw some."

*　　*　　*

That evening after dinner, while the kids were upstairs doing their homework, David took Sue by the hand. "Let's go for a walk."

"Hey," Sue said, "Good idea."

They called up to Megan and Joel to let them know, and ten minutes later they were outside beneath the stars. David pointed up to the sky. "I can always find the Big Dipper, and when I find it I know where to look to find the North Star, but the rest of it I have never been able to see."

Sue pointed straight ahead. "That is Mercury, sinking below those trees."

"But where is Taurus, the bull?"

"I don't know about that."

"Whoever saw those patterns in the sky had a vivid imagination."

"When God moves, it's a wonderful thing to behold." Sue slipped her arm in his and pulled him close. "So, what was the bad part you wanted to tell me?"

"Well," he sighed. "It's not good." He shook his head. "Now I'm not sure I should tell you. It might change your opinion of my father forever."

"I don't think anything you could tell me, one way or the other, could ever change my opinion of Wally Ellis. Go ahead," she urged. "Tell me what you wanted to say."

"It's about Anna."

Sue frowned. "I'm not sure I understand. What did your visit have to do with Anna?"

"Wally told me about things he did to her."

Sue stopped and jerked her arm free. "No," she scowled. "He didn't."

"Yes, he did."

Sue folded her arms across her chest. "Somebody ought to ..."

"What?"

"Never mind. I shouldn't say it. Probably shouldn't even think it." She walked a few steps with her arms still folded tightly across her chest. "I can't even imagine what that must have been like for your sister. And then carrying something like that around all her life." She slipped her arm back in his. "What did you say to him?"

"Holding my anger in check was one of the hardest things I've ever had to do. I took a few deep breaths and pretended he was someone I didn't know, someone who had walked into my office for counseling. Then I told him he needed to ask God to forgive him."

"And did he?"

"He cried and talked and cried some more, and then he prayed."

"Did you tell him that you saw Anna at your mother's funeral?"

"No. I didn't mention the funeral. Neither did Dad."

"Should you have told him about your mother?"

"Maybe. But I didn't think of it, and we had plenty to discuss without getting into that."

"So, what about Anna? What can we do?"

"I want to go up to Chicago and talk to her. If she's carrying around half as much bitterness as I was, she needs to go see Dad and confront him."

"That'll never happen."

"Maybe not." David hugged her. "But I never thought today would happen either."

Sue turned and captured David's hands in hers. "Now, what are we going to do about the doctor and surgery?"

"I'm not sure I need it. They'd probably be glad to operate on me later rather than sooner." He looked down at her. "Sue, I really think God healed me, just like He did when I was a boy and stuttered."

"Okay." She squeezed his arm and rested her head against his shoulder.

"There's one more thing," he said tentatively.

"What's that?"

"You remember when we were walking on the beach this summer, and I told you things were changing."

"Yes."

"I'm not the same guy who came to Belmont Baptist Church ten years ago."

"No, you aren't. But what are you saying?"

"I want to move on."

"I know you do. Things are changing at the church too. I had a conversation with Linda Smith at the grocery store while you were gone. Things have been happening that we know little about. She mentioned a luncheon she was attending at Minnie's house, for wives of the Life Group leaders. They asked her to attend. They never mentioned it to me."

"You're feeling left out?"

"No. It just made me realize that things are changing. Two years ago, I would have known about things like that before they happened. Minnie would have come to me and talked about it before she did it."

"I felt the same way that night Alan came to the hospital."

"That man," she shook her head. "He shouldn't have said all that. Not right there in the hospital room."

"That's just Alan being Alan," David sighed.

They walked along in silence, then Sue looked up at him. "If you leave the church, what do you want to do?"

"Something with Israel maybe. Something with Christians and Jews."

"When do you want to resign?"

"I don't know exactly. Pray with me about it over the next few weeks, and let's see what we hear."

"How would we make a living?"

"I suppose we could find people who feel the same way. Get them involved."

"Involved in what?"

"Reaching out. Building bridges. Come to think of it, that's exactly what I finally told Prime Minister Begin. I told him I was to be a bridge builder. Begin chuckled and asked, 'A bridge builder, huh? A bridge like the Brooklyn Bridge?' I said, 'No, Mr. Prime Minister, a bridge of love between Christians and Jews in Israel. That's why God sent me to you.' Begin stretched out his hand and shook mine. 'I will help you build that bridge.' I haven't worked through all the details. I just think this is the direction God is leading me. Maybe all we have to do is obey Him, live in His truth right now, and be available for the next thing He wants to show us."

"I know. But don't we need a plan?"

"Maybe the plan is just to be available." Sue did not respond immediately. David looked down at her. "Isn't that what we're supposed to do anyway?"

"I was thinking more about how to pay the electric bill. Not that God won't do that, but in the past we've always had a plan for how things will work out."

"Maybe part of the change is to step forward without a plan."

They walked a little farther, and then Sue spoke again. "When did you want to see Anna?"

"The sooner the better. Thanksgiving will be here in a few weeks and then Christmas. If I don't go now, it'll be next year before I see her. I don't think this can wait that long. Does it scare you for me to just quit at the church without another job to go to?"

"A little, I guess." She looked up at him. "But that doesn't mean it's not the right thing to do. And besides, your calling is your job."

David stopped and turned toward her. "I love you." He leaned down, kissed her tenderly, and wrapped her in his arms.

"I love you," she replied.

chapter 31

At first Anna was hesitant to see David when he asked if he could fly up to visit, but he persisted and she reluctantly agreed. He flew to Chicago, and they met at her apartment in Lincoln Park, which was right on Lake Michigan. He arrived at three in the afternoon. They sat in the living room—Anna at one end of the sofa, David in a wingback chair a few feet away—and talked over hot tea and sweetbread. She set the service on a table in front of the sofa. David reached for the cup Anna handed him. He thought she looked pale but hesitated to mention it.

"What time did you get in?"

"Late last night. Cheaper flight. I stayed at a hotel near the airport."

"You could have stayed here. I didn't mean to be rude when I suggested you might come some other time. It's just that I have a lot going on at work. Are you staying tonight too? You're welcome to sleep here."

"I have a flight out tonight."

They sat in silence, sipping tea. Finally, she said, "I need to ask your forgiveness. I was angry with you."

"For what?"

"For getting out. For having a life."

"I wanted to take everyone with me, but that wasn't possible."

"I know that now. I didn't know that then." She took a sip of tea. "You took the worst beatings. You would bear the heaviest burden." She offered him a cookie. He shook his head. She continued. "But you seem to get stronger every year."

"Grace is a powerful antidote for misery." David looked at her. "But you were wrong. Not about me failing, but about which one of us bore the worst of it."

Her eyes darted away. "What do you mean?"

"I talked to Dad."

"Oh? And what did he have to say?"

David couldn't bring himself to press the matter with her. Instead, he turned the conversation in a different direction. "I asked him to forgive me."

She looked puzzled. "You asked him to forgive you? For what?"

"For hating him. I'm not saying what he did was right. I'm just saying I shouldn't have hated him."

"Some people deserve to be hated." Anna set her cup aside.

"Hatred and bitterness are powerful forces."

"Well." Anna had a wry smile. "I must be a powerful woman."

David could no longer avoid the reason he had come to see her. He leaned forward and looked her squarely in the eye. "He told me, Anna."

"He told you what?"

"Wally told me what he did to you."

She shuddered and looked away. "Then you know why I can never forgive him."

"You can't hold onto the hate without holding onto him."

She glared at him. Her eyes were sharp and piercing. "You think you know what it was like?"

"I don't know what it was like to experience what you did. It made me sick when he told me. But I do know what it's like to carry around the hatred. All my life I hated him. It was a chain binding me to him, and I didn't even know it. Everywhere I went I was carrying him with me, like some dead stinking body tied to my back."

"So, how did you figure it out?"

"Actually, Yona helped me. And some others too. A friend at our church. A guy I met in Israel—"

"A guy you met in Israel? A perfect stranger? I suppose you think that was from God."

"Sometimes the people who know the most about us are the ones who see us the least."

Anna sighed. "I suppose."

"I didn't want to forgive him, but everywhere I went I met people who kept pointing me back to forgiveness. Grace. Mercy."

"He doesn't deserve mercy."

"None of us do. Remember the words of Jesus in Matthew 18:21. It says, 'Lord, how often should I forgive someone who sins against me? Seven times?' Anna, unforgiveness is like drinking poison while hoping it will make your enemy sick. I know...I've done my share of hating. But the more I resisted grace and mercy, the more I bore the marks of my past in my body. It started with nightmares, then panic attacks, then spasms and tremors in my neck."

"And now?"

"And now, most of that is gone." David touched her hand. "Hatred doesn't make you powerful, it exerts power over you. Hatred tells you it's right to feel that way and gives you the illusion you are damaging someone, but in the end you only destroy yourself."

David picked up the teapot from the table and offered it to Anna. She shook her head. He filled his cup and stirred in a lump of sugar. "After the funeral, when you left, I went with Yona to her house for lunch."

"Do you remember her?"

"No." David shook his head. "But she remembers me. She remembers all of us. She had pictures of us on the wall at her house."

"But who is she?"

"I don't know." He had his own ideas, but in his spirit he felt prevented from sharing them.

Anna grimaced. "I thought it was all a little weird, her being there and talking to us as if we should remember her."

"She told me about Mama and Aunt Eliana and about their child-hood, about a day when they were girls in Russia, when the Christians came and burned the synagogue to the ground. Nailed the doors and windows shut, then set the place on fire."

Anna's eyes were wide. "They burned down the building?"

"Yes. With the congregation inside." Anna covered her face. David continued. "Our grandmother and great-grandfather were burned alive that day."

"Aunt Eliana and Mama saw it?"

"Yes," David nodded. "They had plenty of opportunity to hate. For most of her life, Mama took advantage of that opportunity. Aunt Eliana chose grace and mercy."

"Aunt Eliana had Jacob. Mama had Wally." She said bitterly. "Parents aren't supposed to treat their children like Wally treated us." Tears filled her eyes. "That man owes me a lot more than just an apology." Her eyes darted toward him. "And if he told you what he did, then you know why."

"But Anna, forgiving Wally is the only way to get past this."

"You think I'm not past it?"

"No, I don't. I think it's eating you up inside and every day it devours more and more of you. Soon, there won't be anything left."

"And if I get past it, what do I find?"

"Peace. Freedom. The woman you were meant to be."

"You sound like a preacher."

"I don't mean it that way. I mean, you were not created to be bitter. You were not created to hate. You were created to enjoy life fully alive. Not to sit around waiting for the end."

"Endurance is all I can offer myself." Tears dripped from her cheeks. "It's all I have left."

"Forgiveness will give you so much more."

"I can't," she cried. "I just can't do it." David moved to the sofa and slipped an arm around her shoulder. She leaned against him and sobbed.

chapter 32

Instead of returning home that evening as he had planned, David booked a flight to Hartford for the next morning. He found a motel room near O'Hare and called Sue. He then used the remainder of the evening to gather his thoughts. He felt that Yona had surely been sent by God to lead them toward resolution with Wally and to show them the way to freedom from their past. But who was she? And how did she remember so many details from their lives? For an answer to those questions and others, he had to return to his hometown.

When he arrived in Hartford the next morning, David rented a car and drove to Indian Orchard. He crossed town to the funeral home, where he and Yona had first met. From there he retraced the route to the house on Davis Street where he had had lunch with her. With little difficulty he located the house and brought the car to a stop at the curb out front.

An oak tree grew in the front yard, scattering its leaves across an unkempt lawn. Cobwebs grew under the eaves. He stepped from the curb to the sidewalk and made his way up the front steps. Through a window by the door he saw the living room was empty. From another he had a view down the hall to the doorway that led into the kitchen. The nook where the table sat at the end of the counter was bare. All that remained of the table were the indentations made by the legs in the linoleum tile.

"It's a nice house," a voice said from behind him.

David spun around to see a man standing at the sidewalk. "Yes. It is nice."

"Is it yours?"

"No." David came from the porch. "You know the owner?"

"I was hoping it was you."

David crossed the yard and stood near the man. "How long has it been empty?"

"Seven or eight years, I think. Long as I've lived here."

"And you don't know the owners?"

"No. We've been trying to find them. We'd like to get it spruced up and occupied. It's the only house on the street that's empty."

"Anybody ever come around to look after it?"

"A guy comes over to look after the yard. That's about it. It could be a nice place to live." The man glanced toward the street. "Good neighborhood. Great place to raise a family." He turned away. "Let me know if you're interested. I live next door."

As the man continued up the sidewalk, David turned to face the house. He thought about seeing Yona at the funeral home, talking to her that afternoon, and standing with her at his mother's grave. He wondered now if it had all been real. Fragments and pieces of conversation—words and phrases, the touch of her hand, and the sound of her laughter—drifted through his mind as he looked through the window. His eyes wandered over the house. Minutes ticked slowly by as he searched for an answer, a sign, some indication that what he had seen and heard were real, but all he heard was the early autumn breeze rustling through the trees above him. Finally, he turned away and started toward the car.

* * *

David drove back across town. There were many things about his past he had chosen to forget. He knew that now. He had forgotten—no, not merely forgotten but pushed his past so deep into his subconscious mind that he could not remember ever having known it. At first he had ignored the problem, thinking it would go away, telling himself it made no difference. Then came the panic attacks, the muscle spasms, and finally the dream with Joel and Wally and the black stones he wanted them to take. Now he meant to put all that to rest, to remember, and not just a few things but all of it. As he turned the car onto Pasco Road he whispered a prayer. "Let me remember whatever it is I need to become the man You want me to be."

In the few memories he had, the houses on their street were large, with yards big enough to give a young boy the space he needed to play and grow, but now he found them small and cramped and jammed tightly together with postage-stamp yards. He searched from house to house for a landmark—the store on the corner, the house where their neighbor Hank lived, anything to remind him of the neighborhood he had tried hard to forget—but all he saw were the fading shadows of a past his mind seemed reluctant to visit. Most of the houses stood vacant, their windows and doors boarded shut. Empty and faded, they bore little resemblance to the ones he remembered. With nothing else to guide him, David counted off the house numbers until finally he reached it.

"There it is," he said out loud, "77 Pasco Road."

The screen door hung open, dangling from a single rusted hinge. Windowpanes across the front were cracked and broken. Faded paint peeled from the eaves, and the yard was littered with trash and bottles, but there was no mistaking it. This was the place. David brought the car to a stop at the curb and climbed out.

Old voices rushed at him as he made his way slowly toward the steps. His father yelling at him, "You stupid Jew bastard. You'll never amount to anything." The screams of his sister, "Daddy! You're hurting him." The anguished silence of his mother. David pushed them all aside and stepped onto the porch.

Through a cracked windowpane to the left he looked into the empty living room. Even from a distance he could see the dirt and cobwebs. A broken chair sat in the dining room. Empty bottles and trash were piled in the corner. A torn, soiled blanket lay nearby. Between the fireplace and the stairway, his eyes came to rest on the place where his father's chair had sat. As he stared at the empty spot, he heard Wally's voice once again. "Moron! What did you do that for?" And he heard the whap of a belt against his bare skin.

He glanced to the right and saw the dining room. For an instant he saw his mother standing at the kitchen sink beyond it, and he had a glimpse of the dining table where his father played cards with his friends, their empty beer bottles stacked at one end. He saw the images in his mind as clear and sharp as if they had only just happened. Then, in the next instant, they were gone.

David moved from the window to the door and twisted the knob. To his surprise, the door was unlocked. As he pushed it open, the smell of dust and decay rushed through the doorway to greet him. His heart quickened as he stepped inside and glanced around. A tattered curtain hung from the window in the dining room. Broken glass was strewn across the floor. Near the door to the kitchen a black garbage bag lay open on the floor. Rats and mice had ripped holes in it. Droppings marked their trail. Everywhere there was a coat of fine, powdery dust that drifted into the air each time David took a step. The acrid stench of urine stung his nose.

He crossed the room to the stairs and looked up to the open doorway that led to his room on the second floor. Memories crowded his mind. The shout of Henry as his father whipped him with a brush. The scream of Peter as his father pulled him down the hall by the hair. The sound of his father's voice over it all. "I'll show you somethin' you won't forget!" Deep inside he felt the urge to turn and run, but he pushed it away, took hold of the banister, and started upstairs. With each step he whispered the words he had said in the car the week before as he drove from Wally's trailer. "I forgive him for all he did to me. And I forgive him for all he did to them."

Like the living room, the second floor hallway was littered with trash and coated with dust. David picked his way past the refuse and stepped through the doorway to the room he had shared with his brothers. He stopped just inside.

His bed had been against the wall to the left. Pete and Henry shared bunk beds on the wall beside the door. To the right, at the far end of the room, the closet door stood open. Across from the door, light streamed through the room's lone window, its grimy panes still intact. Here and there, in between, faint swatches of green-striped wallpaper peeked out from beneath the dirt and mildew covering the walls.

David slowly crossed the room to the window and looked down at the wooden sill. He slipped his fingers beneath the edge and gripped it with both hands, then gave it a tug. The left end of the board swung free, revealing a cavity in the wall. David knelt beside it and glanced inside to a brace that supported the wall. Lying on the board was a pocketknife. He reached inside and took it out. "Not just any knife," he said to himself, "but a genuine Case knife." It was a simple little folding knife, but something every boy coveted and few had—at least in his neighborhood.

One day on the way home from school, his best friend Johnny had wanted to stop by the hardware store to look at a new bike. The beautiful red bicycle with chrome wheels and a big basket on the front was all he talked about at school. Johnny had already counted the money he was going to earn delivering newspapers and running errands for people in the neighborhood. By springtime, that bike would be his.

Sure enough, it was everything his friend had promised. Sitting there in the window of the hardware store, it was the most beautiful bicycle David had ever seen. There was even a bell on the handlebar to warn folks that they were about to be run over by a speeding rider.

David had lingered at the store as long as he could, said goodbye to Johnny, and then turned toward home. He had taken just a few steps when a man brushed past him, running to the bus stop. The man reached into his pocket for a bus token, and as he withdrew his hand something shiny fell into the snow on the sidewalk.

As the bus pulled away, David stepped quickly toward the fallen object, certain he was about to find a shiny new quarter. What he found was even better: a bone-handled, triple-blade Case knife. By then the bus had turned the corner and moved out of sight. David snatched up the knife and rubbed his fingers over it, then reverently slipped it into his pocket.

That night at the dinner table David proudly laid his newfound treasure beside his dad's plate and smiled expectantly.

"Where'd ya' get that knife, boy?" His father's face twisted in an angry scowl. "You stole it, didn't you?" He snatched the knife from the table and shoved it into his pocket. "Who'd you steal it from, boy?" While he bellowed and cursed, his hands unbuckled the belt from his waist. "Who did you steal it from?" he repeated. "I ain't gonna have no thief in this house. You'd better tell me the truth!"

"I-I f-f-found it in the s-snow."

"You're lying to me, stupid! You stole that knife. If you'd found it in the snow, it'd be rusty. I'll teach you what happens when you steal and lie to me about it. I ain't havin' no liars in this house neither. I'll beat you 'til you tell me the truth even if I gotta beat you to death!"

David pushed back from the table. His chair tipped over and fell to the floor. "I d-d-didn't s-s-steal it!" he screamed as he backed away.

"Boy, don't you even think about running from me." Wally's voice went deathly quiet. David edged toward the back door. All the while his father kept coming toward him. Then, just as David felt his back against the doorknob, his father reached out with one hand, grabbed hold of his shirt and slammed his fist into David's mouth. "You're a liar. God hates liars, and I do too! You won't get away with it. Now, tell me the truth!"

David fell to the kitchen floor with a thud. He tried to get up, but the room was spinning. Then he heard his father's menacing whisper. "Where you think you're goin', boy? I ain't through with you yet."

The meaty hand grabbed the back of his shirt collar just as he heard the whistle of a coat hanger descend toward his back. Again and again the blows fell, until at last the hanger slipped from Wally's sweaty grip and went flying across the room. As David lay on the floor, his arms covering his head, he felt the thump of Wally's boot against his side. Air rushed from his lungs, but before he could catch his breath, Wally kicked him again. Not a sound escaped from Henry or Peter or Anna. Their mom sat with her head bowed.

David didn't know how long the tirade lasted. He only heard his own hysterical cries and felt the blood oozing from welts on his arms and back. When his father finally tired, he shoved his hand in his pocket. "Hey moron," he scoffed. "You want this stupid knife? Here it is!" He opened one blade, grasped the handle between his fingers, and with a flick of his wrist threw the knife in David's direction. The point of the blade stuck in the floor inches from David's head.

Now, years later, David stared at the knife in the palm of his hand. "I forgive you, Dad." He rubbed the dust from it with his thumb, and then shoved the knife into his pocket. "I forgive you."

chapter 33

David moved to the hallway and made his way downstairs. When he reached the bottom he turned to see Yona standing in the living room. His heart skipped a beat, and he froze in place.

"Good morning, David," she smiled. "How are you?"

"I'm fine, but how did you—"

"Come here," she said, cutting him off with a nod as she gripped his arm. The smell of her perfume filled the air. "You found the knife?"

"How did you know about the knife?"

"David, I remember many things about your past, things you have worked hard to push from your mind." She gestured with her free hand, clinching it in a grasping motion. "I caught those memories as they slipped from your conscious mind."

"How?" He looked over at her. "Who are you?"

"Don't be silly. I am Yona. I have known you all your life." She pointed with her index finger. "You remember now the afternoon you found the knife?"

"Yes."

"Good. You will keep that memory now. It's a handsome piece, isn't it? The knife."

"Yes," David replied. "It is."

"May I see it?" David pulled the knife from his pocket and held it in his open palm. "Here," he said, gesturing for her to take it.

"No, no, no." She shook her head. "I do not want to touch it. I only want to see it." She looked down at the knife, whispered something David did not understand, and then reached up and patted him on the shoulder. "Okay. Now put it back in your pocket." She slipped her hand over his and folded his fingers around the knife. "And when you get home you can put it on the dresser next to your Bible."

"How do you know—"

She patted him on the chest. "Never mind about that now." She took him by the arm and turned him away from the door. "Look this way." David turned to face the room. Yona continued. "You remember coming home with the knife? And you remember dinner?"

"Yes, but how do you know all this?"

"You thought you could give the knife to your father and, for once in your life, he would be pleased."

"Most fathers would have been happy," David replied. "And most of them would have refused the gift and let their son keep it."

"That's right," she nodded. "They would have handed it back to their son and said, 'This is a wonderful expression of love, but I want you to have it.'"

David sighed. "That's what most would have done."

"But not Wally."

"No," David shook his head. "Not my dad."

"Instead, he screamed at you, accused you of stealing the knife, and beat you mercilessly."

Tears filled David's eyes. "Yes," he nodded.

"Good. You remember it well."

"Why do I have to remember it? I've already forgiven him."

"You forgive him even now?"

"Yes."

"When you were in the bedroom? You said the words?"

"Yes," David nodded. "I said the words."

"Good. This is not about him. It's about you. You have asked him to forgive you for hating him. And you have forgiven him for what you know. But you have not reached the depth of your pain. Those memories you locked away to protect yourself from the pain still hold the pain. It was the best your mind could do, and it helped you for a long time; but now those memories and the pain they hold have become an emotional abscess. You need to open up and allow it to heal with the balm of forgiveness."

"How?"

"By remembering." She gestured toward the room with a sweeping motion and then ushered him toward the kitchen. "And do you remember this one?"

From the doorway David's eyes scanned the room and he nodded. It was dusty and drab, but as he stared into the blank space a shaft of brilliant light streamed in through the window above the sink. Slowly the room came to life. The table appeared in its place beneath the overhead light. On it was a pot. An assortment of vegetables lay next to it. A hand reached for a potato and then he saw his mother sitting there, carefully, methodically peeling it. Footsteps came from behind him. David jumped when Yona touched his back. "It's all right," she whispered. "I have you."

Wally pushed his way through the doorway and stood over Leah. Without a word he drew back his fist and slammed it into the center of her back, striking her squarely between the shoulders. Leah never moved, but continued sliding the knife across the potato, rolling back the skin in thin, even strips.

"You Jew whore," Wally shouted. He drew back his fist once more, this time slamming it into the side of Leah's face. She staggered backwards, her head rocked to one side, but she kept right on peeling the potato. "That kid upstairs is why I don't believe nothin' you say! He's proof of what you done, and I hate you for it every day. You hear me? Every day!"

Yona squeezed David's arm tighter. Suddenly, Wally and Leah were frozen in place. Yona's lips were at David's ear. "You heard what he said?"

"Yes," David nodded. "I never realized I was the reason he hated her."

"That is what he said, but it was not your fault. That was something between Wally and Leah."

"What was it? What happened to make him hate her?"

"I cannot show you that. I can only show you your memories."

"Then how do I know it wasn't my fault?"

"Did you ask to be born?"

"No."

"Your birth was someone else's choice. Wally wanted you to believe it was your fault, because he would not face his responsibility for what happened between him and Leah. Do you remember the first time you ran away from home? You were four years old, and your father had frightened you. He was screaming and throwing things at your mother."

"I remember. I ran to the park."

"Who did you see there?"

"A group of senior citizens. Just old people sitting in the sunlight feeding the ducks. I was barefoot. It was fall, and leaves were everywhere. A nurse with the group caught me by the arm as I raced by her. She asked me if I wanted to feed the ducks. I was so scared of my father that I pulled out of her grasp and shouted at her, 'I don't want to feed no stupid ducks! My dad was screaming and throwing stuff! Leave me alone.' But she didn't. She drew me closer and put an arm around me. She said, 'There, there, little one. What's your name?'

"'D-D-David,' I answered.

"'Well David,' she said, 'did you know you have a beautiful light in your eyes?'

"I felt such peace standing there by her. Some of the others came over and started talking to me. But where did the hatred come from? Why was my dad so mean? Why did he have to scream all the time? Later he began to beat me for the smallest thing...talking too loud, banging the door, running up the stairs. He gave me fear and broken bones but never the gift of his love. I guess he never really gave us anything."

"David, every parent gives gifts to their children. He gave you many things, few of them pleasant. The things he gave you were things that had been given to him. Most fathers would have sorted the good from the bad and given only the good. Wally passed on to you everything he had received from his father."

Suddenly David remembered the dream, Wally with the rocks for him and Joel. He turned to Yona, but she gently turned him away.

"We have more to do."

The light from the window was gone, and the room was empty again, but before him was the door to the cellar. It was ajar, and through the opening between the door and the frame he could see only thick, black, darkness. Yona guided him toward it. David's heart began to race. "Where are we going?"

"Do not be afraid," she said softly.

He dug in with his heels and resisted her attempts to move him forward. "I don't like this."

"You must open the door."

"It's already open."

"You must open it wide, and go all the way to the bottom."

"N-n-no," he stammered. "I can't." He shook his head from side to side, and his voice became that of a little boy. "The cellar's a bad place. A bad place. I can't go down there. I'm not allowed." Yona nudged him forward. He looked at her with imploring eyes. "Why would I want to go down there? Why would you make me?"

"You must face it, David." She inched him closer to the door. "Take hold of the doorknob and open it wide."

With a trembling hand David reached out and gripped the knob. Slowly, he pulled it toward him, swinging open the door. Sights and sounds from the past swirled around him as the heavy, musty air of the cellar drifted up from below—his father dragging him by the arm across the kitchen floor as his mother looked on from her seat at the table, the clink of the buckle as his father took off his belt and doubled it for a beating, the smell of alcohol on his father's breath, his spit hitting David's cheeks as he swore at him …

"No!" David shrank back. "That's enough!" He jerked free of Yona and darted from the kitchen. He rushed through the living room, pushed open the front door, and hurried outside.

chapter 34

David sat at the edge of the porch and rested his feet on the steps. He propped his elbows on his knees and buried his head in his hands. Tears flowed down his cheeks. Yona sat beside him and laid her hand on his back.

"You were born for a purpose. I think you're finding that to be obvious."

"But my own father didn't want me."

"Your Father in Heaven wanted you, David. God is your Father."

"What does that mean? He wants to beat me with an extension cord?"

"You know what it means. You're a father yourself."

"Not like him."

"That's right," Yona assured him. "You aren't like Wally at all. Do you know why?"

"Jesus."

"Yes. Jesus made all the difference in your life. Since that night when you uttered a prayer of despair in your bedroom, saw His Light, and heard His voice, you have never been the same."

David looked at her. "How do you know about that?"

Yona smiled. "I have been guiding you toward that Light all your life. I have not always done a perfect job. The Enemy has tried to interfere, but I have done my best, and it will be enough. There is only One who is perfect."

"But aren't you Jewish?"

"Jesus was a Jew." She patted him on the back. "As are you."

David took a deep breath and stared out at the street. What she said made sense, but still he had a nagging uncertainty about who she was. "Pinch me," he mumbled.

"What?"

"Pinch me."

"You want me to pinch you so you will know I am really here? There was laughter in Yona's voice. "You think because you do not remember me, you might be sitting here talking to yourself?"

"The thought crossed my mind."

"Even though the words I tell you ring true in your heart." She thrust out her arm defiantly. "You pinch me."

Her response startled him. "What?"

"You pinch me." She jiggled her arm to encourage him. "Go on. Pinch me." David reached out with his right hand and gently pressed the warm skin of her forearm between his fingers. "Pinch it," she demanded. David squeezed the skin tightly and let it slip past his fingertips. "Ouch!" Yona exclaimed. She snatched back her arm and rubbed it. "I said pinch it. I did not say rip off a piece for lunch."

David laughed. Yona grinned. "Now you see I am really here?"

"Yes," David replied. "You're really here. So, tell me, why do I have to go down to the cellar?"

"God wants to unlock the hurt so He can bring healing. To do that, He has to unlock the memories that hold the hurt." She pointed toward his chest. "The hurt is contained in the memory. The memory is buried inside you. You must go into the cellar so you can remember."

"I don't want to remember."

"The memory can't harm you. The memory is just that—only a memory. It exists only as a thought inside your head. Your father isn't here. He's in North Carolina." Yona rolled her eyes. "Probably at that awful bar down the road from his miserable little trailer."

"You know about the bar too?"

She patted him on the leg. "You are not in physical danger."

"What's in the cellar? Can't you just tell me?"

"Lessons in life must be learned. Come on." She rose and tapped him on the shoulder. "Let's go see."

David wiped his eyes and stood. He followed Yona inside the house and through the dining room toward the kitchen. The door to the cellar loomed ahead. In spite of what Yona had told him, and in spite of how true he knew those words to be, his heart beat faster and faster with each step.

At last they were in front of the cellar door. Yona gestured toward it with a nod and a wave of her hand. David took hold of the doorknob and pulled open the door. She held it as he moved past and placed his foot on the top step. He hesitated and looked back. "Aren't you coming with me?"

"I'll be right here," she replied. "You are not alone."

David took another step and began the long descent toward the bottom. Dank, musty air rose up to meet him. Down below, shafts of pale late-morning light filtered through the narrow cellar windows and fell in streaks on the dirt floor. He braced himself with a hand against the wall and continued slowly, moving carefully from step to step, the boards springing beneath his feet. Finally, he reached the bottom.

To the left he saw the empty shelves on which his mother had stacked canned goods. The furnace stood to the right. Next to it was the water heater. David felt his heart pounding. The veins in his neck pulsed and his fingertips throbbed. He moved around to the right, between the stairs and the furnace, and then he heard his father's voice. "Something's startin' to stink down there, boy. Go get it and throw it in the garbage."

"W-w-what is it?"

"Don't make no difference what it is," Wally snapped. "I just told you to go clean it up. Now get movin' before I beat the livin' daylights outta ya."

David gasped as he saw himself open the cellar door, flip on the lights, and stumble down the steps. As he got closer to the bottom he could see something lying on the floor. "No," he whispered, and hurried to the furnace. There he found Freckles, lying in a bloody, furry heap. "No, no, no!" he wailed. He knelt beside the lifeless form and cradled it in his arms. Tears flooded his eyes, and deep, wracking sobs consumed him as he buried his face in the bloodied fur. His father had slit the pup's throat with his hunting knife. The bloody weapon still lay on the floor by the stairs.

He picked up Freckles and carried the puppy to the kitchen. "Throw it in the trash," Wally growled. "Ain't gonna have no dog peein' in my house. Should have killed that good-for-nothin' mutt when ya'll spoiled my dinner." He shouted at David as he walked past. "It's your fault the thing's dead!"

Instead of throwing the puppy's body away, David dug a hole in the backyard behind the garage. He laid Freckles in the ground and sat there for a long time, thinking, wondering, and struggling to make sense of what had happened. When he had no more tears to shed, he covered Freckles' body with dirt and patted it in place to keep the neighbor's cat from digging it up. The next day he nailed two pieces of scrap wood together to make a cross and shoved it into the ground above the grave.

David backed away from the furnace and sat on the cellar steps, staring at the place where Freckles had lain all those years ago. He thought about his father, about the horrible darkness inside a man who would kill a child's pet. Tears filled his eyes as he felt the pain of that day.

A shaft of clear light appeared through the center cellar window. The room glowed with a brightness David hadn't seen before. In the midst of it was Wally standing just a few feet away. Slowly, the scene changed. Shelves to the left were filled with jars of vegetables David's mother had canned. Laundry hung from a wire strung from wall to wall.

A washing machine stood against the back wall. Wally was in front of it snorting like a raging bull. David, eleven years old, lay at his feet.

Wally roared down at him, "Think you can talk to me like that and get away with it?" Before David could respond, Wally lifted him by the collar and slammed his fist into the young boy's jaw. "Think you can smart off to me in front of my friends, huh?" David's head hit the floor and bounced. Wally stood over him and pressed his foot down against David's chest.

"I-I c-c-can't breathe," David gasped.

"Shut up!" Wally drew back his foot and slammed the toe of his boot against David's rib cage. Pain shot through David's side. He screamed.

"Shut up!" Wally shouted. "Shut up!" When David began to cry, Wally jerked him up from the floor and slapped him across the face. "I told you to be quiet, you little Jew moron!"

Wally let go, dropping David to the floor. His head struck the dirt with a sickening thud. David curled on his side and tried to scoot away. "I -w-w-wish you were d-d-dead!"

Wally leaned over. "You wish I was dead, huh? Maybe you're just the one who can do it. You gonna kill your old man? Huh?" He grabbed David by the arm and twisted violently. There was a snapping sound and more searing pain. Wally grabbed an empty whiskey bottle from the garbage can by the steps, and with a sneer, smashed it against the stairway railing. Shards of glass fell to the floor. In the next instant, the broken bottle sliced through the air as Wally swung it toward David's face. In the nick of time, David covered his face with his hands and felt the white hot pain as the jagged glass cut through his palms.

Again, the bottle sliced through the air, this time catching David in the side and tearing a gash that gushed with hot, sticky blood. David rolled over on his stomach and clutched his burning side with his bloody hands. "D-d-don't k-kill m-me," he yelled. "P-please d-don't k-kill m-me."

Wally dropped the bottle, grasped David's arm to lift him from the floor, and brought his fist down on David's jaw. Blood gushed from his nose and broken teeth fell to the ground. David rolled into a fetal position as the steel-toed boot smashed into his other arm, breaking the bone and driving it through the flesh. Wally swung his leg and kicked David again. The foot connected with his ribs, the edge of the sole widening the gash in his side. Then with his heavy leather belt, Wally lashed David's back, tearing through the shirt and ripping the flesh from his back in a maniacal frenzy.

As the beating continued, Wally screamed and shouted. "Does it hurt, moron? Can you feel it now? I'll beat the hell outta you. It's my Christian duty. It won't hurt much longer. Pretty soon, you won't feel a thing, you worthless little piece of crap." Wally laughed a cold, chilling laugh. "You wonder why you was ever born. To tell you the truth, I got no earthly idea!"

*   *   *

An instant later the light receded. The shelves were empty and the washing machine was gone. David sat on the bottom step and watched as the last images of his father faded from sight and the realization of what his father had done sank deep into his soul. His father, lost in a drunken rage, had tried to kill him. "Why?" he sobbed. "Why did he do that?"

The steps behind him creaked. Startled by the sound, David jerked around to see Yona beside him. She took a seat next to him and draped her arm over his shoulder. "The question you want to ask isn't why were you born, or why Wally did this, but why did God let it happen. Isn't that really what you feel?"

David looked up. "I suppose."

"You know why your father beat you."

"I guess he was just passing on what he'd received."

"Yes. He was giving you what he received when he was a child."

David wiped his eyes. "But what about God? He could have stopped it."

"You confuse God's power with God's character."

"He had the power to stop it."

"But He also has character."

"Doesn't His character compel him to protect me? A little kid?"

"Perhaps. But you must remember this. God loves Wally as much as He loves you."

"That isn't easy to grasp."

"It is a mystery of life." She squeezed his shoulder. "Did you forgive him?"

"Forgive God?"

"No. Forgive Wally. Did you say the words?"

David took a deep breath. "I forgive him." He closed his eyes and breathed even deeper. "I forgive you, Dad." He opened his eyes and looked again at the place where he had laid at Wally's feet. "I forgive you, Dad."

They sat there in silence, David staring at the empty cellar windows, Yona staring at him. "Did you forgive God?"

David frowned. "I didn't know it worked that way."

"Forgiveness opens every door. Say the words."

David closed his eyes, "I forgive You, Lord." He looked over at her. "That seems too strange."

"Say it again."

David closed his eyes once more. "I forgive You, Lord." He said it again. "I forgive You." And again as a whisper, "I forgive You."

As he sat there on the step the light through the window grew brighter again, filling the room and surrounding him with its glow. The warmth of a long, slow embrace filled his heart, and his mind seemed as light as an early spring breeze. He felt as if he would rise up off the step and float through the air. He reached out to catch himself against the rail. Then, a moment later, he seemed to settle back inside his own skin. His feet were once more on the earthen floor, his hips once more against the wooden step.

"Now, you must go to Anna." Yona spoke as if she had not seen what just happened to him.

David looked at her, his eyes wide with amazement. "Did you not see the light?"

"We were just talking about Wally and what you—" She stopped in mid-sentence. "You saw it again? Just now?"

"Yes."

"This is good," she smiled. "You are moving beyond the past." There was a distant look in her eyes. "Things are changing. Something new is opening." She stood. "Come. You must go back."

"I told Anna I went to see Dad."

"And did you tell her what he told you?"

"Yes. She said if I knew about all he did to her, then I knew why she felt she couldn't forgive him."

"She is trapped. You must help her."

"She won't listen to me."

Yona tapped him on the shoulder. "Come with me."

David stood. "Where are we going?"

"I will show you." Yona made her way up the steps toward the kitchen. David lagged behind, unsure of what was happening and whether he wanted to follow. She glanced back at him. "Come on. Time is short."

chapter 35

David followed Yona from the kitchen, through the dining room, and around to the staircase. She paused there and pointed to the room. "What do you see?"

"An empty living room."

As he watched, sunshine through the front windows changed from morning glare to the soft light of an afternoon. The dining room table appeared. Around it were the straight-backed chairs. Slowly the scene came to life as Wally and his brothers appeared at the table. Wally took a drink from a bottle of beer. "You boys want to go double or nothin' on the next game?"

"I don't know," Clarence groused. "You've got all my money."

"Deal me in," George snapped. "And get me another beer."

Wally gave a sideways look in David's direction. "Get him a beer, you moron. Didn't you hear him?"

There was a knock at the door. Wally looked around, "Who's that?"

George rocked back in his chair and pushed the curtain aside to see out. "It's that preacher."

"What's he doin' here?"

"Maybe he wants to play," George mused.

"Maybe he wants a drink," Clarence laughed.

"Shut up, both of you." Wally jumped up from the table. "Hide the booze and throw out them beer bottles." He grabbed Clarence by the shoulder and shoved him toward the kitchen. "Go out the back and take them cards with you." He looked over at David. "Shove my spit can behind that chair." He turned back to his brothers. "Go on. Get out of here. We'll settle up later." Wally grabbed the money off the table and stuffed it into his pocket.

On his way to the door he leaned over the chair and spit his mouthful of tobacco in the coffee can. He grabbed a piece of chewing gum and popped it in his mouth to disguise the smell of alcohol, then opened the door and called out jovially, "Brother Roberts, praise the Lord. It's good to see you!"

"Just on my way to see some shut-ins down the street," Roberts said, "and I wanted to stop by to tell you how much I appreciate you bringing your children to church on Sunday. I know it's difficult when you have an unbelieving wife."

"Well, I do the best I can."

"You're a real role model for other fathers in our church."

"Thank you, Preacher. We had devotions just like you said."

"Great."

"The kids was real happy to do it. And they read real good. Can't seem to get my wife saved, though. Pray for her."

"We will. But you're doing a good job with your children."

"You know, I love that scripture, 'Spare the rod, spoil the child.' Ain't got no spoiled kids around here."

"You're a good man, Wally Ellis." The pastor shook his hand. "I'm proud to have you in our congregation. Well, I better run. See you next Sunday."

Wally closed the door and turned in David's direction. "What are you starin' at, moron? Get me a beer."

Then, as quickly as it came, the image faded from view leaving only the empty, dusty room. Yona stood at David's side. "You remember Pastor Roberts?"

"He had no idea what Dad was doing to us." David looked over at Yona. "It was his job to know."

She nodded thoughtfully. "I suppose it was." She folded her hands together at her waist. "Did you forgive him?"

David closed his eyes and pictured the pastor at the door. Anger rose inside. "He doesn't deserve forgiveness."

"It's not about him; it's about you. Why do you find it so hard to forgive him?"

David opened his eyes. "He's was a preacher. A minister of the Gospel. He got paid to look after people like me. He only reinforced what my father did. It was a sacrilege. An affront to the Gospel."

Yona wagged her finger. "You cannot go back and redo the past. You must deal with it as it comes to you now, in the present. And now, you must forgive."

David took a deep breath and let it slowly escape. "I forgive him." He closed his eyes and said the words again. "I forgive him." Images of Pastor Roberts standing at the pulpit in church appeared. "I forgive him." He saw the look on Roberts' face as he greeted them at the door. "I forgive him." Slowly at first, a sense of peace swept over him, building to a tide of relief as forgiveness washed away the guilt and pain and shame.

He felt Yona's hand against his elbow. "You are ready now?"

"Yes," David nodded.

Yona led the way as they moved across the room and up the staircase to the second floor. When Yona turned right and started toward the end of the hall, David hesitated. "Where are you going?"

"Down here." She gestured with a wave of her hand. "Come on."

He shook his head. "We shouldn't go in there."

"We must," she replied.

"That's Anna's room."

"I know."

Yona reached back and took him by the arm. "Come," she insisted with a tug. Reluctantly, David followed her through the doorway and into the bedroom.

"You remember this?" She gestured with a sweep of her arm.

"Yes," he nodded. "I remember it. Anna slept there." He gestured toward the opposite side of the room. "Her bed was beneath that window."

A window looked out on the back yard with a view of the garage and the end of the driveway. As David stood there in the center of the room, light through the window faded and the room became dark. A bed appeared beneath the window and on it were two formless shapes. They tussled and thrashed against each other until one overpowered the other. David's heart sank as he heard the rhythmic squeaking of the bedsprings. Then there was the rustling sound of the sheets and faceless forms came into view. Anna lay on the bed. Tears glistened on her cheeks. Her lips quivered.

Wally rolled over and swung his feet to the floor. He stood, pulled his pants up to his waist and buttoned them. "Not a word to no one," he said in a coarse whisper. "Or so help me, I'll beat ya' like your brothers."

Those words stabbed deep into David's chest. Anger rose up from deep inside him. He clinched his fists and waited as Wally started toward him. When he was just inches away, David drew back his fist and swung with all his might. His fist sailed through the air straight for Wally's jaw, then passed through his face with such force and momentum that it spun David's body to the left. His fist struck the wall with a loud whack.

"Ouch," he exclaimed. The room was empty. The dusty floor was barren, and light shone again through the dirty windowpanes.

Yona stood a few feet away, hands on her hips, a scowl on her face. "Was that an act of forgiveness?"

"I should have been her defender." He rubbed his knuckles. "I should have made him stop."

"As I have told you before, you cannot go back to the past and set things right. You must address the past in terms of the present. Forgiveness is the business of the present. Have you forgiven your father for what he did in here? Pretending all your life that you have forgiven him makes it worse, not better."

Anger still lurked in his heart. "That is more difficult than what he did to me," he huffed.

"You must allow God's love to reach the inner recesses of your heart. You can allow no dark spaces to remain."

David took a deep breath. "I forgive him," he grumbled.

"Once more. This time close your eyes and concentrate."

David squeezed his eyes shut. "I forgive him," he repeated through clinched teeth. "I forgive him." Tears filled David's eyes. "I forgive him." He felt the pain and anguish evaporate. His jaw relaxed. "He only gave what he had to give. He was as much a victim as we were." David opened his eyes. "I forgive him."

"Good," Yona smiled. "You must share that with your sister."

Yona stepped to the end of the room near the closet. "Come here." David hesitated. "Come on," she insisted. "We haven't much time left. The present is approaching and you are becoming free." David stepped forward and stood by her side near the closet door. "Reach up there," she said, pointing overhead. "Reach above the door on the inside and tell me what you feel."

David stood inside the closet doorway and felt along the header above the frame. The closet wall was unfinished. His hand ran lightly along the rough boards. "I feel only splinters."

"Come this way a little." Yona pointed to the left.

He moved in that direction, patting his hand against the boards above the door as he worked his way toward the corner. Then his fingers touched something soft. He took hold of it and brought the object out to find it was a doll no larger than his hand.

Yona had a grim expression on her face. "You recognize it?"

Once more, tears filled David's eyes. "Yes," he nodded. "I remember it."

It wasn't much of a doll, with plastic legs and arms and a cloth body, but he had seen it at a store downtown a few days before Christmas. By then he knew their parents weren't buying any gifts for them. He went home that evening and counted all his money. He had four dollars and seventeen cents. The doll cost three dollars. With the extra money he bought his brothers chocolate candy. On Christmas day they awoke to find the floor around the tree empty. They ate dinner that day with the usual dishes of turkey and gravy and all the trimmings, but it was tough explaining to the kids on the block why they received nothing for Christmas. That afternoon they watched as Wally drank himself into a stupor. Then, when everyone was asleep, David brought the doll and the candy as Anna lay in bed.

David held the doll gently in his hand. He'd forgotten that memory. Recalling it now sent tears trickling down his cheeks once more. Yona looked at him. "Take that to Anna. Give her the doll. Tell her I showed you where she'd hidden it, and tell her again she must forgive her father. It's the only way."

David brushed the dust from the doll's face and wiped it against his shirt. "How did you know it was there?" The room was silent as David ran his fingers over the doll's hair to smooth it in place. "I didn't know she'd hidden it there. How did you know it was there?" He looked up, wondering why Yona hadn't responded, but she was not there. He spun around, searching. "Yona!" he called out, but there was no response.

He walked into the hall and looked over the edge of the banister. The living room below was empty. The house was quiet, and Yona was not there. For a moment he wondered if he had really seen her or whether it had all been nothing but a dream. He glanced around at the vacant, dusty house. "Am I losing my mind?" Then he sniffed the air and felt something tickle his nose. "Her perfume," he said to himself. He sniffed the air once more and grinned. "I smell her perfume."

chapter 36

Late that evening David caught a flight from Boston to Charlotte. On the plane he settled into his seat and took out a pocket copy of the New Testament. Because it was so old and fragile, he had packed his beloved Gideon Bible in his suitcase. As he thumbed through the pages, he came to Paul's second letter to the Corinthians. He began reading through it, letting the words wash over him and allowing the Holy Spirit to minister to him and refresh his spirit. His eyes ran over the familiar words until he reached a verse in chapter five. "All this newness of life is from God, who brought us back to himself through what Christ did."

The words went straight to David's spirit. He felt them quicken him. *And God has given us the task of bringing people back to him. This is my work*, he thought. *A ministry of renewal. God is calling me to bring individuals, families, even nations to a place of renewal and restoration.*

For the remainder of the trip home, David thought about what that might be like—a ministry of renewal. Ideas rolled around inside his mind, and he thought about writing a book, a book about his own journey toward personal renewal and peace. He would tell people how God used that journey to move him beyond his own comfort zone. He would exhort the Church that we can't simply be in the business of selling religious goods and services, but in actually doing the will of God in a broader, more strategic sense.

David's flight arrived in Charlotte after midnight. Sue was waiting in the car as he came from the terminal. He slid onto the front seat and leaned over to kiss her. "Where are the kids?"

"At home."

"By themselves?"

"Megan's old enough to baby-sit. She ought to be able to look after her brother."

"Joel can take care of them both."

Sue put the car in gear and steered it away from the curb. "How was Boston?"

"It was okay."

"Did you go to the house in Indian Orchard?"

"Yeah, and it was a little tough."

She rested her hand on his thigh. "Are you okay?"

"I'm fine." He turned sideways on the seat. "In fact, I've never been better. No spasms, no nightmares."

"Honey, that's wonderful! So tell me what happened at the house." David smiled at her. She nudged him with her hand. "What?" she said insistently. "What happened?"

"Yona was there."

Sue looked surprised. "You saw her again?"

"Yes." A wide grin spread across his face. "I don't know what it means, but she was there."

"What did she say?"

"The door was unlocked. So I went inside the house and went upstairs. Made it to my room and found this." He reached in his pocket and took out the knife. "It was under the window sill where I hid it."

"Under the sill? You knew it was there?"

"I was pretty sure that's where I left it." He slid the knife back in his pocket. "When I came downstairs, Yona was in the living room."

"Then what happened?"

"She made me go into the cellar."

"Why?"

"Because of Freckles. The dog that goes with that collar you found in my old Gideon Bible."

Sue looked concerned. "Should we wait until we get home to talk?"

David shook his head. "It's better to talk while we drive. That way the kids won't overhear. I didn't want to go down there but Yona insisted. So, I opened the door and started down the steps, and when I got down there, the place came alive. It was like I was living it again."

"What happened?"

"Dad had slit Freckles' throat."

Sue was stricken. "No."

David pointed to a parking lot outside a restaurant. "On second thought, maybe you'd better pull over here." Sue steered the car from the pavement and brought it to a stop. David continued. "I had forgotten about Freckles and a lot of other stuff. Yona told me I had to remember it so the Holy Spirit could heal the pain. The pain was locked with the memory inside me. So we went through the house remembering."

Sue ran her hand over his shoulder. "So the dog was dead."

Tears came to David's eyes. "Wally sent me down there to clean up the mess he made when he killed the dog. Afterward, I was mad, and he saw how angry I was. He hit me with his fist, then dragged me into the cellar and tried to kill me."

"What happened after you remembered?"

David took a deep breath. "I forgave him, and the weight of all those memories rolled off my back."

"Did you get a chance to go back to Yona's house?"

"Sue," David smiled at her. "It was empty! A neighbor said it hadn't been lived in for a long time."

Sue's shoulders slumped. "Who or what is this woman?"

"I think we both know what she is."

"Maybe. Did she tell you anything more about your father?"

"No. Why?"

"I still wonder if Wally really is your biological father."

"I'm not sure he is," David said as he turned away and stared out the window. They sat in silence a while. "It was tough allowing myself to remember. After that, the rest came easier." He sighed. "Wally only gave us what he got from his father."

"That's no excuse."

"No, but it is an explanation." He pointed to the highway. "We better get going. The kids will wonder where we are." Sue put the car in gear and drove from the parking lot.

When they reached home, Megan was waiting for them in the kitchen. "Someone named Tom called. I think he said his name was Tom Carter."

"Who is he?"

"I don't know. Said he was calling about Anna Ellis." Megan had a quizzical look. "That's our aunt, your sister, right??"

"Yes," David replied. "Come on, Megan, what about her?"

"He wants you to call him back." Megan handed him a scrap of paper with a telephone number on it. "Something about Anna being in the hospital."

David picked up the phone and dialed the number. Tom answered on the third ring. "Hope I didn't wake you."

"No. That's okay. I was hoping you would call."

"What happened?"

"Anna's in the hospital. Cook County Medical Center. She has cancer."

"Cancer! Have the doctors told you anything?"

Tom replied. "She was in bad shape when I found her. She's pretty heavily sedated right now."

"You found her?"

"When I came in she was on the floor unconscious. A neighbor from across the hall heard me yell for help and called for an ambulance."

"I saw Anna at our mother's funeral not too long ago, and she seemed fine."

"Yeah, but there was more going on than I realized. Apparently she's known for some time. Any possibility you could come back up here?"

"Yes. I've been out of town this week. I'll have to check in at the office in the morning, but I should be able to get there by tomorrow night."

"Okay. That would be good."

"Where is she?"

"Cook County Medical Center."

David hung up the phone and looked at Sue. "Anna has cancer," he said quietly. "They want me to come up there."

"Who does?"

"Her friend Tom." David ran his hand through his hair. "I've been away from the church a lot this year." He folded his arms across his chest. "Vacation, Israel, the trip to Boston."

"Vacation doesn't count." Sue countered. "It's part of the package."

"It's still time away from the office." David realized Megan was standing at the door. He looked over at her. "I need to talk to your mother."

"I can handle it, Dad." She had a defensive tone in her voice. "I'm not a little girl anymore."

"It's not that. We need to talk about something else." He put his arm around Megan's shoulder and kissed her on the head. "Go on to bed."

"All right," Megan sighed. "I'm old enough to look after my brother and answer your calls, but not old enough to talk about this."

"We'll talk about it later."

Megan trooped off to bed. David and Sue listened for her footsteps as she moved upstairs. Sue looked at him. "Your sister needs you."

"I know. I should have stayed in closer touch with her—with all my siblings. Time just gets away before you know it."

"David, go. Pray for her. Hold her hand. Share the love of Jesus with her. If Tom and her doctors think you should be there, you should be there."

"I suppose."

"Why are you hesitant? Is there another issue?"

David wrapped his arms around Sue and lowered his voice. "I think it's time to resign from the church."

"What does that have to do with going to see Anna?"

"In the past six months I've been to Indian Orchard twice, Israel, Boston, Chicago, and now I'm going back to Chicago again. In between we had vacation, a week in the hospital, and a woman named Yona—who we suspect may be an angel—has appeared to me. Running the church is a fulltime job and my life, our life, is taking us in a totally opposite direction. I want to do what I've been doing these last six months—follow God totally."

"Is that your idea, or is that something you sense when you pray?"

"Both. I'm going to meet with Steve and Alan about it when I get back from Chicago."

"Think you can talk to them without it getting out to everyone?"

"We'll see." He looked at her. "We've followed the Holy Spirit every step of the way. We did everything we thought He was showing us. I think this is the next step."

"People will think we're crazy."

"But if God is speaking to us—and I'm sure He is—then we have to obey. And the consequences will sort themselves out."

"Okay." Sue paused to take a breath.

"What are you thinking?"

"About packing all those boxes when we move." She gave him a quick hug. "Go take a shower. You smell like you've been riding on an airplane." She turned away and opened the phone book. "I'll call the airlines and see what they have for a flight to Chicago in the morning."

chapter 37

Late the next afternoon David arrived in Chicago. He rented a car and drove to the hospital. An aide at the front desk directed him to the fifth floor, where a nurse met him at the elevator and escorted him down the hall toward Anna's room. "This won't be easy for you." Then she pushed open the door.

Overhead lights inside the room were out. The curtains were drawn over the windows. A nightlight in the corner provided the only illumination. David made his way to the end of the bed and looked down at his sister. What he saw was more grim than he had expected.

Anna laid motionless, eyes closed, feet wide apart, hands at her side. It seemed an odd position for one to sleep. David was shocked to discover she was in restraints. Webbed straps fastened to her ankles and attached to the bed frame kept her feet anchored to opposite corners of the bed. Straps on her wrists tied her arms to the bedrails on either side. The thought of being confined like that made David feel claustrophobic. He moved near the window and pushed back the curtain to look out.

"They like them closed," Anna whispered.

He turned to see her eyes focused on his and smiled. "Will they give me demerits?"

Tears filled her eyes. "I didn't mean for you to come back so soon."

He moved near the bed. In spite of Anna's restraints, he reached down and took hold of her hand. "I wouldn't be anywhere else."

Her lips trembled and tears seeped from the corners of her eyes. "I'm sorry. I feel so ashamed."

"No," he whispered, patting her hand gently. "You don't have to be ashamed."

"Yes," she nodded. "I do. I should be stronger. Like you."

David rubbed the back of her hand. "You are strong. Why the restraints?"

"I guess Tom told you about the cancer—a brain tumor. Sometimes I have seizures. They don't want me to hurt myself or fall out of bed," she sobbed.

"What happened?"

"I don't know," she grimaced. "I was so dizzy." She looked away. "And then I guess I collapsed. Tom found me on the floor. They've given me something to help me sleep. Otherwise terrible things happen when I sleep."

"Like what?"

"Things come alive."

"What kinds of things?"

"Awful things." She moved her head to the side and sniffed.

David took a tissue from a box on the table by the bed and wiped her nose. "Thanks," she chuckled. "You didn't have to come all the way back up here to wipe my nose."

"Don't worry about it." David dropped the tissue on the tabletop and took another. "Here, let's wipe it again." He ran the tissue over her nose.

"In my dreams I'm always a little girl. I'm asleep ... lying in my bed and a man comes in the room. I hear him breathing and smell his breath. He stops at my bed, and I want to scream, but I can't. Then the next thing I know, I'm outside and I hear voices yelling inside the house. I run to the window and look inside and see a man beating Mom." She glanced at David. "Then the man looks up and sees me, and I see his face. It's Dad's face, and he starts toward the door, yelling at me."

"What does he say?"

"I can never hear the words. I mean, I hear him yelling. And he's saying words. But I can never quite make them out."

David squeezed her hand. "I had dreams like that, only he was kicking and beating me."

Anna had a startled look. "You had them too?

"Yes."

"Why? Why did he do that? Why did he do those things to us?"

"He gave us what he had to give."

Anna snapped, "What exactly does that mean? He knew what he was doing was wrong."

"Yes, he did."

"Then why, David? Why?"

"I don't know." He turned the conversation back to her. "You dream about this every time you sleep?"

"Almost." She tipped her head back and sniffed again. "That's why I'm glad the drugs they're giving me make me sleep."

He leaned over and kissed the back of her hand. "I'm glad Tom found you."

"Why?"

"We need you here with us."

She stared at him as if she didn't know what to say, then she pressed him. "And you had bad dreams?"

"Yes. But not now."

She looked curious. "How? How did you get rid of them?"

"I went to see Dad."

Her eyes opened wide. "You saw him?"

"Yes," David nodded, concerned. He had told her all of this when he had visited her just a few days ago. Maybe the brain tumor was affecting her memory.

"What happened?" she asked.

"I asked him to forgive me."

Anna was angry. "What for? What did you ever do to him?"

"I hated him."

She looked up at the ceiling. "I hate him too," she sighed. "I used to think I didn't, but I realize now I do. Whenever I said I didn't, what I really meant was I knew I wasn't supposed to." She turned her eyes toward David. "But I do."

"I realized I hated him too, and I realized that wasn't right. God wanted me to repent. So, I went out to his trailer and asked him to forgive me."

"What happened?"

David smiled. "A ton of bitterness rolled off my back."

"Wow. What did he say?"

"He said he should be asking me for forgiveness."

Her eyes opened wide. "He said that? That's...like...admitting he did wrong."

"He did," David nodded. "He admitted it."

Her eyes darted away. "I wish he would tell *me* he was sorry. He did terrible things to me. Almost every night. Right there in the room. With you and the boys sleeping just down the hall. Every time he came in I tried to make myself small, so maybe he couldn't see me." She moved her feet and tried to reposition her hips in the bed. "I can't get comfortable. Can you take the straps off my ankles?"

"I don't think I should."

"Yeah, I guess you're right." She took a deep breath.

The door to the room swung open. David turned to see a woman, a little over five feet tall, with brown hair and green eyes. She wore a dark blue dress and over it was a white lab coat. Her eyes darted from David to Anna and back to David. She thrust out her hand. "I'm Dr. Janet Harper, Anna's neuro-oncologist. You must be her brother."

"Yes, David Ellis," David replied, shaking her hand.

"Your sister has been through quite a lot." The doctor moved around the bed to Anna's side. "But I think we've got her stabilized." She looked back at David. "Would you excuse us for a few minutes?"

"Sure." David backed toward the door. He looked at Anna. "I'll be out in the hall."

Twenty minutes later the doctor emerged from the room. "I gave her something to help her sleep now. She was pretty excited by your visit. If you want to say goodnight, you'd better go in now to see her."

"Okay." David went back into the room and saw that Anna was fading fast. "Hey, I'll come back in the morning. We can talk some more."

"Okay," Anna replied, her voice already groggy. "We can talk some more. I just can't…hold my eyes…open right now."

David moved beside her and squeezed her hand. "I love you, Anna."

With her eyes closed, her breathing slowed to the regular rhythm of sleep. David stood quietly beside her, watching her as she slept. In his mind he saw her as the little girl he remembered, always so alive and ready for whatever came their way. A sense of sadness swept over him as he realized that playfulness had been stolen from her. "I forgive him," he whispered. "I forgive him for stealing the joy."

David backed away from the bed and crossed the room to the door. Dr. Harper was waiting in the hall when he came out. "Asleep already?"

"Yes," he replied. "I think so."

"Thanks for coming all the way up here. You live in North Carolina?"

"Yes. Charlotte."

"I wanted to ask you some questions about her." They started down the hall. The doctor straightened her lab coat. "Anna mentioned she was having nightmares. She was so hysterical that when I asked about them, she told me most of them involved her father. Were you aware of that?"

"Not until just now. I haven't seen much of Anna in the last ten years. She and I have always had a good rapport, but we haven't visited much. I was the oldest and got away from home first. I guess maybe my siblings felt abandoned. Anna was right. Our childhood wasn't at all pleasant."

"How did you get away?"

"Joined the army."

"And you're a minister now?"

"Yes."

They stopped near the elevator. Dr. Harper checked her watch. "Would you like some coffee?"

"Sure," David nodded.

"Let's go downstairs." She pressed a button for the elevator. "I have a few more questions I'd like to ask. It's important that I know as much as possible about Anna. When someone is as ill as she is, we need to treat the whole person—mind and body."

chapter 38

David rode in the elevator with the doctor to the ground floor then walked with her down the corridor to the cafeteria. It was all but deserted when they arrived. They got a cup of coffee and sat at a table on the far side of the room. He took a sip and looked across the table at her.

"What did you want to ask, Dr. Harper?"

"Anna was unconscious when they brought her in. When I went in to see her before bedtime, she talked about the nightmares. They kept recurring and got so bad she couldn't sleep. She thought maybe they were the result of the tumor."

David looked down at his coffee cup. They sat in silence a moment before the doctor continued. "Tell me more about your father and why he has such a hold over Anna."

"What about him?"

"What was he like? What did he do?"

"He was in the construction business."

"He had his own company?"

"Yes," David nodded. "Excavation business. He had a bulldozer, couple of tractors, a truck or two to haul them around." David took a sip of coffee. "Our mother actually ran the business. She kept the books, looked after the money. He can't read or write well."

"Anna must have worked hard to convince herself she had a typical childhood."

"How long have you been seeing her?"

"About four months."

"Four months?"

"Yes. Why? You seem surprised."

"She was at my mother's funeral, back in the summer. She didn't tell us then that she was seeing an oncologist." He paused. "Well, I guess, to be more accurate, I should say she implied that she was seeing someone. I don't know what I thought, but it certainly wasn't a cancer specialist."

"Interesting. So David, tell me about your childhood. I gather it wasn't typical?"

"Hardly! Our father says he's a Christian. Our mother was Jewish. He hates Jews. She hated Christians. He beat our mother and he beat us boys—there were three of us."

Dr. Harper had a pained expression. "You mean, with his fists?"

"Fists, coat hangers, belts. His favorite thing was an extension cord."

Her eyes were wide. "An extension cord?"

"An electrical extension cord. Used it like a whip. It drew blood rather quickly."

"I had no idea," she gasped. "He beat your sister?"

"Not to my knowledge. I found out later that he did much worse to her. He raped Anna. She was still pretty young when I joined the army."

"When you say he raped your sister, you mean this happened on one occasion?"

"No. It apparently occurred regularly. He came to Anna in her bedroom, which was next to the bedroom where my brothers and I slept."

The doctor shook her head. "That explains a lot about the nightmares."

"And it explains a lot to me too."

"What do you mean?"

.

"She has been trying hard to give the appearance that she's coping with her past, dealing with it, not afraid to delve into it to find answers. But really, all she's been doing is giving the outward appearance. She hasn't dealt with much of anything. Can that hamper her chances of a full recovery?"

"It can take away her will to live and make my work even harder." She took another sip of coffee. "Does the word 'Pasco' mean anything to you? I was in her room last night when she was moaning and crying? She kept repeating Pasco."

"That was the street where we lived. In Indian Orchard, Massachusetts. Why?"

"As she was regaining consciousness she kept saying that word over and over. Pasco. And it sounded like she was saying something else with it, but I couldn't understand it, and she didn't remember it once she was awake."

Tears filled David's eyes. "Don't take me home to Pasco," he whispered in sing-song fashion, "until I've had my dough-no's, from Dunkin' Ds."

Dr. Harper's face lit up. "That's what she was saying. Say it again."

David smiled sadly. "Don't take me home to Pasco, until I've had my dough-no's, from Dunkin' Ds."

"What is that?"

David wiped his face with his hand. "Our father made us go to church with him on Sunday mornings. Halfway through the service they sent us out to Sunday school. We went to the class at first, but after I got older, I realized no one would check up on us to see if we were really there. So I convinced my brothers and Anna we could go down the street to Dunkin' Donuts and get back before anyone noticed."

He wiped his eyes with a paper napkin. "Anna was a little girl at the time. She was always making up some rhyme about whatever she was doing. She made up that ditty one Sunday when we were walking down there. It didn't exactly rhyme, but we couldn't stop her from saying it. She said it all the time around the house." David smiled. "I was afraid Dad would hear her and realize what we had been doing, but he never did."

She looked at him. "What was it? Say it one more time."

David felt his cheeks grow warm with embarrassment. "Don't take me home to Pasco, until I've had my dough-no's, from Dunkin' Ds."

Dr. Harper slid her chair back. "That does give me a bit more insight. I'm sorry, I wish we could talk more now, but I have another patient to see. Thank you for sharing so much of your childhood with me. I'm hopeful this will help me in treating Anna."

They stood and walked back to the elevator. David joined her when the doors opened. "I want to look in on my sister once more."

"Of course," she smiled.

When he walked into the room Anna's eyes opened. "I'm sorry. I didn't mean to waken you."

"It's okay. I doze off and on. I'm glad you came back."

David reached into his pocket. "Anna, I brought you something. I found it at the house on Pasco Road."

"What could I possibly want from that old place?"

David placed the small doll on the bed beside Anna and watched as tears filled her eyes. "I can't believe it was still there. You remember that Christmas? This was the only gift I got." She yawned, and she looked exhausted.

David stroked her hair back from her forehead. "Rest now. I'll see you in the morning."

chapter 39

David left the hospital and drove across town to Anna's apartment. A tall, slender man with curly hair and broad shoulders answered the door. David greeted him with a smile.

"You must be Tom."

"Yes. And you are?"

"David Ellis. Anna's brother."

"Tom opened the door wider and stepped aside. "Come on in. I was hoping you'd come by."

David stepped inside. Tom closed the door and pointed to a chair across the room. "Have a seat. Could I get you anything?"

"No. I'm fine."

David took a seat on the sofa. Tom sat in the chair to the left. "I'm sure Anna was glad to see you."

"She seemed to be."

"I told her I had called you."

"Good." David glanced around the room. "I talked to Dr. Harper. She said you stayed with Anna until the ambulance arrived."

Tom looked away. "I didn't know what happened at first. Then, after the ambulance came they started asking questions, and I told them about the cancer. I've been sleeping here on the couch since her pain has gotten so much worse. She's been having some really bad nightmares. Kicking and yelling. It was really scary sometimes. I guess it's the tumor." A whistle from a teakettle interrupted him. He glanced over his shoulder in the direction of the noise then looked back at David. "You sure you don't want something? I was about to fix a cup of hot tea."

"That would be great."

Tom stood. "Just a minute and I'll get it." He moved across the room and disappeared around the corner. "I have regular old Lipton and Earl Grey," he called out.

"I'll have whatever you're having," David replied. He stood and wandered over to a bookshelf on the wall by the door. On it he found a row of science fiction novels and three books about Scientology.

Tom entered the room carrying a tray with a teapot and two cups. David turned from the bookshelf and gestured over his shoulder. "You a follower of Scientology?"

"No." Tom set the tray on a table near the sofa. "That's Anna's book. I do read the science fiction, but I'm not into L. Ron Hubbard."

David sat back down and reached for the cup Tom handed him. "This is Earl Grey. I was never much of a tea drinker until I met Anna. She drinks hot tea all the time."

David took the cup. "I think it must be a family trait." He stirred in a spoonful of sugar and rested the cup on his hand in his lap. "Was she really into Scientology or just interested in the book?"

"Dr. Harper got her into it." Tom took a sip of tea. "She said she thought it might help her to find peace." He shrugged. "I'm Catholic. I don't go for that kind of thing, but Anna needed some help, so I didn't say much about it."

"Was she just grasping for something?"

Tom gave David a knowing look. "She was pretty much into it, or as into it as you can get in a month." He set his teacup aside. "You want something to eat with your tea? We have some muffins. Anna made them day before yesterday."

"No," David shook his head. "I'm okay." He took a sip of tea. "Did she think all this Scientology stuff was working?"

"It seemed to work for a while, at first."

"Is she still able to work?"

"Some. She had a job at CBOT for a while. In the back office."

"CBOT?"

"Chicago Board of Trade. Big commodities trading house downtown. Corn, wheat, cattle futures. She worked in the back office, processing paperwork for all the trades on the floor. That's where we met."

"You worked with her?"

"I'm a trader."

"Sounds interesting."

"A little intense, but it can be profitable."

"So, when did Anna go to Dr. Harper?"

"She said she wasn't feeling quite right—like she was a few degrees off center. She saw one doctor who just thought she was depressed. Anna seemed to know instinctively there was something more. Finally, another doctor suggested she see a neurologist."

"Good advice. How'd she find Janet Harper?"

"My mother has a friend who sees her."

They talked a little longer about Anna and her struggle to cope with life in the '80s. It all had a cloak of sophistication, but no doubt it was a big part of Anna's inability to find peace. He wanted to say more, but in his spirit he felt a restraint. Instead, he sipped from his cup of tea and listened.

Finally, it was time to go. David set the cup on the tray and stood. Tom rose from his chair. "Sure you won't spend the night?"

"No," David replied. "Thank you. I already have a room at a hotel near the hospital."

"Where are you staying?"

"At the Holiday Inn."

"Be careful. That area isn't too safe at night."

"I'll be asleep before the nightlife gets active."

"I've tried to do what's best for Anna, without just telling her what to do."

"I understand." David stepped toward the door. "Thanks."

As David moved down the hall toward the elevator, he whispered a prayer. "Lord, break through this confusion. Wipe away the lies and deception. Let Your light shine on Anna and on Tom. Please let them know You are the only way, the only truth, and the only source of life." He pressed the button for the elevator. "Reveal Yourself to them in a strong and powerful way. And break this disillusion from Anna's mind."

chapter 40

David returned to the hospital the following morning. "I was hoping you'd come," she smiled brightly. He sat on the edge of the bed, slipped an arm around her shoulder, and gave her a hug.

David noticed that her restraints were gone. "How was your night? Did you sleep well?"

"Yes, I did," she replied. "I had an interesting dream. Tom called. I was just telling him about it."

"It wasn't a nightmare?"

"No." Anna shook her head. "I was standing in the yard. There was shouting and screaming from inside the house, but I was watching you walk down the street, away from me. And there was this really bright light. You were walking toward it, and it was swallowing you up."

David propped his hand against the frame of the bed. "How did it make you feel?"

"Peaceful. Even though everything at the house was still the same, I was feeling really peaceful."

David slid off the bed and walked to the window. He inwardly prayed and then turned to her. "Anna, maybe you should talk to Dad. Bring the things that happened into the open instead of hiding from them. And let God heal you from the pain that's locked in those memories."

Anna looked startled, but she paused to think before saying, "I've never heard of such a thing. Will it work?"

"That's what Yona's been telling me."

"Yona?"

"The lady we met at the funeral. Said she knew Mom and us."

Anna leaned her head back against the pillow. "Do you remember her? Because I sure don't."

"I don't know who she is or how she knows what she knows." David leaned against the window.

"Maybe we're both going crazy," Anna whispered weakly.

"Or," David suggested, "Maybe God is speaking to us."

"Would you stop with that God stuff," Anna complained.

David had a twinkle in his eye. "What if she is an angel?"

"I wondered how long it would take for you to suggest that."

"Don't you remember the stories we used to talk about in Sunday school when we were kids? About angels who looked like ordinary people? Like in Scripture. 'Entertaining angels unaware.'"

Anna sat with her eyes fixed on a spot in the corner. "I tried to forget whatever they said at that church. Those people were so blind. Not one of them realized what was happening to us." Then she grinned. "I only remember the doughnuts."

"You remember the doughnuts?"

"Yes." She stared up at the ceiling. "I was so scared Dad would find out what happened, but I loved those doughnuts."

"Do you—" David started to ask her about the ditty she used to sing as they walked from church, but then thought better of it.

Anna looked back at him. "So, if Yona is an angel, and God is speaking to us through her, then what is He saying?"

"He's telling us we should forgive Dad."

"Maybe I could talk to him." Anna looked thoughtful. "I could even see him, but I don't know if I could ever forgive him. There was a time when I didn't even want to acknowledge he existed. He would have kept doing all those things to me, too, if Mother hadn't stopped him."

"Stopped him?" David frowned.

"Yeah," Anna nodded. "That's why she left him. She saw him coming after me one night. She threatened him with the fireplace poker and said she wasn't letting that happen again." Anna bit her lip and looked at David. "Not again."

"She said that?"

"Yes," Anna insisted. "She said she made a mistake with all of us, letting him beat us and be mean to us because she was too scared to do anything, like maybe it would bring peace if she just took it, or maybe he would quit if she didn't confront him. But she said she was wrong, and she'd been wrong all along, and she wasn't taking it any more."

David shook his head. "Every time I talk about what happened to us it gets more and more real."

"You got out." Anna's voice was curt. "You didn't see the half of it."

"He tried to kill me."

"A lot of things died in that house," Anna grumbled. "But that's when she packed us up and we went to Aunt Eliana's house. Then Aunt Eliana took us to that cousin's house in New York."

"You remember going to the cousin's house?"

"I do now. We didn't stay there long. I can't remember his name."

"Richard," David offered. "Richard Holberg."

"Yeah." Anna's face brightened. "That's him. And then we moved into that apartment in Brooklyn. I think about that place a lot." For the first time that morning Anna smiled. "Mom and I had one bedroom. Henry and Pete had the other." She shook her head. "That place was small." She had a faraway look in her eyes. "I saw Dad one time after that."

David moved his hands to his side. "When was that?"

"He was on the street one day. Sitting on a bench outside our apartment."

"Why was he there?"

"I don't know. I didn't talk to him. I think Mom talked to him, but I don't know what they said." Anna smoothed the sheet with her hand.

"I haven't talked to him since the day we left. He went to work, and as soon as he was gone, Mom told us to pack up." David's eyes widened in recognition and Anna's face lit up again. "See. You do remember it."

"I didn't before you started talking about it. Mom wrote to me that she had left Dad. She told me where to write her." David paused and walked over to take her hand. "This is why we should talk to him. I know it's painful, but we can't get rid of the pain by forgetting. The pain has to come out, or we'll just continue suffering from trying to hold it inside."

chapter 41

David spent the remainder of the day visiting with Anna and asking Dr. Harper questions. That evening he found a local restaurant and finally took time to eat. As he sat at a table that overlooked Chicago's waterfront and Lake Michigan, his mind was far less serene than the view. He was startled when he felt someone tap him on the shoulder. David turned in his chair and there stood Yona, all five feet of her.

David was stunned. "Yona! What are you doing in Chicago?"

"I'm here for Anna. A close friend told me she was in the hospital."

David hurriedly stood and pulled out a chair. "Please sit. Will you eat with me? I'll get a menu."

"David, David, slow down. First, I'm not hungry. And secondly, you need to take a deep breath, relax, and tell me what's going on with you."

"I'm concerned about Anna," David began.

"Is she better now?"

"I'm not so sure. She's better now than when they took her in. I'm not so sure about her doctor, though, Dr. Janet Harper."

"You don't like her doctor?"

"She seems nice enough, and I think she knows what she's doing as a doctor, but she's gotten Anna involved in Scientology. Anna hasn't really dealt with all the pain of her past, and she's looking for a panacea.

She hasn't found a release from it, and she's not going to find it in Scientology." He took a drink of water.

"Anna is on the way to getting better. You'll see. Just trust in the Lord with all your heart, David, and don't lean on your own understanding."

David was stunned. She was repeating the same scripture to him that he was given before his mother's funeral. "Yona, I was with her all day. We talked about a lot of things, but we never talked about the cancer or her prognosis. We ignored the elephant in the room and just talked as if it didn't exist. We spent the entire day talking about our childhood. I thought of things today I haven't remembered in years."

"That was good."

"I guess so. She's been having nightmares too. Apparently they've been getting worse and worse. She said she was sleeping better in the hospital, but she still isn't ready to deal with the cause or the thought of talking to our father. You and I both know we can't ignore what happened to us or what it's doing to us now."

Yona looked intently at David. "When the time is right, David, she will listen to the truth. And she will be set free."

David paused long enough to take long drink of water. "I've had nightmares for as long as I can remember, three and four nights a week, all of them about Dad chasing me, beating me, trying to kill me. It got so bad I woke up a few months ago and thought I was having a heart attack."

"But you weren't."

"No." He wiped his mouth with the napkin. "It was a panic attack. Not long after that, I started having muscle spasms in my neck and shoulders. I'd be doing whatever I normally do and suddenly my head would jerk all the way to one side, or down until my chin banged against my chest. It was terrible. They ran a bunch of tests, wanted to do more, and were talking about surgery. But I suspected what the problem was. I was just too scared to face it. And I didn't want to finally acknowledge the fact that our lives really were a mess. I mean, it's one thing to know you had a tough time. It's another to finally see yourself as a wounded person."

"Wounded. When I hear that word I always think about that wonderful scripture in Isaiah, 'He was wounded for our transgressions, bruised for our iniquities...and with his stripes we are healed.' God doesn't plan for us to go through life wounded—but healed. Anna is not hurting your father by hating him. Quite the opposite. Hatred kills from the inside out."

"I know." David took a bite. "That's just it." He paused to swallow. "We think that by hating him we're doing something to him. But actually, we're only doing something to ourselves. That's why I had to go to see him—to forgive him and ask him to forgive me. The first time I went out there, he didn't answer the door, so I opened it. He was asleep in his recliner. When I saw him, I got so scared I could hardly breathe. It was like I was a little kid all over again."

"What did he say when he saw you?"

"He leveled his shotgun at me and ordered me to leave."

"But I thought you said you asked him to forgive you?"

"I did. But that was later. After the panic attacks, the hospital, and all the tests. And after the trip to Israel. But it didn't accomplish what I wanted. I told myself I could work things out by learning about my Jewish heritage. Find out what it meant to be a Jew. That sort of thing. I learned a lot, but everywhere I turned, things kept pointing me back to Dad. Have I mentioned the guy I met in Israel to you before? Avi? He's a counselor. We hit it off. Spent an afternoon together. Saw things you can't see on the tour. And while we were doing that we talked."

"That made it easier, I'm sure," she nodded. And you don't have to worry about running into him at the grocery store. He said you should forgive your dad?"

"He said forgiveness could reach all the way down to the depths of those memories, and I could find healing."

"You remember now?"

"Not everything. But as I do, I forgive him each time. I say the words 'I forgive you.'" David took another bite and swallowed. "I say it out loud. 'I forgive you.'"

"And the spasms and the nightmares haven't come back."

"No, they haven't. I still have a twitch now and then. The nerve condition is real. It's affected by stress, and it's actually a diagnosable, physical condition. But the nightmares are gone, and the panic attacks are gone."

"And your wife? How did Sue react to all this?"

"Sue has been a rock. She helped me, encouraged me, held my feet to the fire, made me face things I didn't want to face."

"She's a strong person."

"Very strong. You should come visit us. You'd enjoy the chance to get to know her better."

Yona nodded and asked, "How are your children?"

"They're fine. Growing up fast." David smiled at her. "I'm serious. Thanksgiving is only a couple of weeks away. Come visit us. Eat some turkey. See North Carolina."

Yona smiled cryptically. "Maybe."

chapter 42

After two days in Chicago David stopped by the hospital to tell Anna goodbye before catching a noon flight for Charlotte. He was amazed at how much better she looked. She was still weak, but Dr. Harper had said she could go home in a couple of days if she continued to gain strength.

As they said their farewells, David leaned down and kissed her on the forehead. "If you can, will you think about coming to be with us on Thanksgiving? I know you don't feel like doing anything right now, but just think about it. You don't even have to call. If you're up to it, just come."

"I won't make any promises, but I'd love to see your family and spend the holiday with you. I'll think about it and let you know, okay?"

"Sure, Sis. And I'm praying for you. God loves you, and so do I!"

After another hug, David backed out of the hospital room and gave Anna a last wave. He drove to O'Hare Airport, checked in his rental car, and boarded his flight to Charlotte. Sue picked him up at the airport and drove him to the church. David had called Alan Scruggs from Chicago and asked if they could meet as soon as he got home. He and Sue arrived at the church a little before four.

"You want me to wait?"

"No." David leaned across the seat and kissed her. "Just pick me up in an hour."

"Think it won't take longer than that?"

"I don't think so." David climbed from the car. He glanced back at her. "And pray."

"I already am."

The receptionist was gone from her desk when David entered the building. He gathered his phone messages from the box and started down the hall. Alan and Steve were waiting for him when he arrived in the office.

Steve looked up as he entered. "How was Chicago?"

"Good. I think my sister is doing better."

Alan took a seat in front of the desk. "Great news. Now, what's this about?"

David moved behind the desk and sat down. "I think you both know that my life has been going in a different direction lately."

"You've been out of the office a lot," said Steve, sitting in the other chair across from him.

"Right. But it's not just being out of the office. I've been growing in other directions. When I went to my mother's funeral, I began to embrace my Jewish heritage. And more has been happening with me than just that. I think you two have sensed the changes yourself. Some of the members have as well."

"Yeah," Steve shrugged. "There has been some talk about why you're taking Torah classes at the synagogue. But that's not really a problem. And, I've told the ones who came to me about you being gone so much that you were dealing with physical challenges and, of course, the death of your mother as well as the illness of your sister."

Alan spoke up. "Well, I've heard some of them wondering why they don't see you in the pulpit as much, or see you around the church." He crossed his legs. "I mean, it's true. You've been gone quite a lot. We've had to shift more duties to Steve to cover everything."

David leaned forward. "I'll make this as uncomplicated for you as I can. I'm not the same man I was when I came here. And I'm not the same man I was six months ago. I think it's time for us to acknowledge that God is moving me in a different direction. And, to acknowledge that He is moving Steve in a new direction as well."

Steve sat up straight, a concerned look on his face. "You want to resign? When?"

"Christmas is approaching. I don't think it's a good idea for me to leave now. Not that you can't handle things, but it seems rude to drop a transition like this on you, the staff, and the congregation right now, when everyone's focusing on the holidays."

Alan propped his elbows on the armrest. "I agree, but I don't think it's a good idea to have you here and not here at the same time. I mean, from an organizational point of view, if you're here people will always come to you first, and if they disagree with Steve they'll come to you to take their side." He glanced over at Steve. "And you'll be tempted to defer to David whenever a question arises."

David laced his fingers together. "What do you suggest?"

Alan leaned back in his chair. "You've taken this church places no one thought we'd ever go. What we've become came straight from your leadership."

"That was the Holy Spirit's leadership."

"Just the same, you were the guy on the ground getting it done. I think we should honor what God has done here through you. I suggest we move you to a transitional status beginning in January. Keep you on salary until...the end of June. You can continue to live in the parsonage until then, and we'll keep you on the medical plan. What do you think?" He glanced over at Steve and then back to David. "In January you would move all of your things out," he gestured toward the room, "and let Scott set up his office in here; but I think we should help you do whatever it is God is calling you to do, rather than just saying goodbye."

David's eyes were full. "That would be a blessing."

"It would be a blessing to you and to us. We'd have time to figure out our direction while you're still around in case of an emergency, and you can use the time to get things set up for what you're doing too. What do you plan to do?"

"I'm not sure how the details will work out, but I think I'm going to do something with Israel. Building bridges between Christians and Jews. That sort of thing."

"On your own? We should probably talk about not diverting donors from the church to your new ministry. I think if you do, there will be some hard feelings here."

"But there are also some people here who are interested in what I'm doing."

"I'm not saying they can't be involved in both. I'm just saying I don't think it would be right for you to solicit our best financial supporters for your work, to the detriment of the church."

"I would never do that."

"I understand. I just wanted us to talk about it."

"Well, now that you brought that up," David looked over at Steve again, "do you want me to attend church somewhere else during the transition time?"

"I don't know. Maybe we should see how that goes. You could come some, and be away some." He shifted positions. "I think the way to handle that would be to announce this in January, have a Sunday service in February or March when we gather the elders at the altar and lay hands on you and commission you for the work you're moving into. Send you out with a blessing and an anointing. And rather than severing ties with you, we bless what God is doing through you." He looked over at Alan. "I think we should do what you said about salary and benefits, but I think he should get the house for as long as he wants to live there. We're fine living right where we are." He smiled, "I don't think Linda would be interested in moving."

Alan nodded. "That sounds good. I think the board will agree."

"Good," David grinned. "That would be great."

Steve scooted forward in his chair. "I think we should pray for David right now." He reached over the desktop and took David's hand. Alan came from his chair and rested his hands on David's shoulders. Then Steve began to pray.

When they finished praying, David left the office and retraced his steps past the receptionist's desk to the front door. The cool, crisp air made his skin tingle as he made his way across the parking lot. Oak trees stood like stark sentinels, their bare branches gray against the blue Carolina sky. Off to the right the afternoon sun sank toward the horizon. Soon it would be out of sight. He glanced around at the campus with its manicured lawn and stately buildings. He had worked hard to make all this happen. Last year, he would have been devastated to think it might all slip from his control. And now, it seemed as though a great weight had been lifted from his shoulders—like the day he finally asked Wally to forgive him, only better.

"I don't know how I'm going to do this," he whispered, "but I'm not worried a bit."

A car horn sounded. David glanced over his shoulder to see the Caprice on the far side of the lot. Sue waved to him through the windshield. He crossed the pavement and got in on the passenger's side. Sue gave him an expectant look. "Well, how did it go?"

"It went great," David beamed.

"They weren't angry?"

"No, not at all. In fact, they were glad for what we're doing and offered to help. Looks like we can stay in the house as long as we want. They want me to move out of my office in January, but they'll keep paying me through June. They'll keep us on the medical plan until then too."

"They said that? And Alan agreed to it?"

"The salary and insurance was his idea."

"Wow. I'll have to change my opinion of him."

"They want to announce my resignation in January, and then have a commissioning service sometime in the spring. Make it a time of acknowledging what God is doing and of blessing us."

Tears filled Sue's eyes. "I never thought this would happen."

"I know." He took her hand. "It's pretty amazing."

As tears trickled down Sue's cheeks she gestured with her free hand toward the lawn around them. "Look at this. This was nothing but a cow pasture when we got here." She looked across the seat at David. "Do you remember that day? The first time we drove out here. We parked right where we're sitting now and you said, 'This could be a beautiful place for people to find Jesus.' You remember that?"

"I do. I saw it. It was like a vision." He had a satisfied smile. "I saw just about what we have here now. The lawn. The buildings. The trees. And all the people being saved and growing up in God." David rubbed her shoulder. "Something new is happening."

Sue wiped her cheeks with her hands and put the car in gear. "Well, if it's anything like what we've seen so far, it'll be something wonderful." A grin spread across her face. "You know, they have a name for people who get messages from God and encounter Him through visions and voices: Prophet."

"You are my biggest fan," David chuckled. He leaned over and rested his head on her shoulder. "What would I do without you?"

"I don't know, but you better sit up straight. I can't drive with you leaning on me."

chapter 43

A little after eleven o'clock on Thanksgiving morning, a taxi slowed in front of David's house. He watched through a window in the dining room as it turned into the driveway and came to a stop. The rear door swung open and out stepped his sister, Anna. A grin spread across David's face. He called to Sue. "Better set another place at the table."

"Why?"

"Anna's here."

Sue started from the kitchen. "David, that's wonderful! The guest room's ready for her. Thank God she must have felt well enough to come."

Megan walked into the room carrying a handful of cloth napkins. "Why is that taxi in our driveway?"

"Anna's here." David walked toward the front door.

Megan placed the napkins on the table. "Aunt Anna! The one who has cancer?"

"Yes, apparently the chemo and radiation have helped. She called last week and asked if she could come, providing she felt like it. I told her we'd rejoice with her if she could make the trip," Sue replied. "Set another place."

David opened the door and started outside. Anna stood by the taxi, her back to the house, a suitcase at her side. She looked frail, but there was a resoluteness about her despite her head being wrapped in a colorful scarf. David supposed she had lost her hair as a result of the treatments.

Joel came behind David. "I'll get her bags," he offered. David tousled his hair as he moved past.

Anna paid the driver then turned to face David. "You said to come see you for Thanksgiving. I didn't think about calling until I was already in the air."

"This is great," David beamed. "You don't know how happy you've made me. I'm so glad you came."

By then Joel was at Anna's side. She looked at him. "You must be my nephew."

"Yes, ma'am."

"Hi Joel. I'm Anna, your aunt."

"I'm glad to meet you," he smiled. "We've heard a lot about you."

"Oh, you have?"

"Yes, ma'am."

"Well, I hope you believed the good and forgot the bad."

Joel grinned. "It was all good." He picked up the suitcase and started toward the house.

David slipped an arm around Anna's shoulders and gave her a hug. "I hope you're hungry."

"I am, actually. I've gotten a little of my appetite back."

"Good. Sue likes to cook for the holidays, and we're so happy to have you here. There's time for you to have a rest before dinner if you'd like."

"That sounds good. I think I will."

David smiled as he led his sister inside the house and upstairs to the guest room. *Maybe God will open the door, and I'll have a chance to share my faith with her while she's here.*

That afternoon, after everyone had eaten their fill of turkey and dressing, potato-and-cheese casserole, seven-layer salad, and made-from-scratch yeast rolls topped off with apple dumplings and ice cream for dessert, Sue rose from the table. "Megan, you and Joel come help me in the kitchen."

While they were busy in the kitchen, David turned to Anna. "Feel like a short walk?"

When Anna nodded that she did, he grabbed her coat. "Then let's go."

They made their way down the front sidewalk to the driveway and then out to the street. David shoved his hands in his pockets. "I really am glad you came to see us."

"I thought about what you said."

"What was that?"

"About how we've all tried to repress the memories from our childhood, and how that just locked the pain of those events inside. And then it comes out somewhere else."

"That's what happened to me."

"I suppose you're right."

"You seem to be better, though."

"That's just it. I'm not."

"What's wrong?"

"The doctor says the cancer has metastasized. I now have cervical cancer."

"Anna, no!" David was stricken and stopped. He took his hands out of his pockets and drew her to him.

"Yes." She rested her head on his chest. "Isn't it ironic? I've never been with anyone else, only our father. And now I have cancer of the cervix."

"I'm so sorry." David shuddered at the thought of the misery she faced. A feeling of helplessness swept over him. "It's not supposed to be like that."

"I know," she sighed. "But it is. And I wonder if somehow it isn't because I kept everything bottled up inside."

"Perhaps." David left his arm around her shoulders and they began to walk again. "When did they diagnose you?"

"Not long after you left."

He stared down at the pavement. "What kind of treatment are they giving you?"

"They aren't."

David looked up, his eyes alert. "What do you mean?"

"It's rather advanced." Anna sighed. "And I didn't want to go through all that again anyway."

David sighed and prayed inwardly. Then he asked, "Were you thinking about seeing Dad?"

"Don't you think I should?"

"Yes. I just don't want you to go out there thinking it will cure your cancer. I know I got better after I saw Dad, but it doesn't always work that way."

"Well, I guess I know that. Maybe that's why I came. But I need to see him anyway, even if it doesn't." They walked a while in silence, then she said, "You think he'll be home tomorrow?"

"I'm sure he will. If not, he'll be down the road at Tiny's."

"Who is that?"

"It's not a who. It's a what. Tiny's is a beer joint."

"Oh. A tavern."

"In Chicago it might be a tavern," David laughed, "but here it's a beer joint."

"Is it safe?"

"It will be in the daytime."

David spotted an empty bench at the bus stop on the corner and steered Anna in that direction. They sat and conversation lagged. Then Anna asked, "So, what was that about the church? Everyone seemed to be talking around it at the table. They fired you?"

"No," David shook his head. "I resigned. We'll announce it in January, but that's what they were alluding to."

"You quit? Why?"

"I'm no longer the man they hired. I've changed. I think it began when I sat down next to Yona in the funeral home."

"She reminded you that you were Jewish."

"Yes, and she reminded me of things I'd always wanted to do."

"Like what?"

"I don't know, specifically. Just bigger and broader and…more strategic things. I know, it sounds silly."

"It sounds scary, just quitting like that with no real job to go to."

"I'll work until the end of the year. And they're going to continue to pay me through June. Also, we can live in the parsonage as long as we want."

"Still, it's a little risky."

"God isn't safe, Anna. Everyone wants Him to be the safe, loveable grandfather-in-the-sky. He's not safe. He's always good, but following Him isn't always a safe path."

"What about Yona? Ever figure out who she is?"

"I think she's an angel."

"I thought they had…wings or something."

"Some do. But the ones described in Scripture aren't all the same. Like we discussed at the hospital, some were so familiar they went unnoticed."

"I never thought of it like that."

"I just know Yona was at the funeral and at the house at 77 Pasco Road. And I know she was in Chicago. When I asked her who she was, she said she had been guiding me toward the light all my life. And she had me pinch her."

"Pinch her?" Anna asked.

"Yes. I told her to pinch me, so I could see if she was real or not. She stuck out her arm and told me to pinch her instead."

"And what did you feel?"

"The flesh of her arm."

Anna shivered and pulled her coat up around her neck.

"Getting cold?"

"A little."

"We should head back to the house." They turned around and started back the way they came. "Whoever Yona is, she led us into truth."

"Are you talking about the Bible again?"

"No. I'm talking about truth in a broader sense. The truth about our past, about our memories, about who we are. Jesus said, 'You shall know the truth, and the truth shall set you free.' He didn't just mean truths like you read in Scripture; He also meant the actual things that are true about our lives. I recovered the truth about my childhood, and rather than killing me it set me free."

"And Yona started you in that direction."

"Yona was doing what I guess she's always done." David shrugged. "That's how I see it."

chapter 44

After breakfast the following morning David and Anna walked from the house to the Caprice. She opened the door on the passenger side and paused to look at him over the top of the car. "You still think this is the right thing to do?"

"I know it's scary for you." He smiled at her. "But it's the right thing to do."

"You'll be there with me?"

"Yes." He nodded. "I'll be right there beside you. But you have to say the words."

"Okay."

They rode north into the rural countryside. A little over an hour later David turned the Caprice from the paved road onto the dirt road that led to Wally's driveway. At the mailbox he said quietly, "This is it."

Anna shifted positions in the seat and glanced out the window. "Does anyone live over there?" She pointed to the house beyond the overgrown fencerow.

"Yes," David replied. "It looks abandoned, but when I was out here before, someone actually spoke to me from over there. That's how I found out about Tiny's. The man told me where to find him."

"Maybe it was Yona."

"Maybe," David grinned. "I never thought about that. Though the voice sounded like a man." He eased the car past a mud hole at the end of the driveway and brought it to a stop near the front door of the trailer. He switched off the engine and looked over at Anna. "Are you okay?"

She took a deep breath. "I can tell you I'm more than a little nervous."

"It's all right. You aren't a young girl anymore." He touched her arm. "And I'm right here with you."

"Okay." She gave him a forced smile. "Let's go."

They got out of the car and walked to the steps that led up to the trailer door. Anna stood to one side. David rapped on the door. In a moment, the door opened and Wally appeared, dressed in dirty khaki work pants and a once-white t-shirt. His eyes darted from David to Anna and back to David. "Who is she?"

Anna spoke up. "Hello, Dad."

Wally stared at her a moment, then raised his hands in protest. "No." He shook his head. "No. I won't have it." He looked down at David standing near the bottom step. "Why did you bring her out here?" Wally's face turned red. "You stupid moron! Why did you bring her out here?"

"Dad, she ..."

"You did this to get back at me. For all the things I told you I done." Wally held the door with one hand and gripped the frame with the other. He leaned out in David's direction. "You're just like that Jew whore mother of yours!" he screamed. He turned to Anna. "And as for you, get off my property." Then he slammed the door shut.

Anna shrank back. "I had a feeling this wasn't going to work." She looked at David. "It's just too much for either of us."

"No." David squared his shoulders. "It's not going to end like this." He moved quickly up the steps, grabbed the doorknob, and jerked open the door.

He found Wally seated in the recliner. "I told you to leave!" he shouted. "And take her with you."

David was unmoved. "Dad, she's your daughter. She wants to talk to you, and you're going to listen."

"I don't have to listen to nothin' nobody's got to say. This is my trailer, on my property." Wally swung his legs to one side of the recliner and took hold of the armrest to push himself up. "I ain't got to—"

David thrust out his hand and caught Wally in the chest. "Sit back down."

Wally's eyes flashed. "You ain't never touched me and got away with it."

"I'm not a little boy anymore, Dad. You need to hear what Anna has to say."

Wally slumped back in the chair and covered his ears with his hands. "Don't say her name. Don't say her name. Don't say her name."

David pulled Wally's hands from his ears and leaned over at his side. "I think she's earned the right to be heard by you." Wally's eyes were wide. David continued. "Now, you're going to listen to what she has to say. You hear me?"

"I ain't got to listen to nothin'." Wally clamped his hands back over his ears.

David turned away and motioned for Anna. She came up the steps and through the doorway. David gestured with a nod toward Wally. She moved closer. Wally gripped the armrests with both hands and squeezed his eyes shut. Anna said quietly, "Dad, I wanted to talk to you."

With his eyes shut and his hands gripping the armrests, Wally rocked from side to side, a pained expression on his face. Anna nudged David and motioned for him to step back. As he did, Anna came nearer the recliner and knelt beside Wally. She reached out and placed her hand lightly on his arm. "Dad, will you forgive me for hating you?"

Wally's eyes opened. He stared at her a moment, tears filling his eyes to the brim. "I shoulda never done it," he said, slowly. "I shoulda never done those things to you." Tears spilled down his cheeks. "I was worse'n mean and awful, and I knowed better, but I didn't do right."

"Dad," Anna said softly. "I've hated you all my life. I'm sorry. Will you forgive me?"

He cried out, "'Course I forgive you. But I didn't think you could ever forgive me."

"Yes, Dad." She nodded. "I forgive you."

He reached out his hand to touch her then drew it back. "I ain't got no right," he muttered."

Anna took hold of his hand. "It's okay, Dad. It's okay."

"I don't deserve this," Wally sobbed. He looked up at David and back to Anna. "After all I done, I don't deserve to have none of you ever talk to me again."

"It's okay," Anna repeated.

"I don't know how y'all turned out so good and me so bad."

"Grace," David replied. "It was all by God's grace."

They talked a while longer, about Chicago and Anna's life there, about how awful things were in the past, and how it shouldn't have been that way. Somehow the subject of Anna's cancer never came up. Between tears and anguish mercy found a place in their hearts and slowly brought them together.

After a while the conversation lagged, and David knew it was time to go. Wally pushed himself up from his recliner, and Anna and David each hugged him before starting toward the door. As Anna reached to open it, she turned to David. "Tell him about Mom," she whispered.

David turned back to face Wally. "Dad." He took a deep breath. "Did you hear about Mom?"

"What about her?"

"Dad, she died."

"I know," he nodded. "Virgil Ellis called me."

David smiled. "Virgil does keep us all informed."

"Yeah. Me and him go way back. He calls me from time to time to tell me what's going on." Wally sniffed and shuffled his feet. "Anna, I hear you ain't doin' so good."

"No. She isn't," David answered. "Virgil knew about that? How'd he find out?"

"I don't know. Just called up here two or three weeks ago. Told me about it. Virgil's a good man. Me and his daddy was first cousins."

David looked at his father with a new compassion in his heart. "Dad, are you all right?"

"Yeah," he smiled. "I am now."

"I'm better too, Dad. Bye." Anna waved and had tears in her eyes as she went down the steps.

David followed her, and they both got into the car. Wally stayed in the doorway, watching them. David rolled down his window, stuck his head out, and said, "I'll see you again soon."

chapter 45

David and Anna drove back to Wiggins Road and turned toward Mooresville. He glanced in her direction. "Are you okay?"

"Yes. You were right. That was very…relieving."

"Rather ironic. You come away feeling clean, but the place is filthy. I'm not certain he ever takes a bath either." David checked the road then looked at her again. "Remember, the focus of this isn't on him. It's on you. He'll probably always come across as a dirty old man. I don't know. But you can be clean and fresh and new."

"How?"

"Surrender your life to God."

"How do I do that, David? All my life I've been searching for something to take away these feelings of shame." David started to interrupt but her hand went up to stop him. "No, no! I know what Dad did wasn't my fault. I know he was the one who was perverted. But I kept thinking I should have screamed or run away—something—anything."

Anna wiped the tears from her cheeks. "Did you know Yona came to see me in the hospital after you left? In her blunt but loving way she said I should forget all this New Age stuff and seek your God. I've been thinking about that a lot. I just don't know if I'm ready, and yet I may not have much time to make a decision."

David laid his hand on Anna's folded hands. "God is waiting for you when you're ready.

Sue was waiting in the den when they arrived home. David stopped at the kitchen sink to wash his hands. Anna made her way down the hall to the bathroom. Sue came to the counter. "How did it go? He didn't try to shoot anyone, did he?"

"No. Tried to make us leave at first, but I made him see her. I told him she'd earned the right to say what was on her mind, and he had to listen."

"I'm surprised he sat still for that."

"I didn't give him much choice."

Sue glanced over her shoulder toward the hallway and steered David into the den. Before she could say anything, Anna walked out of the bathroom. "I think I'll lie down for a while."

Sue waited until Anna had gone upstairs before asking, "Were you able to talk to Anna about God's love for her?"

"I broached the subject, but she's not quite ready to make a commitment."

Sue slipped her arm around his waist. "You did all you could. Now we just wait. What about your dad? Was he okay when you left him?"

"I guess so. He seemed to be. I told him about Mom dying, but he already knew. Then he said he had heard Anna had been in the hospital. Virgil had called to tell him."

Sue frowned. "How would Virgil Ellis know about that?"

"I don't know. Virgil seems to make our business his business. Some people are like that. There's one in every congregation."

"Maybe you should call your dad and check on him."

"I think I'll wait until morning. He'll probably be asleep by now anyway."

chapter 46

The following morning David drove out to Wally's trailer. Anna was exhausted and planned to spend a quiet day with Sue and the kids. David found Wally in the garage on his back beneath the pickup truck. Only his feet stuck out in view.

"Hey, Dad," David called.

"You come to help me, or ya just gonna stand around 'n talk?"

"What do you need?"

"That filter wrench layin' on the work bench."

David retrieved the wrench and handed it to Wally.

"Whacha doin' out here anyway? You was just here yesterday."

"I just wanted to check on you, that's all. Yesterday was a pretty traumatic day for you."

"I'm fine! I'm a tough old bird. Ya don't have to worry none 'bout me."

David nodded in agreement. "How about we get a bite of lunch before I head home, then?"

"We can go down the road to the burger place. They got cheap burgers." He added, "Let me get this oil in my truck."

Wally finished adding oil to the engine and checked it with the dipstick. Satisfied the crankcase was full, he slammed the hood closed and wiped his hands on the rag once more. "Come on," he said. "Let's go in the house and get washed up. I got somethin' I wanna show you."

David followed him across the yard and up the back steps to the trailer. Wally jerked open the door and stepped inside without waiting. The door bounced off the side of the trailer and swung back to close. David blocked it with his arm to avoid being hit in the head.

The back door led into the kitchen. A refrigerator stood to the left. The sink was next to it with the stove beyond that. The table sat to the right, and beyond was a door that led to the bedrooms. David heard Wally rustling around in the back bedroom. In a moment he returned.

"Here," he said, thrusting something in his hand toward David. "I remembered this last night after y'all left."

Wally handed David a photograph. David stared down at the black and white image of a young man dressed in a suit. His hair was thick and dark, his eyes deep and intense. His skin was smooth with an olive complexion. David felt his heart skip a beat and his mind struggled to make sense of what he saw. The photograph was taken years ago. It looked a lot like a very young Simeon Katz—the man to whom Avi had introduced him while he was in Israel. A frown wrinkled David's forehead. He looked up at Wally. "Where did you get this? Whose is it?"

"It was Leah's. I found it in some stuff she left at the house when she moved out." His eyes darted to the right. "Anyway. It's yours now. I was just too stubborn to give it to ya before."

David gestured with photograph. "Do you know who this is?"

"I don't know his name." Wally shook his head. "I do know one thing." He paused as if weighing whether or not to say something.

"What?"

Wally cleared his throat and pointed with his finger to the photograph. "Near as I can tell. That man there is your daddy."

"What!? What are you talking about? My father?"

"Yeah," Wally nodded. "Leah was married to him before she met up with me."

Images from the past swirled through David's mind. The beatings. Wally standing over him, screaming and shouting. David pushed aside the voices and forced himself back to the moment at hand. "You're sure he's my father, and not you?"

"Yeah, I'm sure now," Wally nodded. "I didn't know she'd been married to this here guy until later. She told me after I slapped her around one night. Said she wished she'd gone to Israel with him." Wally shook his head as if the memory was too much to bear. "Told me he wanted to go back to Israel to live, but she didn't want to leave Eliana. She said when they got divorced she was carryin' you. Leah and me'd been goin' out for about six weeks and got married about a week after she said he had left the country. Since you was born early, I just figured she was runnin' around with him before we said our I do's.

"Is that why you always called me a Jew bastard?"

Wally looked away. "I ought not to a said that. Not to no kid. Don't matter who your father was. You was in my house. I was the one supposed to be raisin' you." He looked down. "I'm sorry for that."

"Look, Dad, all that happened back then…I forgave you the other day, and I forgive you now. It's forgiven."

"I hope so."

David looked back at the photograph again. "You're sure this is my father?"

"Yeah. She met him again just before he left the country. She never told him about you. He didn't know she was a carryin' his child. I seen them together one day. He come up from New York to find her."

"He came to Indian Orchard?"

"Yeah," Wally nodded. "Tried one more time to talk her into goin' with him. She told him no. I think he was about to take off." Wally paused a moment then pointed to the picture. "You act like you recognize him."

David wasn't sure he should tell all he knew. "He looks familiar."

"Looks like you."

"Yeah," David grinned. "I guess he does." He looked over at Wally and gestured with the photograph. "Can I keep this?"

"Yeah, it's yours." Wally wrung his hands again. "Think you'll still come out to see me, now?"

"Yes," David smiled. He stepped closer and laid his hand on Wally's arm. "I'll still come to see you, Dad." He gave Wally a squeeze then turned toward the back door.

chapter 47

When David arrived at home, he motioned for Sue to follow him to the bedroom and handed her the photograph. She glanced at it then looked up at David. "Who is this?"

"Wally says the man in that picture is my father."

Sues mouth fell open. "You're kidding."

David shook his head. "Looks like you might have been right all along."

"He told you?"

"Yes," David nodded. "He said this was a picture of my father. He married my mother, but they divorced when he went back to Israel. Mom didn't want to leave Eliana, so she stayed behind and married Wally. He's pretty sure my father didn't know my mom was pregnant when he left. I don't think she ever told him."

"How did Wally get the photograph?"

"It was in some of the things she left behind when she moved out."

"And he kept it all this time? Why?"

"I don't know. He didn't say. I guess maybe a little bit of his conscience didn't get pickled with the alcohol after all."   .

Sue looked back at the photograph. "But why, if he knew Leah had been married, did he call you those names?"

"Mom didn't tell him she had just divorced or that she was pregnant until after they married. She and Wally had only known each other about six weeks when they married. And then, I was born about seven months later. He thought she had been running around on him before the wedding."

She pointed to the picture. "Who is he? Did Wally know his name?"

"Wally doesn't know his name, but I do."

She looked puzzled. "You know who this is?"

"Yes, sit down on the bed."

"Why?"

"Trust me," David insisted. "Sit on the bed."

Sue took a seat on the edge of the bed and looked up at him. "Is this going to be another strange story?"

"You remember I told you about meeting Avi in Israel?"

Sue's mouth flew open. "This is Avi?" She waved the photo with her hand.

"No," David shook his head. "Just listen." He took a breath. "You remember I told you about Avi taking me to a lecture. The man at the lecture was Simeon Katz."

"I don't remember what you said his name was, but go ahead."

David pointed to the photograph. "I am all but certain the man in that photograph is Simeon Katz, when he was much younger. I overheard my mother and Aunt Eliana talking in Russian one day. I heard her say something about Katz. I just thought she was talking about the cats that lived in the back alley behind our house. I asked her later about the 'cats.' She laughed and said 'No, David, not cats, K-a-t-z. It's the name of a man I knew before you were born."

Sue leaned back and propped her elbows on the bed. "You're kidding." She glanced back at the photograph. "You think this is the same man Avi introduced you to in Israel."

"Yes." David smiled broadly. "That raises an interesting question. Who is Avi and why did he introduce me to Simeon Katz?"

Sue laid the photograph beside her and collapsed backward across the bed. "This is wild." She ran her hands through her hair. "No one is ever going to believe this." David sat on the bed next to her. She looked over at him. "Did you tell Anna about the photograph?"

"No, I haven't told her. And I don't think I will. She has enough on her mind right now."

Sue ran her hand over his arm. "Can you believe it? Your father, your biological father, might be alive and well and living in Israel."

"I think I need to go back and find him."

"You think?" she grinned.

"Maybe this is what Avi and Yona meant when they said I would know what to do when I saw my father." He picked up the photograph. "And now I know what to do. I'm going to find out for certain who this man is."

"You're going back to Israel?"

"I'm going back to Israel."

"Somehow, I don't think that will be the end of it." Sue closed her eyes. "I think you'll find him, but I still don't think that's the end of it." She opened her eyes and looked at him. "Do you?"

"No," he smiled. "I think we've just now reached the beginning of the next thing."

*　　*　　*

Later that afternoon David drove Anna to the airport. He tried to convince her to stay longer, but she had doctors' appointments the following week. When they reached the airport David parked and carried Anna's bag inside.

"We've got nearly two hours before your plane leaves, let's find a place to sit and talk."

Anna smiled up at her big brother. "I'd like that."

They found a quiet corner in the waiting area and sank into the seats. David grinned. "Not terribly comfortable, are they?"

"No, but they'll do for now." She leaned back. "Remember our conversation in the car the other day—about God and surrendering to Him? David, how do I do that? I want the same kind of peace you have."

David took Anna's hands in his. "It so simple, really. The first thing is to admit that you are a sinner. The Bible says that we have all sinned and fallen short of God's glorious plan for us."

Tears filled Anna's eyes. "I know I'm guilty of sin."

"Do you believe that Jesus died on the Cross to pay the debt for your sins?" She nodded. "And do you believe that three days later He arose in victory over death, Hell, and the grave?"

"Yes, I really do."

"Okay. Do you believe He loves you just as you are, Anna?"

Anna's eyes filled with tears. "I believe, David. I believe.

"The Bible says if you confess with your mouth that Jesus is Lord and believe in your heart that God raised Him from the dead, you will be saved. Would you like to do that? Would you like to pray with me?"

Anna squeezed David's hands. "Yes, please. Yes."

As David prayed each sentence, Anna repeated it. "Dear Jesus, I know I am a sinner and need your saving grace. I believe You died for my sins on the Cross at Calvary, and that You rose from the dead three days later. Please come into my heart, take my sin, and make me God's child. Thank You, Jesus. Amen."

As Anna repeated each sentence, she felt the burden of guilt and shame she had carried since childhood lift. When she raised her head, there was a wondrous smile on her face. She threw her arms around David's neck. "I'm saved, David. God has forgiven me."

David returned her hug. "Do you have a Bible?"

"No. I've got books about all kinds of religions, but I don't have a Bible."

David reached into his inside coat pocket and pulled out his New Testament and Psalms. "Take this, Anna. Start in the book of John." He thumbed through the book to show her where it was and marked it with the ribbon in the Bible. "Read one of the Psalms every day. The Word will strengthen you."

"I will, David. Thank you for praying for me all this time."

Anna sat in pensive silence for a few minutes then looked up at him. "What are you going to do next?"

"I'm going to Israel. I have someone I want to visit. After that, I'm not really sure. But I'm going over there and see what happens."

"You would do that? Just fly over there and show up?"

"A year ago I wouldn't do it. Six months ago, I wouldn't have. But that was before Yona came along to show me what to do." He took a deep breath. "Would you care to have lunch?"

"Yes," she said. "I'm starving."

David stood and offered her his arm. She slipped her hand through the crook of his elbow. "Tell me more about that guy you met in Israel. What was his name?"

"Avi."

"What was he like?"

"Are you sure you want to know?"

"Yes. Why wouldn't I?"

"If I tell you about him, your life will never be the same."

"My life's not the same now anyway. Is this some more about the light and truth and religion?"

"No. It's not about religion." David smiled at her.

✳ ✳ ✳

After Anna boarded her flight David drove home in a state of euphoria. He burst through the front door with a grin big enough to light the entire house. "Sue! Sue! Where are you?"

Sue came running from the kitchen. "David, what on earth is wrong?"

"Nothing is wrong! Everything is right!" David laughed, picked her up and twirled her around. "Anna has accepted Jesus as her Savior!"

She laughed as he put her down. "Now I know why I had the feeling that I ought to pray for her after you left for the airport. David, that's wonderful! I believe God has great things in store for her for whatever time she has left. Maybe a healing?"

"It certainly doesn't hurt to pray for that, does it?"

chapter 48

Later that evening as he sat in his recliner in the office, David thought about all that had happened in the last six months and how much those events had changed him. Talking to Yona had set him on a course of reunion with Wally, and in the process brought renewal for Anna and a transformation for himself. Forgiveness was no longer something that happened outside him; it also happened inside. It was no longer merely something to talk about and preach about; it was something he lived. And now there was the possibility that his biological father was alive and living in Israel.

The thought that Simeon Katz might be his father was almost more than David could comprehend. "If that's true, then this whole thing was orchestrated by Avi," he said to himself. *Which means God was leading me in this direction all my life. I wasn't abandoned after all.* He glanced out the window. *It also means I'm not half Jew and half Gentile. Both of my parents were Jewish. I've seen my father. He's in Israel. And now I know what to do. I'm going over there to find out the truth.* "I'm not afraid of the truth. It will set me free."

David got up from the recliner and found Sue in the den. She smiled at him. "Join me? I'm still rejoicing over Anna's conversion."

David dropped down on the sofa beside her. "Yeah, me too."

"We haven't really had a chance to talk about her trip out to see Wally. Was she all right with that?"

"I believe so."

"Did you tell her about the photograph? If not, I really think you should."

"Maybe I'll tell her. I really need some more time to absorb all of this."

"You know, people will think we're crazy." Her voice was terse and not at all sympathetic.

"They already do, don't they?"

"But this time they'll run in the opposite direction." She sounded doubtful. "No one will want to join us."

"What do you mean?"

"You see a woman at a funeral who says she knew you, but you don't remember her. She tells you something to do and you do it. Wally shows you a photograph that looks like a man you met in Israel and tells you that man is your father. And now you're going off to Israel to see him."

"Yeah," David nodded with a grin. "I'd say that just about sums up the last six months."

Her eyes were heavy. "Is this how we're supposed to live for the foreseeable future?"

"You would want to live some other way? What's wrong? You weren't like this earlier this morning."

"I would like to know how we're going to pay the bills after June. And where we're going to live. I don't need you to have someplace to go every day. But I'm just a—"

"We've seen God move in a powerful way. Don't you think He knows about the utility bills?"

"I know," she sighed. "But sometimes it feels more stressful. And this is one of those times."

"What are you saying?"

"I'm saying—"

The doorbell interrupted them. David opened the front door and saw Billy Jones, smiling. "Got a minute?"

David smiled and invited him inside.

Sue came from the den. "Hello, Billy. You want some coffee?"

"Sure."

David led him to the den and pointed to a chair. "Have a seat. What's on your mind?"

"I heard what you did."

"What I did about what?"

"About resigning. The plan y'all have for after the first of the year."

"How did you hear about that?"

"The office door was open when you all were talking. Janitor heard it. He told me."

David glanced away. "I'd rather no one knew about this. I haven't resigned yet, and we weren't going to announce it until January."

Sue handed each of the men a mug of coffee and retreated to the kitchen.

"Thanks, Sue."

"You're welcome, Billy."

I told him not to tell," Billy said grimly.

"Think he can keep quiet?"

"Yeah, he's a good man. But I came to tell you I'm leaving the church this week too."

David put down his mug. "So, why do you want to leave the church?"

"I told you before, when you were in the hospital," Billy replied. "I'd go somewhere else if it meant you could talk to me like you needed to. You're gonna need somebody to help you. If I stayed there, everybody would know what I was doing. I want to be in a position to help."

"Where will you go? What church?"

"There's a little church across town."

"Do they need a preacher?"

"No," Billy shook his head. "You don't want to do that."

"I know. I'm kidding."

"God has more for you to do than grow little churches into big ones."

"Like what?"

"I'm not sure, but I believe your church will somehow be the nation of Israel. Haven't you been going over to the synagogue?"

"Yes. I've been attending Torah classes and have met some wonderful people there."

"Ever think about doing something with Israel?"

David caught his breath. "Well yes, as a matter of fact, I have."

"What are you thinking about doing?"

"I don't know, really. I met someone there I want to go back and visit again. Other than that, I've been thinking about just sitting outside the hotel and seeing what happens. See what God opens up. He's brought me this far without my having a plan. I thought maybe He would show me what to do when I got there."

"Good." Billy smiled. "That's a great place to start. Just show up on the job and say, 'Here I am. What do you need me to do?' I love working with people like that."

"It's a little unsettling, though. To think of just going over there and not having a plan or anything."

"You could lead a tour group. That would cover the cost of your trips. Or, you could just go over there and sit around. Drink coffee in the local cafés. Listen to the people. Figure out what God is doing, and join Him in whatever that is."

David nodded. "That's sort of what I had in mind."

"Great," Billy replied. "I'd like to help."

"What would you like to do?"

Billy glanced around the room. "I heard you and the family're staying here a while."

"They said we could live here as long as we like."

Billy smiled. "I have a rental house. Over near Belmont Abbey. Three bedrooms with a den. Two bathrooms. Nice garage. Big yard. We lived in it until we built the house we have now. Renters are leaving in

May. I'll get it repainted by the end of June. You can move in there if you want to. Stay as long as you like." He took a sip of coffee. "If this place doesn't work out."

David felt a lump in his throat. "Billy. I don't know what to say."

"Just let me know what you want to do."

"Thanks, Billy," David grinned. "I appreciate it."

"I think you'll need an organization too, something people can identify with, give their money to." He took a check from his pocket and handed it across the table to David. "Use this to help with your travel costs."

David glanced at the check. Tears welled in his eyes. "Billy, you have no idea …"

"Oh, I gotta pretty good idea," Billy grinned. "I've started off on a few ventures myself. Nothing like working without a safety net to sharpen your faith."

They talked a while longer, and then Billy stood. "I better get home. Margaret will have dinner ready before long."

David opened the door for him. "Billy, I appreciate your help."

"My pleasure." Billy took David's hand. "Fear will try to change your mind. Just tell it to be quiet and go away."

"I will," David nodded. "I will."

When Billy was gone, David closed the door and stood there a moment with his forehead against it, choking back tears. Sue came behind him and slipped her arms around his waist. "So," she began, "how soon did you want to leave for Israel?"

David turned to face her and wrapped his arms around her. "Can you believe the timing?"

"Yes, I can." She looked up at him. "I'm sorry I was worried before."

"That's okay." He kissed her. "We'll probably both be worried again. More than once. Just promise me you'll talk about it and not keep it inside."

"I promise."

✻   ✻   ✻

A week before Christmas the weather was unseasonably warm, and David was sitting on the patio reading his Bible when Sue called him. "David, Anna's on the phone. She sounds really excited."

David hurried into the kitchen and took the phone from Sue. "Hi, little sister! What's going on?"

"David!" Anna cried, and then burst into tears.

David looked at Sue, who was hovering near the phone, and put his hand over the mouthpiece. "It must be really bad," he whispered. "She's just sobbing."

Finally the cries subsided and Anna took a deep breath. "David, Dr. Harper called me this morning. I had gone back yesterday for a bone scan and more tests to determine how far advanced the cervical cancer is." She paused as if trying to find the words to say. Then she dropped the bombshell. "The cancer is gone! Completely gone! The bone scan was clear. The tests for the cervical cancer are negative. They took x-rays. When the results came back, the radiologist thought he had the wrong ones. They took three different sets. I was sure I would die from the radiation alone. David! There's no sign of the cancer. Even my hair's growing back. God healed me. I know it. He healed me!"

Sue wrapped her arms around David. "Honey, what's wrong? You're white as a sheet. How bad is it?"

"Anna, you're sure you heard the doctor correctly? The cancer is gone?" Beside him Sue gasped and then sank down in a chair at the kitchen table. David shouted, "Praise be to God! Anna! You're healed!"

The brother and sister talked for a few more minutes. Finally David said, "I love you, Anna. I'm so glad you made the commitment to follow God. I'll talk to you real soon."

After he hung up the phone David turned to Sue. "Can you believe it? The cancer is gone."

With tears in her eyes Sue just looked at him and grinned. "Should I say, 'Oh ye of little faith?' This is what we've been praying for, honey! First her salvation, and now her healing."

chapter 49

David, Sue, Joel and Megan had made plans to spend Christmas with Sue's parents in Arizona. Raymond had retired from his teaching post and he and Betty moved to the desert to get away from the threat of hurricanes and the humidity in South Carolina. Her brother, Peter, and his family had been able to fly in from California to join in the fun and festivities. Sue was thrilled to be able to spend some quiet time with her mother in the midst of all the family chaos. They flew home two days after Christmas, and David began to prepare for his next trip to Israel.

Early in January David flew to Tel Aviv, where he stayed the night at the Yamit Plaza Hotel. He wanted to find Simeon Katz and talk to him, but he also wanted to be available—to sense what the Holy Spirit was doing and join Him in that, whatever it might be. So he put his luggage in his room and headed for the lobby. Immediately he spotted Avi sitting on a bench near the front entrance and smiled. Avi smiled back and rose as David approached.

"David," he said, greeting him with a hug. "You had a good flight?"

"Yes, but how did you know I would be here?"

"We have our ways," Avi chuckled. "Your family is well?"

"Yes, they are fine. And yours?"

"My people are as they always are. Some are doing well. Others are struggling." Avi gestured toward the hotel café. "Why don't we have some tea?"

"That would be great," David replied. "I'm still a little buzzed from the flight. Tea would taste great right about now."

They walked across the lobby to the café, where a waiter led them to a booth in the corner. David sat with his back to the door. Avi placed his elbows on the table and laced his fingers together. "So, tell me. What has happened since I saw you last?"

"I went to see my father."

"Good. What happened?"

"I asked him to forgive me."

"And he forgave you?"

"Yes. It was really a wonderful experience."

"Good." Avi took a sip of tea. "It took a lot of courage to go see him."

"I didn't want to, at first. But I started having physical trouble."

"Not just nightmares?"

"No." David shook his head. "Post traumatic stress disorder. Panic attacks. Heart problems. Neck problems. It was scary."

"I'm sure it was. But all that is gone now?"

"Yes. They wanted to do surgery on my neck. But I had a dream—"

"Dreams are important," Avi interrupted. "Not like Freud said, but like God says. When you read in the Scriptures, you see how dreams were often used to guide people. What did you dream?"

"I dreamed that my son and I were standing in the woods. We were waiting for my father. When he got there, he tried to give us each a black stone."

"But you refused."

"Yes."

"Did you understand what the stones meant?"

"Not exactly, but I knew it was bad. And I knew he was trying to give it to Joel, my son."

"And that is when you went to see him."

"Yes. I had tried earlier, before I met you. But I got scared and couldn't do it."

"But you did this time. And you asked him to forgive you?"

"I did. And he did. We prayed. It was really good."

David's eyes darted to the left then back to Avi, prompting Avi to ask, "But what else happened? I can see it in your eyes."

"He told me about abusing my sister Anna."

"That must have been difficult to hear."

"It was awful. At first I wanted to punch him out. But then I forced myself to think and remember why I was visiting him and what the Holy Spirit was trying to accomplish in me."

"So you had to forgive him all over again. Life is like that, David. Forgiveness takes us deeper into God's grace. Then, as we go deeper, we see more places where forgiveness needs to be applied. And that application of grace takes us deeper still."

"Does it ever end?"

"Not really," Avi chuckled. "But it does get a little easier to bear. It becomes a lifestyle." He took another sip of tea. "That dream you had was important. The black stones represented the life Wally received from his father. The Enemy wants to pass that on to you, to keep the generations captive. It was passed from his grandfather, to his father, and then down to him."

"I sensed it was wrong, but in the dream I wasn't really conscious of why."

"And when you awoke?"

"I just knew he was after my son, and I wasn't going to let that happen, regardless of how scared I was or what might happen to me."

A warm smile spread across Avi's face. "This is good. You have learned much, and I can see you have come a long way toward finding the freedom you wanted and needed."

"He gave me this." David took the photograph from the pocket of his jacket and handed it to Avi. "He said my mother had been married to this man before I was born. He's certain this man is really my father. My biological father."

"Biological father." Avi smiled again. "I like hearing that from you. It shows you acknowledge Wally's place in your life. And it also acknowledges that while there may be more to the story, you have not rejected Wally, in spite of all that has happened." Avi nodded his head thoughtfully. "This is good."

"There is still a relationship there." David took a sip from his cup. "I've known the man as my dad all my life."

"Yes. A relationship. As well there should be." Avi leaned back from the table. "Relationship will be an important concept for you."

David pointed to the photograph. "Do you know who this is?"

Avi looked at it again. "You should not get your hopes too high, David."

"What do you mean?"

"Much time has passed. Six months ago when I first saw you, you were very different from the person you are now. And that was only in six months." He tapped the photograph with his index finger. "This man knew your mother fifty years ago. If you have changed so much in six months, imagine how much he must have changed in fifty years."

"Is he the man I think he is?"

"Yes," Avi nodded. "He is." He handed the photograph back to David. "You wish to see him and talk to him about this?"

"Yes, I do."

"I will contact him on your behalf."

"I think I would rather just show up."

Avi paused for a moment in thought, then picked up the cup and took a sip of tea. "As you wish."

The following morning David asked the hotel concierge how he should go to Jerusalem. He hired a driver for the trip, and an hour later he arrived at the Mount Scopus campus of Hebrew University. With little difficulty he located Simeon Katz's office. He paused outside the office door to collect himself, then he knocked on the door. A voice called from inside. "Come." David opened the door and stepped into the room.

Directly opposite the door was a large wooden desk. Behind it shelves crammed full of books rose to the ceiling. Stacks of papers covered the desktop, and files sat beside it on the floor. Simeon Katz sat in a chair behind the desk. David smiled at him as he entered the room. "Remember me?"

"Yes," Katz replied. He had a surprised look on his face, and there was a touch of nervousness in his voice. He rose from his chair and came from behind the desk. "I wondered if we might meet again." They shook hands. Katz gestured to a chair nearby. "Have a seat." He pulled a chair up to the front of the desk and sat next to David. "So, you decided to return to Israel." Katz folded his hands together and rested them in his lap. "I suppose we both know why."

David took the photograph from his pocket. "This is you?"

Katz nodded with a smile. "That is I." He looked at David. "Where did you find it?"

"Wally gave it to me."

"Wally?" Katz looked startled. "Why did he have it?"

"Mom left some things behind when she moved out. This was in one of the boxes."

"And he kept it all these years." Katz had a pensive look. "Perhaps he's not quite as bad as I once believed."

"Oh, he was pretty bad," David said with a wry smile. "But I guess he still has a little bit of conscience."

"So, he told you about me and your mother?" Katz propped an elbow on the armrest of his chair. "I knew there was a connection between us when you were here before."

David was puzzled. "How did you know that?"

"The prime minister's security team did a background check on you."

"Oh yes, I remember. Avi told me about that."

"It is not as extensive as they would like, but they can learn enough about someone to know what sort of person they are." Katz crossed his legs. "They found information about me and your mother very quickly. Begin asked me about it before you arrived. They are really quite thorough."

David's palms were sweaty. "So, are you my father?"

"That is what Wally Ellis told you?"

"Yes."

Katz adjusted his position in the chair. "I met your mother at a synagogue in Manhattan. I was in New York raising money for an agricultural project. I attended a service at the synagogue. She was there. A friend introduced us. I invited them to one of the events I was attending later that evening. They came. She and I danced. I fell deeply in love with Leah. Things went on from there and we were married." He looked away. "This is not easy to talk about."

"I understand. Look, I'm not upset," David assured him. "I'm just glad I found you and found out about this part of her life. My life, perhaps." David returned the photograph to the pocket of his jacket. "Wally said you came up to see her."

"Yes, I did." Katz had a wisp of a smile. "I did not realize he knew about it."

"He told me he saw you with her."

Katz's face softened. "Your mother was the most beautiful woman I had ever seen. So intelligent and witty. She had a wonderful smile, and when she laughed the whole room lit up."

"I have never heard anyone describe her that way." David was overwhelmed with sadness. "And I don't think I ever heard her laugh... or thought of her as witty." An image of his mother seated at the kitchen table flashed through David's mind. "Wally kept her so beaten down. Apparently we never saw much of my real mother."

"And it is such a pity." Katz gave him a kind smile. "For you both."

"You and she had a rather brief marriage."

"It was too brief for me. I think it was love at first sight." Katz took a deep breath. "After we married, I wanted to return here, to Israel. I asked her to come with me but she refused. She did not want to leave her sister. I was devastated when she asked me for a divorce. Right before I left, I went up to Indian Orchard and found her. I asked her again to come with me. I thought her first refusal was just Leah being courageous. I thought perhaps if I came and found her, she would realize how serious I was and it would make a difference."

"But it didn't."

"No. She said she had already married again." Katz looked at David once more. "She never told me she was pregnant."

"You didn't know?"

"Not then. I found out much later, actually after your first trip to Israel. When you were being vetted I found out who your mother was. Given your date of birth, I put two and two together. Our last meeting was awkward for her. I felt that she still loved me, but it was too late for us." Katz ran his fingers over his cheek. "And then, I noticed the bruises on her arm." He pointed to his upper arm. "Large blue ones, just visible beneath the sleeve of her dress. I felt she was probably facing a tough time at home. I wanted to take her with me anyway. Make her go. But she was unrelenting, and there was nothing I could do."

"So, you returned to Israel?"

"Yes."

"Something puzzles me. You said you found out about me when I was vetted, before my first trip to Israel. How is it that you were made aware of the results of the vetting?"

"David, my second wife and I had one child, our daughter Miriam. She would be your half-sister. She is a lawyer, who works for Mossad and happened to be the agent who checked you out."

"I have another sister? Can I meet her?"

"Unfortunately, she is in New York City at this time, assigned to our ambassador to the U.N. Her being overseas has been very difficult for me, especially since her mother passed away a year ago." His face brightened and he chuckled. "But she has told me some very interesting things about you. Nothing classified, of course. She told me you are married to a lovely blonde lady named Sue, and that you have two children, a boy and a girl. Joel and Megan, right?" David smiled and nodded. "And that you were the pastor of a church in Charlotte, North Carolina. I know you just resigned from the church before coming over here. Rest assured, David, Miriam is keeping an eye on you." Katz winked. "If you ever get into trouble, I suspect she may know of it before you do." Then he sobered, "I know your beautiful mother died several months ago, and that her last years were happier than her first. For that I am grateful. She deserved happiness—more than she apparently had with Wally."

"Did you ever hear from my mother again?"

"I received one letter from her. After she divorced your...Wally. But by then my life had moved on. I was married and had a child. The time for Leah and me had passed." They sat in silence a moment, then Katz had an amused smile. "You came all this way just to ask me these questions?"

"Yes. I came to find you and talk to you. But I also came to find the next step in my own journey."

"Which is?"

"I want to be a bridge builder between Jews and Christians. Between America and Israel. I have no idea how to accomplish that, but that is why I am here."

Katz chuckled. "Begin liked your answer, by the way. When he asked why you were here. He liked what you said."

"I sounded like a big, dumb American."

"No. No. No." Katz shook his head. "I think you came across as a most genuine person. He asks about you regularly. I'll tell him I saw you."

"Tell him if he can help me figure out how to build bridges, I would be glad to discuss it with him." David laughed and checked his watched. "I've taken up enough of your time." He reached over to Katz and rested his hand on his arm. "Do you mind if I pray for us?"

"Not at all."

"Lord, thank you for Simeon Katz. You have blessed us with a connection that has reached across fifty years. Help us as we explore the meaning of that relationship and as we work together to further Your purposes in Israel. Amen."

David rose from his chair. Katz guided him across the room to the door. He took David's hand in his and smiled sadly. "Since you did not know about me, you would not have known that my father's name was David Benjamin Katz. Please stay in touch, David."

David shook his hand and nodded. "I will."

chapter 50

When David returned to the hotel in Tel Aviv, Avi was once again waiting for him in the lobby. "How did it go?"

"It went well."

"Did he have answers for you?"

"He filled in a lot of details about how he met my mother."

"Then he is your father."

"He believes he is, and the information he offered confirms it. Where we go from here is up to God."

"Good." Avi breathed a sigh of relief. He smiled at David. "Are you hungry?"

"Starving."

"I know a great place to eat."

They ate at a traditional Jewish café, dining on freshly caught fish and fresh vegetables.

"You have come far on your journey," Avi observed.

"It feels like I have just now reached the starting line."

"The start of something new," Avi nodded, "but the end of what came before. And what have you learned?"

"Well," David mused, "I guess I have learned that one thing unfolds to something else."

"Yes," Avi nodded. "This is really about that. The journey you thought was about reconciliation with your father led you on a quest to find your biological father. Now, have you considered finding your spiritual Father?"

"My spiritual Father?" David asked. "You mean Jesus?"

"I mean Abba. Your concept of father has been renewed as it relates to your earthly father." He gave David a tight smile. "Or fathers." He swallowed a bite of fish. "But you have yet to apply that redemption to your view of God as Abba."

"You mean...I'm not to the end of that journey."

"You have reached a critical stage. Much has been accomplished, and what has been done is now bearing fruit in your desire for service. Your desire to minister the renewal you have found in God's love and forgiveness is a direct result of your journey."

"I just don't know what to do or how to do it."

"In America schools teach their students to manage events and businesses by focusing on the details. Perhaps you should focus on the relationships instead."

"What did you mean about a critical stage?"

"The new relationships you have discovered with Wally and with Simeon Katz have opened doors for a new calling to minister to those with broken relationships. The Enemy will twist that to suggest you have arrived at the end of the journey of renewal. Otherwise, how could you minister restoration to others if you have not already received it? That is a lie. You have come far, but there is one more aspect to which you must apply forgiveness and redemption."

"God as Father, huh? And how do I do that?"

"It will come to you on the journey. Stay focused on doing the next thing, and let it unfold from your relationship with God. He will show you." Avi pointed to David's plate. "Do you like the fish?"

"It is delicious."

"We eat a lot of fish in Israel. It is not really a meat, you know."

"Not a meat?"

"For Kosher purposes, it is not a meat. We can eat it with dairy products if we like." He turned up his nose. "But I do not care for it that way." He patted his stomach. "Too heavy."

David laughed. "I don't know what they did to this piece of fish, but it is excellent."

chapter 51

A few days later David returned home. Sue and the children picked him up at the airport in Charlotte. He was tired but exhilarated from the things he had learned on the trip. The following morning, after the kids were off to school, he and Sue sat in the den and talked.

"You saw Avi?"

David nodded. "He was in the lobby of the hotel. I checked in and went to the room. When I came back down he was sitting near the front door."

"How did he know you'd be there?"

"I don't know," David shrugged. "I asked him, but all he said was 'We have our ways.'"

"He's as mysterious as Yona."

"Yes," David nodded. "He is."

"Do you think he's an angel too?"

"I don't know. He knows a lot about me. He could have deduced some of it from things I told him. But some of it I can't figure out how he knows."

"So the picture really was of Simeon Katz?"

"Yeah."

"Simeon Katz wasn't angry with you for bringing up his past?"

"No. But I didn't even think about it in those terms."

"What terms?"

"His past. I thought of it only as my past."

"Did he shed any light on what happened?"

David chuckled. "Shed light? Everyone is shedding light. He told me about meeting my mom and falling in love with her."

"Did he come to see her in Indian Orchard, like Wally said?"

"He did. He tried to convince her to go to Israel with him, but she wouldn't."

"Why not?"

"She had already married Wally. It was too late for her to change her mind."

"Hard to imagine her having a life other than the one you describe from your childhood."

"It was for me too. He talked about how pretty she was, and that when she laughed she lit up the room." David shook his head. "We never saw that."

"Makes me wonder how other people see us."

"What do you mean?"

"What do they see in us that we don't see?"

"Not sure I want to know the answer to that question!"

"Did you miss me?"

"Yes," David smiled. "I miss you when you walk to the other end of the house."

Sue grinned. "Not always."

He reached over and took her hand. "Always."

chapter 52

As planned Steve Smith held a commissioning service for David in February at Belmont Baptist Church. As the service ended, the deacons gathered around David at the altar to invoke God's blessing and favor. After the deacons prayed Pastor Smith held up his hand. "Brother David, I feel like God wants me to share a very special scripture from Isaiah with you as a benediction: "Do not be afraid, for I have ransomed you. I have called you by name; you are mine. When you pass through the waters, I will be with you; And through the rivers, they shall not overflow you. When you walk through the fire, you shall not be burned, nor shall the flame scorch you."

The Word sank deeply into David's spirit. He claimed it as his own promise from God. Then the service was over, and the congregation lined the steps outside. They shook his hand, tearfully hugged his neck, and sent him off with their blessing. It was a bittersweet moment for him—saying goodbye to the congregation he had led for ten years, launching into a new venture full of promise and challenge—but after months of transition, he was glad to finally be on his way.

David had felt a clear leading to see Simeon Katz in January, but after talking to Katz and learning about his mother's commitment to honoring her vows, he was at peace with the issue of who his biological father might be. Now, he waited on God's direction—and while he waited he worked on the things at hand. One of those tasks was a book about his experiences in finding reconciliation with his father and his past.

Long known in the region, he was invited to preach almost every weekend. That led to additional speaking opportunities during the week. Before long he was busier than when he was a fulltime pastor. In the few spare moments he had between preaching and writing, he took Billy Jones up on his offer to get involved, and together they worked on ideas for an organization to help with the work in Israel—building bridges between Christians and Jews.

In March David and Billy attended a conference on U.S.-Israeli relations held at a center near Wilmington, Delaware. One of the afternoon sessions included a multi-media presentation marking the five-year anniversary of the rescue of Israeli hostages held at the airport in Entebbe, Uganda. The rescue was successful, but during the operation the commander of the Israeli Defense Forces, Jonathan Netanyahu, was killed. While a narrator described the events of that day, an image appeared on the screen. In it, Jonathan's father stood beside the casket as his son's body was reverently carried from a military aircraft. The father paused on the tarmac, shoulders square, head held high, and his chin thrust defiantly forward; but in his eyes David saw the pain and sorrow of a man who had lost a son. The narrator explained that Mr. Netanyahu had received a card of condolence from President Gerald Ford, which read in part: "Do not be afraid, for I have ransomed you. I have called you by name; you are mine. When you pass through the waters, I will be with you; and through the rivers, they shall not overflow you. When you walk through the fire, you shall not be burned, nor shall the flame scorch you."

David's head snapped up, and he leaned over to whisper in Billy's ear, "That's the same scripture Steve gave me at the commissioning service. Do you suppose God's trying to tell me something?"

Billy turned to look at him. "I wouldn't be surprised. I think maybe you just got another confirmation."

As David watched the remainder of the presentation, he thought of his own children and what it would be like to lose one of them. The longer he watched, the more real that loss became. He thought of all the moments in a lifetime wasted on the pursuit of things that don't matter. Not bad things or wrong things, just things that have no eternal purpose or consequence, like turning aside a child's request to throw the ball in order to write a letter, saying no to playing with dolls or watching a television program in order to read a book or make one more outline. He imagined Jonathan Netanyahu's father, standing by that casket, thinking of those moments and wanting them back with all his heart. While the program continued, that fatherly sorrow began to build in David, and he went from knowing it in his mind to sensing it in his heart, then feeling it in his soul so much so that he wanted to run from the conference room, drive home to his own children, and hold them close.

That night he and Billy took a break from the conference and rode into town for dinner. As they enjoyed plates of fried shrimp, they talked about what they had seen and heard that day.

"I can't imagine losing a son like that," said David.

"In fact, Margaret and I did. He did his first duty in Korea. Didn't have tours back then. Not for enlisted guys. You just fought and came home when it was over. Only Frank never came home. He was only eighteen."

"Ah, Billy! You've never told me that. I'm so sorry."

"Time has healed the hurt, David, but the memory is still there. Something else, back at the beginning of World War II, I spent eight months on notification duty."

"Notification?"

"Yeah, driving out to the homes of servicemen who had died in combat and telling their parents or wives or whoever that their soldier wasn't coming home."

"As a pastor, I've had to do some of that. It's rough."

"I was supposed to be there a year. When they assigned me I thought, 'Yeah, sure. This won't be so bad. Beats getting shot at.' But after the first day I knew I wasn't going to make it a year. Six months into it, I started calling everybody I knew and asked them to get me out of there. I thought I would go crazy."

"Good chance for ministry, though."

"Would have been if I'd had anything to minister."

"You weren't a Christian?"

"Only on the forms I filled out."

"What made the difference?"

"A chaplain we had on the base. He rode with us sometimes to see the families. He was a good man. Captain Fitzgerald. Prayed me through to salvation in a little grove of oaks not far from Moncks Corner, South Carolina. We were sitting on the hood of the car. Two months later I was discharged."

"I'm so glad you came to know the Lord, Billy. You are such a blessing to Sue and me. By the way, I'm thinking about another trip to Israel."

"What do you want to do over there?"

"I would like to meet Jonathan Netanyahu's father. While we were watching that presentation about the Entebbe rescue, I kept thinking about that father standing there with the casket, and I had this tremendous sense of isolation, like he was feeling all alone...like no one could possibly sense his pain and feeling like no one cared at all."

"It is an incredibly lonely moment."

"Think I could find him?"

"Maybe. Place can't be that big. I'm sure you could find where they live. Whether they would let you in is another question. What would you do after you got there?"

"I don't know," David shrugged. "Start talking and see what happens, I guess."

Billy smiled. "That's all we've been doing so far, and it's worked out pretty well. You give any more thought to forming an organization for this work?"

"I was thinking about calling it 'Followers of the Light.' It comes from Isaiah 60:1-4: Arise, shine; For your light has come! And the glory of the Lord is risen upon you. For behold, the darkness shall cover the earth, and deep darkness the people; but the Lord will arise over you, and His glory will be seen upon you. The Gentiles shall come to your light, And kings to the brightness of your rising. Lift up your eyes all around, and see: They all gather together, they come to you; your sons shall come from afar, and your daughters shall be nursed at your side."

"I like it, David. It pretty much defines the way the Light has worked in your own life. Would you have people pray for the peace of Jerusalem?"

"Yes. We could organize groups to do that. Recruit churches that would agree to make it a focus of their prayer once a month."

"Pray for the peace of Jerusalem. Where's the verse that talks about that?"

"Psalm 122."

"I like that idea. You want to form a corporation? Fix it so people can give to it and get a tax deduction? Lot of people give for that reason."

"I don't know how to do that."

"There's a guy in Charlotte who can help, a lawyer named Tom King. He's a friend of mine. I'll give you his number when we get back."

"Aren't lawyers expensive?"

"Nah," Billy shook his head. "Not Tom. He won't charge us too much."

When he returned home, David told Sue about the plans he and Billy made to form Followers of the Light. She was intrigued by the idea but a little skeptical that people would be interested in "just praying."

"Well, it might become more than that, but isn't that what we tell people to do? Pray? I think Followers of the Light would be a wonderful name for the organization. Don't you?"

Sue nodded. "I think it would be."

"Think of it like this: Not many people can grab their guns and go off to physically defend Israel, but they can pray. And they will pray. Prayer is more powerful than the armies of the world. I think it's about time we as Christians got involved in using that as an avenue for opening up God's work in the Middle East."

"Nothing else seems to be working."

"That's because this battle is bigger than guns and soldiers. This is a spiritual battle."

Three days after they returned from Wilmington, David met with Tom King at his office in the BB&T Center. Located in uptown Charlotte, the office had a commanding view of the city's business district. From the plush carpet and antique furnishings, David was certain he was in the wrong place, but before he could leave the receptionist notified Tom's secretary that he was there. An assistant appeared from the hallway to the right and escorted him to an office on the opposite side of the building.

Tom came from behind the desk to greet him. "David Ellis," he said with a smile. "I've heard a lot about you."

"I hope it was all good."

"Billy Jones talks about you every time I see him. Traveling to Israel. Leaving your church and trusting God. Sounds like an adventure. Have a seat." Tom pointed to a chair. He returned to his seat behind the desk. "Billy said you wanted to form a business for the things you're doing in Israel."

"Yes." David glanced around nervously. "But I don't think I'm the kind of client you're looking for."

"What do you mean?"

"All I have is a calling and a desire to serve God. I don't have money."

"Well," Tom shrugged, "I think if you had an organization it would be easier to raise money. We can set you up in a corporation, file the forms with the IRS to request a tax exemption, and point you toward an accountant who can help you keep it straight."

"Sounds great, but how do I pay for it?"

"What if we did this—what if I help you get the organization formed. We'll get the documents prepared and filed. You'll be up and running."

"And the bill? How do you make a living doing that?"

"Same way you do," Tom grinned. "I help the ones the Holy Spirit sends my way. Some can pay. Some can't. It all works out."

David was floored. "You would do that?"

"I would do that." Tom stood and reached across the desk. They shook hands. The office door opened behind them and an assistant appeared. "This is Nancy. She'll take care of the details we need to get started, and I'll be in touch."

Four weeks later Followers of the Light was officially formed. David opened the company's bank account with a check for one hundred dollars. When he got home that day, there was an envelope in the mailbox from Tom King. Inside was a check for five thousand dollars. A note with it said simply, "I consider my life worth nothing to me if only I may finish the race and complete the task the Lord Jesus has given me. Acts 20:24." Tears filled David's eyes as he read it. In his spirit he sensed God whispering to him, *"I have many people who are ready to join you."*

David also applied what he had heard at the conference to his own life—about being a father. He began turning down some of the weekday speaking engagements to spend more time with his children. In the evenings after dinner he sat with Joel and Megan on the sofa in the den and watched their favorite television shows. In the afternoons he tossed the football and baseball with Joel in the back yard. And he went for long walks with Megan and listened to her conversation about the girls in her class and heard about the boys she liked. He spent time with them and entered their world, their relationships, their thoughts and dreams and worries. And every night as he went to bed, he remembered that somewhere in Israel there was a man named Netanyahu who could no longer have that pleasure with one of his children.

One night late in April, as he lay in bed and stared up at the ceiling, he finally put words to the thought he had had for weeks. "I want to see him," he sighed.

"Who?"

"I want to see Benzion Netanyahu."

"Who is he?"

"Jonathan Netanyahu's father."

Sue rolled on her side to face him. "You saw a slide show about a soldier from Israel who died rescuing airline hostages, and now you want to make a pastoral visit to his father?"

"Yes."

"His father is Jewish."

"Right. When I saw those images of him standing there, watching soldiers unload his son's body, I had this sense that he was feeling isolated. Like he was facing this tragedy without a friend in the world. I think that's how Israel as a country feels, like they are facing the world all alone. When I resigned at the church, I said God was calling me to build bridges. That's what this is about. I don't know how it fits. I don't know what it means. But it's about building bridges."

"Has Israel become your church?"

David arched an eyebrow. "That's what Billy mentioned to me a while back. It didn't really hit me then, but now that you mention it, I think it has."

"You plan to just walk up to his door and ring the doorbell?"

"If I wanted to see the father of an American soldier, would anyone stop me? Would they have guards at the door?"

"No. But America isn't Israel."

"I think I could find him. I hope he would agree to see me."

"Why?"

"Because I think this is what God wants me to do. He used Mr. Netanyahu's story of the death of his son to change me and help me see the need to spend time with my family. He used it to teach me about being a father. But he also put that man on my heart for a reason. I don't know what it is, but He does." He turned to face her. "We have the money for the ticket."

"Yes. We have the money."

"This is what God is asking me to do, so I'm going over there, and I'm going to do it. I'm going to see him. Even if I look foolish to men, God will count it as obedience."

chapter 53

Early in May Sue and David dropped Meagan at the college
and Joel at his high school. The two had grown and matured over the
three years since David's first trip to Israel. Meagan was finishing her
second year at Queens College and Joel was on the track team. Both
were saving for their first cars, but neither had quite reached their goal.

David said goodbye to them as they got out of the car, then Sue
took him to the airport in Charlotte. She brought the car to a stop in
front of the terminal and leaned toward him. "God is doing a new thing
in and through us."

"I know," David replied.

"This is an important trip…1982 is going to be a banner year for
you, David. I know it."

"Crucial," he nodded. "Are you praying?"

"Since the day I married you," she smiled.

"Good." He kissed her. "I'll be back in a week." He smiled at her.
"Don't forget to come pick me up."

She took hold of his arm. "Don't forget to come back."

David settled back in the seat and smiled at her. "You are the most
beautiful woman in the world."

"And you better go," she nudged him, "or you'll miss your plane."

"You're right." He kissed her once more then stepped from the car.
Fourteen hours later he arrived in Tel Aviv. A taxi took him to the Yamit

Plaza Hotel, where he checked in to his room, tossed his suitcase on the bed, and pulled back the curtains from the balcony door. Down below, the blue waters of the Mediterranean Sea shimmered in the afternoon sun. It shone brightly against the sandy beach below and bore down on the hotel in a blinding glare.

David suddenly felt very small and insignificant. His mission to find the father of a soldier who died five years ago now seemed silly. Thoughts crowded his mind with a withering blast of doubt and pity. In the space of a few minutes he went from a confident man of God on a mission to an eleven-year-old boy cowering in the cellar, waiting for yet another beating. Then slicing through the confusion he remembered a line from the Psalms. "For the Lord is a sun and shield." David repeated those words to himself. He said them again as he opened the suitcase and took out his Bible. The line was from the eighty-fourth psalm. He found it quickly and read it aloud.

"Better is one day in your courts than a thousand elsewhere; I would rather be a doorkeeper in the house of my God than dwell in the tents of the wicked. For the Lord God is a sun and shield; the Lord bestows favor and honor, no good thing does He withhold from those whose walk is blameless. O Lord Almighty, blessed is the man who trusts in You."

David felt his confidence return. "God, You have sent me. I would rather be here with You, doing what You called me to do, than anywhere else. You bestow favor. No good thing do You withhold from those whose walk is blameless." David paced the floor. "The Lord Almighty bestows favor. I am blameless in this calling if I do what He tells me to do." David snapped the Bible shut. "He will give me favor."

David left his room and walked quickly to the elevator. He pressed the button and stepped back to wait. While he waited, he thought about how he could find Netanyahu. "I could check the phone book," he mumbled to himself. "But I can't read Hebrew. I could ask at the desk."

A hotel housekeeper appeared in the hall. She approached with a concerned look. "You need help?"

"Just trying to figure out how to locate an address."

"You want to go somewhere? Ask the taxi drivers. She chuckled, "They know where everything is."

"A taxi driver," David laughed. "Why didn't I think of that?"

Just then the elevator bell dinged and the doors opened. David caught the door and turned to thank the housekeeper, but she was gone. The hall was empty. He paused, holding the door with his hand and wondering who she might have been, when a passenger in the elevator tapped him on the arm. "You are waiting for someone?"

"Oh," David replied, startled. "Sorry. Didn't mean to hold everyone up." He stepped inside and let go of the door. The elevator began its slow descent to the lobby, where David found a bellman near the front door. "I need a car and driver, please."

"Certainly," the bellman replied. "There is a car out here." He led David through the doors to the driveway and pointed to the right. "He is waiting for a passenger."

David slipped the bellman a five-dollar bill and walked briskly to the waiting car. As he opened the door and crawled into the back seat, the driver turned to face him. "Good afternoon. I am Moshe. How may I help you?"

"Do you know the story about Jonathan Netanyahu and the rescue at Entebbe?"

"Of course," Moshe smiled. "Everyone knows that story."

"Do you know where his father lives?"

"Benzion Netanyahu? He lives in Jerusalem."

David sighed. *This would have been easier if I had stayed in Jerusalem,* he thought to himself. When he was there before and wanted to see Simeon Katz, the hotel concierge made a big deal about the distance and the drive from Tel Aviv. They had insisted on hiring a driver with a car. He looked at Moshe intently.

"Can you drive me there?"

"Certainly." Moshe turned, put the car in gear, and steered it away from the hotel. An hour later he brought the car to a stop at the curb in the Nachlaot section of Jerusalem. He turned to look at David. "This is the home of Netanyahu," he said, pointing.

Out the window to the right David saw a residence, partially hidden behind a sandstone wall. In the center of the wall was an iron gate, and through the gate he glimpsed a courtyard with flowers and three small trees. "How do I get past the gate?"

"Push on it," Moshe suggested. "It might be open."

David opened the car door. "Can you wait for me?"

"Sure." Moshe switched off the engine. "I'll be right here."

David pushed the door open wider and stepped out. With a few quick strides he was across the sidewalk and in front of the gate. He grasped the latch and pressed the lever with his thumb. The latch popped open. With the slightest nudge, the gate swung back. David glanced over his shoulder at Moshe. Moshe grinned and waved.

The gate opened to a courtyard filled with lush flowers. Afternoon shadows made it cool and inviting. David felt awkward at entering without an invitation, but he had come too far to stop now. He pushed the gate closed behind him and made his way to the door. His heart pounded as he pressed the doorbell button.

The door was opened by an elderly man. David gave him a broad, friendly smile. "Benzion Netanyahu?"

"Yes," the old man nodded. "I am Benzion."

"My name is David Ellis. I'm a pastor from North Carolina, in America. I was wondering if I could talk to you for a moment."

Benzion's eyes focused on David, boring in on him with unusual intensity. Then his face softened, as if he had seen something that satisfied his mind about his visitor. He gave the slightest nod of his head. "Would you like to come in?"

"That would be an honor," David replied.

Benzion stepped back from the door to let David enter. After David passed, he closed the door behind them and led the way through the house to a room in back. He pointed to an overstuffed chair. "Have a seat."

David sat down, and Benzion sat a few feet away. David glanced around nervously. "Now that I'm here, I'm not sure where to begin."

"Perhaps you should begin at the beginning."

"Yes," David chuckled. "That would be a good place." He took a deep breath. "I attended a conference a few months ago about American-Israeli relations."

"The conference in Washington or the one in Wilmington?"

David was surprised by the question. "Wilmington," he replied. "You know about that conference?"

"Many of my friends were there."

"In one of the sessions they gave a presentation about the rescue at Entebbe and your son's role in that mission."

Benzion nodded slowly. "My friend Nathan Mileikowsky created that presentation."

"He did a good job. It was very powerful."

"Powerful enough to bring you all the way from America to my home?"

"Yes."

"Which part did you find most interesting?"

"A picture of you, standing on the tarmac at the airport, watching as they brought Jonathan's casket from the plane."

Benzion's eyes brimmed with tears. "That was the worst day of my life."

"I could see it in your eyes. You held your head high. Your jaw square. But your eyes showed the pain of a father who had lost a son."

"You are a father?"

"Yes," David nodded. "I have two children."

"I pray you never see the day when either of them dies. What are their names?"

"Megan and Joel."

"I suppose you know that in Hebrew Joel means 'Jehovah is Lord.' Those are good names."

"And they are good children too."

A door to the left opened and a young man appeared. About thirty years old, he was dressed in a suit and carried himself with purpose. He glanced at David as he entered the room. "I heard your American accent and wondered who was visiting us today."

Benzion gestured with his right hand. "This is David Ellis. He is a minister from North Carolina." Benzion turned to David. "This is my son, Benjamin."

David stood and the two men shook hands. Benjamin said, "A preacher?"

"Yes," David replied.

"What brings you to our home?"

"I was just telling your father, I attended a conference a few months ago in Wilmington. They had a presentation about the Entebbe rescue."

"Yes. Nathan Mileikowsky put that together." Benjamin took a seat on the arm of a nearby chair and David sat down again. "You are interested in the relationship between America and Israel?"

"Yes. My mother was Jewish."

"And your father?"

"Actually, my biological father was Jewish, but the man who raised me was not. Long story." David smiled.

"Interesting," Benjamin nodded. "You were intrigued by the story about Jonathan?"

Benzion looked at Benjamin. "A father's loss of a son can only be understood by a father."

David was inspired by Benzion's words and turned back to him soberly. "I wanted you to know that you are not alone. You do not face the loss of your son alone. And Israel does not face her enemies alone. You have friends who stand with you. I think God wanted me to come here and tell you that, and so I have come."

Benjamin folded his arms across his chest and gave David a curious look. "You flew all the way over here just to tell my father he has a friend? Because God told you to do it?"

"Yes."

Benjamin smiled wryly. "And does God have a message for me?"

David looked Benjamin in the eye. His pain at the loss of his brother was palpable. In an instant he felt the words rising inside. He stood slowly, put his hand on Benjamin's shoulder, and said, "You loved your brother Jonathan as Jonathan of old loved his friend, David. From the ashes of your despair will come strength from God."

The sound of his own voice seemed strange, but the words kept coming and rolled off his lips like water cascading over the rocks. "Yet unlike Jonathan of old, who died in battle defending his country, you will accede to the seat of power. One day you will become the prime minister of Israel, not once but twice. And the second time will be the most crucial in Israel's history." When he finished David felt suddenly weak, as if delivering those words had drained all energy from his body. His face was wet with tears as he sat down in his chair.

The smile had vanished from Benjamin's face. His forehead wrinkled in thought. David wiped his face and smiled at him. "It is a word from the Lord."

Benjamin nodded. "We shall see if you are a prophet." He stood. "Lucky for you, we do not live in ancient times. You know what happened to the prophet whose words did not come true."

"Yes," David grinned. "I am not afraid to be held accountable for the words God has given me." He pushed himself up from the chair. "Gentlemen, I appreciate your hospitality in allowing me into your home like this." He reached out for Benzion's with one hand and rested the other on Benjamin's shoulder. Without asking, he invoked an ancient Aaronic blessing. "The Lord bless you, and keep you. The Lord make His face to shine upon you, and be gracious unto you. The Lord lift up his countenance upon you, and give you peace. Amen."

"Amen," Benjamin repeated. "Come. I will walk you to the door."

chapter 54

David left the house and found Moshe still sitting in his car. When he climbed into the back seat, Moshe glanced at him through the rearview mirror. "You had a good visit?"

"I had a great visit."

"They are good people," Moshe agreed. "The entire family. Very good people."

"They were very good to me."

"Benzion Netanyahu taught in America. At Cornell. And his son, Benjamin, studied at MIT and Harvard. Did you know that at one time he was the chief marketing officer for a furniture company?"

"Wow." David arched an eyebrow. "I'm impressed."

"Yes. They are impressive people."

"Do you know them?"

"No." Moshe shook his head. "I just have a knack for interesting trivia." He put the car in gear and started forward. "You wish to return to the hotel now?"

"Yes." David rested his head against the seat. "Take me back to Tel Aviv."

David watched out the window as they wound through the streets of old Jerusalem and then turned onto the highway. Somewhere in the Israeli countryside he fell fast asleep. He was awakened by a tap on his knee. His eyes popped open to see Moshe grinning at him. "We are here."

David sat up and glanced around. "I slept the whole way?"

"You must be tired."

"I am." David leaned over the seat to pay him then shook his hand. "Thanks for the ride."

"It was my pleasure."

David climbed from the car, entered the hotel, and crossed the lobby to the elevator. He realized he had been in Israel for a day and still had not seen Avi. When he reached the room he took Avi's business card from his pocket and tried the number. It rang a dozen times with no answer. He shrugged and dined alone in the hotel restaurant.

* * *

The following morning David was awakened by the telephone. He groped on the table beside his bed and lifted the receiver. "Hello."

"David, you were sleeping?" It was Simeon Katz.

"Long day yesterday. What time is it?"

"Nine o'clock."

"How did you find me?"

"I called your home. Your wife told me you were here."

Now David was wide awake. "What's up?"

"The prime minister asked about you yesterday in a meeting. He wanted to know if you needed help building bridges. It made me think of our conversation, so I called your house to talk to you."

"Great! We should get together."

"I was calling to see if you could meet with the prime minister this afternoon. He has time for a short meeting at three."

"Simeon, I would be honored. It's hard to imagine that Menachem Begin actually remembers me."

"He asks about you often, David." Katz laughed. "I will send a car for you. They will pick you up at one this afternoon."

"I'm in Tel Aviv not Jerusalem."

"David," Katz replied wryly. "I called you, remember?"

"Yes."

"I know where you are."

"Okay," David chuckled. "I'll be waiting."

David pulled himself up and sat on the side of the bed. He rubbed his hands over his face and ran his fingers through his hair. After a moment to collect his thoughts, he headed to the bathroom for a shower.

✳   ✳   ✳

At one that afternoon David was waiting by the hotel entrance. He watched as a black Mercedes limousine came to a stop beneath the hotel canopy. Through the windshield he saw two men seated in front. The man on the passenger side opened the door and stepped out.

"David Ellis?"

"Yes."

The man opened the rear door. Simeon Katz was seated in back. David crawled inside. They greeted each other with a handshake. Katz seemed genuinely glad to see him. "How have you been?"

"I have been well."

"I heard you went to see Benzion Netanyahu yesterday."

"How did you find out about that?"

"The security detail did a check on you. They followed up to see what you had been doing. Miriam had asked a friend to let her know if you came back to Jerusalem. She informed me you were here."

"When do you think I might meet Miriam?"

"When the time is right, you will meet." Katz gave him a smile. "You can rest in the knowledge that she is keeping an eye on you.

"Did you really come all this way, David, just to see Benzion?"

"That's all the purpose I knew at the time I left home. I was to see him and share my heart with him about his son Jonathan. It was a good visit."

The time passed quickly as they talked, and they arrived at Menachem Begin's office just before three. An assistant greeted them and led them into the prime minister's office. Begin was seated at his desk when they entered. He smiled up at them. "A man who builds bridges across the ocean."

"Mr. Prime Minister. Thank you for seeing me."

"No. Thank you for coming," he smiled. "You have been here only one day and already you have made an impression."

"I hope it was a good one."

"Well, it is certain no one will forget you." They shook hands. Begin looked David in the eye. "How are you? Well, I hope."

"Yes," David nodded. "I am well."

"Please." Begin pointed to a chair. "Sit, David." He returned to his seat behind the desk. "So, this is now your third trip to Israel. Finding any more of your roots?"

"They are finding me."

Begin laughed. "I like that. Your roots are finding you." He looked at Katz. "This man has a sense of humor." He leaned back in his chair and focused his attention on David. "You have a good idea. Building bridges. We have not enough friends in the world."

"And Christians in America need a deeper appreciation for the historic and strategic connection between Judaism and Christianity."

"You have a way to give them that appreciation?"

"I'm working on it. My first step is to recruit churches and groups that will pray for the peace of Jerusalem."

"Prayer," Begin nodded. "We need much prayer. We also need young minds to stay right here and help us." He gestured to a row of pictures along the wall. "We are getting old, those of us with ties to the beginning. The next generation has to step up and take their places."

"I met a young man yesterday who needs to be involved. Benjamin Netanyahu."

Begin nodded. "He is a fine young man. But he withdrew from public life after the death of his brother."

"Someone needs to bring him out."

"You think he is ready?"

"I received a prophecy yesterday while I was visiting with them."

"A prophecy?" Begin laughed. He looked at Katz again. "The prophets have returned to us, Simeon. They've been living in America all this time." As his laughter died away Begin looked back at David. "And what was that prophecy, my friend?"

"That Benjamin Netanyahu would one day be prime minister. Not just once, but twice. And the second time would be more crucial than the first."

The laughter evaporated from Begin's eyes. "You think this is true?"

"Yes. I do."

"And how do you know it?"

"In my spirit."

"You do not find it a problem that God would reveal to a Christian a prophecy about a Jew who does not follow Jesus?"

"God is not finished with that story, on either side."

Begin leaned forward in his chair, his head cocked in a thoughtful pose. "And how did he react to your prophecy?"

"He said it was well that I did not live in ancient times, when a prophet paid for his life if he was wrong."

Begin thought a moment longer, then stood. "My friend, I am glad to have this time with you." He came from behind the desk and embraced David. "I hope we can enjoy many more times like this together."

The prime minister stretched out his hand and clasped David's. "I will help you build that bridge."

"Mr. Prime Minister, before I go may I pray for you?"

"Yes, David, by all means. I need all the prayer I can get."

David gripped his hand. "Please, pray with me, Mr. Prime Minister. "My God, guard my tongue from evil, and my lips from speaking falsehood. May my soul be silent to those who insult me; and my soul be as lowly to all as the dust. Open my heart to your Word, so that my soul may follow your commandments. Speedily defeat the counsel of all those who plan evil against me and upset their designs. Do it for the glory of Your name; do it for the sake of Your power; do it for the sake of Your holiness; do it for the sake of Your Word."

When David finished, the prime minister repeated the prayer in Hebrew. "*Elohai, netzor leshoni meira, usefatai midaber mirma; Velimkalelai nafshi tidom, venafshi ke'afar lakol tihiyeh. Petach libi betoratecha, uvemitzvotecha tirdof nafshi; Vechol hachoshvim alai ra'a, meheira hafer atzatam vekalkel machashavtam. Aseh lema'an shemecha, aseh lema'an yeminecha, aseh lema'an kedushatecha, Aseh lema'an toratecha.*"

Begin reached up and put his hands on David's shoulders. "Thank you. I love that ancient prayer. I am deeply grateful."

✳   ✳   ✳

On the ride back to the hotel David and Katz passed a street corner where police had three people detained. Two police vans were parked nearby, and as the car moved by a dozen officers rounded the corner to help. David looked in their direction. "Will the day come when terrorism—the sort Mossad deals with—comes to America?"

Katz glanced down at the floorboard. He traced his finger along a seam in the upholstery of the seat. "America has the power to fight terrorism but not the will. Terrorists have the will to destroy both our countries but not the power."

David nodded. "In spite of all our technological development, the Atlantic Ocean has been America's single greatest defense."

"But all of that could change," Katz replied. "Revenue from the trade in oil purchases more than tents in the desert."

"Their power is growing?"

"Yes. And their determination with it." Katz leaned back against the seat. "We face very different situations. In the West you kill a fly and rejoice. Here in the Middle East we kill one fly and a hundred attend the funeral." He looked across the seat at David "Yes, I fear it will come to you."

David turned away from the window. "How much time do we have?"

A smile flickered across Katz's face. "If I could predict that, I would be shouting it from the rooftops."

"Any idea how they would strike? Or where?"

Katz shook his head slowly. "That is hard to say. Islamic militants are infatuated with symbols. They would do their best to strike at the icons of your power—symbols of your economic, governmental, and military might."

"Washington, D.C.?"

"Perhaps. But they are also practical, which makes it difficult to predict. They would make their best effort to reach the most important symbols possible. But they know their limitations. So, while they might prefer the Treasury Department to the local bank, they would not avoid the local bank if that was the most they could do."

"So nothing is safe?"

"No, probably not. The center of your economic power is in New York, the financial district and the surrounding area. Your government and the military, of course, are primarily located in Washington, D.C. Those are the places to be guarded most carefully, in my opinion."

"How do you convince the powers that be in Washington that the U.S. is in danger?"

"Keep building bridges," Katz smiled, "and perhaps you will one day meet the people who can help."

As they neared the hotel Katz asked, "Can we park on the street and talk for a bit before you go back to the hotel?"

David looked at his birth father and nodded. For over an hour they proceeded to talk about their families and lives. Simeon was very curious about David's relationship with God and his ability to hear from Him. David was only too happy to share his faith with Simeon. He had great hope that one day his birth father would truly share his faith.

As their conversation wound down David wondered if Katz knew what had transpired after his first meeting with Prime Minister Begin. "Did Miriam tell you about my meeting in New York City with the prime minister a couple of years after our first meeting in Jerusalem?"

"She mentioned that you met with him, but the details were sketchy."

David leaned back against the car seat. "On an October evening in 1981 my phone rang at my home in North Carolina. Prime Minister Begin asked me if I would host a delegation of evangelical leaders to meet with him and his cabinet members when they came to New York later that month.

"I flew up to New York and met with the prime minister and Reuven Hecht. They were scheduled to meet with President Reagan, and I could tell they were worried about how things were going to go. Our secretary of state had told Begin that he would not fare well in talks with the president. Hecht told me Reagan thought Begin was a hardheaded Jew whose brain had been baked by the Holocaust. He had heard from the attorney general that, in fact, a meeting might not even take place."

Katz sighed. "I remember what a difficult time that was for Menachem."

"I sensed that. During our conversation, Mr. Begin asked me if I ever talked to my Jewish relatives. I told him I didn't know I had Jewish relatives other than mom's sister and her husband, my Aunt Eliana and Uncle Jacob.

The prime minister stammered, 'I thought you must have more relatives on your mother's side.'"

Katz looked searchingly at David. "Maybe the prime minister knows more than I give him credit for. Maybe he's been looking over Miriam's shoulder. He knows about my marriage to Leah."

David glanced at Katz. "I suppose that might have been why I was vetted before my first trip here. But back to my story about the New York City meeting. As I sat with the prime minister a sense of restlessness overshadowed me. Then a scripture in Matthew came to mind. It says, 'If two of you agree down here on earth concerning anything you ask, my Father in heaven will do it for you.' It talks about forgiveness bringing God's blessing. When I asked Reuven to tell me about the proposed meeting with Mr. Reagan, he replied, 'The cabinet members will meet with the prime minister's advisers. Then the president and prime minister will meet privately for about fifteen minutes.'

"I looked at Reuven and said, 'I believe God has a message from His Word for the prime minister. In the Oval Office last year for a gathering of ministers, I saw a photograph on the president's desk. It had supposedly been given to him by the International Red Cross. It was a child with no arms. Reagan had been told that the Israelis had caused the injuries to the little boy, but he was actually born that way. Nevertheless, the president thinks your countrymen did it. His advisers have told him that the prime minister is a stubborn Jew. Is that right?' Hecht responded, 'Yes, that is correct. I have heard the same assessment.'"

Katz laughed sarcastically. "That is the general consensus among those who hate the Jews."

David nodded and continued. "'Dr. Hecht,' I said, 'Prime Minister Begin needs to share the scripture in Matthew with President Reagan.' Hecht looked at me as if I were crazy."

Katz leaned forward with a twinkle in his eye. "I cannot imagine why."

"Seriously, I told Dr. Hecht, 'The prime minister should say this to President Reagan: Both our countries were founded on religious principles; they are both inhabited by people with a belief in the God of the Bible; the peoples of both our lands offer prayers for divine intervention and protection; and the peoples of both our lands believe God is in control of their destinies. Given all we agree upon, how can our two countries not find a way to move together toward peace and security in the world? We both believe in God. We both believe God has a great plan for our lives. God has a great plan for our countries. We have both faced death. Would you pray, Mr. President, that God's will be done in our meeting today?'

"Dr. Hecht paused and said, 'That is brilliant. I will tell him.' And, as you probably know, the meeting between the president and the prime minister went well."

Katz laid his hand on David's shoulder. "David, no matter what, do not ever be afraid to follow what God tells you to do—no matter how far-fetched or difficult it may seem."

David smiled and was warmed by the affirmation. "Well, I guess I'd better get back to my hotel room. I want to give Sue a call tonight. Thank you for this time together. I do hope someday soon to be able to meet Miriam."

"I know she would like that very much. It's just that her schedule is so uncertain. She never knows where she will be sent or when."

"Well, maybe you and I can see each other from time to time."

"I hope so, David. I hope so. Shalom and goodbye until we do meet again."

David clasped his birthfather's hand. Katz gripped his son's hand tightly before David opened the door and climbed out of the car. With a final wave he walked into the hotel lobby.

chapter 55

As the wheels lifted and the aircraft rose from the ground, David felt a twinge of sadness. Though he had stayed in Israel not quite seven days, it had begun to feel like home. He had made new friendships and strengthened the bonds with those he already knew. Going home seemed more like leaving home.

He propped his head against the airplane's window and wondered about Avi. He'd seemed so mysterious before, appearing in the lobby as if he knew exactly when David would arrive. David had expected to see him on this trip, but he had been mysteriously absent. Still, things had gone well, and he was pleased with the progress. Perhaps Avi was correct when he suggested relationships were more important than details.

When he arrived back at the airport in Charlotte, David made his way through the airport terminal to the luggage claim section. He grabbed his suitcase from the carousel and headed out the door. Sue and the children were waiting in the Caprice. At the sight of them his melancholy mood lifted. He put his suitcase in the trunk and got in the front seat. "Anybody miss me?"

Sue leaned over for a kiss. "I did," she smiled.

Joel reached over from the back seat and tousled David's hair. "I made the summer baseball team," he announced.

"Great," David replied. He turned to look over his shoulder at Megan, who was in her cheerleading uniform. She smiled at him from the back seat. "Looks like you've been to cheerleading practice." Megan raised her foot to show an Ace bandage wrapped around her ankle. Her eyes were full, and she was on the verge of tears. David looked concerned. "Does it hurt?"

"Yeah," she nodded.

"When did that happen?"

"This afternoon."

"I'm sorry." David reached over the seat and took her hand. "When were tryouts?"

"Yesterday," she smiled.

"So, you made the squad?"

"Yeah," she nodded. "I made the squad."

"Great," David grinned. "This calls for a celebration."

"Tony's Ice Cream!" Joel announced.

"Tony's it is," David agreed.

Sue steered the car from the airport. "You sure you don't want to just go home and sleep?"

"A shower would be great," David replied. "Right after some strawberry ice cream."

"Hey, Dad," Megan spoke up. He turned in her direction. She smiled at him, "Great to have you home," and she patted his arm.

*   *   *

Sue came into the bedroom and sat on the bed while David put on his pajamas. "Anna called yesterday."

"How is she?"

"She is doing extremely well. She's found a little church in Chicago, a Messianic Jewish group, and is diligently studying the Word. I told her you'd call when you got home."

"Okay, I'll do that right now." He picked up the phone and dialed her number. "Hi, Sis! Sue tells me you are doing well."

"I've never been better. Did you have a good trip to Israel?"

"Yes."

"How many times have you been over there now?"

"This was my third trip."

Anna laughed. "You're becoming an Israeli citizen," she quipped.

"It's feeling more like home every time."

"I'm glad you called. I wanted to talk with you some more about what we discussed last time."

"Which part?"

"Praying."

"What did you want to talk about?"

"I didn't really want to talk about it. I wanted to do it. David would you pray for me?"

"I do pray for you, Anna, daily."

"No, I mean pray with me."

"Sure, what shall we pray about?"

"David, I'm puzzled. I've prayed to receive Jesus. I'm going to church regularly."

"Yeah, Sue told me."

"But sometimes the anger still pops up at the most unexpected times. Yesterday, I saw a family walking by. The father was holding the little girl and smiling at her. I wondered if he really loved her, or if he was like my father. How do I get rid of the anger, David?"

"By forgiving him every time you have a bad memory. Say the words aloud, 'I forgive you.'"

"Is it really that easy?"

"No, but pretty soon it becomes second nature. You know, Anna, forgiveness doesn't mean you forget. It just means that the pain of the memory no longer has the power to hurt you. The memory may remain, but the pain is gone. Every time you consciously forgive Dad for his acts against you, you drive one more nail into the Enemy's coffin. Keep praying, keep forgiving, and the pain of the past will give way to the joy of the future.

"Let's pray. Jesus, in Your Word You say that You will give us beauty for ashes and the oil of joy for mourning. Cover Anna with the garment of praise to battle this spirit of heaviness that sometimes threatens to overwhelm her. Show her that for the beauty to come forth, she has to make an exchange. She has to hand over the old, dirty ashes of the past to You and let You turn them into beautiful, sparkling diamonds. Daily give her Your peace that passes man's understanding. In Jesus' name, amen."

After a long pause, Anna spoke again. "Thanks, Big Brother. I appreciate your prayer. Speaking of prayer, did you ever meet Hilda? She was the lady who came in and helped me when I was the sickest after chemo and radiation."

"I haven't met her."

"Yesterday I found out that she was an angel is disguise. Well, not really an angel, but you know what I mean. God sent her to help me. He was watching out for me all that time, and I didn't know it!"

"How did you meet her?" David asked

"I was in the store one day. Hilda helped me reach a can on the top shelf. We started talking, and she told me she liked to cook. We made a date to get together at the house. When she found out what I was facing, she just came back every week. I bought the groceries, and she cooked. What I didn't know was that Hilda was a Christian and was praying for me."

"Wow! That tells me that while Sue and I have been praying for you, God has been faithful to send you help. Please tell Hilda how much we appreciate what she has done for you."

"I will. I love you, David. Tell Joel and Megan hi for me and give Sue a big hug. She's one special lady, you know."

"That I do know, and I'll be more than happy to pass on the hug and the hi."

David hung up the phone and grabbed Sue in a bear hug.

"What on earth is this for?"

David grinned. "Oh, just a hug from Anna. She asked me to pass it on."

chapter 56

A few weeks later David and Sue packed up the Caprice for the family vacation. Two weeks at Carolina Beach gave them time together and a chance to rest after a busy and life-changing winter and spring. They returned home to find the mailbox filled with mail. David brought it to the kitchen table and sorted through it. One of the letters was of particular interest. It was from the Lebanese Christian Foundation, an organization in Atlanta that supported Christian groups in Lebanon. Sue looked over his shoulder while he read. "What is that about?"

"They've been having trouble getting supplies and aid to their groups in Lebanon. They want to know if I can help."

"How did they find you?"

David pointed to the letter. "Says they heard about me from Jeff Howell."

"Who's he?"

"Steve Smith's cousin."

"That's an interesting twist. Think you can help them?"

"I don't know anyone in Lebanon."

"But you do know a few people in Israel."

"Jews helping Christians smuggle aid across the border into Lebanon."

"No," Sue replied. "Friends in Israel, helping a friend in America, reach a group in Lebanon."

"But who could I ask?"

"Let's see," she mused playfully. "There's the prime minister of Israel. Or his best friend. Who else do you know?"

"I'll pray about it," David agreed. "But I'm not rushing into this just because it sounds good. The people I know in Israel are all people I met for a reason. I have to make certain this is one of those reasons. Think I'll go for a walk and pray about this."

"Want some company?"

"Would you mind if I said not right now?"

"Of course not," she smiled.

He opened the back door and stepped outside. The summer sun was hot, and he was soon wet with sweat as he walked past the driveway onto the street. He was also soon deep in prayer. As he made the block, and made it again, he began to sense the Holy Spirit moving. He had friends in Israel. They might be willing to help if he was willing to ask. He hadn't thought of it that way, of building friendships as a way of working in the region. He had just thought of it as working with Israel. As he continued to pray he heard Avi's voice. *"You worry too much about the details. You should concentrate more on the relationships."*

On the third lap through the neighborhood David began to think about those he might contact for help. Menachem Begin had the power to make things happen, but the prime minister of Israel couldn't get involved in something like this. Lebanon was in the midst of a long-running civil war, much of which spilled over into Israel and created a serious challenge to Israel's security. If the prime minister helped a group of Christians smuggle supplies back across the border and something went wrong, it might be seen as a provocative act against Lebanon's sovereignty.

Simeon Katz was an obvious choice, but he was close to Begin. If anyone found out what was happening and connected it to Katz, it might embroil Begin in the controversy. "Lord, I want to help, but I don't want to damage what You are doing."

As he made yet one more lap around the block, he thought of Benzion Netanyahu and of his son Benjamin. "That might work," David muttered to himself. The Netanyahu family had relationships with many influential people in Israel. A phone call from them to the right people might open a way for the project to move forward. At the same time, they had no official connection to the Israeli government. If something went wrong, there would be less chance it would become an international incident.

Or I could just go over there myself, drive to the border, and try to get across. If it works, good. If not, or if I get caught and get in trouble, I could always apologize later. He thought about it a moment longer, then shook his head. *Not a good idea.*

A few days later David traveled to Atlanta and met with the leaders of the Lebanese Christian Foundation. He toured their offices and learned more about their work. That night he had dinner with the foundation's president. Afterward, he rented a room at a motel on the east side of town. As he passed the registration desk he picked up a copy of the *Atlanta Journal Constitution* and took it to his room. In bed that night he began to read it and came across an article about the war in Lebanon. The article mentioned patrols conducted by the Israeli Defense Force and allegations that those patrols had made incursions deep into Lebanon's territory. It quoted an official from the Israeli embassy in Washington, D.C. That official was the newly appointed deputy director of the diplomatic mission, Benjamin Netanyahu.

David grinned. "Menachem Begin gave him a job after all." He folded the paper and laid it on the nightstand, then slid under the covers. "Netanyahu would be the perfect person to contact. If I ask him for help, he won't get involved on my word alone. He'll have someone investigate the Foundation, and they'll do a more thorough job than I could ever do. That would protect us both." He reached over and turned out the light. "I think Benjamin is the man for this job."

Later that week David placed a call to Netanyahu's office and requested a meeting. An hour later a secretary from the embassy called to say Netanyahu could see him the following Monday afternoon. That day he was met in the lobby by a guard who escorted him upstairs to Netanyahu's office. Benjamin was standing near the door when David arrived.

"We meet again."

"Yes," David replied, shaking Netanyahu's hand. "Good to see you."

Netanyahu closed the door behind them. David looked around the room. "Nice office."

"I suppose I have you to thank for it too."

David said sincerely, "You were too good to spend your life marketing furniture."

"Well," Netanyahu shrugged, "we do what we have to." He moved behind his desk. "But thanks for mentioning me to Begin. How may I help you?"

David took a seat. "There's a group in Atlanta that works with Christians in Lebanon. They've been working there a long time, but their primary contact was killed a few months ago and they're having trouble getting supplies into the country. They asked me if I could help."

"What are they sending?"

"Blankets. Books. Food. I think they'll probably include an envelope of cash too."

Netanyahu turned his chair sideways and rested his arm on the desktop. "Have you ever done this sort of thing before?"

"No." David shook his head. "Never."

"These things can be tricky."

"That's why I came to you."

"How are they sending them?"

"Packing boxes in Atlanta. Loading them on a flight to Tel Aviv. Driving them to the border."

"Would they be willing to let someone inspect the contents of the boxes?"

"I'll tell them they have to."

Netanyahu nodded his head thoughtfully. "The cash. Will it be U.S. currency?"

"Should it?"

Netanyahu threw back his head and laughed. "You really have not done this before, have you?"

"Hey," David grinned. "I'm being totally honest. I've never done anything like this in my life."

Netanyahu pushed back his chair from the desk, stood and smiled. "I will see what I can do, my friend."

"That would be a great help," David stood and they shook hands.

Netanyahu guided him toward the door and opened it. "But do me a favor. Do not tell anyone."

A week later David received a plain white envelope in the mail. It was addressed by hand and bore a return address in Maryland. He opened it to find a single page. On it was written, "Cross north of Rosh Hanikra. Before 1 August."

chapter 57

Mid-July found David once again onboard a flight bound for Tel Aviv. This time he brought Billy along. They had been working together, developing Followers of the Light, and Billy had spent many hours accompanying David to meetings. His help allowed David to concentrate on the work at hand and freed him from some of the details. They arrived in Tel Aviv before noon and brought their luggage and boxes to the Yamit Plaza Hotel.

While Billy rested in his room, David went downstairs and found the bellman. "When I was here before, there was a driver named Moshe who took me to Jerusalem. Do you know how I could find him?"

"Certainly." The bellman started toward the front entrance. "He is right this way." David followed him out to the drive in front of the hotel. The bellman gestured to the right. "He is seated over there. His car is for hire."

David walked over to the older black Mercedes. He opened the rear door and crawled into the back seat. Moshe turned to greet him, his eye wide with surprise. "Hello. I remember you."

"Yes?"

"You are the preacher from America. I took you to see Benzion Netanyahu."

"Right."

"Where would you like to go today?"

"Nowhere today. But tomorrow I need to go to Rosh Hanikra. Can you drive me there?"

"Yes. I can do it."

"I will have one other person with me. And six boxes. You can do that?"

"Yes."

"Good," David nodded. "I'll be waiting for you at six in the morning."

"I will be here."

*   *   *

The following morning David and Billy awoke before the dawn and ate breakfast in the hotel café. Afterward, they returned to David's room and loaded the boxes on a luggage cart. Moshe arrived just as they wheeled the cart outside. Three of the boxes fit in the trunk of the car. Three were stacked in the back seat beside Billy. David rode up front.

Moshe followed Highway 4 north from Tel Aviv. The ride to Rosh Hanikra took about an hour. As they drew near, he looked over at David. "You wish to visit the caves?"

"No, not this time." David shook his head and pointed out the windshield. "Stay on the coast. Toward the border."

Moshe looked concerned. "You are traveling to the border?"

"Beyond."

Moshe lifted his foot from the gas pedal. "I do not have documents for the car. We cannot cross the border without permission."

"It will be fine." David pointed again. "You'll see. Let's go."

"No." Moshe shook his head. "We cannot."

"We must. These boxes have to reach Lebanon."

"If we cross into Lebanon with these boxes, we will be arrested for aiding the enemy."

"Israel is not at war."

"But Lebanon is. A civil war. And we must not get involved."

"Look. These boxes have blankets, medical supplies, and books.

They are going to a group of Christians who live in Lebanon." He reached across the seat and rested his hand on Moshe's arm. "Just drive to the border. If the guards stop us, we'll go back to the hotel." Moshe gave David a wary look. "Just to the border," David urged. "We'll see what happens when we get there." Moshe turned away and pressed his foot against the gas pedal. The car picked up speed.

A few minutes later they were at the border crossing. A truck blocked the highway. Moshe brought the car to a stop. A soldier approached. He was dressed in combat fatigues with what appeared to be a Galil assault rifle slung over his shoulder. He came to the driver's window and leaned down to look inside. He said something to Moshe in Hebrew and then looked at David. "You are Americans?"

"Yes."

"Let me see your passports, please."

David took his passport from his pocket. Billy handed his over the seat. The soldier glanced at Billy's then opened David's. He scanned them quickly then handed them back through the window. He turned away and shouted to a group of soldiers standing near the truck. One of them climbed into the cab. The others scrambled out of the way.

Moshe looked over at David in disbelief. "They are letting us pass."

"I know." David pointed. "We better go while we can."

Black smoke belched from the truck as the engine started. Slowly it moved forward out of the way. The soldier who had approached them signaled with his arm to motion them past. As the car started forward he shouted something through the open window.

David glanced across to Moshe. "What did he say?"

"Be back before nightfall."

"That shouldn't be a problem."

"Where are we going?"

"Naqoura."

"That is quite a ways."

"Not any farther than we've come."

"Farther than I have ever been into Lebanon," Moshe grinned.

They arrived in Naqoura after noon. After a few wrong turns, David found what he was looking for. A blue BMW parked outside the Ya Libnan Café. Their contact, Abdul, was waiting inside. The exchange went smoothly. In an hour the BMW was loaded. David, Billy, Moshe and Abdul sat down for an early dinner at the café. Billy paid the café owner for the meal and the four men walked outside. After saying goodbye, Abdul climbed into the BMW and took off. The other three men walked down the street to Moshe's car and got inside for the ride back to Tel Aviv.

Suddenly Moshe asked, "Where is everyone?"

David looked around. "What do you mean?"

"The streets." Moshe gestured. "They are empty."

"I don't like it," Billy spoke up.

Moshe started the car. "We should go." He made a u-turn from the curb and drove away from the café. As they turned the next corner, a bomb exploded behind them. The sound was deafening. David felt the concussion.

"What was that?" Billy screamed.

"Car bomb."

"How can you tell?"

"The size of the explosion," Moshe explained. "It was too large to be carried by one person."

Emergency vehicles traveling in the opposite direction passed them. All around them they heard the wail of sirens. Then came the sound of gunfire. Moshe pressed the gas pedal to the floor and hunched over the steering wheel. He whipped it back and forth like a madman as they barreled through the streets, dodging people and cars at breakneck speed. It seemed to take forever to find their way out of town through the mass of people and vehicles hurrying toward the explosion.

David shouted, "I don't know which will kill us first, the shooting or your driving!"

"Don't let up," Billy called from the back seat. "We don't want to get stopped."

Finally they turned onto an open highway and sped away from town. David glanced out the window at the countryside. "This isn't the way we came."

"I know," Moshe replied. "But it should get us back to the border faster."

"We have to cross at Rosh Hanikra."

"We have to survive first."

"Do you think it will take us to the crossing we came through?"

"I hope so."

"Do we have enough gas?"

"I hope so."

Several miles south of town, the paved highway became a dirt road. Fear lurked at David's side. He thought of all that could go wrong: Lebanese soldiers on patrol. Random gunfire. A mortar round striking their car. He looked out across the countryside and began to pray, and as he opened his heart to God he remembered a line from the ninety-first Psalm. He whispered the words. "I will say to the Lord, He is my refuge and my fortress, my God, in whom I trust. You will not fear the terror of the night, nor the arrow that flies by day, nor the pestilence that stalks in the darkness, nor the plague that destroys at midday."

As the evening faded and night began to fall bright lights suddenly zipped overhead.

"Tracers!" Billy shouted. And then the sky was on fire with them. Billy turned to look out the back. "Somebody's shooting at us?"

David turned to look, but just then the car sputtered and slowed to a stop. Panic rose inside. He looked at Moshe. "Gas?"

"I do not know," Moshe shrugged. "I thought we had enough."

There was a tap at David's window. He turned to see an old man dressed in a white robe and wearing a *kaffiyeh* on his head. Deep lines ran across his forehead and around the corners of his mouth. He stared at David a moment, then walked around the car and removed the fuel cap. Seemingly from out of nowhere, a fuel can appeared and he emptied the contents into the tank. An instant later, he opened the rear door and crawled inside next to Billy. "*Rouh! Alatool!*" he commanded.

Moshe turned the key. The engine came to life. David cut his eyes at Moshe. "What did he say?"

Moshe pointed, "He said, 'Go! Go straight on!'" He gunned the engine and the car sped forward.

They rode in silence, the old man seated next to Billy, David seated up front with Moshe. A few miles farther they came to a road that led off to the right. The old man grunted something and pointed. Moshe turned the car to the right and continued on.

As night fell the old man barked something from the back seat. Moshe brought the car to a stop. The old man opened the door and stepped out. He walked around to David's side of the car. David rolled down his window, and Moshe translated as the old man patted David's arm, "You are safe now. The Light that resides in you will guide you." He smiled and then stepped back from the car.

Billy leaned forward. "What did he say?"

David turned his head to one side. "He was telling me we're safe now."

"I heard that. But what was the part about the Light?"

"I'll tell you later."

Moshe put the car in gear and they started forward. David turned to the right to wave, but the old man was gone. Billy glanced out the rear window. "Where did he go?"

Thirty minutes later a familiar smell wafted through the car. David sat up straight. "I smell salt in the air."

Billy frowned. "Salt?"

"Sea air. The beach."

After driving a few more minutes they topped a hill. Before them, the Mediterranean Sea glistened in the moonlight. Moshe turned the car to the left and headed south toward the border at Rosh Hanikra.

chapter 58

It was nearly eight o'clock when they reached the hotel. After David paid Moshe for the trip, he and Billy went to their rooms to change clothes then walked down the street to a restaurant for dinner. They sat at a table near the window and ate while watching the passersby on the sidewalk outside.

Billy wiped his mouth with a napkin. "Who do you think that old man was?"

"I think," David smiled, "he was an angel." He took a sip of water. "What did you think when he got in the car?"

"I thought we were going to die. Then I looked at his face."

"What did you think then?"

"That he was just trying to help."

"But how did he know we needed help?"

"Car stops in the middle of a gunfight." Billy shrugged. "I guess he figured something was up."

"Or he was an angel."

"That's possible too."

"Did you ever see an angel?"

"I don't know, for sure. When we were in France we got pinned down one night. They called in an air strike right on top of us. A shell exploded just a couple of yards away from me. I thought I was gone, but a hand came over my shoulder and grabbed the front of my shirt. I could feel an arm pushing me into a foxhole. The shrapnel went right over my head. When I recovered, there was no one around. I was in that foxhole alone. Were you scared today?"

David nodded. "I've been praying since that bomb went off in Beirut."

"I wasn't praying then," Billy grinned. "I was too busy staying down until we got out of town. I really started praying when I saw those tracers overhead."

When they finished eating dinner, David and Billy walked back to the hotel. As they walked through the front door, David saw Avi seated in the lobby. After introductions Billy excused himself to go to his room.

Avi gestured toward the door. "Let's go for a walk." David followed him outside. They turned right and started up the street. "You had quite an adventure today."

David nodded. "I did."

"Don't you think it's time we talked about angels?"

"I think we saw one today."

"What better place than Israel."

David nodded. "What drew them to us today?"

"It is not just today," Avi replied. "Even in your short lifetime, you have had a number of encounters with angels."

David gave him a skeptical look. "I believe in angels, Avi. I think the man we saw today might have been one. And I think there might have been one or two others. But besides that, I don't think it's been a regular occurrence for me."

"Do you remember that time when you were four years old, you ran away from home? You were frightened of your father and you decided to leave. Do you remember that?"

"I remember. But how do you know about that?"

"Never mind how I know. We will talk about that later. You remember the incident?"

"Yes."

"You ran to the park, and what happened?"

"There was a group there. Older people. Senior citizens."

"And what did you do?"

"I ran right through them."

"And a nurse with the group caught you by the arm and asked if you wanted to feed the ducks."

"There's no way you could know about that."

"Trust me. I know. You were scared, and you jerked free of her grasp and yelled at her. 'Leave me alone.' Only she didn't."

David remembered it as if it had just happened. She leaned close and asked his name. Then she smiled at him. Others from the group gathered around him and started talking to him. A neighbor found him there, and with the nurse's help convinced him to go back home.

"She stopped your headlong rush toward the pond," Avi explained. "Had she not intervened, you would have fallen in and drowned. Abba sent those people with their nurse to the pond to stop the Enemy from destroying you. Even then Abba had a plan for your life, and it didn't include drowning in a duck pond."

David had a puzzled frown. "That nurse was an angel?"

"Yes," Avi nodded. "They were not there by accident. Abba sent them out there to keep you safe." They walked in silence a while, then Avi asked, "What happened when you went to school each morning?"

"In elementary school I walked six blocks to the corner and crossed the street. We lived really close to the school."

"Who was at the corner?"

"The crossing guard, Mrs. Panelli." Avi gave him a knowing smile. David shook his head. "Are you telling me she was an angel?"

Avi smiled the enigmatic little smile that David had seen so often. "What did she say to you almost every morning?"

David swallowed the lump in his throat. "She would always wink at me before saying, 'Good morning, young man. I see the light in you.'"

Avi leaned closer. "Remember the car? The one that nearly ran over you."

"They said some guy had a heart attack just before he reached the crosswalk. I remember looking up and seeing the grill of that big, old car coming right at me. The next thing I knew, I was standing on the curb beside Mrs. Panelli."

"Mrs. Panelli," Avi said quietly. "Your guardian angel swept you up and deposited you on the curb without a scratch. I know you faced some real hardships and terrible abuse, but Abba preserved your life, David. He wanted you to know His light was in you, that you were not a child of the darkness but a child of the light."

"I never thought of it like that."

"Here's another one for you," Avi continued. "One day you raced out of a store into the street and ran right into the side of a car. The jolt threw you backward onto the pavement. You could have been seriously injured, but a man standing nearby caught you before you landed on your head. You walked away without a scratch."

"An angel?"

"Some of them were angels. Some of them were Abba orchestrating the events of your day to protect you."

"So, what about Yona?"

"You already suspect the truth about Yona. Do you really need me to tell you?"

"I guess not. But what about the house?"

"Which house?"

"Her house, where we had lunch."

Avi came to a stop. "That will have to wait for another day."

"Why?"

Avi pointed. "We are back at the hotel." David spun around to see the hotel right behind him. Avi laughed. "It is late, my friend."

"I would rather stay and talk."

"And we shall talk more. But not tonight."

"When?"

"Come back in the spring. And we will go on a trek to Sinai."

"Mount Sinai?"

"Yes. Mount Sinai. You have but one more thing to learn about your Father, and then you can move on from this part of your journey to the next."

"What will that be?"

"We will discuss that when you return."

David turned toward the hotel. He took a step and then remembered they hadn't set a date for the trip. He turned back to ask, but Avi was gone.

chapter 59

After David and Billy returned home, Billy called one afternoon to say they needed to talk. "It's important, David," Billy urged.

"Come on over. There's nothing going on right now."

Ten minutes later Billy was sitting in David's living room. His old friend looked intently at him. "I have a story to tell you. Please just listen. I told you about our son who was killed in Korea. Well, after he died we collected on his insurance policy—two hundred thousand dollars. We'd never seen that much money before. Our hearts were broken, and it seemed a poor substitute for Frank, so we just invested it—some in the market, some in CDs. We've never touched it. It's just been sitting there gathering interest.

"Margaret and I have been praying about what to do with it. We've each been feeling like we knew, but it wasn't until this morning that we finally sat down and talked about it. We are agreed, David. We want to invest it in Followers of the Light."

David was stunned. "Billy, I can't take your money."

"It's not my money, David; it's God's money. He wants you to have it. You can't argue with Him, now can you?"

David leaned back against the sofa cushions. "I don't know what to say."

Billy pointed up toward the ceiling. "Just thank Him. It's His idea."

He pulled a card from his wallet. "Now, here's the name of my lawyer. He's a good guy. You'll like him."

David took the card from Billy and looked at it. "Michael Cohen. Attorney at Law. Lindberger, Mann, and Liddle."

Billy stood. "I'd better get on back home. Give Michael a call. He'll take care of you and get this all squared away."

David stood and shook his hand, then he walked Billy to the door. After he closed the door he called out, "Sue, where are you?"

"In the kitchen."

David hurried down the hallway and into the kitchen. "You'll never believe this. Billy and Margaret are making a donation to Followers of the Light. He said something about a couple hundred thousand dollars."

Sue turned white and dropped into a chair. "I don't know what to say. How can that be?"

David recounted the story of Billy's son and the insurance money. "He said God spoke to both him and Margaret. They are in agreement to give the money to Followers of the Light. I'll call the attorney tomorrow and find out what I need to do."

"God does provide, doesn't He? And He'll bless Billy and Margaret for their faithfulness. I know it."

The next morning David called Michael Cohen and made an appointment to stop by his office that afternoon. After he arrived, David spent most of the time signing papers and telling Cohen about his trips to Israel. Two weeks later David received a letter from the attorney. All the details had been settled. Stapled to the letter was a check. David staggered into the den and collapsed in the recliner.

When Sue heard the loud "thump" she came running. "Is something wrong?"

"No," David sighed. He handed her the check. "Nothing at all."

Sue's mouth fell open. In her hand she held a check for eight hundred fifty thousand dollars. "Wow." She dropped to the arm of the chair. "I don't know what to say."

"Thank you, Lord."

"Yes," Sue agreed. "Thank you, Jesus. I think there's a trip to the bank in our near future."

David slipped his arm around Sue and stared at the check in her hand. "Thanks to Billy we have the offer of a house should we need it and the operating capital for Followers of the Light. We have enough money to do just about any kind of work that's needed, and we don't have to worry so much about the cost of an airline ticket." David paused and looked at Sue. "Did I tell you Avi invited me back to Israel in the spring?"

"For something in particular?"

"A trek to Mount Sinai."

"You'll like that," she grinned. "Why does he want to take you to Sinai?"

"He said there was one more thing I needed to learn about my Father."

"Your Father? You know, he doesn't mean Wally."

"I know. And he doesn't mean Simeon Katz, either."

"Are you ready for a hike through the desert?"

"I can get ready."

David spent the fall and winter preaching, recruiting supporters for Followers of the Light, enjoying the regular Torah Study, and polishing the manuscript for his book. He also started jogging and working out regularly at the gym. He had never been on a desert trek, but he was certain it would be physically demanding. He wanted his body ready for the challenge.

Finally, in late March he made a reservation for the flight to Tel Aviv. That same afternoon, the phone rang. The call was from Avi.

"You are ready for the trek?"

"Your timing is impeccable, Avi. I just made a reservation."

"Good. Tell me the date and time of your arrival."

David gave him the flight information, and they discussed the equipment he needed to bring.

"I'll have a backpack and sleeping bag waiting for you at the hotel.

All you need to bring for the trek is a good pair of boots and several changes of socks."

"That's it?"

"That's it. And remember," Avi added. "Whatever you bring you must carry on your back. So pack lightly."

chapter 60

David arrived in Tel Aviv in late April. After a good night's sleep he arose before dawn. As he dressed, the reality of what he was about to do finally hit him. *What in the world have I gotten myself into? I don't like to sleep on the ground. I don't like to eat sand. The desert is full of scorpions and who knows what else.*

He slipped his feet into his boots. *I wonder if it's too late to back out.* He pushed his toes all the way down and pulled the laces tight. *Why would I intentionally go off into the dark? I hate the dark.*

Dressed and ready, he slid open the door to the balcony and stepped outside. A blinding rainstorm had blown across the city during the night. As the sun rose behind him, long rays of sunshine slowly spread toward the horizon in the west. A rainbow appeared in the sky, followed by a second, and then a third. His heart leaped in his chest. "Rainbows are a sign from Heaven," he said to himself, "a promise from God that He is at work to renew and restore all of His creation. And that includes me."

A knock at the door brought David from the balcony. He crossed the room and opened it to find Avi. "*Boker tov!*" he said in a loud voice. "Good morning, my friend. Are you ready?"

"I hope so."

"Well, if you're ready and willing, let's go."

David picked up his backpack from the end of the bed and slipped his arms through the straps. "Don't walk too fast."

"I'll make sure you keep up."

Avi held the door while David stepped into the hall. He pulled the door closed then led the way to the elevator. Downstairs he stopped at the desk and turned to David, holding out his hand. "Give me your wallet, your passport, and your watch."

David was taken aback. "Why?"

"You must travel from here without them."

"I don't want to give up my wallet."

"You must." Avi wiggled his fingers. "Hand them to me, and we will put them in the hotel safe."

Reluctantly David slid the watch from his wrist and took the wallet from his hip pocket. He handed them to Avi, who passed them over the counter. The clerk placed the items in the safe and gave David a receipt. Then Avi motioned for David to follow. He led the way across the lobby and out the front door.

Outside a silver Land Cruiser was parked in front of the hotel. "This is ours," said Avi. David opened the rear hatch, stowed his backpack next to Avi's, and then climbed inside. Avi introduced David to the driver, Benni Mazur. He leaned back as Benni steered the big vehicle onto the busy street.

Once underway, David turned to Avi. "I saw a triple rainbow this morning."

"You are fascinated by light."

"Yes."

Avi smiled at him. "When the Savior appeared to you, it was in the form of a shaft of light breaking through the gloom of your dark bedroom. You have discovered over your own lifetime Abba's light can never be extinguished. No matter what comes our way—sickness, death, prosperity, poverty, depression—His light shines even in the darkest hours. It is impossible for darkness to overcome the light. You are a follower of the Light!"

The two men sat in silence, each deep in thought. Finally, Avi spoke. "Abba doesn't want the redeemed just to sing to Him and shout hallelujah throughout eternity. He wants fellowship with His sons and daughters in the light of Heaven. Many think of Heaven only as a place with streets of gold, no more tears, seeing family members who have gone on before them."

"That's how Scripture describes it."

"Yes, but the point is not just about seeing others. It's about seeing Abba. He will be the first in line to welcome you home. Abba loved you so much that He penetrated the darkness of your life to reveal Himself to you. He wants you to live in the light, in the brightness of His Son. Now you know why the Savior called you son."

"It's a little difficult to think of God that way. Every time I hear the word father I think of Wally." He shook his head. "Not a good image for that word."

Avi patted him on the leg. "We are going to work on that image now."

David nodded blankly as he sought to understand the depth of what Avi was saying. "I felt His love there in my room. He actually said, 'I love you.' The first one to believe in me was Jesus." He paused a moment, then said, "The second was Sue."

"No, David," Avi replied. "The first to believe in you was Abba. Before He created the Heaven and the Earth, He believed in you and loved you. It is time you accepted that."

David turned away and looked out the window. The early morning light cast a rosy glow over the landscape. The sky was aflame with reds, oranges, and yellows. He looked in amazement at the awesome display of the power of a loving God, the One who existed in light. Seeing it now left him feeling small and insignificant.

Avi spoke in Hebrew to Benni, then he eased back in the seat and turned to David. "Our drop-off point is just ahead. We're almost to the northwestern gulf of the *Yam Suf*."

"The Red Sea? So, we must be near the Egyptian border, right?"

Avi nodded. "We will retrace some of the Exodus journey." He gave David a long, careful look. "I am glad you agreed to come. I think this will be an important few days for you. We will be following the footsteps of Moses for a part of the trip. He lived in the dark for a very long time…until the Light shined on him through the burning bush."

"I'm looking forward to whatever it is you think I need to learn."

The Land Cruiser slowed. Avi turned around to look out the window "Ah," he smiled "We are here."

They came to a stop, and in every direction David looked there was nothing but rocks, sand, and in the distance, a line of craggy hills that looked like jagged teeth. He had heard the region described as the "great and terrible wilderness." Now he knew why.

Avi opened the door and went around to the back of the vehicle. Benni was already opening the rear hatch. He helped Avi shoulder his pack then did the same for David. A few minutes later David watched as Benni got back in the Land Cruiser and pulled away. Soon there was nothing in sight except the barren Sinai Desert stretching away on all sides.

"So Avi, this is it? Just you and me?"

"You expected more?"

"Well, to be honest, I had no idea what to expect. But from all this gear, I'd say we're making a major trek."

Avi nodded. "As I hope you will see, a desert walk has not only a physical dimension but a spiritual one as well. We will end at Mount Sinai, and along the way…well, we shall see." He turned, adjusted the straps on his pack, and started walking.

David followed. "Don't we need a map or something?" Avi made no reply. He just kept walking. David did his best to match Avi's pace. "So, I guess you've done this before? I mean, we don't have a guide or a base camp." Avi just looked straight ahead.

chapter 61

David followed a few paces behind Avi, plodding across the desert. As the physical stress of hiking settled into his shoulders and legs, he began to feel forgotten and shunned by Avi's unwillingness to talk. *I've flown the better part of seven thousand miles, and now I'm being ignored. If I had a way to get back to the hotel, I'd go. But I don't even have my wallet.*

As the morning wore on David's mood improved. He began to see the wisdom of silence. It saved breath for walking. The weight of the pack and the unrelenting glare of the sun against the sand forced him to conserve his resources, expending no more energy than necessary to keep moving forward.

It's a good thing we're doing this in the spring. This place must be like a furnace in the summer.

Ahead of him Avi moved at a steady pace. Of average build, he looked like any ordinary middle-aged Israeli man, but there was no questioning his stamina. His gait was consistent, his breathing deep but regular, and he moved with the confidence of one who knew exactly where he was going and exactly the amount of effort needed to get there.

What would it be like to live that way? To be so at peace with yourself that you could make a decision and not have to worry about second-guessing yourself? To some people it would seem like arrogance, but that's not the feeling I get when I'm around Avi. Not arrogance, just certainty. Complete certainty.

As the hours passed David became even more introspective. The desert slipped from his conscious thought. He heard nothing but the sound of his breathing and felt nothing but the jarring thump of his boots against the rocky soil. His eyes were focused on the ground as he concentrated on placing each step at the same angle, beginning each stride on the same part of his heel, fitting his gait to the momentum of the pack rather than fighting against it. Soon he fell into a trance-like state and became a creature of the desert, oblivious to its harsh beauty and immersed in its quiet stillness.

After a while Avi motioned to the right. David lifted his head to see a rock outcropping up ahead. Avi led the way around it to the shaded side. He slipped his pack from his shoulders and nodded at David to do the same. Gladly David popped the buckle of the waist strap and shrugged the pack from his shoulders. He set it on the ground and took a seat beside it, then reached inside and took out a bottle of water.

They sat side-by-side, leaning against the rock, and stared out across the arid landscape, neither saying a word. Now that he had the time to talk, David realized he no longer wanted to speak. Then, all too soon, it was time to move on.

With Avi in the lead, they walked until the sun slipped down the western slope of the afternoon sky. Around them shadows reached across the desert in the purple glow of evening. Even though his muscles ached and his feet were sore, there was a part of David that wished they could walk on through the night and watch the moon climb up past the jagged peaks that rose to their left.

At dusk they made camp at another outcropping of rock near the base of a small hill. The wind that had come up with the setting sun died away and the air became still. Finally, Avi broke the silence as he unrolled his sleeping bag. "It was a good day, yes?"

David could only nod in response. Although he had exercised at home and was in good physical shape, he found his legs unprepared for the physical endurance of a hike across the desert. He unrolled his sleeping bag and collapsed on it to watch Avi prepare for the night.

Avi glanced in his direction. "People have grown accustomed to being immersed in sound. They awaken to the sound of the alarm clock. They listen to the news as they drive to work. And in the churches, where people go to meet Abba, it is the same. The band is thumping, the preacher is shouting, the choir is singing until the last amen. Then the people jump up and start talking and laughing before they even leave the sanctuary. How can Abba speak to them in a still, small voice if the din is so great they cannot hear Him? Have you ever wondered about this?"

"I hadn't really thought of it that way," David mused, "but you're right. Noise is so prevalent, we hardly even notice it any more."

Avi unzipped his sleeping bag. "Silence is part of the healing process. It is like the pause between heartbeats. Or the calm of sleep that readies us for the day ahead." He gave David a measured look. "And that is why sometimes, when you demand an answer from Abba, His best and most loving response is silence." Avi crawled inside his sleeping bag. "I suggest you zip up tight, David. The desert looks desolate and vacant, but there are many small creatures out here that would like to share the warmth of your bed. It could get crowded before morning."

David zipped his bag up against his chin and lay there staring into the night. Overhead the sky was ablaze with the light of more stars than David had ever seen before. *I've spent most of my life in the city. I never realized how many stars are visible once you get beyond the reach of the urban haze.* His eyes grew heavy. *And to think, I'm staring up at the same sky seen by the Magi on their way to Bethlehem.*

Sometime in the night David awoke in desperate need of a bathroom. The wind that had died away at nightfall now howled through the rocks. He unzipped the sleeping bag and made his way to a large rock twenty yards away. He relieved himself and returned to find that the harsh wind had picked up his sleeping bag and tossed it several hundred yards into a grove of acacia trees. He hurried after it and grabbed it just as another gust lifted it from the ground. Rather than trudge back to camp, he stretched out the bag near the trees and crawled inside.

The next morning David awoke to the nudge of Avi's foot against his leg. Avi smiled down at him. "You slept in the acacia trees?"

"Long story," David yawned.

Avi squatted beside him and picked up a branch. He pointed to the branch's sharp thorns. "You remember the crown of thorns placed on Jesus' head?" David nodded in response. Avi continued. "It was made from the branches of the acacia tree. Look at the size of those thorns. Can you imagine them being pressed down onto your head?" Avi winced. "The pain would be excruciating." He tossed the branch aside. "The cruelty of doing such a thing to someone is almost unimaginable."

"The crown of thorns that Jesus wore was made from those branches, weren't they, Avi?" David asked. He looked up at the sky as dawn broke over the desert and whispered a prayer of thanks.

"Yes, David, but it was a willing sacrifice."

David crawled from his sleeping bag and rolled it up. A small fire burned near the rocks where they had set up camp. He secured the bag to his pack and joined Avi as he laid another stick on the fire.

"If you look in your pack, you'll find packages of pita and some dried fruit. A perfect way to break your fast."

For the first time David realized they hadn't eaten since they had left the hotel the morning before. He unsnapped the side pocket of his pack and found pitas and dried dates in a sealed package. David tore open one of the packages and bit into the bread. After a day of hiking, even prepackaged pita was delectable.

Avi glanced at him. "How did you sleep?"

"Like a baby for part of it." David popped a dried date in his mouth. "I didn't think it would be possible on this hard ground. But I rested quite well, until nature called."

"I'm glad to hear it. You will need your strength today."

David moved closer to the fire. The warmth of the small blaze felt good in the cool morning air. He knelt before it and popped another date into his mouth.

Avi looked around. "When Moses came this way, he did not enjoy much silence. His people were grumbling, 'We should have been so lucky to stay in Egypt, where at least there was a bit of shade. And to eat, what do we have? No garlic! No leeks! Nothing but this wretched manna and some skinny quail.' What Moses would have given to have spent a day as you and I did yesterday, taking a nice, quiet stroll in the desert."

David laughed. "You tell it like you were there."

"Yes." Avi gave him a broad grin. "I remember it like it was yesterday."

When they had readied their packs for the day's hike, Avi stomped out the fire and scattered the ashes. David took a seat on the rock ledge and pulled the laces of his boot tight.

Avi bent down and picked up a pebble no bigger than the tip of his little finger. "Today, I want you to walk with this in your boot." He offered David the pebble.

David frowned. "Why would I hike with a pebble in my boot?"

"I did not say *you* wanted to," Avi replied. "I said *I* wanted you to. Trust me. There is a good reason."

David shook his head. "I barely kept up with you yesterday, and today you want me to walk with a pebble in my boot? That doesn't make sense."

Avi smiled and looked away. "How long, I wonder, will humanity insist on good sense over wisdom?" He looked back at David. "If you had cancer, and I were an oncologist advising you to take chemotherapy, would you question the sense of poisoning your body in order to cure it?"

"Probably not. But that's kind of an extreme analogy, isn't it?"

"Extreme?" Avi arched an eyebrow. "As extreme as an unnamed terror that lands you in a trauma center with symptoms of a heart attack? As extreme as being so afraid of something hiding in your past that you, a grown man, will not go into the cellar of the house where you grew up? Is that what you mean by extreme?"

David's mouth dropped open. "How do you know—?" His hand went up, "I know. We will get to that later."

Avi smiled and straightened his shirt. "You are on a quest for knowledge. And that is what I offer." He held out the pebble once more. "If you will trust in my instructions, by the end of the day this pebble will seem to you like the pearl of great price."

David reluctantly took the pebble. He slipped off the boot from his right foot, dropped the pebble inside, then pulled the boot on and laced it up.

chapter 62

From the rocky ledge they continued on, the sun rising above the jagged mountain range that rose in the east. The pebble in David's boot rested between his toes. He hardly noticed it was there.

At mid-morning they rested near the bottom of a wadi, in the scant shade of a scrub acacia. They sipped from their water bottles and munched on dried dates. Avi was the first to break the silence. "The desert is where some of Abba's best work is done," he began. "Think of it. Moses, Elijah, your namesake King David, the apostle Paul...all of them spent time in seclusion and isolation with Abba. In a desert of the soul, if not a desert like this one."

"And Jesus," David added. "Forty days in the wilderness."

"Yes," Avi sighed. "That much at least, and more besides."

David looked at Avi and wondered again about his friend. Then, as if he heard the unspoken question, Avi gave him a knowing look. "You will have to decide that on your own." He stood and shouldered his pack. "Shall we move on?"

From the *wadi* the trail grew rougher, and the pebble in David's boot slipped free of its place between his toes. With each step the tiny stone grew and grew into a painful rock. He tried every strategy to accommodate it, shifting it to the side, maneuvering it into the space between the ball of his foot and his heel, then back into the space between his toes, but nothing helped. Every step became an exercise in futility, pain, and endurance.

All the while Avi talked. "Not too far from here is the place the wandering Hebrews named *Marah*, Bitter Waters." Avi sounded like a tour guide as David limped along behind him. "They arrived there after three days of travel in the Wilderness of Shur. They endured the desert and found a place with water, but it was too alkaline to drink." He gave a gesture of frustration. "Then the complaining started. 'This water is bad! Why have you brought us out here, only to die in the desert?'" He glanced over his shoulder with a grin in David's direction. "Moses, as you can imagine, was less than pleased."

David thought to himself, *Moses and I have a lot in common.*

"Think of it," Avi continued. "Only three days earlier the children of Israel were singing a song of victory as they crossed the Red Sea. They were shouting praises to God for their miraculous deliverance from Pharaoh's army. Then, after a little heat and a lot of walking, they where whining about the lack of water." Avi shook his head. "How short a memory people often have."

By then the pebble in David's shoe had graduated from painful rock to excruciating boulder. David found it difficult to allow Avi such easy moralizing. "On the other hand," he countered, "think of the mothers whose children were thirsty. Think of the animals that needed to drink. What were they supposed to do?"

Avi abruptly halted and turned to face him. "Trust, David," he said flatly. "They were supposed to trust in the One who had already shown His intention to save and preserve them."

As Avi's eyes locked with his, David knew with disquieting certainty that Avi wasn't speaking about the children of Israel. He glanced down at the ground. "Sometimes it is hard, even when you know better."

"I know, David." Avi turned away and continued walking. "And in the gracious mind of Abba, that difficulty is always taken into consideration. Just as a loving mother delights in her child's halting attempts at taking that first step, Abba rejoices when you make even the most hesitant move toward acting in faith rather than retreating in fear."

The day grew hotter and they continued in silence until Avi pointed to a clump of trees in the distance. "We will stop there and camp for the night." David felt relieved. The sun was still well above the horizon, and there would be plenty of time to rest his feet before night. Then Avi turned to David with a smile. "I have something I want you to do. Don't worry. It does not involve physical discomfort." The smile became a grin. "Not too much, at least."

"I hope not," David groused. "I've had about all I can stand for one day." He made his way to the clump of trees and lowered his pack to the ground. He dropped down and eased off his right boot. With the boot upside down, the pebble tumbled onto the dusty dry dirt. David picked it up.

"Look," Avi pointed. "It is still the same size as when you put it in there this morning!"

David gave him a sour scowl. "Easy for you to say."

"Yes, I suppose," Avi nodded. "And I commend your effort. You carried on like a trouper with the little princess-and-the-pea exercise I gave you." He patted David on the shoulder. "Keep that pebble for a bit."

"Thanks," David grumbled as he slipped the pebble into his pocket.

Avi removed his pack from his shoulders and set it near David's. "When you have rested, and while there is still plenty of daylight, I would like you to gather up twelve stones and pile them together. Will you do that?"

"Yes," David replied. "Just give me a minute."

When the discomfort in his foot had subsided to a dull throb, David eased his boot back on and headed out in search of the rocks. He found twelve, each roughly the size of a basketball, and carried them to the center of the campsite. There he stacked them on each other and looked to Avi for approval.

"Perfect," Avi smiled. "Now I want you to take the pebble you had in your boot and place it atop the altar you just built." David retrieved it from his pocket and laid it on the makeshift altar. "Very good," Avi nodded. "Sit down and relax. Drink some water. Later, we will talk."

As the sun began to set, a light breeze sifted through the trees. The rustling of the branches provided a soothing backdrop to the evening. They dined again on pita and dried fruit, while listening to the sounds of the desert as the animals came out to forage. David lay back on his sleeping bag and stared up at the fading blue sky.

After a while Avi spoke. "Tell me what you were thinking today, as you walked with the pebble in your boot."

"Mostly," David replied, "I was thinking about the rock. How it felt, the discomfort it was causing, how I could move it around to the least painful place."

Avi nodded. "I wonder…did you notice, during the day, that a skim of cloud covered the sun as we walked, providing a bit of relief from the glare? Did you see all the different birds? The Desert Lark, Hume's Tawny Owl, the Rose Finch with its delicate, rosy feathers? And the Spotted Sandgrouse, the Hebrews' main staple during their wandering? There were even a couple of Osprey soaring overhead, searching for dinner. Did you see any of that?"

"No." David shook his head. "I missed them."

"And how about the others?" Avi continued. "The hyraxes to our right. A small herd of gazelles in the distance. The Blue-Headed Agama lizard that lay on the rocks, and the sand snakes that slithered across our path. Did you see any of those?"

"No," David shook his head again. "I had my head down and my mind on trying to make my foot comfortable."

"What a pity," Avi smiled. "There was so much to see today, and you missed it. All because of a tiny pebble in your shoe."

David stared at the ground and said nothing. Avi pointed to the stack of twelve stones. "Now, look at the pebble, where you placed it on top of your altar. Do you see it?"

"Yes," David replied."

"It is so small," Avi continued. "Insignificant really, and yet it changed your vision. It altered your perception and blinded you to the wonder and beauty that surrounded you." He gazed intently at David. "And that is precisely what the pain of your past has done to you."

The observation hit David hard. He had come so far from his childhood, done so much more than he had ever hoped or dreamed or imagined. And now he realized he had missed a large portion of his life. Still, Avi kept going.

"In spite of all you have accomplished, for much of your life the pain you experienced as a child has been your focus." Avi's observations again fit perfectly with David's thoughts. "And that focus has caused you to experience only a part of the world around you and only a part of the people in your life. By the grace of Abba, you have managed to avoid much of the harm you could have done to yourself and others. But you have lived half a life."

The revelation was more than David could bear. "You speak so freely of the grace of God," he replied, "yet you told me yourself, you aren't a Christian."

"David," Avi retorted. "This is not about me. Do not try to change the subject." David looked away. Avi began again. "What I hope you will learn is that there is so much more to see and to know than what is contained by the limited horizon you have allowed yourself. Do you remember when Yona told you to deal with the past in terms of the present?"

"Yes."

"She was telling you that what is behind you is much less important than what lies before you." He grasped David's chin in his hand and turned it toward him. "Your future is unlimited." He looked David in the eye. "And it begins now." Avi stood. "Come with me."

David rose and followed him to the altar. "Place your hand over the pebble." David did as he was told, then Avi placed his hand on David's. "I want you to leave your pain on Abba's altar. You took a huge step in this direction when you humbled yourself before your father and asked his forgiveness. You took another when you returned to the house and went with Yona from room to room. Now I want you to take the final step. I want you to let go of the fear, the shame, all of it. From now on I want you to live in the unbounded love of Abba." He paused a moment then said, "Follow me in this prayer."

Slowly, hesitating at first, David repeated the phrases. "Abba, Father. I bring you the pain of my past, and I lay it here before You. Free me from the misery inflicted by others. And set me loose to know Your presence in my life as the one true Father. Amen."

Avi placed both of his hands on David's forehead. "Breathe in Abba's gracious forgiveness. Pull it into yourself until it fills every cell of your being, until it becomes as much a part of you as your own DNA." He was silent a moment. "Now breathe out that same gracious forgiveness on others. Inhabit every moment in Abba's grace."

As he stood there with Avi's hands on his head, David felt a sense of weightlessness wash over him. He seemed to float, as if on a bed of air, in the most peaceful state he had ever known.

chapter 63

David awakened the next morning tucked inside his sleeping bag with the zipper pulled up to his neck. He glanced around, confused and unsure of how he got there.

"Good morning!" Avi called. "How did you sleep?"

"Sleep?" David laughed sardonically. "What? With the wind howling and me worrying about scorpions and venomous snakes looking for a warm spot in my sleeping bag, why wouldn't I sleep?" He unzipped the bag and ran his hands over his face. "But actually I did fall asleep and had an amazing dream. The last thing I remember was standing by the stone altar."

"And you were transported to a place of peace and joy."

"Yes." David rolled aside the sleeping bag and stood. He reached for his boots and shook them out carefully, then slipped into them. Still drowsy, he stumbled to the pool by the spring and splashed water on his face. The cool water made his cheeks tingle. He thought about the evening before and about how it felt as Avi prayed. Still, he wondered how he got from the stone altar to the sleeping bag.

Wide awake now, he moved near the fire and took a seat. Avi handed him a package of dates, followed by a cup of hot tea. "We shall not travel today." Avi poked the fire with a stick. "We can enjoy some quiet moments together."

"Sounds good." David took a sip of tea and popped a date in his mouth. He found a package of pita in his backpack and brought it out. The flat taste of the bread was a welcome contrast to the flavor of the date.

Slowly the sun rose. Glare from the sand wiped away the brilliant colors of sunrise. They sat in silence, enjoying the solitude of the morning. As the sun moved higher in the sky, David shifted his position on the ground and leaned back on one elbow. "I have a question about something we discussed last night."

"We talked of many things. What in particular is troubling you?"

"When I first encountered Jesus, I thought the abuse would end." David set the cup on the ground in front of him. "It was never as bad as it was those nights in the cellar, but my dad continued to beat me, especially when he was drunk. And I've struggled ever since with the question of why God didn't stop the abuse."

Avi pulled his feet up under him and rested his chin on his knees. He stared across the fire at David. "You are still angry with Abba, are you not?"

"Yes, I guess I am," David admitted. "I didn't realize it until last night. but I am. I feel like He didn't answer my prayers. He rejected me."

"This goes back to the question of the hurt and pain we discussed. You see only the pain. God sees only you. You deal in fairness and equity. God resides in holiness and power."

"But I was a little boy. I would never let something like that happen to my son."

"No, you would not," Avi agreed. "But you are not God. Do you not suppose that God felt the same way as He hung on the Cross?"

"God? Don't you mean Jesus?"

"No, David. I am not talking about God the Father; I mean God the Son. He was God in the flesh, who dwelt among mankind. Then there is God the Holy Spirit. They are three, yet they are one. That is why it is sometimes called the mystery of the Godhead. You see Jesus as love, but you see God the Father as being angry like your earthly Father. Is that not true?"

Yes," David sighed begrudgingly. "I guess so."

"When you asked Yona that question, she told you that you confused God's power with His character."

"It didn't make much sense then either."

"His power gave Him the ability to create. His character gave Him the will. And yet He could not create man in any likeness other than Himself." Avi gestured with a broad sweep of his hand. "All that exists reflects His character in some measure." He pointed to David. "Including you. And Wally."

"I understand all that. It's just that—"

"When He made man in His own image, He gave man the ability to choose. He gave him limited autonomy."

"Limited autonomy." Sarcasm dripped from David's voice. "There's a contradiction."

"But it is the truth," Avi insisted. "That bit of autonomy is a reflection of Abba's total autonomy."

"You mean He is capricious?"

"He has the power to be capricious, but His power is bounded by His will, just as is yours."

"I'm not God."

"No. But you are not powerless either. You have the power to choose good or evil. It is at your hand to do well or ill to others." Avi took a deep breath. "That power is a gift from God. He gives it to every person. It is as much a part of Wally Ellis as it is of you. And God cannot easily contradict it."

"But He *can* contradict it."

"He can, and He does. But only by His sovereign choice. Sometimes He comes by invitation. Sometimes He comes because His autonomy is not limited and He has reserved for Himself the final outcome."

"The final outcome?"

"The Revelation of John. If you skip to the end you will see; mankind does not get to destroy God's creation."

"Okay."

"Sometimes Abba intervenes for the sake of our own circumstances. And sometimes He intervenes for His own purposes. But always the choice is His."

"That's not a comfortable answer."

"It is not given for your comfort. It is given for truth."

"But Jesus appeared to me in my bedroom. Why didn't He show up and stop my father from beating me?"

"You think that seeing Him in all His glory would have made a difference?"

"It made a difference for me."

"Remember when Abba hovered over Mount Sinai in a thick cloud?" David nodded in agreement. "The people could readily see the sign of His presence, and yet when Moses ascended the mountain to receive the commandments written by the very finger of the Almighty, what happened?"

"They made a golden calf, and they worshiped it instead of God."

Avi pushed himself up from the sleeping bag. "There was a gap of four hundred years between Jacob moving his family to Egypt and Moses' birth, and in that time the descendants of Israel went from the palace to the slave tents. They went from being the relatives of Joseph, second only to Pharaoh, to making mud bricks and barely surviving. Then Moses was born and he lived eighty years before he led them from Egypt. Do you suppose some of the people of Israel might have felt the same as you?"

"Perhaps," David replied.

"But God was not silent. He just was not speaking to the Hebrews."

David frowned. "What do you mean?"

"Why did they go to Egypt in the first place?"

"To escape the drought and then the famine that followed."

"And who provided for them? In earthly terms, who sustained them?"

"Pharaoh," David answered slowly.

"And so during that drought and famine, God was keeping them alive through the work of the Egyptians and the decisions of Pharaoh. Was that for Israel's benefit? And was it God at work?"

"Yes."

"So we cannot say that merely because He is not speaking to us, or intervening to free us from our circumstances, He is not working on our behalf. He was far more interested in preserving Israel than liberating the people from physical misery." Avi leaned close to David. "And He was far more interested in having you here, alive and active in human history, than He was in alleviating the circumstances of your childhood."

"That sounds harsh."

"That is the reality of the world in which you live and the struggle into which you were born. God kept you alive. You survived by His grace. The hand of evil that came against you did not prevail." Avi took a deep breath. "Up!" he shouted. "Up!" He gestured with both hands. "On your feet and praise Him!" Reluctantly, David forced himself to stand. "Lift your hands," Avi shouted.

"I don't feel like it."

"It does not matter what you feel. Lift your hands!" Obediently, David raised his hands over his head. "Now move your feet!" Avi shouted even louder.

Plodding at first, David moved his feet from side to side. He had never danced like this before, and it made him feel uncomfortable to do it now, even though they were hundreds of miles from the nearest humans.

As David made a feeble attempt to dance, Avi began to sing. His voice was rich and full and the melody like none David had ever heard. Soon they were both dancing in a circle around the campfire, David with his feet stumbling along, Avi as light as the breeze. And as they danced, David felt the burden of his soul lift. His feet became lighter. A smile crept across his face. And then he threw back his head and laughed.

David and Avi continued to dance until they were exhausted and collapsed on the ground. By then the sun was low on the horizon. They lay on their backs and watched as the last rays of light streaked across the sky. As dusk descended, Avi raised himself up and brushed the dust from his trousers. The campfire had long since been reduced to a few glowing coals. He gathered a handful of twigs and tossed them on the hot embers, then dropped to his hands and knees and leaned his face low to the ground. He blew against the coals, and in a moment a flame appeared. He coaxed it to a blaze and added a few more pieces of wood.

From his backpack Avi produced a white linen cloth. "I thought by now you might enjoy a change from pita and dried fruit." He spread the cloth on the ground and set out braided rolls sprinkled with sesame seeds, soft white goat cheese, galia melon that, when sliced, sent a delicate aroma of mingled spice and banana into the air, a cluster of plump purple grapes, fresh figs, and even a small bottle of wine. When it was all arranged, it looked like a feast fit for a king. "Come, eat." Avi motioned for David to join him.

They ate in leisurely fashion, propped on their sleeping bags like Bedouins. As David polished off the last of the goat cheese, Avi took one of the rolls in his hand. Holding it gently in his palm he glanced at David. "Will you share communion with me?"

"Yes." David sat up straight. "Of course."

With his eyes closed, Avi recited the ancient Hebrew blessing of the bread. "Blessed art Thou, Lord God, Ruler of the Universe, who brings forth bread from the Earth. Amen."

"Amen," David echoed. Avi broke the bread and handed a piece to him. He ate, chewing slowly, allowing the taste to fill his mouth, his mind, and his heart.

Avi poured a bit of the wine into their cups then prayed, "Blessed art Thou, Lord God, Ruler of the Universe, who creates the fruit of the vine. Amen." Avi handed him the cup.

David took a sip. He stared down at the fire as he rolled the wine across his tongue and swallowed. "Today," he said quietly, "while we were dancing, for the first time in my life, I caught a glimpse of God as Abba Father."

Avi nodded. "You are being released from your past. You are

embracing more and more the fullness of God." He set the cup aside and, as he had the night before, placed his hands on David's head. "Abba desires to trade the ashes of your childhood for the beauty of His loving care. He wants to turn your mourning into joy. May your heart be filled with dancing and your spirit with the light of His presence. Amen."

chapter 64

The next morning they angled toward the southwest along the line of jagged hills that began the rise toward the crest of the Sinai Peninsula. "Tonight we will stay at a place near the monastery of Saint Catherine." Avi gestured to their surroundings. "I love this land. It has been a place of renewal and rebirth for as long as man has been alive."

David nodded. "I'm starting to see that."

"Good," Avi smiled. He pointed to the left. "Careful here. The rocks along this ridge are prone to sliding from under your feet."

Shortly before noon they came upon a small oasis in a dry wash at the base of the ridge separating them from the Saint Catherine Protectorate, a national park that had been established by the Egyptian government. Avi pointed toward the intense blue sky. Floating effortlessly above them was an eagle, its wings locked in place as it soared on a thermal draft. Off to the right a massive thunderhead rose into the troposphere. David shaded his eyes with his hand and squinted at the magnificent bird. "How high can it go?"

Avi continued to watch. "As high as it takes to go over that storm." He lowered his gaze and looked to David. "Which is what Abba wants you to do, David. He wants you to rise above the storm on His very breath, to catch the *ruach*, the breath of His spirit, and rest on His provision."

Before long they arrived at the chapel at St. Catherine's. Avi explained that it was a monastery, built at the bidding of Empress Helena, the mother of Constantine. "For many years it was so secluded that the monks in residence were often totally ignorant of world affairs. That all changed with Israel's Six Day War, and since then St. Catherine's has become the destination of many tourists." All the sudden hustle and bustle made David long for the peace of the desert.

A Bedouin tent was pitched on the edge of the oasis. Avi led the way toward it, and as they approached, a woman burst from the tent. She held a bundle in her arms, and she was wailing as she ran toward them. David watched her with alarm. As she came closer, he could see the bundle in her arms was a small child. A glimpse beneath the blanket told him the child's head was badly burned. The forehead was blistered and charred, and the smell was putrid. David felt his stomach roil as the woman spoke in a torrent of Arabic. "*Men fadlak! El-hauuni! El-hauuni.*"

"She is asking that we help her," Avi translated. "The child fell into the fire a few days ago. There is no doctor nearby, and when the damaged flesh began to seep, the little girl's father tried to sear it with a hot knife to burn out the infection, but it did not work."

The woman was clutching at David now, staring frantically at him, pleading for him to do something, anything, to save the child's life. "*Men fadlak, men'fadlad. El-hauuni!*"

Avi said, "We must pray for the child. Place your hands on the child's head."

David reached out to the child and gently placed his hand atop her head. Avi put his hand over David's and began to pray. "Abba, I call Your attention to this innocent child. I ask that You pour forth Your healing upon her, and I invoke Your protection over her. Grant peace to her mother's heart and health to the child, that she may grow up to bless Your name."

The words were simple and brief, but as Avi spoke the mother stopped weeping and the child grew calm. Avi withdrew his hand. David slowly drew his away. Still, the child's scalp was the same as before—seemingly burned beyond help.

The mother's eyes darted from David to Avi and back to David. Then, with a look of sadness, she turned back toward the tent. Avi nudged David. "We should go. Tomorrow, we will stop and see how she is doing."

✳   ✳   ✳

They camped that night a hundred yards from the tent. David went to sleep thinking of the little girl. He knew God could heal, and he wanted her to get well, but in his mind he wasn't sure it would happen.

The following morning he awakened to find their campsite surrounded by dozens of Bedouin tents. During the night sojourners had slipped in and silently set them up. He crawled from the sleeping bag and stood. With his arms stretched wide he gave a big yawn. "What's for breakfast?" Avi pointed to a group of men standing at a fire pit in the distance. David looked on. "What are they cooking?"

"Camel," Avi replied.

"They eat camel?"

"Roasted whole over the fire." Avi gestured. "Come with me."

Across the compound they came to a tent crowded with women. As they drew near, David heard the sound of weeping from inside. He looked at Avi in horror. "The little girl is dead? Are they here for her funeral?"

"Go inside," Avi urged.

David's heart pounded as he pulled back the tent flap and ducked inside. The smell of smoke and unwashed bodies stung his nostrils. As his eyes adjusted to the smoky haze, he saw the tent was filled with women, all of them seated on the floor. They weren't weeping but gently singing.

From across the tent, the mother rushed toward him, her daughter clasped in her arms and tears streaming down her face. "*Shukran! Shukran! Shukran!*" she repeated.

Avi was behind him. "She is saying, 'Thank you, thank you.'"

The mother gently pulled back the blanket from the child's head to show the forehead covered with smooth soft skin where the oozing burned flesh had been the day before. David was dumbfounded.

"*Alhamdulillah*" the mother cried.

This phrase David understood. "Yes," he agreed. "Praise God." He ran his fingers lightly over the child's forehead and whispered a prayer. After a moment, he turned to leave. As he bent to step through the tent opening, the woman caught his arm. He turned to see in her hand a rusted cup. Steam rose from a dark liquid sloshing inside it. With a big smile she offered the cup to him. David hesitated.

Avi leaned close and whispered. "She is offering you the best she has—a cup of hot, sweet tea." He laid a hand on David's arm. "Do not refuse the cup. She is offering hospitality and her deepest gratitude. To refuse it would be a terrible affront."

David reached for the cup. As he did so the mother drank a sip from it, then handed it to him. He forced a smile, lifted the cup to his lips, and drained it.

"Good." Avi slapped him on the back. "That was just the beginning. Now you are in for a real celebration." Avi lifted the tent flap. "Tonight we celebrate. Tomorrow, we climb Mt. Sinai!"

✳   ✳   ✳

At dusk a procession of young men came for David and Avi. They were ushered through the compound to one of the tents. A group of women danced and sang in Arabic as they approached. David turned to Avi. "What are they singing?"

"The little girl's name is Hanifah," Avi replied. "Her name means 'true believer.' Because of her miraculous healing, the family changed her name now that they have become believers in Abba. They sent word last night for their entire family to gather for a betrothal celebration. While you were being refreshed with sleep, I shared the Word of God with them all. Many wished to become members of Abba's family. They are joining themselves with Abba."

"But what are they singing?"

Avi grinned. "In English it means, 'Abba is God; Abba is good; Abba heals; Abba restores; Abba is love and mercy. Praise to Abba! Praise be to Abba!'"

David paused to listen. Avi pulled him along. "Come, we are going to be late for the celebration."

The party lasted long into the night, with eating and singing and dancing, and more eating and singing and dancing. When David and Avi finally emerged from the tent with the adults, they were surrounded by dozens of children all dressed in their finest—little boys in traditional Arab dress and little girls with beads and jewels braided in their hair—dancing and singing around a huge campfire. As the embers from the fire floated into the night sky, David realized that Avi was laughing with abandon and had joined the dancing and singing children. The crowd was whirling and chanting, "Abba, Abba, bless us, Abba."

David caught the hand of an old man standing near him and said, "No, his name is Avi not Abba."

The man shook his head and grinned at David. "Not Avi! Abba! My Abba!"

David's forehead wrinkled in a frown at the response, and he stood there watching, perplexed by their reaction to his friend and by Avi's response to them. Before long the children clamored to be held by Avi. They tugged and pulled at him and jostled him from side to side. Finally Avi sank to the ground and wrapped them in his arms. David watched from a distance.

In a little while Avi came to him, still laughing from the joy of the celebration. His clothes were wet with sweat and his chest heaved as he worked to catch his breath. "I have some gifts," he said between gasps. "Gifts for everyone." He slapped David on the back again, his eyes alive with joy. "This is all very new to you, is it not?"

"Yes," David nodded. "Very new."

"Perhaps you will get used to it," Avi smiled.

"Perhaps I will," David replied with a grin.

Avi slapped his back once more. "Come with me, and help me distribute the gifts."

David followed Avi away from the crowd to rows of camels tethered at the edge of the compound. They were laden with bundles of food and clothing. David's mouth fell open in amazement. "What is this?" He stared at the boxes and bags strapped on the backs of the camels. "Where did all this stuff come from?" He looked over at Avi. "How did you do this?"

Avi shrugged. "I trust Abba. Not only has He given our new friends hope and peace and life, He has also supplied their material needs as well." He tapped a camel on the shoulder. Slowly, it settled to the ground. Avi moved alongside it and loosened a bundle from the camel's back. The Bedouins formed a line and began passing the items from hand to hand. David watched as the line wound around the compound to their tents.

"David," Avi called. "Help me." He stepped quickly to Avi's side. Working together, they unloaded each of the camels, sending the food and clothing down the Bedouin line.

As the last of the gifts was placed in one of the tents, Avi turned once more to David. "It is late, my friend. The guides will collect us well before sunrise for the ride to the base of the mountain. You had better get to sleep."

chapter 65

Avi took the lead as the two travelers moved across the oasis to their campfire. He turned to look over his shoulder at David. "If I gave you one word that had the power to bring physical, emotional, spiritual, and financial healing into your life, would you want it?"

David chuckled sarcastically. "Would I want it? What kind of question is that? Of course I would."

"There is a word that has the power to do that in your life. Come! Join me here by the fire. We will have a bite to eat before we turn in for what little sleep we will get tonight."

As David dropped to the desert floor, Avi continued, "I do have a word that does have the power to do that in your life." He reached into his pocket and extracted a miniscule bit of paper and a pen and painstakingly wrote something on it. He folded it in half once and then again before closing his fist over the fragment of paper. "Are you really sure you want to know what this word is?"

David shook his head. "Anyone would want the one word that could bring them the things you mentioned. I do want it."

Avi opened his hand and looked again at the tiny scrap of paper. "Most people feel as you do, David, but then when confronted with the truth of this word change their minds."

"I'm not most people."

"Well, let us not move too quickly. Enjoy your meal. Eat the hummus and bread and the roasted meat the Bedouins cooked for us." Avi laid the fragment down beside his plate.

David was frustrated. "Come on, Avi! Give me the word. Did you write it on that piece of paper?"

"No, no, let us eat first. I really want to be certain of your determination to have this knowledge."

When the meal ended and Avi had offered the traditional Hebrew blessing for the food, David could sense his piercing gaze directed at him. He looked up to meet Avi's eyes and watched him lift the tiny slip of paper. "Are you still so sure you want this word?" David nodded. Avi stood, laid the bit of paper in the middle of the linen cloth, and walked away. David was left alone with the revelation.

He tentatively reached down to retrieve the slip of paper, wondering what word would bring physical, emotional, spiritual, and financial healing. He gently picked it up but didn't open it. He held it tightly as he stood and walked over to his sleeping bag. David slipped inside and pulled the zipper halfway before reaching for his flashlight. Balancing it on his legs, he began to slowly and carefully unfold the bit of paper. It was pitch black around him, but the beam of light shone on the lone word carefully written by Avi ... *forgiveness*. He closed the paper and snuggled down into the sleeping bag. Tears soon slid from the corners of his eyes and pooled in his ears. David looked up through the misty blur. The stars seemed more a montage than individual lights piercing the night sky. It seemed as though he could reach up and touch the blanket that hovered over him. He felt emotionally exhausted and drifted to sleep.

In what seemed like minutes, David felt the nudge of Avi's boot against his leg. "*Boker Tov!* Good morning. I will not ask how you slept. I could hear you snoring! Come on, the water is on and I am making you an omelet—a special desert omelet."

David climbed out of the sleeping bag, washed his face with a handful of cold water from his canteen, and came to the fire. Avi handed him a steaming cup of hot tea and a plate filled with eggs and toasted pita bread.

David smiled his thanks. "I read the word last night. It reached down into the very depths of my soul."

Avi asked gently, "Do you know why?"

"I think I do. I've struggled with unforgiveness all of my life."

"Yes you have. There are still two that you have never forgiven—Abba and yourself."

David dropped his head. "I know that now. That's why I was reduced to tears last night. I've never forgiven myself, nor have I forgiven God the Father. I've tried to pretend forgiveness, but I know it's not true. I've allowed the hurts to cultivate a seed of bitterness that has colored my relationship with Abba and kept me from forgiving myself."

"David, your religious training taught you that Abba is an angry God waiting with raised fist to hurt you like your angry father. The truth is, He is a loving Father, full of compassion and mercy. You have been so harsh and critical of Him, and of the little boy you were. In a perverse way, you felt you deserved the treatment you got. You were made to believe it was your fault when your father beat you."

"Avi, I want a close relationship with Abba. I love the way you talk of Him. Your voice reverberates with love. And I want to forgive myself so I can move on with my life in total peace, prosperity, and joy. Help me to understand how to do that, please."

Avi smiled his enigmatic little smile and simply pointed at a large stone. "Put that in your backpack, David. I want you to carry it up the mountain. You learned with the pebble in your shoe that little foxes can spoil your view of the world around you and take your focus off God's goodness. It was a source of constant irritation, shifting your focus from the beauty around you to the pain in your foot. Now it is time to learn another, greater lesson.

David walked over to the rock. He tried to roll it into his backpack, but he quickly realized it wasn't as easy as it looked. Although it was a little smaller than his pack, the rock was far heavier than he had anticipated. "I can't carry this rock up the mountain; it's much too heavy. I'm not even sure I can get it in my pack. How much does this thing weigh, anyway?"

"Ah, about 200 pounds—the same as you."

"Impossible! I can't carry two times my own weight up the mountain."

"It is possible, David. Just do it."

David finally managed to inch the rock into his backpack, fastened the straps, and then tried with all his might to lift it to his shoulders. "Can you please help me? There's no way I can lift this thing by myself." His patience was quickly waning.

"Of course, I will help you. Sit down." Avi easily moved the backpack behind him, fitted David's arms through the harness, and secured the straps around his waist. Then he helped David to stand. David's legs almost collapsed beneath him, and he started to teeter backwards from the weight. "Lean forward, David."

David staggered forward, his chest tightening and his breath coming in harsh gasps. "Avi," he wheezed. "Can't stand. Can't climb. No way." The weight of the stone began to pull him backward again. Avi grabbed David from behind to stop his fall. Then he released the harness from his back.

"You are right, David. *You* cannot. There is no way you can tote that burden to the top of the mountain. You have been a burden to yourself. You have been trying to carry the weight of your sin. You have refused to love unconditionally what God loves. God knows everything about you...and He loves you unconditionally."

Avi emptied the rock from David's backpack as if it weighed no more than a handful of feathers. Pulling a blue, felt-tipped marker from his pocket, Avi wrote on the stone, "Unforgiveness...Whatever you resist persists. Abba equals peace, prosperity, and joy." He added the date.

Avi urged, "Come, let us rest a while longer before it's time to climb the mountain together."

David suddenly felt exhausted again. He lay down on his sleeping bag and fell into a deep sleep until Avi nudged him again. As he rolled up his sleeping bag, he realized the night was cold and the desert wind was quickly draining the warmth from his body. Hurriedly, he pulled on his clothes. Six layers to ward off the cold.

Avi called to him, "The camels are here to take us to the foot of the mountain." David hurried to join him. Avi laughed. "You waddle like a duck. In a few hours you will be shedding all those clothes.

In less than an hour they reached the trailhead, where they left the camels and began to climb toward the peak nearly nine thousand feet above. Avi's plan was to arrive there by first light. To make it, they could not hesitate. It would be an arduous hike through the dark and windy predawn hours, but well worth it to see the sunrise over the desert from Moses' vantage point.

On the first leg of the ascent the wind howled and shrieked between the rocks. At times David felt as if he might be blown right off the trail into the valley below. Good climbers had fallen to their death doing exactly what he and Avi were attempting. He had brought along a flashlight, but its feeble glow was nearly consumed by the inky blackness surrounding them.

Avi called back to him, "Turn off the flashlight. You can see the trail better without it. Give your eyes time to adjust to the light Abba has provided."

David switched the light off and was immediately lost in total darkness. He flipped the switch back on. Avi was insistent. "Turn the light off, David. It takes more than a moment for your eyes to adjust. Just stand still and wait for it to come." David's hands trembled as he switched off the light. Just as Avi had suggested, his eyes soon adjusted and the trail appeared before him. He put the flashlight back in his backpack.

As they climbed upward, the trail became narrower, weaving in and out between large boulders. A little farther, the trail swung out along a narrow ledge. David hesitated, but Avi was already well ahead.

He took a tentative step forward, halting and cautious. The corner of the backpack rubbed against the rock cliff that rose above them. David felt it pushing against him, forcing him to lean to the right, over the edge of a narrow precipice. Fear swept over him. In spite of the cold morning, his palms were damp and his skin clammy.

He turned his back to the precipice and crabbed sideways, clinging to the rocky face of the cliff. Slowly, carefully, he inched forward, gingerly placing one foot beside the other. Below, there was only the darkness and a long fall to the valley floor.

In the midst of that terrifying moment, anger seized him. "Avi, where are you?" he demanded. "I can't see you. You're too far ahead of me on the trail. I can't walk in the dark! Don't you understand? I'm afraid of the dark! And I'm stuck here on this ledge." There was no response. David scooted one foot forward, followed by the other. Then it happened.

David's feet slid from under him and he began to slip over the edge. He twisted to the left and grabbed in the darkness for something, anything to save himself. As his weight shifted over the edge for the long drop to the bottom, he caught hold of the ledge and held on with both hands. "Avi!" he screamed. "Avi! Help me! Avi!"

David hung there, his feet dangling in the air. Muscles in his arms ached as he did his best to hold on. Then, through the confusion and fear, he heard a still, small voice. "David, let go and grab my hand."

"I can't let go!" David protested. "I'll fall! I can't see you! Where are you, Avi?"

From somewhere in the darkness above him, Avi whispered again. "Trust me, David. Trust Abba. Just let go and reach up to me. I am right here above you."

David was afraid, but he couldn't hold on much longer. In desperation he summoned all the strength that remained and, in a quick motion, let go of the rock and reached up for Avi's hand. For a moment it seemed as though he was falling backward, but in the next instant he felt Avi's hand lock around his wrist and pull him to safety.

The momentum of Avi's lift pulled David from the ledge and into a cleft in the rock, sheltered from the wind and cold. David leaned over, hands on his knees, gasping for breath. Avi took a thermos from his pack and poured David a cup of hot, sweet tea.

"My friend," he said quietly, "you have been on the very edge of the valley of the shadow of death, but We are with you. We have preserved your life." He gestured to the night sky. "And now, all of Heaven rejoices at your deliverance. You can always look to the Light with confidence and complete trust."

David looked up at the night sky, ablaze with the light of innumerable stars. "It really is You?" he whispered.

"All in good time, my friend. Sip your tea." Avi patted him on the shoulder. "And then, we must hurry if we are to view the sunrise from the top."

chapter 66

When they reached the summit, Avi opened his own pack and emptied it. David was stunned to see the rock he thought they had left by the campfire. It bore the same inscription.

"You carried that up the mountain. Why?"

"I carried it for you, David, because I love you. I bore all of your sins so you would not have to face Abba weighed down by them. I told you the only way to get this stone up the mountain was to recognize that you could not do it in your own strength."

David could feel heat radiating from the rock as the sun's rays touched it. As he felt the warmth of Abba's love touch his heart, David realized they were not alone on the mountaintop. Others had made the trek to the top to watch the sunrise from the place where Moses had once stood. Off to the left a group was singing, "Amazing Grace." From the sound of their voices David was sure they were Americans. To the right a cluster of bare-chested men stood arm-in-arm, facing east, their eyes set on the horizon.

Avi stood next to David. His voice was low and soft. "This is more than the mountain of Moses. This is the mountain to which Elijah fled to escape Queen Jezebel and King Ahab." He looked at David. "Abba has a word for you, my brother. He says, 'Well done, good and faithful servant. You have been faithful in your assigned tasks.'"

"But I thought you said I had missed half my life."

"Yes," Avi nodded. "But you followed the path you were given. You might not have noticed all that you passed along the way, but in spite of the pain you carried, you pressed on against the fear. When you were shown the way, you did not shrink back from following."

"I shrank back from Wally."

"Only that first time," Avi countered.

"And I wouldn't go into the cellar."

"Eventually you did, and prevailed against them both. And when you felt God leading you into something new, you did not hesitate to quit the work you had been doing to follow Him." Avi rested his hand on David's shoulder. "As I said before, you focus on the details. Abba focuses on the relationship. And in that, you have done well.

"David, your earthly father's words hurt you. Abba's words healed you. When you heard the Word of God at age eleven, it was literally Abba speaking to you. He has been speaking to you for over fifty years now. When you marked promises in your Bible, dated them, and saw those things come to pass, did you fully understand the significance then?"

David shook his head. "No, I guess I didn't."

"Those very promises were the same ones you held to tightly in war zones. In your darkness you experienced great light. It is always that way. In your darkest night, the light is the brightest. That is why you must focus on the Light, not the darkness.

"You know there have been times in your life when you felt you could not see the Light. Like another David, you were in the valley of the shadow of death, where the light could not penetrate. During those dark days you had to walk by faith and know beyond a doubt that Abba was holding you close ... that you were in the palm of His hand. He spoke to you through His Word. Each scripture you underlined was from Abba...not a verbal voice, but His voice nonetheless."

While Avi was speaking, the dark night sky slowly gave way to hues of gray. "This is a new day. Taste the immeasurable greatness of

Abba today. What He has for your future is greater than anything He has done in your past."

To the east the jagged range of mountains stood as a dark outline in the predawn light, like a child's drawing on the blank page. Then dawn began to unfold across the desert, a scene painted by the very hand of God. A dash of pink, followed by brilliant red, and then the sun broke over the peaks in a glorious burst of light.

Overcome with emotion, David raised his arms heavenward. Tears ran down his cheeks as he basked in the majesty of the view before him. Only Abba could have designed such a magnificent greeting.

From the left the group that had been singing before lifted a familiar Psalm heavenward:

I will lift up mine eyes to the hills

from whence cometh my help,

my help cometh from the Lord,

the Lord which made Heaven and Earth.

Others on the mountain joined them until all were singing that same refrain, including David. As the sun rose higher in the sky, the vivid colors gradually faded to desert pastels. By then the chorus had faded too. Filled with gratitude at receiving such a wonderful gift, David turned to wrap his arm around Avi's shoulders—his Friend, Counselor, Teacher, and desert guide.

"There is so much more I want to say to you." Avi slipped an arm under David's and put his hand on David's shoulder. "But time is short."

"Short?"

"Yes," Avi nodded. "Indeed, you are free now, and I must be going."

David pulled away. "Will I see you again?"

"I will always be with you."

"But I wanted to—"

"I know," Avi nodded once more. "You have many questions. And they will all be answered in due time."

Suddenly a shaft of light appeared, so brilliant David raised his hands to block the glare. Then, through the glare of the light, two hands reached out to him. Palms scarred, they looked as though they had been terribly wounded. One hand rested on David's shoulder. The other gently touched his head.

A human form appeared, clothed in white, with a familiar face smiling at him. David whispered, "Avi."

Avi answered, "Son, I love you. And I am fulfilling a great plan for your life."

Then, just as suddenly, the light was gone and David stood alone on the mountain. A breezed swirled around him, and when he looked down, the valley floor below seemed far away. He glanced around, searching for Avi, but in his heart he knew he was not there. Fear rose inside. How would he get down? How could he—

David pushed those thoughts aside and remembered the lessons he had learned while trekking across the desert. "I know the way to the bottom," he said aloud. "I climbed it in the dark. I can surely find it in the light." He took a deep breath and forced his mind to remain in the present. "I will not let fear rob me of this moment. I will no longer live half a life." He gazed out over the desert, searing the images in his mind. The skiff of clouds that drifted past. The Osprey soaring high above.

Finally he turned away and started toward the trail. "And when I reach the bottom, Benni Mazur will be waiting with the Land Cruiser. And my family will be waiting for me at home." He grinned. "My Abba has it all arranged. He speaks to me through His Word. My task is simply to follow the Light."

Epilogue

The sunny day was cool and lovely. Native New Englanders call it Indian Summer. Sue had finally gotten her wish to see the beautiful foliage around Massachusetts. They were spending a few days in Indian Orchard. David was glad he had arranged to purchase the old home place. It was high time to make good memories there, especially since David and his father had reconnected.

The whole neighborhood had been reborn as people bought the old places and restored them. The renovation of 77 Pasco Road had taken a lot of hard work, but it hardly resembled the old house that once stood there. Now it had room for David, Sue, and their family when they came to visit. With both kids married and with children of their own, it was proving harder to get everyone together at the same time.

David sat outside on the back steps, enjoying the cool, fall morning. It seemed he could almost see the leaves turning various shades of red and gold. He leaned back, snagged the edge of the screened door, and called to Sue, "Honey, how'd you like to go down to the park and feed the ducks?"

She walked over to the door, leaned against the facing, and grinned down at her husband. "Sounds like fun, and I could use the exercise. Let me get my sneakers, and I'll be right with you." Sue slipped back inside the kitchen.

Smiling to himself, David called after her, "Have we got any old bread we can take to toss to the ducks?"

Sue's voice came from the pantry. "In the sack under the sink. I'll get it."

David smiled as Sue walked out the front door and closed it firmly behind her. As they started down the steps, he turned back to look at the new façade adorning the old house. They walked along the paved pathway that led to the park and talked about the progress that had been made on the house, the beautiful fall weather, and their plans to host their extended family—including David's birth father and step-sister—at Thanksgiving.

Sue squinted up at the trees that formed a bower above them. "I'm so glad we finally made it up here during the fall. The colors are fantastic. It looks as if God painted them with a special brush. He really is the Master, reminding us of Himself. 'For since the creation of the world God's invisible qualities—his eternal power and divine nature—have been clearly seen, being understood from what has been made, so that people are without excuse.'"

David nodded as the words from the book of Romans soothed his soul and smiled down at his wife.

There wasn't anyone else near the benches by the pond, and the ducks waddled toward them as soon as Sue began rustling the bread bag. In just a few seconds the bench was an island in a sea of clamoring birds. She laughed as she tossed pieces of bread to the eager mob. When the sack was nearly empty, she leaned back within the circle of David's arm and sighed with deep contentment. "Thank you for bringing me here. I know this park has special significance for you."

"Yes, it does. I believe this may be where I had my very first encounter with an angel." In the corner of his eye David caught something moving and looked over to see a little boy with his head down, dashing straight for the pond. He passed the fringes of the duck feeding frenzy at a dead run, and David could see that if he didn't put on the brakes pretty quick, he would tumble into the water.

David jumped up from the bench and took two long strides to clear the horde of ducks, then sprinted to catch up with the little boy, grabbing him around the waist just as he neared the edge of the pond. "Hold on there, buddy." The boy struggled against David's hold. "You'd better watch where you're going, huh?"

"Lemme go! Lemme go!"

David realized the boy was crying, and then he noticed the blood on his lip. The little boy had skin the color of creamed coffee, and his black hair was matted with dirt and traces of the blood from his lip that he had apparently smeared as he ran.

"What's the matter, pal?" David pulled out his handkerchief and daubed at the boy's lip. "Did somebody hurt you?"

"Lemme go," the boy cried, but weaker this time. He seemed to be relaxing slightly in David's grip, as if he wasn't so sure he really wanted to be released.

"You want to come over here with my wife and me? We're feeding bread to the ducks. You could help us, if you want to."

The boy said nothing, but he had stopped struggling. David carried him toward the bench and set him on his feet beside Sue, who smiled brightly at him. "What's your name?"

"Dillon," the boy's eyes were downcast.

"I'm Sue," she said, and held out her hand to shake his. He took it tentatively and then gave her hand a quick squeeze.

David sat next to Sue. "Well Dillon, how about it? You want to throw some bread to the ducks? We've got plenty, don't we, Sue?"

"I don't want to feed the stupid ducks."

Sue held out a tattered piece of bread. His eyes squinted in a frown, and then he took it. After holding it for a few seconds, he tossed it halfheartedly at the ducks, which squabbled loudly over it.

David prayed a silent prayer: *Dear Abba, I don't know what has happened to this little guy, but I plead with you to protect him from whatever it is that sent him running to this park.*

Dillon tossed another piece of bread into the mob of ducks. "So, Dillon," David asked quietly, "tell me: Are you okay? Do you need some help, maybe?"

The child didn't answer.

"Listen to me, son. I know you're scared and hurt right now, but it doesn't have to be that way. And you know what? I didn't want to feed the ducks, either, when I was about your age." Very slowly Dillon raised his eyes to David's and looked for a long time. "You've got happy eyes. I've never seen eyes with sparkly light before. How'd you do that?"

David gently wiped away the remaining traces of blood from the little boy's mouth and the streaks of dirt from his forehead. He looked at him intently. "I want to tell you something, Dillon: Abba loves you, and He has a wonderful plan for your life ..."

The people who walked in darkness have seen a great light;
those who dwelt in the land of the shadow of death,
upon them a light has shined.

Isaiah 9:2

Acknowledgements

My sincere thanks to Joe Hilley, Lanelle
Shaw-Young, Arlen Young, Thom Lemmons,
Peter Gloege, and a host of others who had
input in making this book happen.

Thank you for the hours and hours of time
devoted to *The Light*.